CUSTER'S BROTHER'S
HORSE

Novels by Edwin Shrake

Blood Reckoning
But Not For Love
Blessed McGill
Peter Arbiter
Limo (with Dan Jenkins)
Strange Peaches
Night Never Falls
The Borderland
Billy Boy

CUSTER'S BROTHER'S
HORSE

BY EDWIN SHRAKE

JOHN M. HARDY PUBLISHING
ALPINE & HOUSTON
2007

First Printing: October 2007

1 3 5 7 9 10 8 6 4 2

ISBN 0-9717667-8-9

Printed and Bound in the United States of America

Cover Photo - Bill Wittliff

Cover Design - Leisha Israel

John M. Hardy Publishing
Houston, Texas

www.johnmhardy.com

For Jerre and Melba Todd

Thanks to Father A. A. Taliaferro

One

THE FOG COMING OFF SHOAL CREEK was pouring through the prison yard in pearl-colored puffs that made him think of cannon smoke. Captain Jerod Robin lay on his back in the caliche mud with his head leaning against the south wall of the stockade. The Leatherwoods had smashed his pocket watch, but he thought it would be nearing a wet dawn if he could see the sun.

A chain around his ankle locked him to the steps of the gallows platform. Robin's ribs ached from the stomping that had been laid on yesterday evening by Santana Leatherwood and his three nephews. Massaging his sore heart with his fingertips, Robin touched the letter the nurse at the hospital in Tennessee had sewed into the lining of his butternut coat. Several buttons had been torn off the double row down the front of his coat, but the letter was safe. If the Leatherwoods had found and read the letter they would have murdered him yesterday on Pecan Street instead of beating him and throwing him into the bull pen and waiting for the judge to come and hang him to make his death what now passed for legal around here.

As Robin's fingers rubbed the outline of the letter, he felt comfort in those folded pages of words. His life had been so distorted for the past three years—since Shiloh—that he might have been dreaming his existence. The letter was a real thing that confirmed the one hope that through it all had brought him back from madness and given him reason to return to the world—the hope that he still had a home at Sweetbrush and people there he loved who loved and needed him.

A smell of rotted meat floated through the fog, and then a groan.

"Help me," a voice cried. "Will someone help me, for God's sake?"

"That's a laugh," yelled another voice.

"Please. For God's sake help me."

"Tell it to your preacher and let him holler up at heaven with your sad story."

Laughter drifted around through the fog. Then silence settled as prisoners brooded their fates in the dark. The fog grew thick as snow to the touch and turned cool. Robin realized he was feeling rain on his hands and heard drops tapping on his hat. He lifted his head and opened his mouth and licked the moisture off his lips.

"Bastards coming," shouted a voice in the fog.

More voices shouted, "Bastards coming. Bastards coming."

"Quiet down, you putridity," yelled a voice Robin recognized as Santana Leatherwood. Robin heard the chink of spurs. He saw a disturbance in the fog where forms began to appear coming toward him.

"Jerod Robin, where you at?" called out Billy Leatherwood, the youngest and smallest of the three brothers approaching him in the fog. They were dragging a sack that had something heavy in it.

"Over by the heel-fly, Billy. He's chained up over that way," said Santana Leatherwood, looming out of the mist behind his three nephews. There were gold tassels on the band of his wide brim campaign hat that he wore tilted forward onto his forehead. His neck scarf and suspenders were yellow against the faded blue of his Seventh Cavalry uniform shirt. Six silver conchos, Mexican style, ran down the outside of each of his black leather boots. His spurs were silver with two-inch rowels, mean ones.

"Here he is, captain," Billy said. "Laying here like he's on a holiday with nothing to do. Why I believe he's asleep."

"Give him a kick," said Santana.

"Don't touch me, Billy," Robin said. "I'm keeping score on you."

"Get up then. The captain has brought you a new friend."

Robin pulled his knees up and made it to his feet as the two elder Leatherwood brothers hauled their sack toward him. Robin was tall and pale, with sleepy blue eyes. In the fog he could barely make out the sullen features of the middle Leatherwoods under their round-top felt hats. Vapor floated around their faces. Santana stepped closer to Robin and gestured toward the sack.

"This fool stole General Custer's brother's horse," Santana said.

What Robin had taken in the fog to be a sack he now saw was a man with his chin fallen onto his chest. Blood dripped from a black patch in the man's gray hair and plopped into the dirt. Luther and Adam Leatherwood were holding him up by the armpits. His legs disappeared behind into the fog.

"This fellow is as big a fool as you are, Robin," Santana said. "You and him are going to pay the same price for your foolishness. You'll be jerking in the sky side by side, you and this foreign idiot. Put the horse thief down, boys."

The Leatherwood brothers let go and the prisoner hit the ground on his face.

"Chain him up next to young Robin," Santana said. He bent near enough that Robin could see above Santana's left ear a bit of silver plate that was a marker from battle in a war previous to the one that was now ending. "Well, Robin, life is uncertain, ain't it? Full of twists and turns. When they talk about odd twists of fate, they mean you and me, don't they? Seems like yesterday you was a rebel officer with a history and a future. But today you are a doomed fool chained up with an idiot who thought he could make off with Tom Custer's famous horse from in front of Dutch John's Saloon in the middle of the night."

"This thief has to be real stupid," said Adam.

"I mean he's dumb as a stump," Luther said.

"The horse he tried to steal is the very same horse Tom Custer rode at Namozine Church and three days later at Sayler's Creek when we were chasing you rebel cooters through Virginia three months ago. You'll be glad to know I got back into action in time for the finish of this war. I saw Tom Custer win two Medals of Honor in one week on the back of this very horse. This is a legendary horse. Can you picture the confusion in the mind of a person who thought he could climb on Tom Custer's horse and ride out of town?" Santana said.

Billy was fastening a chain on one of the horse thief's ankles.

Billy said, "Robin, you should of heard this thief trying to talk his way out. He was talking an owl out of a tree is what he was doing. It was comical."

"So you bashed his head," Robin said.

"Adam bashed his head. Then Luther let go another bash," said Billy.

"I got him good," Luther said. "He might be dead."

"He ain't dead. Look at him. He's bleeding," said Adam.

"Uncle Santana just now done that gash with his spurs," Luther said.

"Still. You ever seen a dead man bleed?" said Adam.

"Plenty of times," Luther said.

Round splatters dappled in the dirt as heavy raindrops fell through the fog.

"You never," said Adam.

"Don't give me that cockeyed look," Luther said.

"You boys pay attention here," Santana said.

Billy wrapped the horse thief's chain around a post of the gallows platform and locked it with a click. The two older Leatherwood brothers wore red bandanas knotted at their throats to show they belonged to the company of Home Guard that was cooperating with the Federal regiment that had begun arriving in Austin to start imposing law. Outside the prison gate there was disorder and fear. The elected governor of Texas had fled to Mexico. Buildings had been sacked. Returning rebel soldiers were passing through the capital city, often barefoot and injured and penniless, with anger in their hearts and exhaustion on their faces. Citizens and refugees were rushing through the streets carrying bags of coffee, flour, sugar, salt, bacon, cloth, rope, leather, cotton, whatever they could snatch. The public mood was to catch what you can and hold fast to what you get.

The horse thief lifted one hand and spread his fingers and touched them to his hair. His fingers felt blood and froze. The rain shower was passing but the fog was dark and wet. The Leatherwood brothers stepped back from the prisoner and became half lost in the mist. Santana looked down at the bleeding head of the fallen horse thief and then raised his eyes to Robin.

"In far off Tennessee you had thirty mounted men under your command." Santana's eyes sparked with humor and intelligence. He grinned and showed a healthy set of white teeth. "Now you come back home to Texas, and what do you find? You find a date with a rope. A cruel ending to your story, but fitting. You and I both know you are without honor. You deserve to die like a rat."

"What charge could you hang me on?"

"I made a list. Murder is at the top."

"You know I didn't kill that old man," Robin said.

A loud sharp bang crackled through the fog. It was an explosion from the south part of town where the river turned toward the southeast and headed for the Gulf of Mexico two hundred miles away.

Santana said, "We've got quite a few guerrillas that need to be subdued. In Texas the war ain't over no matter if General Lee and Joe Johnston and Jeff Davis and every cracker in the whole rest of the south may have quit. They still love to string up abolitionists here. Appomattox is just a tick on a hog's back as viewed from Texas. But when the people here do learn they've lost the war they'll keep fighting anyhow because fighting is their nature. You've known my nephews since they was children down on the bayou. You ever remember a day when they wasn't spoiling for a fight?"

"I remember a day they showed pure yellow," said Robin.

"Not in history has there ever been any yellow in any Leatherwood."

"The day the recruiter came gathering men to fight the war, your nephews ran and hid in the forest," Robin said.

"Because you're on the wrong side, Robin. You're fighting the rich man's war."

"You're a traitor to Texas," said Robin.

Santana licked his teeth and then spat onto the horse thief's back.

"See what a fool you are?" he said. "I am Texas now. You are done."

Santana turned and took two steps and vanished in the fog with his silver spurs chinking and his nephews following. Billy looked back, shook his head, and chuckled. He said, "Jerod Robin, you are sure going to suffer for your sins today," before the gray mist covered him.

Robin knelt and gave his attention to the horse thief.

Two

IN HIS MIND VARNEY WAS BACK in Afghanistan.

He was hearing drumming and screaming. His skull was throbbing and his stomach flopped like he'd drunk too much of that bloody fermented whatever the hell it was the Ghilzai head man served in that blasted bone cup that looked like his grandmother's knee.

Varney had woken up from a concussion to find himself sprawled in the snow in a clearing surrounded by mud huts with rusted tin roofs made from British ammunition boxes. The wild Ghilzais were squatting on their haunches in the snow, clutching their knives and long rifles, smoking and laughing at him. He sensed now that his head was bleeding as it had been that morning in the village in the Hindu Kush near the pass where the British army and their women and children and servants were being slaughtered that very day on their retreat from Kabul, all killed, all sixteen thousand dead. Varney's fingers felt wet and sticky from touching his scalp, not at all a good sign.

He opened his eyes into a squint and peeped out, expecting he was going to see the bearded Ghilzai warriors capering in their pantaloons, their sheepskin cloaks scattering snow, swinging Varney's ruby amulet on its gold chain in a loop around their turbans and fur caps, the head man mounted on Varney's beautiful horse Athena, prancing in the snow.

But he saw cool gray smoke enveloping him instead. He heard voices cry out from somewhere in the smoke on the far side of wherever this was. One voice screamed, "Mother of Jesus, get away from me or I'll kill you." This sounded like what you might hear in Kabul, but Varney began to realize it wasn't smoke he was seeing, and these cries were not in the Pathan tongue but were in English of a sort, the slurred tones of the southern mountains, the flat drawls of the west. He began remembering that Afghanistan was years ago, though it seemed recent and was always near the front of his mind. He was among a different breed of savages now. He was in Texas.

"My God, this bloody fog is worse than London," Varney said. "Who would have believed it? I can't see the end of my blasted feet."

Varney tried to move his right leg and discovered he was chained. Behind him, hidden by the fog, Robin stood and watched. Varney grasped the chain in his strong right hand and yanked, but it rattled and held. He reached out with both hands and tugged again. Robin saw the swell of muscle in Varney's neck and shoulders. Varney dropped the chain. He licked blood off his upper lip. He touched the bleeding lumps on top of his head where the hair had gone thin, a patch of it torn out.

Somewhere in the fog a voice yelled, "Please, I'm asking, will somebody help me?"

Another voice yelled, "You're in hell. What do you expect?"

Varney looked at the blood on his fingertips. His face had a patrician aspect, a heavy brow, a well-drawn nose and chin. Robin was thinking this horse thief's head looked like a long-buried bust of an ancient Roman senator, with the dirt still on it, but the body was sturdy and blocky like that of a laboring man. Robin guessed the horse thief to be about fifty years old, about twice Robin's age. The horse thief's left earlobe was pierced by a green earring that looked to Robin like jade laid on silver.

Varney shouted into the gray curtain, "If you think this is hell, you have sorely underestimated the devil. I have visited the afterlife and have returned. This isn't hell, you bloody yobs. This is only Texas."

The prisoner's accent sounded familiar to Robin. It was an upper middleclass English preciseness like that of Robin's mother, who had been born in St. John's Wood in the north of London.

Despite nearly thirty years in Texas, Varina Hotchkiss had maintained the sound of London in her accent. The rhythms of the prisoner's voice reminded Robin of her.

Varney looked down at his fist wrapped around the chain. "Hullo," he said, noticing another chain. He clutched the second chain in both hands and began to haul it in like a fisherman retrieving a net. Twelve feet away at the other end of the chain was Robin's right boot.

"What's this then?" Varney said.

The prisoner peered at Robin emerging from the fog so close by. Robin could see he was struggling to clear his mind from the blows that had been lavished onto his head by the Leatherwoods.

"Let me take a look at your wound," Robin said.

"Are you a physician, or merely morbidly curious?"

"I have some experience with wounds, but if you'd rather not, the hell with you."

"I've already been to the afterlife," the prisoner said.

"I heard."

Varney studied Robin, looked him up and down with a curiosity that would have caused offense in almost any other circumstance. Varney's eyes were large and gray and somewhat protruding. At first his look was fierce, but his attitude softened as a pain struck behind his eyes. Varney thought this young man he was looking at seemed sincere. The youth was tall and blonde, wearing a gray hat and a yellow-brown uniform coat with two rows of buttons over a dirty cotton shirt, denim trousers, and boots.

"Well then, please. Have a look at my nog. Awfully kind of you," Varney said.

Robin bent over and scraped away the sparse hair around the two lumps which rose like little purplish volcanoes surrounded by gray thatched jungle. Blood had dried on the two lumps, but two fresher deep scratches were oozing on the horse thief's scalp high on his forehead. The horse thief's hair hung down over his ears. He reached up and combed it back with his bloody fingers. Robin smelled whiskey on the horse thief's breath.

"Santana Leatherwood raked your head with his spurs," Robin said.

"Pardon?"

"I'm surprised he didn't yank that earring out of your ear."

"This earring is protected by a powerful spirit."

"Do you remember how you got here?"

"I'm starting to, yes, up to a point. I was having a discussion with four Hittites on horseback and suddenly one of them belted me with a club and another whacked me with a shotgun barrel. But I don't understand why I now find myself chained to a gibbet in this bloody fog."

The prisoner rolled over, got onto his knees, gathered himself and stood up. He brushed his clothing with his hands. His knee-length jacket was filthy, bloody and ripped, but it was expensively tailored. His boots were scuffed and worn but made of fine leather by a master craftsman.

"Have you seen my hat?" Varney asked.

"You weren't wearing one."

"My satchel? My dispatch case?"

Robin shrugged.

The prisoner rattled his chain by shaking his leg.

"If I should snap this chain, what next? What lies around us concealed in this fog?"

"A stockade fence fifteen feet high," Robin said.

Varney swept the yard with his gaze. He used his imagination to see through the fog and render a picture of his surroundings. He nodded. He said, "Well then." Varney looked at his chain and at Robin's chain. "This is quite an unexpected pickle. I must think this situation through. Do you have any tobacco?"

"No."

A dizziness struck him, and Varney said, "Sitting down sounds a proper idea." The horse thief traced one hand along the gallows plat-form until he touched the wooden steps leading up. Varney tugged at his chain and found it was just long enough that he could sit down on the second step. The fog was beginning to fade. A crack of light showed in the east. Varney looked up at the hanging arm of the gallows. He said, "How many souls do you reckon have climbed these steps into the great mystery?"

"None yet. The Yankees just now finished building this gallows.

The style in hanging, around here, is from a tree limb."

Varney touched fingers to his scalp and said, "What is your prognosis for my nog?"

"You've had no fracture. You'll heal."

"Did you say someone put the spurs to me?"

"Santana Leatherwood left his mark on you. Those are good Mexican spurs."

The fog was lifting fast and the late spring sun began to light the prison yard. Other forms began to emerge as the mist faded away. Men were rising, stretching, spitting in the dirt. Several were pissing against the fence. Varney saw there were about thirty prisoners inside the stockade. Tents and shelters had been erected by the prisoners. Blankets and bundles lay strewn around the perimeter like an undisciplined military camp. But these were not prisoners of war, Varney saw. They looked to him like robbers, thieves, murderers, drunks, brawlers, degenerates, the failing and fallen. Varney searched with his eyes for the wretch who had been crying out for help, but the voice was silent now. The prison yard was circular, about seventy-five yards across. The fence posts were pine logs planted in the ground end-first, and there were two guard towers and a main gate.

"I don't see chains on any of the other chaps," Varney said.

"You and I have been set apart for special treatment."

Varney's face lit up with a wide smile that wrinkled the corners of his eyes.

"Then we must become chums," Varney said. "Edmund Varney is my name."

Varney wiped his right palm against his chest and then stuck out his hand. Robin was impressed by the strength of the older man's grip as they shook hands. The name sounded vaguely familiar, but Robin couldn't recall where he might have heard it.

"Jerod Robin."

"Tell me, Mr. Robin, why are we in chains?"

"Santana Leatherwood intends to hang us."

"Good Lord, why me?"

"You for stealing a horse."

"It was a misunderstanding. My embassy will be contacted."

"In Texas, horse thieves don't have any rights, Mr. Varney."

"Why you? What have you done to be hanged for?"

"I offended Santana Leatherwood."

"How did you do that?"

"I ran him through with a sword in battle in Tennessee."

Varney's white-tufted eyebrows lifted. He scraped a handful of damp dirt and stood up from his seat on the gallows step. He scrubbed his hands with dirt in an effort to remove the dried blood. Varney grinned and said, "Worse and worse. Worse and worse." He dusted his hands and patted his pockets. He scowled. Varney searched his pockets more carefully. "Gone," he said. "By damn, it's gone."

Robin thought of his letter from Sweetbrush that was sewn into his coat.

Varney bowed his head and pinched the bridge of his nose. The lumps on his head now appeared more like small blue eggs. The spur scars were red but had stopped bleeding. Varney's shoulders slumped. He shook himself. He raised his head, lifted his chest and squared his shoulders. Robin was reminded of watching a bare-knuckle boxer who gets up after being knocked down, gathers his wits and his courage, and is game to continue the fight.

"How would I get in touch with this Santana Leatherwood fellow?"

"He'll be coming to see you soon enough."

"I am remembering now—the chief of the Hittites. You put a sword through him, eh? How Byzantine."

Varney paced to the end of his chain and back. He scratched the gray bristles on his chin. Varney again studied Robin from boots to hat with a curiosity that would have provoked a brawl if this had been Dutch John's. To Varney, Robin looked like a prime young Scots-Irish southerner, a well-reared Celt on his way home from the war.

Varney said, "Clearly you are a soldier." He paused. "You have the air of an officer." Varney squinted and sniffed. "You have the look and smell of a horse person. I can tell. I am a horse person myself. So you encountered this Santana Leatherwood in a skirmish and thrust him through?"

"It was more than a skirmish," Robin said.

"A battle then. What was it called?"

"Snow Hill."

"I haven't heard of it. When was this battle?"

"Last Christmas Eve."

"In Tennessee, you say?"

"In the Great Smoky Mountains along the North Carolina border."

"You were in a backwater affair. The battle at Nashville ended in the middle of December. Sherman had gone from Tennessee long before Christmas Eve. The major fighting had moved toward the sea. With respect, Snow Hill must have been a skirmish."

"I was at Nashville. Then we went east to the mountains. That's where Snow Hill is. We judged our fights by how nasty they were," Robin said. "It was a battle."

"I do understand about war, old son," Varney said. "I did a career turn for Her Majesty's horse soldiers and the East India Company in India and Afghanistan in my younger days that were not so long ago, it seems to me."

"Is that what you call hell?" asked Robin.

"India and Afghanistan were merely a warm-up for the real thing. But I do accept your definition of battle. Snow Hill was a battle that I never heard of. Am I correct in assuming you are going to tell me about it?"

"No."

"Later perhaps?"

"I don't see us having a later," Robin said.

"Last Christmas Eve you nearly slew the Hittite?"

"Nearly."

Varney paused and smiled at a memory.

"I was in Spain last Christmas Eve," mused Varney. "While you were fighting the Hittite, I was in a cave in the Pyrenees."

"You get around," Robin said.

"Indeed."

Varney yawned. He drew in a deep breath. Robin noticed the creases in Varney's forehead and between his brows. From what Robin knew of London from stories his mother told, and from books in the library at Sweetbrush, he speculated that Varney might be a high-born confidence man fleeing from a serious misadventure back home.

They heard the cry, "Bastards coming!"

Around the yard prisoners turned their heads to hide the identity of voices that began yelling, "Bastards coming!" The fog had thinned away. In Texas in June, the weather could change quickly from cool, wet and green to hot, yellow and dry. A guard in a blue Seventh Cavalry uniform raised the bar and pulled open the main gate. Little bowlegged Billy Leatherwood entered carrying a scattergun that almost reached his chin. He stopped and spoke to the guard and pointed toward Robin and Varney. Robin could see that Billy had tied around his neck a red bandana like those worn by his brothers in the collaborator Home Guard Company.

"Liiittle bastaaaaard comiiing!" a voice whinnied like a mule.

"You think that's funny? Using that kind of language?" shouted Billy Leatherwood.

The Englishman said, "There's something familiar about that bandy legged chap."

"He's one of your Hittites. Coming for us."

"Ah yes." Varney raised an eyebrow and said, "Into the crucible then. I do wish I had my hat."

Three

THE THREE LEATHERWOOD BROTHERS, wearing their red necker-chiefs that marked them in Robin's eyes as traitors, marched the two prisoners, both still dragging ankle chains, through the gate of the stockade and headed toward town on a road called Pine Street. Behind them to the west lay two miles of forest and streams that ended on the east bank of the Colorado River. Beyond the river rose white limestone cliffs and green hills.

"This is your lucky day," Billy said to the prisoners. "The county judge has swum the river on horseback so he could get here to hold court first thing this morning. You're lucky to be brought up before a real judge in these lawless times. Lt. Tom Custer will be in court in person to get a firsthand look at what kind of stupid idiot would try to steal his horse. His brother, General Custer himself, will be showing up here in Austin with the rest of his regiment in a few days, Uncle Santana says. Too bad you fellows will be dead by then. You, Robin, you would be thrilled to see the Seventh Cavalry riding into the capital of Texas with their flags and bugles and drums."

Billy laughed.

"Be a good chap and let me have a drink of water?" asked Varney.

"Got none to spare," Billy said.

They walked past young boys fishing in Shoal Creek. The creek was wide and flowing from the wet spring. The boys kept a cautious distance between where they stood with their cane poles, and the position of four blue-jacketed Federal troopers who were watering their horses. Further up the creek was a gathering of tents, and more Federals were walking about. The boys and the soldiers stared at the procession going past, as the Home Guard marched the prisoners toward court. One of the fishing boys hooted and yelled at the Leatherwoods, "Red-throat sons of bitches." Two rebel soldiers, looking haunted and hungry, sat beneath an oak tree and watched without interest as the prisoners went past. The soldiers had already seen the worst of nature. The Leatherwood brothers fell into a proud step as if they could hear a military drummer. They had avoided serving in the military, but they enjoyed playing soldier. Luther poked Robin in the ribs with the knobby club he had used to lay out the Englishman.

Luther said, "Step smart there, Jerod Robin."

"I'm keeping score, Luther," said Robin. "Every time you touch me goes into my ledger to be repaid."

Luther whacked him on the back with the club and knocked a puff of dust out of Robin's coat.

"Be sure and don't forget that one," Luther said.

Varney rubbed his throat and looked at Billy's water bottle. During his three days in Austin, Varney had observed the mood of the town to be taken over by that old devil fear. Citizens who had opposed the war had lived for four years with the cold comfort of their consciences and their reasons and they still feared the nightriders who burned the homes of Unionists. Already, Varney knew, the winners had begun satisfying their need for revenge. Anyone might be a target. From his window in the Avenue Hotel on Congress Avenue, Varney had heard shootings. Grudges were being settled without honor. The sounds of shouting and brawling were frequent interruptions in the nights. A fog of anxiety hung over the town. Varney enjoyed the sensations of this kind of place. The tensions reminded him of Kabul.

They saw an old man staggering across the road, bent by the weight of three saddles that he carried on his back. The saddles were tied together with a rope that stretched across the old man's forehead. Varney wondered if he had stolen the saddles, or was he hurrying along to hide them from thieves? Daylight robberies were common. There was randomness to life. Half a dozen girls in spring dresses stood inside a picket fence and watched the prisoners being marched east on Pine Street. A large Georgian house with white columns rose among the trees on a hill behind the girls. The house reminded Robin of his home at Sweetbrush. One of the girls cried, "You stupid red throats, you dirty Judases."

Robin smiled at the girls and waved to them.

"They hate you Leatherwoods," Robin said.

"They're just a bunch of trash. What do I care about them?" said Billy.

"They whores," Adam said.

"They're not whores. Just trashy Austin girls," said Billy.

"No, they whores with smelly, swampy cooters," Luther said.

The Leatherwood brothers whooped.

"Cooters," Adam yelled at the girls. "Swampy cooters."

"I wonder if I might have a nip from that water bag?" the Englishman said.

Robin looked around at the scowl that was pinching Varney's face. If Varney had been drinking at Dutch John's until he tried to steal Custer's brother's horse in the middle of the night, he couldn't have had any sleep except for the time he was unconscious, and that would not have been restful. Varney licked his lips. He was trying to decide which headache hurt the worst. He had the sick headache that follows from the poison of too much whiskey. He had the pulsing headache that came from the blows to his skull by the Leatherwood brothers and their uncle. But topsys among his problems was this awful thirst. He must have water. He thought of his journey across the plains of Punjab the summer when even the bloody camels were suffering on the march. This morning was no topsys for that ordeal, but he could feel last night's alcohol drying and shrinking his tissues. His body's cry for water was more urgent than the hurt of a few more lumps on a head that had already taken so many.

"I'm saying, friend, what about a tug at that bag of water?" said Varney.

"Don't give him nothing, Billy," Luther said.

"We can't be stopping. The judge gets mean if you make him wait," said Billy.

Robin saw a small shudder go down to Varney's boots. He wondered how a man like Varney, obviously educated and claiming a military background, had found himself accused of stealing a horse in Texas. Robin knew quite a lot about England from his parents—his father had sailed to London and married his mother there—and from books in the library at Sweetbrush. During his two years at Austin College in Huntsville, Robin was reading for a history degree. For nine months of the year before the war, Robin came home and taught at the two-room white-pine school his father, Dr. Junius Robin, had built for the children of the workers—slaves and Mexicans—at Sweetbrush. Soon after Dr. Robin had opened the school, young people had begun coming down the red dirt roads from other farms and plantations, along with the children of property owners and merchants who did business in the town of Gethsemane, four miles through the forest by road but closer by boat on Big Neck Bayou. By the time young Robin returned from college to help his family at Sweetbrush and took over teaching school three mornings a week, there were from ten to forty pupils, Negro, Mexican, and white, in class, depending on the season. The Leatherwoods lived in a two-story house near the church in town. Pastor Horry Leatherwood, their father, the Mayor of Gethsemane, sent his three sons to the Sweetbrush school even though he had become an enemy of young Robin's father, the doctor. Adam and Luther would sprawl spraddle-legged in their cane chairs in class and listen to Jerod Robin with dull-eyed distaste, but little Billy was fascinated when Robin told them about British history, about the Magna Carta and the Crusades and the two American wars of revolution in the last eighty years against British Colonial rule and the abuses of royalty. In particular Billy had loved stories about the Crusades.

"I'm asking you one more time for water," said Varney.

"Or you'll what?" Adam said.

"I hate Englishmen," said Luther. "Give me a look and I'll bash you."

"I'll do it again, twice as hard," Adam said.

Billy said, "My favorite Englishman is Ivanhoe."

This was unexpected news to Robin. He had not taught Sir Walter Scott at the Sweetbrush school. Robin remembered Billy bent over a book on English history, slowly picking out each word and

forming it in his mind to grasp and keep it. Later Robin discovered
Billy had torn out the chapter on knights and the code of chivalry
and had taken it with him when he ran away into the forest. Now
Robin wondered if Billy might have slipped in and stolen Ivanhoe
from the Sweetbrush library.

Billy said, "I like how Ivanhoe whipped that Boy Gilbert and
rescued the beautiful Jew girl."

"Bois-Guilbert?" asked Varney.

"Boy Gilbert is how you say it," Billy said. "This ain't France."

"You are a fancier of romances, are you?" said Varney.

"Of what?"

"Of romantic novels."

"Not that crap. No," Billy said. "I don't have time to waste on
imaginary stories. I like to study the real English history. You ask
Captain Robin if I don't."

"It's true," said Robin. "Billy is a great admirer of the Crusades."

"I wish they would have another Crusade. I'd sign right up," Billy
said.

"You're eager to kill Mohammedans?" said Varney.

"I'll kill whatever they got over there," Billy said.

Robin was watching all along the road for any intervention of
luck or fate that would give him a chance to grab Billy's shotgun and
turn the weapon on the Leatherwoods. Robin could not flee
because of the chain that locked him onto the chain of the
Englishman. Sweat rolled down his chest inside his butternut coat.
He could feel the letter from Sweetbrush against his heart.

"So to you Ivanhoe is an historical figure?" Varney said.

"What do you mean?" said Billy.

Varney's tufted eyebrows lifted, and furrows trotted across his
brow.

"I am a great admirer of Wilfred of Ivanhoe, just as you are,"
Varney said. "Yes, I am a fan of Ivanhoe, indeed. Powerful chap.
Handsome. Fearless. He fought in the Crusades against the Arabs
beside Richard the Lion Heart. Am I correct?"

"That's right," Billy said.

"Tell me if I am correct that Ivanhoe returned from the Holy

Land to England and was betrayed and taken prisoner by the Norman barons. His friend Robin Hood helped him escape, if I recall the story truly."

"You know your history," Billy nodded.

Varney said, "The mysterious Black Knight appeared at the jousts as the champion of the beautiful prisoner Rebecca and in fair combat killed Sir Brian Boy Gilbert, thus saving Rebecca's life."

Billy was excited. "Boy Gilbert was going to burn the Jew girl at the stake. But the Black Knight knocked him around and then stood over his hacked up body. The Black Knight took off his helmet and it was Ivanhoe underneath. Ivanhoe looked at the damsel and told her to take her old Hebrew daddy and go back where they come from. He didn't even rape her."

"That was stupid of him," said Luther.

"She was what is known in history as a damsel. He was a knight. Why the hell you think they called him Sir Ivanhoe? He don't rape damsels," Billy said.

"He's really stupid then," said Luther.

"Who ever heard of a Jew damsel?" Adam said.

Varney said, "Wilfred of Ivanhoe always kept his prisoners well supplied with water. It was known by all—even the Arabs in the Holy Land knew it, that if you were nabbed by Ivanhoe you would never die of thirst. He might throw you off a castle parapet, but a man of great heart and humanity like Ivanhoe would never withhold water from a prisoner."

"He's making fun of you, Billy," said Adam.

"No, he ain't," Billy said. "That's the kind of fellow Ivanhoe was."

Billy unhooked the goatskin bag of water from his belt and passed it to Varney, who emptied it with three gulps. Robin's tongue touched his lips unbidden, but he would not ask the Leatherwoods for any favors.

"Where's your uncle?" Robin said.

"He's somewhere oiling up a new rope just for you," said Luther.

"You shouldn't of stobbed him. He was hurt real bad for a while. He almost died," Adam said. "If you was going to stob him with your sword, you should of stobbed him good and killed him dead. Uncle Santana don't forget and he sure as hell don't forgive."

"He's got a huge dent now where his right kidney used to be," said Luther.

"He keeps his shirt on when he takes the ladies to bed," Adam said.

"And he does lots of that," said Luther.

"Not as much as he used to," Adam said.

Varney gave the water bag back to Billy and said, "Thank you. This earns you a shiny gold star in heaven."

"I've already got my ticket to heaven. Our daddy is a preacher. He keeps us prayed up and ready to go. But I ain't ready to go just yet," said Billy. "You prisoners step smart now. People are watching. You don't want to look sloppy or scared."

The odd little procession crossed West Avenue and passed into the heart of the town. Here in Texas they called it the Capital City, but to Varney it was a small town. Several small boys fell in behind and marched along kicking up dust, mocking the prisoners and the red-throated Home Guards. The procession turned north on Colorado Street, walked a few minutes to Mesquite Street and then turned east again. Swallows flitted overhead. The birds were making nests on the limestone walls of the old Capitol. Pigeons ruffed up their feathers and strutted and cooed. At dusk clouds of bats would fly out from the building. Men peered into the morning from doors and windows of saloons. In front of a Methodist church built of pine logs, a flea market was spread across the grass. Robin's eyes searched the faces, hoping to find an ally who might help him escape. But the people were involved with their own daily despairs and turned away from the spectacle of three Home Guards marching two chained prisoners to confront their fate.

Four

A FOUNDRY IS A PLACE FOR CASTING metal, but this foundry was closed for business because the owner had been murdered in his sleep by his wife. Temporarily the building was being used as the county court. The foundry was a two-story gray fieldstone set in a four-acre clearing in a forest on the sunrise side of town. To arrive there the prisoners and the Leatherwood brothers climbed a hill on a road through oak trees and then went down, followed by a dozen citizens who had fallen into their wake. On the road they could smell the sweet purple grapes of the mountain laurels. Tiny green worms of early summer hung in the air on invisible strings and stuck to the faces of the marchers.

They heard the crack of axes from woodchoppers clearing another road beyond a stream that ran over rocks east of the foundry. Their boots crunched on gravel as the procession came toward the building. Wagons were drawing up in front, their leather harness squeaking and the horses wheezing and blowing and clopping. Six mounted men galloped up in a body, all of them armed with rifles and wearing wide-brimmed hats. Women with children in hand were coming out of the forest and walking toward the foundry. A dozen Negroes—slaves who had been freed by Lincoln but not by Texas—gathered at the windows outside so they could see into the courtroom and hear the proceedings. Robin glanced at the Englishman. Varney stood erect again, his shoulders square, taking in the scene with curious eyes, studying the faces that were excited at the prospect of watching the prisoners be judged and most likely condemned.

Robin saw Santana Leatherwood waiting for them at the doorway. Santana was straightening the golden cord on his hat band. His thick black hair was wet and combed back. Santana's forehead was pale, but his face was brown from sun and wind. He noticed Robin and broke into a wide white toothed grin. There was a streak of handsomeness in the Leatherwood family; Robin had always admitted that much. To Robin this demonstrated that beauty and good do not necessarily go together.

Santana said, "Welcome to the house of justice."

"You have no right to hold me," said Robin. "Cut me loose and we'll settle our score just between you and me, the way we would back home."

"You're not only without honor, you're real primitive, Jerod Robin. You're a savage at heart. You could get away with your behavior in the old Texas because of your birth. But in the new Texas we have laws and courts to deal with people like you."

"There's no evidence against me."

"I am the evidence. Don't worry about your sweet little wife, Laura, after you're hanged. She won't be without the comfort of a man. I hear she's gotten very hospitable, with you gone for so long. I'm thinking I might call on her myself, next time I get down that way," Santana said.

Robin lunged at Santana. Adam and Luther each grabbed one of Robin's arms and hauled him backward.

"I'll kill you if you set foot on Sweetbrush again," Robin said.

"You tried killing me, but I'm too tough for you," said Santana. "I look forward to hearing what you have to say in your defense before we take you out and break your neck."

Adam and Luther pushed Robin into the courtroom. Robin's chain jerked against the chain of Varney, who dug his heels and planted himself in front of Santana, lifted his chin and looked into the officer's face with stern gray eyes. Varney seemed to grow bigger in the chest.

Varney said, "You stole my wallet. You stole my clothing. I shall have an accounting of those items later. But I insist that you return my notebook immediately." Varney patted his jacket pockets to reassure himself one more time that the notebook was missing. "I must have my notebook. Where is my notebook?"

"Billy left your notebook in the thunderbox," Santana said.

"The thunderbox?"

"I imagine the paper is all used up by now," Santana said.

Varney's large gray eyes blinked as he absorbed what he was hearing. His lips mumbled to form words that did not come out. Rage began to shake his shoulders.

"You barbaric, criminal bastard," Varney said. "Do you have any idea what the bloody awful hell you have done? What an atrocity?"

"Boys, throw this loudmouth into his seat," said Santana.

"History will scorn you for this," Varney shouted.

He wrestled with Adam and Luther. They shoved him into the courtroom and thrust him down upon a wooden church pew beside Robin. The Leatherwood brothers were surprised at Varney's strength. They thought of him as an old man. The Englishman looked about the same age as their father. Pastor Horry Leatherwood was strong and could be rougher than any of them in a wrestling match, even at his age, but the boys regarded their father as a special case, a natural champion.

In the struggle Varney was pushed past Robin and fell onto the pew and winced at the sharp runner of pain that shot up his spine. He leaned left from the loss of balance, and became aware from the soft feel of flesh that he had not fallen against some wretch from the bull pen.

"Don't you be laying all over me, hey?" she said.

Varney smelled sweat and ginger as he turned to look at her. She was a girl in her teens. Her eyes drew him in. Her skin was nut colored and her eyes were green as the ocean. At the ends of her earrings dangled tiny bits of ivory that at first appeared to him to be Buddhas, but on closer look became talismans of some sort. She wore a green turban wrapped around a fuzzy crop of black hair. Varney had leaned against a bare arm that curved out of a bright blue blouse. Her skirt was mustard colored, made of soft hemp cloth, and her bare feet spread against the stone floor, toes splayed, determined to hold her position on the pew.

Billy Leatherwood made a grab for Robin's hat. Robin slapped Billy's hand away.

"Show some respect for the court," Billy said.

Upwards of fifty people had found places to sit or stand in the room. Negroes looked in from the windows. Robin could see there was a crowd outside with horses and wagons. Judgment day was a popular entertainment. The judge rode a circuit and could hold court here once in ten days, depending on the weather. There was an odor of sulfur from the iron cauldron behind the empty judge's table. Billy hooked a finger inside his red neckerchief and loosened it a bit. The morning was heating up. Luther and Adam took up positions beside Santana at the door.

Billy looked down at the seated girl and said, "Too bad you are only a nigger and not a damsel. There won't be no knight in armor coming to save you today, I imagine."

The girl rolled her eyes to look at Billy. The intensity of her gaze disturbed him.

"I'm just joking about the olden times," he said. "This horse thief can tell you what I mean."

"You ignorant runty brute, what have you done with my notebook?" said Varney.

"I read some of it."

"Where is it now?"

"I forgot and left it in the outhouse."

"Go get it," Varney said.

"Well, the truth is I only used part of it. Other people came along and used up the rest."

"You read it first and then you used it?" Varney's voice rattled with anger. "You knew what it was before you used it—and still you used it?"

The girl's gaze remained fastened on Billy. She said, "You are going to die today, hey? You hear me? You will be dead by nightfall."

"With my hands around your nasty little throat," said Varney.

Billy stepped back and said, "You don't scare me. You're just hollering in the graveyard. You two is doomed. Well, maybe this here colored witch ain't doomed, I don't know, but you are sure one doomed Englishman."

Billy turned away as the judge stepped out from behind the cauldron, where he had changed into dry clothes and unpacked his black gown. A week's growth of beard shaded his round red face. His belly made a mound under the black judicial robe. The robe was caught up at his right hip by the butt of a pistol which stuck out of his trousers.

The judge said, "Announce me, Billy."

Billy took three steps to the judge's table, did a military turn and looked out at the crowd. Billy removed his hat and held it against his chest.

Billy said, "The court is now in session. The Honorable Judge P. M. Dingus presiding. Judge Dingus would like for all you men to take off your hats in court."

"No, I wouldn't, Billy, damn it. Look at me. I'm wearing a hat myself."

The judge pointed to the dirty black bowler on his head.

Billy ducked at the wave of laughter from the crowd, but he kept his hat off. Judge Dingus pulled up a chair and sat down behind the table. He scowled as he turned through a stack of papers. He picked out a piece of blue paper and squinted at it. He turned it upside down.

"I know this is from the female because who the hell else would use blue paper to write a complaint on?" the judge said. "But I can't read this name or make out what the problem is, other than what I obviously see before me in the front row. Stand up, girl. Identify yourself to this court."

The colored girl rose slowly, with dignity. Her blue blouse was loose and concealed her form, but her arms were brown and smooth with muscle.

She said, "My name is Flora Bowprie."

Judge Dingus studied her for a moment. Her bare feet caught his attention. He picked up an ink pen and traced its dry point against the letters in the name on the blue paper document.

He said, "That is spelled B-e-a-u-p-r-i-e-u-x?"

"No, your honor. It is spelled B-o-w-p-r-i-e."

"That is slave spelling. Where did you run away from? Who is your owner?"

"I am a free person," she said.

"You are wrong about that, girl. By law there are no free nigras in the state of Texas. If you are a nigra in Texas, somebody owns you. That is a fact of life. Prima Facie. Are you telling me you are some kind of Hindu and not a nigra at all?"

"No sir," she said.

"How old are you, anyhow?"

"Sixteen."

"Old enough, then, to know right from wrong."

Judge Dingus looked into the faces in the courtroom. His eyes passed over Robin and Varney on the front row and moved to the women and children behind them and then to the rough men in the pews and leaning against the walls, and finally to the black faces peering in the windows.

"You nigras out there at the windows, you listen to me," the judge said. "I am going to tell you the facts of life as it is lived today. You come here this morning to see justice done, feeling that now you have an interest in this old flag, which was never an emblem of justice or freedom to you before now."

The judge gave them a moment to look at the United States flag, which now hung on the wall behind the cauldron.

He said, "You nigras hear reports that you are free, or soon will be, and freedom to you is like heaven to the poor people—a place where there is a great deal of singing and no work to do. But you will find yours will be a freedom that gives you no holiday for headaches, sideaches, backaches, and bellyaches. If you nurse and physic these afflicted organs hereafter, it will be at your own expense."

Flora Bowprie said, "Your Honor—"

"You'll have your turn to speak," said Judge Dingus. "You would be wise to keep standing there and listening to me with a respectful attitude and heeding what I am saying. All you nigras out there at the windows, you go tell your aunties and cousins what I am saying this morning. One day soon the state of Texas will be forced to proclaim that all nigras are set free. You nigras will celebrate and dance and sing and play musical instruments. But being new to freedom, you do not understand what freedom entails. Once you are set free, you will have to pay the doctors to kill you and the sextons to bury you, just as white people do."

The judge drank from a tin cup of water that Billy poured for him. Varney leaned forward and stared at the water pitcher. Robin licked his lips. Flora Bowprie stood with her arms folded and cocked her head and looked at the judge.

Judge Dingus said, "I have myself paid more of your nigra doctor bills than Jesus ever would have paid, I swear to you. I have clothed and fed and cared for ten nigras to get the work of two. I am not going to do it anymore. You nigras must pay for your own cursed awkwardness and carelessness, which have generally caused financial ruin to your masters. You people never were worth a damn as workers anyway. I have seen you broken down in the cotton fields and fainting in the wheat fields, far behind in your work, laying out in the rows. So you nigras go to your homes and make your arrangements to work longer and harder and do better work for what comes down to less pay as soon as you are free and on your own, with no security in this world whatsoever."

The judge studied the crowd.

"There is a widespread belief among you nigras that on freedom day in Texas each nigra will receive forty acres of land and a mule free of charge paid for by the Confederacy."

Several white men in the crowd shouted disapproval.

"But I am here to tell you," the judge said, "that you nigras and all your aunties and cousins will go through a million hells before that ever happens."

"Let 'em know about it, Judge," yelled a man on the back row.

Judge Dingus turned toward Santana Leatherwood, who was standing in the doorway with his hat under his arm and kept glancing back in the direction of town, waiting on something.

"To you Yankee officers I want to say I know what's coming—the government is going to send among us a horde of dwarf schoolmasters, politicians, administrators, lawyers, and editors who have been falsely taught up north that all us whites in Texas did before the war was sit in the shade and drink lemonade while nigras labored all day in the hot sun and in the ice of winter and did all the work," the judge said. He slapped the table. "Are you listening to me, Captain?"

"I am, yes sir," Santana said.

"You Yankees will have your delusions dispelled in a hurry," said Judge Dingus. "This is a hard country down here. We keep our patriotism, and by that I mean our love of Texas, in our hearts right next to our love of family and just a notch below our love of God. Up north you have a very divided faith. You have Universalists, Shakers, Dunkers, Spiritual Rappers. You have Mormons and Catholics and Jews. Here in Texas we have only Methodists, Episcopalians, Iron Jackets, and a few others of little consequence. God has seen fit to give us just enough Jews to energize trade, and most all of our Catholics are Mexicans. There might occasionally be a shaky brother on some article of faith in Texas, but we never exhausted our well of faith during the long and bloody war."

Louder than before, Flora Bowprie said, "Your Honor—"

"Judge Dingus warned you to keep your mouth shut," said Billy.

"Your judgment is coming, girl. Don't be in such a hurry for it," Judge Dingus said.

"What do you be judging me for? I didn't come here to be judged," said Flora Bowprie.

"Nigra insolence will not help your case," the judge said.

Judge Dingus took off his dirty black bowler hat and wiped sweat from the bald area high on his forehead. He scratched his belly. He regarded the girl standing before him. He looked out at the crowd, the white and colored faces. He cleared his throat.

"I was making the point that up north they are confused by many faiths," the judge said. "Here in Texas we have just one abiding faith. We believe in the divine word of God Almighty and His son Jesus Christ as revealed to us in the Holy Bible. Our faith has carried us through years of terrible war. Our faith will carry us to Kingdom Come. We enlisted God without paying any bounty money. Our faith was not shaken when General Lee surrendered his army at Appomattox two months ago in far-off Virginia, when soldiers, women, children, and dancing, shouting little nigras ripped the last garment and divided the substance of the stricken Confederacy. Lee surrendered an army; he didn't surrender our cause. This is the will of God for now. Texas is on the side of God always. Amen."

"Amen to that, brother," yelled a man from the back of the room.

"The main fact of life I am trying to explain today to all of you people is that when the late President Lincoln decreed that no one shall have chattel interest in nigras, it does not mean that nigras are no longer required to work, as many of you seem to believe. Nigras ask to be equal citizens with us, and I say by your labor and your attitude shall you earn your keep in this world. I am not paying nigras' living expenses anymore, not in fact and not by taxes, either."

Judge Dingus turned toward Santana Leatherwood.

"Captain, what is your charge against this girl?"

"I have none, sir. I didn't bring her in."

"I haven't seen you here before, Captain . . ."

"Captain Leatherwood, sir. I arrived here eight days ago."

"You don't sound like a Yankee. What part of the north are you from?" asked the judge.

"Just north of Houston."

"Houston?"

"Yes sir."

"Houston, Texas?"

"Yes sir. On the bayou."

"What in the hell are you doing in that Yankee uniform?"

"I am in command of the prison stockade until civil authorities are in shape to take over, sir."

"I mean what is a Houston man doing wearing the Yankee colors?" said Judge Dingus.

"I joined the United States Army to fight in the invasion of Mexico."

"That was nearly twenty years ago," the judge said. "You don't look old enough."

"I enlisted at age seventeen."

"Did you fight against the Mexicans?"

"All the way to Mexico City with General Scott, sir."

The judge nodded.

"The world of man gets more insane with each breath I take, but war is a constant thing. I suppose there is a good reason why you remained a Federal instead of joining your Texas brothers for the last four years?"

"I have one Texas brother, sir, and he believes slavery is a sin against the intention of God."

"Your brother knows the intention of God, does he?"

"He preaches it every Sunday and many Wednesdays," Santana said, glancing outside again. "My brother is the founder of the town of Gethsemane and is the only mayor the town has ever had. His church is the only church. My brother is a hero of the Texas revolution. What he knows, he for damn sure knows."

"How does your brother identify his faith?"

"He is pastor of the Zanzibar Church of Gethsemane, Texas."

"Baptist?"

"The Rock of the Truth, sir."

"He is an Iron Jacket of some kind, I take it."

"True Believer, sir."

"What do you keep looking at?" asked the judge.

"I'm expecting Lieutenant Custer, sir."

Flora Bowprie said, "Judge—"

Judge Dingus thumbed through the papers on his table and peered again at the blue sheet.

"Who brought in this nigra girl?" he said.

The room was silent for a moment.

"Now may I speak?" said Flora Bowprie.

Five

FLORA BOWPRIE SAID, "I CAME to this court seeking justice. I have traveled alone from New Orleans in my wagon on a difficult and dangerous journey, but it was not until I got close to this capital city of Texas that I was attacked by a gang of outlaws. They stole my wagon and my mules and all my worldly possessions. They had in mind to rape me, but I escaped through the tall yellow flowers into the cypress trees and swam across a creek and then walked all night through a forest, hearing the howling of wolves. At dawn I came across some of my people who were on their way here to watch justice being done, so I have brought my case directly to the judge himself, hey?"

Rich and theatrical presentation, Varney was thinking, surprising for such a young girl. He was delighted by the lilt of her voice. Her accent fit his recollection of New Orleans and the races that mingled there. The muttering, coughing and clanking of the crowd was stilled by her voice. Robin sat up straight and stared at her. Santana Leatherwood was watching from the doorway. Adam and Luther stood on either side of their uncle. Billy took a step away from the table to get out of the girl's sight line.

Judge Dingus lifted a hand for silence. He looked again at the piece of blue paper.

He said, "I see now that this pleading is written in French. No wonder it looked peculiar to me."

"I learned French from birth. My pen naturally writes in French."

The judge waved the piece of blue paper.

"What does this say?"

"I'm asking you to send the law to catch those outlaws and return my wagon and my property, including my professional equipment."

The judge grinned. He thought he knew the answer before he asked his next question.

"What profession would that be?"

"I am a future teller," she said.

That was not the answer he expected.

"Is that what prostitution is called in New Orleans?" he scowled.

There was laughter from the crowd. Flora turned and fixed her gaze on a man who was heehawing in the third row of pews. Something in her eyes caused him to gulp and cover his mouth. Varney admired the girl's poise. He liked it that she spoke French. He imagined she could be of use to him in his quest, if they could manage to get out of this courtroom.

"Would you like me to tell your future?" Flora asked the judge.

Still scowling, Judge Dingus reached down the neck of his robe and found the stump of a cigar. Billy moved to strike a match, but the judge brushed him aside and bit off the ragged end of the cigar and spat onto the floor behind the table.

"Who owns you?" the judge asked.

"I was born free in New Orleans. I am a free citizen."

"Hah! Not in Texas!" said Judge Dingus. "I suppose I could hold you in custody until we find your owner, but if you have no owner then you would have to remain in custody until Texas frees the slaves."

"I am the one whose mules and wagon got stolen," Flora said. "I am not the guilty one, hey."

"You are illegal is what you are, young missy," said the judge. "You shouldn't keep taking a too smart tone with me. You say you are a fortune-teller? Tarot cards? Crystal balls? The wet leafs of orange pekoe tea? What kind of fortune-teller are you?"

"The kind you fear the most," she said.

"Oh yes? You think you know what I am feeling? You know what awaits in my future? You're too young for such things. How could you pretend to know anything at all about me?"

"As I watch you and listen to you I foresee what will become of you," she said. "As you think in your heart, so you are and so you cause things to happen to you."

"Tell me then, what is my future?" said Judge Dingus. He stuck the cigar into the corner of his mouth, put his elbows on the table and leaned toward her. Then suddenly he lifted both hands in a gesture of fending her off. "No, no, wait! Never mind that. I don't want to hear it. You're using this as a trick to vent your nigra mind in my court. I don't care what you think of me. You don't know my future. I'd sooner trust the throw of the dice than your imagination."

"I had some dice in my wagon," she said.

"Your request of this court is preposterous," said Judge Dingus. "The people of this county have a tough time defending their own property. Do you think I am going to ask them to form a posse and leave their homes unguarded while they pursue the stolen crystal ball of a runaway slave?"

"I told you I am born free."

"Regardless, you are ipso facto in violation of Texas law that says there are no free nigras in this state. So I am declaring you a runaway slave. But I will say this in your behalf. You are the most interesting criminal I have seen this week, and certainly the prettiest."

Flora Bowprie said, "Judge, I didn't make this journey just to fore-tell your future. I am searching for my father."

"He a runaway, too?"

"My father is French."

"So you already know his name?"

"Of course I know his name. Henri Bowprie is his name."

"You've not come here to accuse anybody of anything?"

"Hey, I said they stole my wagon and mules and all I own, didn't I?"

"How old are you?" asked the judge.

"Sixteen."

"What color is your father?"

"What shade is his skin?" she said.

"I mean is he a French nigra?"

"My father is white."

"Then you are a mulatto and thus technically not an authentic nigra. I will take that into consideration as I deliberate your case," said the judge.

A commotion at the door drew the judge's attention.

Santana Leatherwood stepped outside and exchanged salutes with a slender young man, a boy in looks despite his mustache. His sandy hair was parted in the middle and hung over his collar in the back. He wore the tabs of a first lieutenant on his clean blue blouse that was smartly pressed. A vivid red splash colored his left cheek. Jerod Robin looked curiously at the freshly washed and ironed blouse—fit by a tailor—and at the red splash, which he recognized as a bullet wound. The hero Tom Custer stood erect, shoulders back, pelvis slung a bit forward. His eyes were puffy from sleep, and his lips turned down in what Robin took to be a surly manner. Robin was thinking, so this skinny boy with the fancy haircut and the clean blouse is the famous Tom Custer?

Robin was in a hospital two months ago in Knoxville when he began hearing stories about Tom Custer. Robin believed there is a hierarchy of the foolishly brave in war. Robin had become an initiate at Shiloh early in the war, when he was the same age Tom Custer now appeared to be, and Robin had won his membership in the same way as Custer, except in raids behind the lines that were unseen by generals and unrecorded by the newspapers. In the hospital in Tennessee, Robin heard wounded men repeating tales of the recent fights at Namozine Church and three days later at Sayler's Creek in Virginia. One man claimed he had been in the front rank at the church when the Yanks charged. "A crazy boy mounted on a beautiful chestnut horse come running straight into our guns," the man wheezed as the nurse wrapped a clean bandage on his chest. "We killed a terrible number of Yanks that day, mowed them down like wheat, but this crazy boy jumped in among us, shooting and slashing and screaming, and grabbed our colors and made it back to his own people with our flag. We saw him give the flag to his brother, the general. Our snipers took shots at him but only knocked a twig off a tree by his head. He's got luck with him."

A man who lay on a pallet in the corner with a hunk of muscle gone from his right thigh, sat up on his elbows and said, "Tom Custer is who it was. My brother is in Virginia. He wrote me that Tom Custer leaped the breastworks at Sayler's Creek on a beautiful chestnut Arabian horse and plunged in among our boys and stuck his pistol against the chest of our color bearer and shot him dead and captured our flag. My brother fired the bullet that hit Custer in the face, but Custer kept his seat in the saddle and that big chestnut horse carried him back out of there before my brother could finish killing him. My brother said he had to take his hat off to the crazy son of a bitch."

Robin sized up young Tom Custer standing at the courtroom doorway and decided if they should ever be matched against each other for their lives, Robin would get the best of him.

"Order! Order! What the hell is all this?" shouted Judge Dingus. He pounded on the table.

"That is Lt. Tom Custer," Billy said.

"I don't care what his name is," the judge said. "He is disturbing my court."

"Your Honor, I am here to see the man who stole my horse," said Custer.

There was an off-tone in Custer's voice that carried the flavor of a long night of drinking whiskey, and indicated he may have had another taste before coming to court.

"What part of the north are you from, Lieutenant?" the judge asked.

Flora Bowprie cried out, "Hey, hey, you still have me to deal with, Judge. You can't up and decide to proclaim me a slave. If you want to change the rules, it can't be done by mouth alone. These soldiers are here to protect my rights."

"You are sorely trying my patience," said the judge. "Put her down, Billy."

Flora stared at Billy, who did not move. She remained standing for a moment to make her point. After a silence she sat down beside Varney on the other side of Robin. She noticed the dried blood on Varney's ear. She looked at his earring. He gave her a slow wink.

Judge Dingus looked back at Custer.

"Now tell me. What part of the north are you from?"

"New Rumley, Ohio."

"Is that near Cincinnati?"

"New Rumley is on the opposite side of the state from Cincinnati. The far eastern side. New Rumley is in Harrison County, near the West Virginia border."

"But you are a genuine Yankee?"

"I am indeed."

"The son of General Custer?"

"Younger brother, Judge."

"What did you say about your horse? Somebody stole your horse?"

"Yes sir. My horse Athena was stolen last night."

"Do you see the thief in this courtroom?"

Custer looked at the three prisoners in the front pew. Custer's eyes found the eyes of Robin and held for a count of two. Robin felt that they were recognizing each other as members of the brotherhood. Then Custer broke the gaze with Robin and moved his eyes onto the face and form of Flora Bowprie. He smiled directly at her, pleased at what he was seeing. The crowd was bending forward like stalks in the breeze, straining to see the Yankee officer and hear what he was saying.

After a pause to consider the charms of Flora Bowprie, and flirt with her with his eyes and his smile, Custer looked away from her and into the blood-flecked gray eyes of Varney.

"Edmund Varney? What are you doing here?" Custer said, surprised.

Six

VARNEY STOOD UP. Despite his torn and tattered clothing and the knots and bruises on his gray head, Varney looked more like a judge than anyone else in the courtroom did, Robin thought. Varney smiled at Custer and said, "Good morning, Tom."

"You look a sight, Edmund," said Custer.

"There has been an embarrassing misunderstanding," Varney said.

"Hold on now," said Judge Dingus, "Let's go in order here. Prisoner, identify yourself to the court."

"My name is Edmund Varney."

"What is that on your left ear?" the judge asked.

"An earring."

"It is tarnished."

"It is jade."

"Why would a man wear an earring?"

"It is a gift from my late wife. I wear it in her memory." Varney glanced at Santana Leatherwood. "Her spirit keeps the hands of robbers off it."

"What would be your trade, craft, or profession?"

"I am a romancer."

From his seat at the table the judge beheld the speckles of blood on the dirty, battered face of the Englishman.

"A romancer? You mean you are a gigolo? I warn you, we don't approve of gigolos in Texas."

"I am a writer of romances. I am a novelist, and a journalist as well."

"Like Charles Dickens?"

"Exactly."

"You couldn't be exactly like Charles Dickens, or I would have heard of you," said the judge.

"In my own country the name Edmund Varney is known from coast to coast and from bottom to top. Stop any person on any road, especially in London, and inquire of Edmund Varney, and you will get an earful."

Suddenly Robin knew why the name had seemed familiar when Varney had introduced himself in the prison yard. Robin's memory began to scan the titles of the books on the shelves in the library at Sweetbrush.

"In Texas the word romancer is liable to get you shot dead," Judge Dingus said. "Also you shouldn't let it get around that you are a journalist, especially not with that foreign accent." The judge laughed. "Frankly, Varney, I don't despise journalists as much as I ought to—as most judges do—which is lucky for you. Now, would you like to have a chance to change your story and tell me what it is you are really up to?"

Custer had been looking back and forth from Varney to the judge.

"Would you vouch for me, Tom?" said Varney.

"Your Honor, I can vouch that this man is a writer of some repute," Custer said. "I have a copy of the London magazine he writes for, with a story by him in it. Also I have in my quarters a novel by Edmund Varney called *By the Sword*. He gave it to me himself and inscribed it for me."

Robin remembered. In his mind he saw a red-leather binding and the title *By the Sword* on a shelf at Sweetbrush. He saw *by Edmund Varney* on the spine of the book. A friend of Robin's mother had sent the book to her from London. It had arrived the same week Robin was saying goodbyes and preparing to go to the war with the First Texas Volunteer Cavalry. Robin had unwrapped the package from London and taken out the book and flipped through the 300 pages and remarked that it was a sturdy job of publishing. Then he handed the book to his mother, Varina, and watched her admiring the red leather binding and the printing and the quality of the paper. With a fingernail she traced the name of the author—Edmund Varney—and smiled, apparently remembering something that pleased her. Varina had been an actress at the Covent Garden when she married Dr. Junius Robin, but she had not stepped on a stage since they left London and came to Texas. Varina was six feet tall and had long blonde hair, nearly waist length, which she kept touched up with peroxide. "How nice, how lovely that she thought of me," she said. She went to a book shelf and placed *By the Sword* next to a well-thumbed volume of plays by Shakespeare, which meant she would soon have a look at it. Robin and his bride, Laura, left for Galveston Island for three days, and then it was time for him to join his brigade. That was nearly four years ago. Robin had been back to Sweetbrush once since—two years ago—but he had never heard the Varney book mentioned and did not remember noticing it on the shelf again.

"Then you are a friend of this self-proclaimed romancer?" the judge asked Custer.

"He is writing the true story of my life for the *Holly Bush Journal*, his magazine," Custer said.

Varney turned to face Custer. From his seat Robin had a close view of one of Varney's hands. The hair on the back of the hand was matted with dried blood and dirt. It was a muscular hand, not the dainty hand Robin might have expected of a writer. Robin looked at the dirt on Varney's fingernails and tried to imagine a quill pen in that hand, scratching words onto paper. Flora Bowprie's lips parted as she watched with her young fortune-teller's way of viewing life, which she had said was that we cause our tomorrows.

"Now we will have to start our interview over pretty much from the beginning," said Varney. "I'm sorry, Tom, but the officer standing beside you stole my notebook with all my notes for your life story in it. He maliciously gave the material to that runt, who wiped his ass with pages that had your name on them. You can imagine what a thrill it must have been for this Home Guard hero to look down between his legs and see the name of a true hero being defiled with feces."

"The pages I looked at didn't have nothing to do with Lieutenant Custer," Billy protested.

"Wilfred of Ivanhoe would be ashamed of you," said Varney. "He respected the act of writing. His life did honor to it."

"That's not fair," Billy said. "The pages was just squiggles that didn't have any meaning. They wasn't even words in the historical sense."

"It's a form of shorthand I use to make notes, you idiot," said Varney.

Judge Dingus took off his bowler hat and wiped sweat from his forehead.

"I have neither the patience nor the time to spare on stolen crystal balls or missing notebooks," said the judge. "There are hideous dangers loose in this county that require my attention. Captain Leatherwood, it says on this charge sheet that you caught this Englishman heading south near the river in the middle of the night on Lieutenant Custer's horse, which you recognized because it is a big stallion. Is this correct?"

"The horse is a chestnut mare," Santana said. "She is a distinguished looking mare with four white stocking feet and a white spot on her forehead and a record for glory in battle. Me and my nephews caught this thief riding toward the river on this beautiful horse."

"What were you and your nephews doing in that area at that time of night? Visiting the whores?"

"We were on patrol, Your Honor. Every night there are reports of robbers and looters. In the moonlight we saw this Englishman cantering along on Lieutenant Custer's horse. Her white feet were flashing. I would recognize that horse by the sound of her gait if I was blindfolded, she is such a great horse. We hailed the Englishman to stop, but he tried to make a run for it. On that horse he could have outrun us, but Adam and Luther angled across the road and cut him off. He began trying to sweet-talk us. I confronted him and called him out for a liar and a thief. He cursed us and pulled his pistol. We knocked him out of the saddle. His satchel tore open and his goods spilled out. The Englishman kept telling us he owned the horse. I informed him he was under arrest and he started fighting again and we were forced to belabor him a bit. We left his goods laying in the road and when Luther went back to get them, they was gone. I know nothing of any notebook."

Robin glanced at Custer, who was listening to Santana and staring at Varney. Custer was trying to make this story fit into his cloudy memory of last night.

"What do you have to say for yourself, Varney?" asked the judge. "Make it short and simple."

Varney rubbed his throat.

"May I have a cup of water, Your Honor?" Varney said.

"Take him the pitcher, Billy," said the judge.

Billy frowned and bobbed his head, a gesture Robin recalled Billy making at the Sweetbrush school when Robin told him to wipe the blackboard. Billy took the water pitcher around the table and gave it to Varney, who placed a hand on either side of the porcelain and drank the pitcher dry.

Varney wiped his mouth with the back of his wrist and said, "Now then. Much better. Let us clear this thing up."

Varney smiled at Custer.

"Last night I checked out of my room at the Avenue Hotel and went to Dutch John's Saloon for a glass of whiskey with Lieutenant Custer," Varney said. "I had been in Austin for three days of rigorous interviewing of Tom Custer and three nights of pounding the bars with him, mostly at Dutch John's, though we did make visits to a few other taverns, as well. Am I correct so far, Tom?"

"Correct," said Custer.

"Tom Custer was in a splendid good humor last night when I joined him at Dutch John's. The bullet wound in his cheek had been causing him pain, but we all understand and appreciate the pain-relieving properties of whiskey, do we not? Tom was quite convivial by the time I arrived in Dutch John's and took a seat at his table. He challenged me to a game of darts. We did have half a dozen games of darts, and traded about even at being topsys. I truly enjoyed Tom's company, and he mine, I feel free to say. Am I still correct so far, Tom?"

"Correct," said Custer.

"Let's skip ahead to the part about how you came to leave the saloon on the wrong horse," Judge Dingus said.

Flora Bowprie nudged Robin with an elbow. It surprised Robin to be included in her enjoyment of Varney's performance.

"Do you remember me leaving the saloon, Tom?" asked Varney.

"I am not certain of that, no," Custer said.

"Are you going to try to tell this court that you got onto the wrong horse by a drunken mistake?" asked the judge.

"I said misunderstanding, not mistake," Varney said. "The misunderstanding is with these four Hittites who assaulted me, not with Tom Custer."

"Where were you going on my horse?" said Custer.

"But you must remember, Tom."

"Remember what?"

"You and I were standing together at the bar, very late. I was telling you of the book I am writing now, called *Playing with the Mortals*. You must remember, Tom. I was saying that to produce a mighty novel, one must choose a mighty theme. You said the mightiest theme of all is death. Remember? I said yes, of course, death is always at one's elbow, like a shadow. But the real question is what is life? Why are we alive and what is this happiness we seek, and why do humans drive themselves to folly? Those are my themes."

"Oh, is that all?" the judge said. "Why don't you tackle something serious?"

"Like God? God is too big for me."

"What do you mean by folly?" asked the judge.

"By folly I mean our rush to do things that cause our destruction, despite being warned and having better courses of action available, refusing to use common sense, and persecuting those Cassandras who try to save us."

"Like what, for example?" asked the judge.

"Like the citizens of Troy opening their gates to the famous wooden horse covered with smelly cowhide and full of killers."

Judge Dingus studied Varney for a moment.

"You are not, by any chance, in any way, referring to the Confederacy as a folly?" asked the judge.

Varney raised his hands in surrender.

"Your Honor," Varney said. "I must admit because we are under oath—we are under oath, I assume?—that last night Tom Custer expressed his opinion that it was folly for you rebels to launch war against the Union, and I had to agree with much of what he said. However, Tom did salute your gallantry and your dead who fell to Northern steel and your cities that were blasted into burning rubble."

"You did, eh?" said the judge, looking at Custer.

Custer nodded slightly. Recalling a conversation from a drunken night in a saloon was like trying to restart an idea that had occurred in a dream.

"I told Tom that I felt obliged to visit Mexico. How could I presume to write a romance dealing with human folly without going among the Mexicans? Mexico is thousands of years of unrelenting folly. Tom said yes, by God, you must go and see the Mexicans. He thought it a topsy idea. The more we talked, the more he liked it. Tom and I have become quite friendly. Three days of conversation and three nights of roaming the bars together will make men friends if their personas mesh, as ours did. Tom is not a surly, antagonistic drinker but a conversationalist of wit and humor and generosity. I enjoyed his company very much. I mentioned that my horse is some-what lame. Tom threw an arm around my shoulder and said why Edmund, you take my chestnut mare and leave your crippled old gelding and I will doctor up your horse so handsomely he will be winning stakes races by the time you return."

Varney looked into Custer's squinting eyes and said, "Am I correct so far, Tom?"

"I said you could ride Athena?"

"You insisted on it, Tom."

"Nobody rides Athena but me."

"We sang 'Rowdy Annie from Virginia' and I bought drinks for the house at Dutch John's. There must be twenty witnesses. You poked my chest and said yes, by God, go among the damned Mexicans. You need to be among the Mexicans to learn your lessons about folly. You take Athena and go to Mexico. You said when I come back, you will have healed my horse, and you will have finished reading my romance about what you called my escapades at war in India and Afghanistan. You said upon my return we will throw darts and sing songs and drink whiskey once again. You said probably there will be more questions for me to ask about your life for my story in the *Holly Bush Journal*. In fact, I have thought of more questions already."

"Stop right there," said Judge Dingus. "Do you have any idea how far it is to Mexico from here?"

"Roughly two hundred miles to the border, Your Honor," said Varney.

"But you certainly didn't intend to ride to the border and turn right around and come straight back?" the judge said. "In my opinion, that would be compounding a folly, the original folly being getting on Lieutenant Custer's horse and riding away from that saloon."

Custer stroked his mustache. He was digging into his memory.

"Now that you know I didn't actually even really leave town on your horse, Tom, we need to clear up this misunderstanding," said Varney. "Look at my clothes. I am beggared. My next move today is to the tailor, after a bath, of course. My wallet and my goods and my pistol have been stolen, but the *Holly Bush Journal* will wire money to the bank in Austin, assuming there is a bank in Austin that is open, assuming you have a telegraph that works. I must ask this court to vouch for my hotel bill and livery until my funds arrive."

The judge smiled and shook his head. This was the sort of craziness the Yankees were bringing into his life.

"Yes," Custer said.

"Yes, what? You will stand good for the Englishman's bills?" asked the judge.

"Yes, I remember talking about Varney's war in India and Afghanistan. Rajah something or other. Punjabis. Sikhs. Hindus. Mohammedans, Pathans. I do remember that," said Custer. "That's what *By the Sword* is about. A slaughter of the British. I read a few pages of it. By God, we did talk about India. We talked about the British army massacred at the Khyber Pass. We talked about folly. We talked about the British charge eight years ago at Balaclava, but that's not India, it was the Crimea, and Varney was not there, I don't think. We joked about death. We played darts. We sang songs. I remember."

"Then you vouch for him?" Judge Dingus said.

Custer took a step into the room. His eyes suddenly froze as he looked at Varney.

"Varney, you son of a bitch," said Custer.

In Custer's rising temper Robin saw not the lunatic rage that would make him charge Confederate guns, but the nasty irritability that comes with a hangover.

"You said nothing to me about Mexico," Custer said.

"But of course I did, Tom. You told me to take your horse."

"I may have said you could ride Athena for some brief errand or just for the thrill of sitting on a great warhorse. But it is a whole different thing for you to ride Athena to Mexico. If I say you can ride my horse and instead of going on down the street a little and coming right back you take off for the border, it is the same as stealing. No, that is worse than stealing. That is betraying the trust of a friend."

Custer had made up his mind what must have happened at Dutch John's last night. He must have been robbed.

"I'm very disappointed in you, Varney," said Custer.

"No harm has been done," Varney said. "The horse Athena is returned safely to you. I am the one who has been beaten and thrown into prison on false charges. However, for those who harm me, I forgive them so as not to carry the awful weight of anger. I will stand the bill for an evening of whiskey drinking for you and Captain Leatherwood and his nephews. What do you say to that, Captain?"

"Leatherwoods don't drink whiskey," said Santana.

"Ale, then. Beer. Gin. Your choice."

"We are raised to be teetoolers," Billy said.

"Stay on the subject, Varney," said Judge Dingus.

"Yes, you stay on the subject," Billy said.

"You must remember speaking of Mexico with me, Tom," said Varney. "You made fun of the mob of Confederate politicians and soldiers that is fleeing down to Mexico. We asked if the Mexicans will open their arms? Will the rebels be welcomed by the French puppets Maximilian and Carlotta? Will they be murdered by the campesinos? The last time these politicians and soldiers from the south went to Mexico, it was with cannons firing and bayonets gleaming. You nudged me in the chest with your fist and said, 'good show, Edmund, stick it to the buggers.'"

"To the devil with you and with your magazine," Custer said. "Yes, my horse Athena is safe in my care, but only because of the keen eye of Captain Leatherwood. You, Varney, have betrayed my friendship. No telling what confidences you would betray or lies you might tell in your damned magazine. I want no more part of you."

Custer took out his gloves that had been folded in his belt. He put his gloves on slowly, knowing he had the eyes of all in the court while he was staring only at the Englishman. Varney returned the gaze, his head raised, unafraid. Robin was struck again by how young Custer looked. Other than for the uniform and the red splash made by the bullet that had struck his cheek, he could have been a senior boy at the Sweetbrush school. From the year of classes Robin had taught, two of the senior boys from Gethsemane now lay dead in faraway battlefields. Of all the senior boys only Adam and Luther Leatherwood and their little brother Billy had survived the war unharmed by it. Custer gave his mustache a stroke and fixed his hat firmly atop his new haircut. Custer sighed and shook his head, more melancholy than angry.

"Judge, do not be taken in by this man, as I was. Edmund Varney is a horse thief. Deal with him as is your Texas custom," said Custer.

Custer touched the brim of his hat in a salute and made a quick nod to Judge Dingus, then again found Robin with his eyes wondering if they might have met in the smoke and noise of the recent past. Custer glanced at the colored girl, then looked once more at Varney.

"I remember another thing from last night," Custer said. "You told me you had visited the afterlife but have returned to earth to play with the mortals. Well, Edmund, your stay on earth this trip will be a short one. It's off to hell with you."

"I will take the devil your regards," said Varney, smiling.

Custer turned and went out the door. Robin and Varney leaned forward and watched Custer walk through the grass and gravel to his chestnut mare Athena. The reins were being held by a trooper. Athena observed the approach of Custer with intelligent, arrogant eyes. Robin softly whistled and admired the horse's profile, the gentle taper to her muzzle as she turned. She stood sixteen hands high and had powerful but graceful muscles in her upper legs. Her four white feet danced as Custer swung himself up into the saddle. Athena was an excitable animal that required an excellent horseman to ride her. Athena stepped high and pranced sideways, and Custer smiled and lightly rode the motion. Varney appreciated the figure Custer made in the saddle. A warrior on horseback was near to topsys in dramatic images. But it tore at his heart to see Custer riding away on Athena.

In the courtroom they could hear the diminishing thumping of Athena's hooves.

The crowd had been fascinated by Custer and Varney, but now there was an excited babble. Judge Dingus shouted for silence. He had to shout three times. Billy yelled and waved his shotgun. Santana had stepped outside to watch Custer depart on that magnificent horse, but he came back inside and added his voice to those of the judge and little Billy. Adam and Luther stood solemnly, wondering if they would be asked to wade in and flail away at the crowd in which the Leatherwood boys could see pistols, rifles, shotguns and one man who carried a hoe as a weapon. Robin caught a whiff of what smelled like ginger as Flora Bowprie bent close to him. He realized she was chewing gum.

"The romancer, he crap now, hey?" she whispered.

Varney was still standing as the crowd settled down. He raised his hands to his breast and clutched the lapels of his coat and adjusted the fit of it, ragged and dirty though it was.

"In conclusion, Your Honor," said Varney, "my defense is as simple and straightforward as you wish it to be. Last night Tom Custer was drunk and generous. This morning he is sober and remorseful, and above all, forgetful. I demand to see the British ambassador."

"Sit back down there beside that nigra while I decide upon this," Judge Dingus said.

"History will long note your decision here today," said Varney.

Flora Bowprie edged over against Robin as Varney sat down on the other side of her. She was touching shoulders and arms with both men.

Judge Dingus pulled up the black robe that was snagged on the butt of his pistol. He reached under the fold of his stomach and produced a gold-plated pocket watch. He opened the case and frowned.

"I've got lots of docket to get through today. Let's be moving on," the judge said.

He picked up another piece of paper, read it for a moment, then looked at the prisoners and said, "Captain Jerod Robin?"

Robin stood up.

"I am Captain Jerod Robin."

"You look like a fine Texas gentleman to me," said the judge. He glanced at Santana Leatherwood and looked back at Robin and held up the sheet of paper. "I am shocked by what I read here, Captain Robin. This charge alleges you broke into Klein's Jewelers on Guadalupe Street yesterday afternoon and murdered old Fritz Klein. Whatever could have possessed you to do a thing like that?"

Seven

ROBIN HAD EXPECTED THE WORST. Santana Leatherwood's threat of hanging had not been lightly regarded by Robin, not for a moment. But at the word murder Robin felt a freezing shock. Hearing the name of the victim—old Fritz Klein—gave the charge a jolt, and for a moment Robin wondered if he might have had a fit and done the crime. Over the past three years Robin's picture of reality had grown airy. There had been spells when he felt like a passenger on a runaway railroad train. Landscapes and events flashed past the windows. Darkness fell, electrical storms flickered. Sunlight broke out again with brightness that made him dizzy. Robin ate, slept, rode, fought, bled, hated, suffered, loved and somehow lived from day to day often without feeling part of what he was doing any more than he was part of the images going past the car windows. There were also vivid periods when he knew he was precisely and violently and agonizingly at the center of everything that was of any importance in the world—a use of the mind that can drive people completely insane. Robin didn't know old Fritz Klein, but he had killed men like him, some might say murdered them, for the flag and from his own madness.

What oddity had brought Robin onto Pecan Street yesterday afternoon at the very moment the Leatherwoods happened to be there? What exquisite timing had led him down from the Great Smoky Mountains into Memphis and then across Arkansas where he caught a ride on a train of freight wagons heading for Austin? How had he chosen the exact moment after arrival to set out looking for a meal and transportation for the final 170 miles southeast to Sweetbrush on the Big Neck Bayou? If he had arrived at the corner of Congress and Pecan a few minutes earlier or later, the Leatherwoods may never have seen him passing. Had he come along the plank walk a few minutes earlier, his presence might have prevented the robbery and murder of old Fritz Klein, whose body lay on the floor of his jewelry shop with the four Leatherwoods standing around it when Robin walked by. Thinking back, Robin reassured himself that he had not had anything to do with the murder of old Fritz Klein. But his participation in the deaths of men like Fritz Klein in the last three years had put him on the long curious path to Pecan Street at the particular wrong moment, that's for sure, as if he was getting what he deserved.

Before Robin could answer the judge's question, Santana spoke up.

"Your Honor, it is my duty to tell you that Captain Jerod Robin may look to you like a fine Texas gentleman, but the truth is he is a savage. I have known him all his life. He was a dangerous bully as a boy. His daddy owns a large cotton plantation and thirty or forty slaves. The boy Jerod was a swaggering dandy who hid from community justice behind his mother's skirts. We all hated him. Yesterday when I saw him lurking at the window of the jewelry store, I realized who had murdered Fritz Klein. There he stands with no remorse. Captain Jerod Robin, as cold-blooded a killer as ever came out of Texas."

"How is it that you have known him all his life?" asked the judge.

"My brother is the pastor of the church in the town of Gethsemane, a few miles from the Robins' fields. My brother is, as I have said, the founder and mayor of the town of Gethsemane, but his calling above all is preaching. Pastor Horry Leatherwood was in the Robins' house the night Jerod Robin was born. I was a boy of eleven, waiting outside. I heard his first cry on this earth. I know Jerod Robin for what he is, not for what he appears to be."

"Did your lip curl when you said that?" Judge Dingus said. He planted his elbows on the table and leaned forward and peered at Santana. "Are you trying to make me out as stupid?"

"I am testifying to the true facts of Jerod Robin's character."

"A Texas man wearing a Yankee uniform needs to tread lightly in this court." The judge turned toward Robin. "Well, Captain Robin, how do you plead?"

"Is this a true legal proceeding, your Honor?" said Robin. "This is a county court. I was arrested in the city."

"You are accused by the military and the Home Guard. The jurisdiction is mine. How do you plead?"

"I am innocent."

It was a strange feeling for Robin to hear his own voice saying he was innocent. He felt the colored girl's eyes staring up at him, as if she knew he was guilty of so much.

"Your Honor," said Santana, "it was only last December that this man led his gang of cutthroats into eastern Tennessee and captured the town of Snow Hill. Robin held the entire town for ransom. When the people of Snow Hill couldn't pay what he and his thugs demanded, Robin hanged the mayor and the banker and, I say with emphasis, the judge; he hanged the judge, Your Honor—and then he burned the town to the ground."

Varney looked at Robin with renewed interest, as did everyone in the court room except the Leatherwoods.

"Is this true, Captain Robin?" Judge Dingus asked.

"Put into simple words, that is a true story, but there is much more to it than that," said Robin.

"What ransom did you ask?"

"Food for my men and horses."

"Nothing more?" the judge said.

"Blankets, whiskey, morphine," Robin paused, "Also their gold and silver, not their paper money."

"For this you hanged three men?"

"Not for the money, no. Our bunch had passed through Snow Hill weeks earlier on our way to the battle at Nashville. The mayor, the judge and the banker swore they were friends of our cause, but while we rested in their homes at night, they sent word ahead to the Federals that we were coming. We rode into an ambush the next day and lost three dead. When we returned to Snow Hill after the battle of Nashville, we demanded their treasure and three of their lives. I chose the three. The fire was an accident."

"Did you take their treasure?"

"They had none."

Robin turned his head and looked at Santana. It had been shortly after Robin's men blasted open the vault and found less than fifty dollars in gold and silver that Santana and his troopers attacked in Snow Hill on Christmas Eve night.

"What are you now doing in Austin?" asked the judge.

"Looking for transport. I am going home."

"Home from the war?"

"Yes sir. Home at long last."

"Do you bear wounds on your body?" asked the judge.

"Yes sir."

"Have these wounds been causing you pain as recently as today?"

"Yes sir."

"Our cause was righteous," the judge said.

"My cause is the freedom of Texas from Yankee rule and is righteous yet," Robin said.

"You wouldn't murder an old man like Fritz Klein, would you?"

"I wouldn't murder him, no sir."

"And if you had done this crime, you wouldn't be lingering at the scene, would you?"

"No sir."

Santana Leatherwood said, "Judge Dingus, I can show you why Captain Robin came back to the jewelry store while Fritz Klein's body was still warm on the floor."

"I wonder how many killings have occurred in Austin in the past month?" asked the judge. "Do you know the answer, Captain Leatherwood?"

"I haven't been here for a month yet. I don't know," Santana said. "Show him the envelope, Billy."

"What would you guess? Ten or twelve killings? More? Including street fights and barroom fracases. Maybe eighteen or twenty?"

"Billy, I said show him the envelope," Santana said.

Billy was feeling his pockets.

"Why would Captain Robin murder old Fritz Klein?" said the judge. "For his money? Fritz had no money. For his diamonds? Fritz sold his last diamond a month ago. The only thing keeping his shop open was Fritz's mule-headedness, believing things are going to get better. It's close to impossible for me to believe that Captain Robin would do this crime."

Santana shouted, "Billy, show the judge the damned envelope. Open it for him."

A brown envelope fell out of Billy's shirt onto the floor. Billy picked up the envelope, tore it open and shook out its contents. He held up a button.

"Here it is," Billy said. "Says FTVC on it. That stands for First Texas Volunteer Cavalry."

"This button was clutched in the fingers of the dead man. Fritz Klein ripped it off Jerod Robin's coat during his death struggle," said Santana. "I figure Jerod Robin came back to the shop to retrieve this piece of evidence. There's not many of these FTVC buttons left in existence."

Billy rushed around the table and held up the button against the front of Robin's coat. Several buttons were missing from the coat, but the remaining buttons were an exact match for the one in Billy's fingers.

"He's guilty. Look at this button. He's guilty as he can be," Billy cried.

"What do you say to that, Captain Robin?" asked the judge.

"They must have torn off that button in the fight when they jumped me on Pecan Street," Robin said.

Judge Dingus made a noise that began as a sigh and turned into a growl.

"It's clear to me that there is a feud going on here," said the judge. "I suppose it may be an old feud between two families. I don't know what this personal bitterness between you is about, but I don't want to know. I don't care. It is no business of mine. God knows I have enough to worry about."

The judge looked at Flora Bowprie and said, "You ain't the only person in this court who can read minds. As for foretelling the future, let me take a stab at it. I predict Captain Robin or Captain Leatherwood, or both, will be buried in the Texas earth within a very short time. Only the Good Lord could guess how many of their kin will fall with them. But this feud will not be settled or even perpetuated in my court. Captain Robin says he is innocent of the murder of Fritz Klein, and I am inclined to believe him. Captain Leatherwood contends that Captain Robin is some kind of savage monster, but I don't see any proof of that. I see a Texas gentleman, an officer who fought for the Bonnie Blue Flag. I know the reputation of the First Texas Volunteer Cavalry. They rode from one bloody battle to the next for four years. When I hear a Yankee officer say the First Texas Volunteer Cavalry are savage monsters, I swell with pride."

"Hear! Hear!" yelled voices in the courtroom. "Amen to that!"

"Judge, you can't be thinking about turning this man loose," Santana said.

"That sounds like a threat," said the judge.

"I am the arresting officer. I collected the evidence. Robin is guilty of murder. I say we march him back to the bull pen and string him up."

"I decide what happens in my court. Does the Yankee army dispute me?"

"You figure it out," Santana said.

"I damn sure will," said the judge.

Judge Dingus chewed on his cigar.

"Captain Robin, do you have family praying for your return?" the judge asked.

"My wife. Our child that I have never seen. Others."

Robin didn't mention his mother or father. He was annoyed to have learned for the first time that Pastor Horry had been at Sweetbrush the night he was born. Why had Dr. Robin allowed his enemy into the house? Why had Varina allowed it? He thought of the letter from Laura that was sewn into his coat.

Judge Dingus stood up. He was a boulder of a figure in his black robe that was hitched around the butt of the pistol in his belt. The judge threw his stub of a cigar onto the floor and ground it under his boot heel. He looked past Robin into the faces of the crowd in the courtroom.

"Men of Texas," the judge said, "we are bound to support the Union flag now that Texas has become occupied territory."

Voices called out, "The hell with that! The Yankees ain't telling me what to do!"

There was a clanking and bumping of metal striking the wooden pews as men in the crowd angrily shifted their rifles, pistols and shotguns. Santana Leatherwood studied the crowd with a calculating eye.

"Men of Texas," said the judge, "do you back me as your judge, or do you back the will of the Yankee army?"

"You're our judge," the men cried. "We're behind you, judge."

"What is the point of this?" said Santana.

The judge said, "Stand up, Varney. Stand up, Flora Bowprie."

Varney and Flora rose beside Robin. The chains that bound Varney together with Robin stretched across the bare ankles of the girl.

The judge said, "Perfect justice is beyond the attainment of this court or any other court, but I do my best. Captain Robin, a button torn off your coat does not decide me that a man like you would murder old Fritz Klein. I see no purpose for you to do a terrible crime like that. Edmund Varney, I believe you did try to steal Lieutenant Custer's horse during a drunken night at Dutch John's Saloon, but you are a foreigner and that would cause me a world of trouble down the road if I hang you. As a writer of books and magazine articles you are more dangerous to me than an ordinary horse thief, if my jurisprudence gets off half-cocked somehow. And you, Flora Bowprie, are by law a runaway slave, but don't think I do not see the absurdity of your situation in case you truly do not have an owner."

Judge Dingus turned to Santana and said, "This court instructs you to bring a wagon around to the door at once. I want two Yankee soldiers to come with the wagon."

"No need for more soldiers, Judge. Me and my nephews can do whatever you got in mind."

"No," said the judge. "This court orders you and your nephews to keep away from these prisoners. I order that these three be driven to the Travis County line by the United States army and dumped over in Bastrop County in the piney woods. These three will become somebody else's problem, not mine."

"Judge, I am warning you not to do this," Santana said.

"Men of Texas, do you hear what he is saying? This turncoat of a Yankee is warning me that the power of this court does not belong to your elected judge."

The men in the courtroom let out a roar. They leaped to their feet, many of them brandishing their weapons. Women hugged their children close, watching with anticipation as if beholding some carnival act. Negro faces peered in through the windows, big-eyed, enjoying the spectacle of justice being done.

"I insist you turn Jerod Robin over to me," Santana said.

"This crowd of men won't let you have him, Captain," said Judge Dingus. "You get busy and carry out the will of this court."

Eight

SEVENTY THOUSAND TEXANS put on the Confederate uniform to fight for the Bonnie Blue Flag—the Lone Star on a field of brilliant dark blue—against the Yankee army, while twenty-five thousand able-bodied Texas men between the ages of sixteen and sixty avoided military service. Most who entered the military went to battlefields far from home. Others served in the rebel army at Texas posts, or in the navy on the Gulf of Mexico. Some who did not enlist and somehow evaded being conscripted by the military draft formed companies of Home Guards. Some who refused to serve fled into the forests and hid and became known as brushmen. Many Texans in conscience avoided going into the military because they disagreed with the war for moral or political reasons. For others the war meant financial ruin. Some used the war to make themselves wealthy by supplying goods at high prices to the troops and to an increasingly desperate public.

For Pastor Horry Leatherwood, the act of fighting a war to preserve slavery was evil and ignorant. Pastor Horry had preached against slavery from his pulpit in Gethsemane for many years before the war. Those who denounced Pastor Horry as unpatriotic or disloyal discovered he did not show the other cheek or use a soft answer to turn away wrath. His courage and his allegiance to Texas had been proved during the revolution of 1836 when he charged the Mexicans at San Jacinto, running side by side, step for step, with

Dr. Junius Robin, and was seen to slay a red-coated officer bare-handed by snapping his neck after Leatherwood's pistols had fired and his saber had broken in half. But Pastor Horry refused to support the Confederacy. He encouraged his three sons to hide in the forest when the conscriptors came. The presence of the Leatherwood clan along the bayou discouraged patriotic vigilantes from pursuing them. People were afraid of the Leatherwoods. A few months before the war began, with feelings at the boil during a period known as the Great Fear, Pastor Horry's brother Santana came home on leave. Santana walked down the middle of the main street in Gethsemane in his blue Federal regular army uniform, wearing his black boots with the Mexican silver conchos and the big silver spurs that he had taken away from a Mexican general, and nobody dared step out to oppose him.

When Santana encountered Jerod Robin at Snow Hill, Santana was an officer of cavalry with the regular army. After the battle of Snow Hill, while Santana was surviving surgery in a hospital, General Briggs visited his bedside and awarded him a medal for valor. The general advanced Santana in rank to brevet captain. Upon his return to active duty following the removal of his right kidney and three months of recovery, Santana was assigned to the Sixth Michigan under General George Custer and was sent to join the regiment in action in Virginia. After Appomattox he volunteered for the new Seventh Cavalry, which was being formed up and sent to Texas as an occupying force. Santana came home to Texas with it on his mind to eventually look up Jerod Robin and take his revenge. With their father's blessing, Santana's three nephews left the bayou and journeyed up to Austin to welcome their uncle and quickly they joined the Home Guard to serve alongside him without the inconvenience of actually being in the army.

"I tried to do this in a legal way," Santana said to his nephews, as they watched Robin climb into the wagon with Varney and Flora.

"It's not right to let him go," said Billy.

"Them men with guns think it's right," Luther said.

"But we got the U. S. Army on our side," Adam said.

The brothers looked to their uncle.

"This is a long way from over," Santana said. "We'll catch that son of a bitch wherever he runs."

"I bet he's running home to that tall beautiful mother of his," Billy said.

"Not to his wife?" said Adam.

"Yeah, her, too."

"I'd take the mother," Luther said.

"Yeah, I'd rather have the mother," said Billy.

Judge Dingus stood beside the wagon, his arms folded over his belly, to make sure his orders were being carried out.

Santana saw the grin on Robin's face and called out, "You're the last of an arrogant breed, Jerod Robin. Your day is done. Your high-flown, fancy family is finished."

"Next time I see you I will finish what I should have finished at Snow Hill," Robin yelled.

Santana had the urge to shoot him then and there, but the mood of the crowd was hostile toward the army and the Home Guard. Travis County had voted against seceding from the Union, but now the reality of a Yankee army occupying their capital city was bitter fruit. Among the citizens who had poured out of the foundry, Santana saw two men wearing their gray uniform jackets, another in a yellow-brown coat colored by dye made from butternuts like the coat of Jerod Robin, and several more that were not in rebel uniform but were staring at Santana and his red-throat nephews with hatred on their faces. The Negroes gathered in a separate group. A stout black woman held up her left palm and touched it with her right forefinger in a sign to Flora Bowprie. Varney supposed it was some fortune-teller's message that had to do with the lifeline. Varney snagged his ankle on the chain that bound him to Robin. Varney grabbed the chain in a fist and shook it.

"Your Honor, unlock us!" he yelled.

"In Bastrop County you'll be set free," Judge Dingus said.

"I'd like the return of my pistol, if you please," Varney yelled.

The judge shouted, "Use your imagination, romancer. Invent a pistol."

A Seventh Cavalry teamster clucked and snapped the reins and the two mules started the wagon crunching across the gravel. Another Seventh Cavalry soldier, a husky, baby-faced private assigned to be the guard, laid his Remington double-barrel 12-gauge shotgun across his knees and looked straight ahead, grinning, enjoying this duty. As the wagon rolled toward the southeast, heading into the forest, Robin could see Santana and his nephews looking at him from the growing distance. Robin waved at them. He felt sure he would see them again.

On a rutted, red-dirt road, the wagon entered the shade of oaks and pecan trees, wagon wheels creaking, mules snorting and moving at a steady pace. Birds called from the branches above, and squirrels scampered through the leaves. Once they reached the county line and were turned loose, Robin intended to make his way on foot to the town of Bastrop on the east bank of the Colorado River. The old town of Bastrop, forty miles southeast of Austin, was small but prosperous from coal mining and brick making, and the area was a source of lumber from its vast pine forest that was unlike any other forest in Texas but familiar to Robin and other rebel soldiers who had traveled and lived and fought in the pine forests of the old South. In the town of Bastrop, Robin would catch a ride on a commercial wagon bound for Houston and would jump off near Big Neck Bayou and hurry on to his destination, Sweetbrush. At the thought, Robin touched the outline of the envelope sewn into the lining of his coat. The Leatherwoods had stolen his bedroll, his money and his pistol, but Robin felt he would find sympathetic spirits in Bastrop.

"What do you keep feeling your chest for, hey?" asked Flora Bowprie.

"I'm sort of bruised up," Robin said.

"You have something hidden in your coat," she said.

"It's nothing."

Varney drank deeply from the water jug in the back of the wagon and laid his head against a burlap bag of oats and yawned, but his glittery gray eyes were taking note of the fortune-telling girl and the young captain. Varney had begun fitting them into the romance he was making in his head. The girl was fitting especially well. She had qualities Varney could use. She was young and handsome. She spoke French.

"You have no need to be lying to me, hey. What do you have in your coat?"

Robin didn't like being ragged on by a colored girl.

"Don't carry on with your act. Let it go," he said.

"You believe I don't have the power of foretelling?"

"I don't know. I just said drop it."

"Let me see your hands," she said.

He surprised himself by offering her his hands. Robin had not been touched by a female, except for nurses, since he was last with his wife Laura two years ago. The fortune-telling girl took his hands into her hands and turned them over and then turned them over again, gently pulling his fingers, inspecting his palms. He remembered how it was to be caressed by a woman. He looked into her green eyes. How explain the mystery of attraction? In the opening of her blue blouse he could detect the rising and falling of her breasts. Her lips were red and her breath had a ginger smell from the gum she was chewing.

Robin's thoughts went to Laura, who was waiting for him and needed him at Sweetbrush. He saw Laura standing at the French doors of their bedroom with the curtains on the second floor porch stirring in the breeze off the water. He smelled the fragrance of a rain shower. Laura wore a nightgown. Her hair was loose and full. In the moonlight her expression seemed melancholy. She said, "No matter what happens, I promise I will stay here and raise our child here." Until that instant, he couldn't have imagined it would ever be any other way.

"I see here that you have had a bad disruption to your mind," Flora said.

"Where do you see that?" said Robin.

With a fingernail she scratched a mound of flesh on his right palm.

"Here. Here it is in your palm."

"What else do you see?"

"You fall in love three times in your life," she said.

"Stout fellow," said Varney. "Three loves is beyond the capacity of most."

Varney was looking at Flora and thinking of the Sikh girl he had loved and married in India and who had been murdered by the British on the road to Lahore during the big Afghan uprising. He saw a physical resemblance between his wife and this child, the height and the coloring and the intense blackness of their hair, and the same bright, curious gaze. Aliyah had been sixteen when he first saw her in her father's palace. She was trained in meditation and the language of Sikh scriptures. She had a beautiful singing voice. Aliyah was twenty and pregnant with their first child when she was murdered by the British Army.

"Tell me something, Mr. Varney. No offense intended," Robin said.

"My life is a readily available open book," Varney said. "At least, I keep trying to make it so."

Robin took his hand back from Flora.

"You're an intelligent man. How did you think you could get away with stealing Tom Custer's horse?"

"You didn't believe my story in court?"

"Nobody believed it," Flora said.

"I thought that story might have a better chance with the judge than the truth would have done," said Varney.

"The truth being that you got drunk and tried to steal that beautiful horse?" Robin said.

"The truth is that horse, Athena, is mine."

Robin and Flora both stared at Varney.

"Athena belongs to me."

"How could that be?" said Robin.

"Ten, twelve, no—forgive me, when you reach my age the years go by like hours—let's call it fifteen years ago, I was working for Ranjit Singh as a mercenary, keeping an eye on the British, who were trying to retreat from Kabul and fight their way through mountain passes back into India with all their women and children and servants and baggage and musical instruments for the orchestras, and horse herds, including herds of polo ponies and their packs of foxhounds. I was riding my horse, Athena. We were moving on ridges in the high snows, watching the British column down below. My scouts and I were ambushed by the Ghilzais, the mountain people. I was knocked out of the saddle and hit my head on a rock and went out cold. After that moment I never saw my horse Athena again until three days ago. But I had learned in New York when I arrived in this country that Tom Custer had won two Medals of Honor with two gloriously heedless charges on the back of a chestnut Arabian mare named Athena. So I had to see for myself. Yes, it is she. Athena recognized me straight off."

"That's a much better story for a romancer to tell," Flora said. "The judge would have liked that one the best."

"Ah, but it is the truth," said Varney.

"If you have a piece of paper showing you own this horse, you should have let the judge look at it," Robin said. "Or was it in your lost satchel?"

"Does Tom Custer have a bill of sale for Athena?" Varney said. "He got her the same way I did, as the spoils of war. I took Athena from a rebellious prince we killed in his own garden. The prince died fighting, which was the kindest way he could have died back then, believe me. Ranjit Singh claimed Athena for himself, of course, but at a victory banquet he gave her to me as a reward, along with a ruby pendant that I also lost to the Ghilzais. I rode Athena for two years of fighting Ranjit Singh's enemies, until she was taken from me that day in the mountains."

Robin put a finger to his lips, thinking.

"How old would you say this horse was when you rode her in India?" asked Robin.

"Seven and coming into her prime," Varney said.

"Then this horse Tom Custer is riding would have to be at least twenty-two years old," said Robin.

"Hard to believe, isn't it?" Varney said. "Athena looks seven years old right now. She is ageless."

"You love this horse," said Flora.

"I do, indeed. She is a full sixteen hands tall, weights twelve hundred pounds, runs forty miles an hour, jumps fences I would have a hard time climbing. She has the most seductive eyes, with long lashes. She knows she is the apex of creation. You can love her all you want and she will perform for you, but she is not going to love you more than you love her, not ever."

"Horses love other horses, that's all," Flora said.

"What did you call the horse back in India?" Robin asked.

"Athena. She has always been Athena."

They shifted as the wagon bounced through a rut. The young private looked around at them. His eyes lingered on Flora, and he squinted and speculated. His hands twisted on the shotgun barrel, and then his attention shifted to the side of the road, into the forest. For the Seventh Cavalry soldiers this was hostile country. Dangers lurked in these dark woods.

"She has a small V mark branded on her left hip. I never knew what the V stands for, but Athena had it. This horse has it," Varney said.

"Still and all," Robin said, looking at Varney, "why did you think you could get away with it?"

"But I almost did get away with it," said Varney. "Tom Custer was drunk and asleep with his head on the table. As apparently happened with you at the jewelry shop, it was simply bad luck that I encountered the Leatherwoods on the road. A few minutes one way or the other, and I would have been gone. Riding Athena I would have been a hundred miles away by the time Tom Custer woke up. In another three days, Athena and I would have been in the mountains of Mexico, where the whole Seventh Cavalry could never reach us."

"What are you talking about back there?" the guard asked.

"Horses," said Varney.

"You better not be talking about sex," the teamster said over his right shoulder. "You don't want to get young Huffer here all worked up."

"Shame to turn that girl loose right away," said Huffer. "We fought a war for her. She ought to be grateful and show us some affection. Am I right, Rudy, or do you think different?"

The teamster laughed.

Varney adjusted his seat with his back against the burlap bag of oats and turned his face close to Huffer. Flora and Robin saw Varney in profile, his hair hanging over his left ear and curling over his collar in back, the earring, the knot near the bridge of his nose. Robin was wondering how much to believe of anything Varney had told him since they had met in the prison yard that morning. There was the fact of the book *By the Sword* that would indicate Varney was an author, but Robin didn't know what the book was about—a massacre of the British, Tom Custer had said? And what could be proved by a romance? Flora was watching Varney and wondering if the Englishman was going to charm the baby-faced soldier, or abuse him.

"Where are you chaps from?" Varney asked.

"Michigan," said Huffer. "We're both from Michigan."

The canopy of pines caused shafts of sunlight to reach through the branches and illuminate Huffer's baby-face with its sparse sideburns stretching below the ears. The darkening forest closed in on either side of the road. The air was cool. A flying squirrel spread his wings and glided overhead, making Huffer more nervous.

"Where the hell are you from?" Huffer asked.

"London."

"Where?"

"London, England."

"Do all the people over there talk in that prissy way?" asked Huffer.

"Yes," Varney said.

The wagon creaked and rocked over the red dirt. The two mules pricked their ears, alert to sounds in the forest, which gave cover to panthers, wolves, bears and wild tuskers. The red Indians had mostly been driven out of this part of Texas, but outlaws and deserters and brushmen found sanctuary in these woods. No place in Texas could be thought of any more as safe, if any place ever had been.

"I suppose you must have a loaf of bread and maybe a hunk of cheese in this wagon?" asked Varney. "Biscuits? Bacon? A bite of breakfast for your prisoners? Michiganers are world famous for their hospitality."

Huffer patted himself on the rump and said, "Take a bite of this, England."

The two Yankee soldiers laughed.

They saw a fluttering of Monarch butterflies around patches of yellow flowers. Bunches of wild grapes hung just out of reach. Robin watched Varney who studied the back of Huffer's neck as the wagon bounced along.

"Ignore him," Robin said.

"I don't know if I can do that," Varney said. His eyes glittered like icicles.

"It'd be another case of bad timing," said Robin. "In an hour, he'll be gone from your life forever."

"He's right, romancer, Don't make more trouble now, hey?" Flora said.

Varney turned away from Huffer, inhaled deeply, clenched his fists twice and held his breath for a full minute. Then he puffed his cheeks, blew out a long breath through a small o in his lips. A smile broke across Varney's face. His eyes softened.

"Picked up that technique from a yogi in the Punjab," he said. "It resets your nervous system and dispels anger. There's an incantation you can use with it, silent or screaming, depending on how much anger you need to get rid of. What you say is, 'just for now I let go and surrender my anger to the universe. Just for now my anger is gone, and I am on the same page with God.'"

"Why 'just for now'?" asked Flora.

"I added that bit myself."

"You served in the British army?" said Robin.

"Indeed, I did. I left Oxford after my third year. I had been working on a degree in the moral sciences, trying to make sense of the world, when I ran into trouble with booze and cards and, of course, women. Friends of my father got me into the regiment with a commission. We sailed off to India for a long, bloody adventure, twelve years in all for me—eight for the Queen and the Company, followed by four years of mercenary service as commander of cavalry for Maharajah Ranjit Singh."

"Is this what *By the Sword* is about?" asked Robin.

"Why bless you, dear boy, for knowing of my work."

"Tom Custer mentioned the title in court," Flora said.

"I know of your book because a friend of my mother's sent it to her from London. My mother is English," Robin said.

"Really? And how did your mother like my book?"

"She never said."

"Was your mother born in London?" asked Varney.

"She was born in St. John's Wood. She was an actress."

"Her stage name?"

"Varina Hotchkiss."

Varney tapped his forehead. He broke into a delighted smile.

"I have found her!" he said. "What a wonderful world it is!"

"Found her?" said Robin.

"Some names I don't forget," Varney said. "Varina Hotchkiss is one. I used to go and see her at Covent Garden when I was a student. She was a star. Truly a star. She made her own light on stage. Her Lady MacBeth was famous in the London theatre world. She was too young for the role, and too beautiful, but so charismatic an actress. Very tall and lithe, long yellow hair, large eyes and wide mouth, bewitching manner. I fell madly in love with Varina Hotchkiss. The night I finally went round backstage to meet her, with a bouquet of roses after a performance of Sheridan's *The Rivals*, she had disappeared immediately at the last curtain call. She had quit the play and left London. She never returned to the theatre in England. I wondered why."

Varney studied Robin anew. "So you are the son of Varina Hotchkiss? Yes, now I can see something of her in you. Well, I'll be damned. Where is Varina Hotchkiss today?"

"At home."

"She married well, quite obviously."

"My father is a doctor."

"I should like to call on her, after all these years," Varney said.

"She would probably enjoy that," said Robin.

"Tell me the truth, romancer," said Flora. "That notebook didn't have notes on Tom Custer in it, did it?"

He smiled. "What do you think the notes were?"

"Writings for your new romance," she said.

He nodded. "The notes represented six months of work. I started notes for my new romance last January, writing in a notebook I bought in Barcelona. Every inspiration and thought I have had since then—and there have been many—I wrote in shorthand in that notebook, along with plotting out the events that will illuminate my story. Then little Billy comes along and wipes his ass with it. Little Billy is my cruelest critic to date, and I've had some nasty ones, believe me."

The pines on either side of the red-dirt road grew dense and it became dark as dusk, though Robin reckoned it couldn't be much past noon. The canopy was a hundred feet above them. The air became cooler and smelled of rain nearby. Abruptly the teamster hauled back on the reins and jerked the wagon to a stop.

"I don't like the looks or the feel of this place. I think it's haunted," the teamster said. "There's ghosts in here."

"How far is it to the county line?" asked the baby-faced Huffer, glancing back and forth from the shadows on one side of the road to the shadows on the other, his shotgun ready. Shadows closed in on the wagon.

"How would I know?" the teamster said. "What does a county line look like?"

"Let's throw their ass out right here," said Huffer.

"Look up ahead," the teamster said. "How about that grassy circle? We'll dump them in the clearing."

The wagon rolled for another twenty yards. The teamster shouted at the mules and slapped the reins, hauling hard on the left. He had begun turning the wagon around before they reached the clearing.

Huffer hopped down and gestured at the prisoners with his shotgun.

"This may not be the county line, but it's close enough. We ain't going any deeper into these woods," said Huffer. "Get out of that wagon. The three of you jump the hell down."

The mules continued turning the wagon as the prisoners climbed down out of the bed. Robin took Flora's hand to help her down, though she was a strong, athletic girl and didn't need help. It was awkward for Robin and Varney to leave the wagon while chained together. Varney stumbled but braced himself against the tailgate.

"Get on gone now. Take off walking," Huffer said.

"Unlock us first," said Varney.

"What do you mean?" Huffer said.

"Remove these blasted chains."

"We don't have a key to these locks," Huffer said. He called up to the teamster, "Hey, Rudy, do we have a key?"

The teamster by now had the wagon facing back toward Austin. He twisted sideways to see what they were doing.

"What?" he said.

"A key for these damned locks," Varney yelled. "Where is the key?"

"I never saw no key," said the teamster.

"You three hike it out of here," Huffer said. "Go on now. Get moving."

Varney and Robin picked up their chains and walked a few yards along the road with Flora close behind them in her bare feet on the red dirt.

"Wait!" shouted Huffer.

The three prisoners stopped, and the teamster cupped a hand to an ear, wondering what Huffer wanted.

"You two bastards keep going," Huffer said. "But you, girl, you come back here. You come here to me."

Flora took two steps toward the guard.

"What you want, hey?"

"You're a pretty thing. You owe me some love for killing rebels in your name. You owe me three years worth of gratitude."

Huffer waved his shotgun at Robin and Varney.

"You bastards keep moving on down that road. What I got in my pants ain't for you."

Varney and Robin stood still.

"You taking up for her? You sticking with her? Are you three some kind of gang?" said Huffer.

"We're with her," Varney said.

Robin looked down at the chain on his ankle but made no effort to move away.

From the wagon the teamster called, "Hey, Huffer, let's get out of here."

"I'm doing some love on this girl first," Huffer said.

"Why don't you be smart and get back on that wagon and follow the judge's orders?" said Varney.

"The judge never said I couldn't love on her. You bastards back up now."

"This girl is with us, isn't she?" Varney said. "Don't you see that? Surely it must be clear we are not going to allow you to rape her."

Up on the wagon seat Rudy the teamster took his pistol out of its holster and laid it across his left forearm and grinned nervously.

"Better not argue with Huffer," the teamster said. "He's a killer. He'd as soon blow you to pieces as belch."

Huffer walked toward Flora but kept his shotgun aimed at Robin and Varney.

"I've killed far better men than you two bastards," Huffer said. "I hate this miserable damn Texas. I'd like to rid the earth of you bastards."

Flora was staring at Huffer and her gaze turned intensely feline, as when she had made little Billy afraid in the courtroom. She said, "You don't want what I've got for you."

"The hell I don't," Huffer said.

His left hand dipped into his pants and he began fumbling with the buttons. He held the shotgun in his right hand, the butt tucked against his side, the muzzle looking at Robin and Varney.

Huffer's voice began to moan. "You pretty girl, you pull up that dress and fall down on your back and spread your legs and be nice to me. You two bastards take off running or I swear I'll gut the both of you."

Flora reached into her blue blouse, lifted the garment and edged her fingers down inside the front of her mustard colored hemp skirt, apparently disrobing as Huffer tore open his pants and exposed himself.

Then her hand came out of her skirt holding a derringer. There was a crack and puff of smoke. Huffer's head rocked backwards with his eyes wide and astonished. A hole appeared in his forehead and a spray of blood and matter flew out the back of his skull. He collapsed in his tracks, falling like a sack of meal tossed off the wagon, all the sudden, the way violence happens, the way death often comes, unexpected and all at once.

Up on the wagon seat the teamster's mouth opened in surprise and he loosed a loud pistol shot that flew over the prisoners' heads and rattled into the pines and set off a racket of cries from the crows.

"Great God Awmighty!" shouted the teamster.

He whacked the mules and started the wagon rolling at a fast pace away from the scene on the road and back toward town.

"Shoot him!" Robin yelled. "Shoot him, too!"

Robin saw that the teamster was already out of range of Flora's little derringer. He ran to grab Huffer's shotgun, but was halted by the chain. Varney jumped forward to give him slack. Robin pushed the dead trooper with his boot and rolled him off the shotgun. Robin picked up the Remington 12-gauge and aimed it at the back of the fleeing teamster who was fast moving away, the wagon bouncing in the road, the teamster shouting, "Great God Awmighty!"

The teamster was too far away for the shotgun to reach him. Had he not been impeded by the chain, Robin might have been able to run after the wagon and get close enough to fire a load of pellets that would down the teamster. But now there was no use. He was getting away.

He was the witness. Now the killing couldn't be blamed on guerrillas.

In two hours the teamster would be back in Austin. Robin knew he would tell Santana Leatherwood and Tom Custer and the judge that the three prisoners had murdered the guard. The Seventh Cavalry would be coming after them.

Nine

FLORA BENT OVER THE DEAD SOLDIER. She searched his pockets and found a folding jackknife. She flicked open the long, shining blade.

"You fools sit down and hold out your feet with the chains on them. I can open those locks with this knife," she said.

Quickly she picked the locks. The two men watched her work in silence. The grassy clearing trembled from the claps of the gunshots by Flora and the teamster. The smell of powder hung in the air with drifting smoke.

"I didn't mean to kill him," she said.

"Right through the bloody forehead," said Varney. "You don't play around, do you?"

"It happened so fast," she said. "I was going to scare him, make him back off."

Varney looked at Robin.

"And you, you bloodthirsty bugger, you wanted to kill both of them," Varney said.

Robin shrugged. With cold clarity he realized that one shot from Flora's derringer had changed the course of the rest of his life.

"In two hours they'll be headed back this way," Robin said. "Because of the one who got free."

Robin stepped out of his chain as Flora opened his lock.

"Fact is, I'd just as soon you hadn't shot that son of a bitch," Robin said.

"Yes, murdering our guard is a complication I hadn't reckoned on," said Varney.

"He had in mind to rape me. You heard what he was saying. You saw him tear open his pants."

"You said in court the men who stole your wagon had in mind to rape you," Robin said.

"That's how men are," she said.

"I should imagine Tom Custer will be riding Athena in pursuit of us," Varney said. "I'll have another crack at getting my horse back."

"In pursuit of you," said Robin. "I'm parting company with the two of you right now. I don't want to see that damn horse again ever."

They dragged the soldier's body out of the clearing and into the pines. They laid him on pungent pine needles that crunched beneath his weight. Robin took his Remington shotgun with five 12-gauge loads and his three dollars of money, but left the wallet on the dead man's chest. Robin didn't read the letter Huffer was carrying in his breast pocket, but Varney looked through it. "From his mother. She thinks she raised a good boy," Varney said. In the other breast pocket Varney found a plug of black tobacco and kept it. They left the soldier's trousers unbuttoned. Flora folded the jackknife and tucked it away in the mustard skirt beneath her blue blouse where her .32-caliber derringer was hidden again. Robin had noticed the derringer was a two-shooter with one load left.

"Should we bury him?" Flora asked.

"No time for that," said Robin.

"We must make a plan," Varney said. "I suggest we go to the nearest farm house, steal their horses and be off to Mexico, all three of us."

"I shot him. It's me they want. You two fools better get gone, hey?"

"On the contrary, it's all three of us they will want," said Varney. "Tom Custer will take this personally. If he thinks I stole his horse and then abetted the killing of one of his troopers, he will consider this a mortal insult to his honor. He will want satisfaction from me, all right. As for you, Captain Robin, is there any doubt in what regard the Leatherwoods view you, or that they would love to see you hang? When that teamster gets back to Austin and tells the judge his version of what transpired here, how we menaced and abused the poor Huffer, taunted him sexually and lured him to his death, the three of us will officially become a crew of murderers. The judge will feel a bloody fool for turning us loose. Old Dingus will have to get his hands on us now to save his reputation. You want to take your chance with him again in court? I don't."

Robin studied the tattered romancer with the noble brow and the laborer's body. He looked down at Flora's bare feet, then up to her eyes. He was looking for panic or fear or guilt in the girl's eyes but saw only appraisal of himself as she looked back at him.

"If the two of you want to stick together and try to run down to Mexico, you've got my blessing," Robin said. "I'm going home no matter what."

"You can't go home," said Flora. "The law will be waiting for you there. That Yankee captain, he knows you are going home."

"The first place the law is coming is to this spot where we are standing and chatting and wasting precious time," Varney said. "They'll want to make sure the teamster is telling the truth that his partner is actually murdered. Then they'll pick up our trail from here. As the ranking member of this party, I say we find horses and head for the border."

"Who appointed you the ranking member?" said Robin.

"In the Punjab I was a general in command of twelve thousand Sikh warriors."

"Then you take command of this girl if you want her, but I'm going alone," Robin said.

"Nobody takes command of me," Flora said.

"So I notice," said Varney.

Though she tried to keep the emotion off her face, Flora was shaken by the sudden finality of what she had done. She was sorry about the soldier but he had brought it on himself. He should have listened to her. She felt sympathy for his mother who had written a letter to her good boy, but Flora didn't have a place in her heart at the moment for guilt. She didn't blame herself for a spontaneous act of self-defense. All her life men had wanted to take advantage of her but none had ever succeeded. Growing up in the French Quarter, living in a four-room flat above her mother's fortune-telling parlor on the Rue Iberville, Flora had been approached by a succession of men, some of them her mother's lovers. The men were enchanted by Flora the babe, beguiled by Flora the child, and hoodwinked by Flora the girl. Men had thought they could be in command of Flora, but they never came close.

"Go ahead then," said Varney. "But leave the shotgun with us."

"You've got her pistol," Robin said.

"With one shot in a tiny little derringer? How much good is that? I am requisitioning that shotgun for the greater benefit of the greatest number."

Varney reached for the shotgun, but Robin stepped back.

"Let's not get ugly here, General Varney," Robin said.

"You say ugly as if you don't believe I am capable of ugliness," said Varney. "You say general as if you don't believe I was one. Doubting my ability to do violence could be your most dreadful mistake."

Evaluating the two men, Flora decided to cast her lot with the old Englishman. The young captain was tall and good-looking, but she had seen in his palms that he was dangerously unstable. She also considered that he was the product of a plantation family that owned slaves. How would he be likely to treat her? Flora was born in New Orleans, but her mother was a dark-skinned native of Jamaica and her father was a white Frenchman who had left Europe in a failed attempt to make a business of exporting rum from Montego Bay back to his homeland. Flora had not seen her father since she was ten years old, the afternoon he had packed his steamer trunk and left the fortune-telling parlor on the Rue Iberville. Her father had told them he was going to Texas, but he couldn't take them because of their color. Six years later she had come to Texas looking for him and gotten arrested as a runaway slave. Now she would truly be on the run. So how would this young Texas captain who owned slaves be likely to react toward her? No, the Englishman was the better prospect for the immediate future, which was difficult for her to foretell.

"You fools stop arguing," Flora said.

"That's the third time you've called me a fool," said Robin. "Don't do it again."

"Even though I outrank you, I am offering to fight you for this shotgun, bare knuckles, no biting or gouging," Varney said.

"Hey, I can't help it if you act like fools," said Flora. "Let him have the shotgun, romancer. You come with me. I got you into this, and I will guide you through it and get you out of it."

"You're going to Mexico with me?" Varney said.

"I'm going where this path takes us," she said.

Flora grabbed Varney by the hand. There were three faint trails leading off from Huffer's dead body into the pine forest. Flora chose one that headed southeasterly. It was an almost hidden route that was used by animals and outlaws and recluses from society. Whatever was going to eat Huffer would probably come along this path.

Varney allowed himself to be pulled behind this amusing girl. He was feeling erotically pleased by the day's adventures, not quite topsys in his personal history of thrills but more exciting than most days. He felt keen. Life had a special edge when he faced danger and death. The girl was leading him further into the unexplored territory of his new romance. His blood was racing, his heart uplifted, his imagination flying far ahead. He felt no fear. He had visited the afterlife. He knew what awaits. He had been to hell on earth, had seen betrayal, had seen humans skinned alive, had seen living heads sawed off with short knives and waved about as bloody trophies, and had written and published a romance about that part of his life, but he hadn't told the readers of his magazine the whole truth of what had happened to him last Christmas Eve in the Pyrenees. His readers had been told he stopped on the trail to help an injured man and was robbed and beaten and left for dead but had crawled into a cave in the mountains. He had not written of the quiet people who came to him in the cave to guide him into the afterlife.

In a long magazine story he had described the drama and gore of being attacked by Spanish bandits while hiking toward a mountain monastery, but he had not revealed the spiritual adventure that this particular brutality introduced him into. He had been on the other side, into the afterlife. The true purpose of his new romance was to reveal the way of the afterlife. In the pages of the *Holly Bush*

Journal, published monthly in Hampstead, Varney wrote that he was taking leave from his regular essay to write a book that would feature the charge of the Light Brigade at Balaclava in 1854, Pickett's charge at Gettysburg in 1863, and whichever folly Varney might decide upon in the recent history of Mexico. Unwritten was that the core of his book was his theory that folly was a climactic step in the human yearning for entry into the afterlife, the mad dash to earthly, bodily obliteration that resulted in being reunited with God. The quiet people had come to him as he died in the cave. The quiet people had taken him into the afterlife but only for a visit and brought him back and left him in the monastery with his new knowledge. This charming, lethal girl with psychic powers had used the word guide; she might be his spirit guide, sent by the quiet people. She might not know her purpose. He felt his chest swell with excitement.

Breathing hard, sweating, pushing branches back out of their faces, Flora and Varney had gone a mile on the narrow path when they heard a threshing in the brush to their rear. Varney tugged at Flora's blouse to halt her and then put a finger to his lips for silence, as though it was necessary to tell her. Varney opened his palm and whispered, "The derringer. Give it to me."

She shook her head.

"It's my turn to bag one," he whispered. "Give me the derringer."

"That'll be Captain Robin coming," she said.

"You sure of that?" he whispered.

"This is the path that leads straightest in the direction he wants to go."

Varney leaned against a pine tree and breathed deeply. It was difficult to admit it to himself, and he would not have admitted it to anyone else, but he was winded. At the age of fifty-two, he was very fit, though injured by the heavy whiskey drinking the last few nights with Tom Custer. But he was not up to a rapid forced march. It had been an awfully long day already, and it was still early afternoon. He watched leaves, branches and vines being pushed aside and then saw Robin's face appear, his hat knocked askew, sweat dripping off his nose.

Robin stopped and wiped his face with his sleeve.

"Here. Take this," Robin said.

He handed the shotgun to Varney.

"You're right," said Robin. "You and this girl need the shotgun more than I do."

Flora was thinking that two hours ago she was stroking his palm and feeling him responding to her and now he was pretending he didn't know her name. The old romancer would never behave toward her that way.

"So you chased us down to apologize and turn over the weapon?" Varney said.

"I can't claim that to be the reason, no," said Robin.

With a glance at Flora, Robin pushed past them on the path, forcing each of them to edge back into the brush to let him go.

"I figure this path leads to the river," Robin said. "If you want to come along behind me, I can't stop you."

Robin pushed ahead through the trees. After a moment of looking at each other, Varney and Flora followed. Within half an hour, they could hear the river flowing. It had been a wet spring and early summer, and the current was up and running loud. In another few minutes they could smell the water. The thought of a bath brought a grin to Varney. He was about to suggest a swim when the three of them were halted by a new sound floating through the pines.

It was a loud, keening wail from somewhere ahead.

Ten

ISABELLA MARÍA DE ALVARADO BUSHKIN walked around the round oak dining table, and around again, letting go a wail every third or fourth step as her eyes fastened on the ugly document that lay on one luncheon plate of a table set for two.

Five years ago she had left her home in Barcelona, Spain, on the arm of Jeremy Bushkin, a cardplayer from Philadelphia. They had departed stealthily in the middle of the night. Her father, mother, brothers, and sisters believed Bushkin was not good enough for her. Though she was twenty-seven years old at the time and had never married, Isabella had a bountiful figure, lustrous black hair and perfect skin. It was true that her nose was of prominent length—a trait inherited from her wealthy grandfather, Marcus the banker— but her overall physical appearance was pleasing, her temperament was fiery but invigorating, her dowry was handsome, all in all far too good for a stoutly built, mustachioed gambling man from America who claimed high social connections but always edged out of producing proof in the way of letters or names and addresses.

Isabella married Bushkin in the middle of the Atlantic Ocean preceding a storm that she realized she should have seen as a bad omen. The ship was a sailing vessel with a steam engine. The captain who performed the wedding ceremony winked at Isabella and suggested she would enjoy taking a turn at the wheel before the voyage ended. Isabella spent her honeymoon dinner crouched before a pot-bellied stove for warmth in the dim, smoky salon while wedding guests swilled whiskey at the bar, laughed at Bushkin's stories and jokes, and sneaked glances at his unhappy, long-nosed bride. Late in the evening Bushkin started a card game. On her wedding night Isabella went to bed alone. The floor was rocking as she undressed, put on her lacy white negligée and crawled into her bunk. She was angry enough that it crossed her mind to go visit the captain on the bridge, but by now the storm was tilting the ship. Soon Isabella was keening over the chamber pot, wretchedly ill. Thus passed her honeymoon night. Bushkin won seven hundred dollars before the storm broke up the card game, but his bride never again looked on him with the blind love that had led her to go with him to America.

Having committed herself to marriage and having unwisely turned her broad back on her family, Isabella determined to make a success out of this situation that sex had gotten her into. People never thought of the price of sex until it was too late and the bills came due. Isabella learned that lesson and took it in stride. She was a proud woman. She paid the debts God asked of her. Isabella was not one to return to her family in Barcelona feeling shamed and scorned and weeping and begging forgiveness. Having a long nose had toughened her to criticism.

She discovered her husband was more of a phony than she had believed possible but less of a phony than her family had thought him to be. Jeremy Bushkin did have high-society friends in New York, Boston and Philadelphia. But they were men he had met at gambling clubs. Many were educated and wealthy with aristocratic names. They viewed Bushkin as a shrewd but honest cardplayer and enjoyed his conversation at the tables and at the bar. These men never brought their own wives to the gambling clubs, but Bushkin brought his long-nosed, exotic Spaniard. Isabella had been educated in excellent schools. She had a diploma from the University of Madrid. She spoke four languages and could read in Latin. Bushkin found himself and his wife being invited to dinner parties and restaurants and eventually to the elegant homes of his gambling companions who had always bade him goodbye at the doors of the clubs where they played cards.

Bushkin's husky natural charm and convivial manner combined well with the strange beauty of Isabella. He was a classy and fastidious dresser, and she looked every bit like Spanish royalty. She brought him what every gambler wants—luck. Her family refused to pay a dowry, but Bushkin was way ahead of the game. He'd long had skill. Now he had luck. Bushkin went fifty-six nights in a row of winning at card tables in Boston. Bushkin and Isabella took a train down to New York City. Their suitcases were full of money. They booked a suite at the Broadway Palace Hotel on Fifth Avenue. Bushkin put their money in the hotel vault. Isabella was looking more royal every day, erect and handsome in her new gowns.

There followed weeks of socializing with the gambling elite of Wall Street at clubs, racetracks, private games in mansions of lower Manhattan. Bushkin was careful not to win too much money from his powerful friends, but enough to more than keep up the grand life he and Isabella were living, still in their Broadway Palace suite but spending weekends as houseguests on Long Island. The Bushkins became close to Puffy Rathenberg and her husband Winthrop, known as a wizard on Wall Street. Puffy had been thrilled to discover Isabella knew quite a lot about horses and dogs. Isabella and Jeremy became guests in the Rathenberg box at the polo field. One evening after dinner, while the men were enjoying cigars and Cognac on the broad veranda of the Rathenberg estate in Glen Cove, admiring the moonlight on the waters of Long Island Sound, Puffy was feeling warm and chummy after a bottle and a half of merlot and confided to Isabella that Winthrop was onto a sure thing. He was buying shares in a salt mine because Puffy was one of only three persons in the world who knew the mine would be getting a contract to sell the salt for a fat price to the government to distribute on Indian reservations for the next hundred years. Anaconda Salt was the name of the company. Isabella and Bushkin caught the Wall Street fever. They bought Anaconda Salt. But clever as they were in the gambling world, the Bushkins had yet to understand how easily Wall Street breaks outsiders. Anaconda Salt shares crashed when the government contract went to a rival salt mine. The Bushkins lost ninety-seven thousand dollars. Winthrop Rathenberg had quietly sold his shares in Anaconda Salt before the crash after he received a coded message from his former Princeton roommate who was now in the government. It was as if Rathenberg had traded his soon-to-be-worthless shares to the Bushkins at face value.

In his life as a gambler, Bushkin had lost large sums of money on occasion. He was too proud and canny to complain. But he felt sour toward Winthrop Rathenberg. The more Bushkin thought about getting taken this way, being made a chump, the worse it stung. The evening of the third day after the Anaconda Salt stock crash, Isabella was sitting alone at a table in the bar in the Metropolitan Club, looking royal in her green silk gown, having a glass of wine from a bottle of Sancerre. Bushkin sat at the poker table twenty-five feet away. Loud voices rose from the poker game. Members across the mirrored, overstuffed, red-velvet great-room began looking up from their cards or their newspapers in annoyance. Winthrop Rathenberg was drunk. He was arguing a point with Sonny Redfern of Redfern & Sons. Winthrop glanced over Sonny's shoulder and noticed Isabella. Winthrop said, "Sonny, you fool, that I'm right is as obvious as, well, as obvious as the nose on Bushkin's wife's face." Bushkin jumped up and pulled out that little hidy gun that gamblers carry and shot Winthrop Rathenberg through the chest without hitting anything vital.

This incident was kept away from the police and out of the newspapers, but it was the end of the Bushkins' social and professional life in New York, Boston, and Philadelphia. They were barred from clubs. Choice tables no longer awaited them at restaurants. There were jokes about Isabella's nose having caused a shooting. She was stared at and whispered about in public places as the story of the shooting got around. Three thugs hired by Winthrop Rathenberg caught Bushkin walking alone at night in Chelsea. He put up a vigorous fight, but they broke his arm. The next morning Isabella fetched their remaining twenty-six thousand dollars from the vault and checked them out of the Broadway Plaza. The Bushkins took a steamer to Galveston, in Texas, far from Winthrop Rathenberg's reach. They discovered that Texas was actually a whole different country from New York, Boston, and Philadelphia.

They were starting over. Isabella put herself in charge as the brains behind the Bushkins. She persuaded her husband to run for county commissioner in Galveston. She spent twelve thousand dollars making friends for his campaign. He won. The job paid sixty dollars a year, but it opened many doors. Adapting to their surroundings, the Bushkins became fiery Confederate patriots. Isabella was always at Bushkin's side in Galveston's finest places, looking from any angle spectacular. She was his not-so-secret weapon. Many now believed her to be a cousin of the Queen of Spain. For the next election cycle Isabella decided Bushkin would run for the state senate. The senatorial districts in Galveston and Houston were locked up by powerful politics. Isabella's new friends tipped her to a seat that would open in Bastrop County. She badgered Bushkin into leaving Galveston and moving a hundred and fifty miles to the northwest up the Colorado River to Bastrop, where Isabella bought property on the river south of town to establish residence. With his robust personality and his intriguing wife, Bushkin won election to the state senate. He sponsored the bill that created the East Texas Steamboat Company to further commerce on the Colorado River, and he saw to it that his senate committee was the ultimate authority over all steamboats on all Texas rivers.

Isabella built Bushkin's Landing as a way-station for steamboats. The two- story, white-frame home stood a hundred yards inland from the river. In front of the main home near the water's edge was a white wooden structure of four rooms—three for overnight customers and one for gambling games. The kitchen where the cooking was done occupied its own separate structure because of the danger of fire. There was a warehouse for supplies and freight, and a barn for the farm animals. The Bonnie Blue Flag flew from a pole on a wooden dock. When the first paddlewheel steamboat arrived at Bushkin's Landing, half the town of Bastrop journeyed south to see it. The Bushkins shot off fireworks. River passage from Bastrop to the Gulf should be a bonanza for the Bushkins. These were happy days for Isabella, much more so than for Bushkin, who yearned for the big city life. He missed the fancy restaurants and sophisticated gambling clubs. Bushkin had never cared for storing up money. He believed the gambler who is constantly counting his money is in the wrong trade. Then the war kept going on and things kept getting worse everywhere. The vagaries of the river ruined the East Texas Steamboat Company. There were shifting sandbars and huge rafts of timber blocking the channels. There were floods and, of course, drought. Two steamboats sank and the other just never really worked right. Finally came the news of Lee's surrender, and Jefferson Davis was rushing from place to place on his own railroad train trying to avoid capture, and General Johnston surrendered. Rumors flew that the Yankee army was marching into Texas looking for revenge against the leaders of the stubborn rebels who had fought them for four years. Confederate politicians were to be jailed and possibly hanged.

Now Isabella was walking around the round oak dining table in the residence, and around again, looking down at the document on one of the two plates that Mandy, the maid, had set for the Bushkins's lunch. Mandy and Sara, the cook, and Joseph, the yard man, came running when they heard Isabella wailing, but the sight of her anguish and wrath stopped them from entering the room. They were slaves, but Isabella did not own them. She leased them from Dr. Thatcher in Bastrop.

The document on the plate said:

> *I have gone to Mexico to make a new life and fortune.*
> *I divorce you.*
> *The next man who takes you on will wish he hadn't.*

Isabella's first thought was: after all this, after all I have done for him, he betrays me. I should kill him. I will send for my father and my brothers. They would love to murder Bushkin. Then she thought: no, it's my nose. She went to the mirror on the wall and looked at herself. She was wearing the brown riding skirt she had purchased in New York. Her black hair glistened around her shoulders. Her white silk blouse was unbuttoned down to the third button and showed heaving cleavage. Her eyes were large, brown and clear, her teeth regular and white. Then there was the nose. Face-on in the mirror, the nose was nothing remarkable, but from a side view it was what a nasty newspaper article in The Galveston Herald had called Egyptian from the era of the pharaohs. Bushkin could no longer stand to look at my nose, she thought. But no, she reasoned, it's insane for me to berate myself. It wasn't my nose that drove him away. This wasn't my fault. The truth is Bushkin is a coward. He is running to save his life before the Yankees get here. He is leaving me here to face the revenge of the victors.

Mandy spoke up hesitantly from the doorway.

"Miz Bushkin, they's a dirty, rough-looking man at the door asking to see the head of the house."

"What does he want?"

"I doan know. But Joseph is holding a gun on he."

"Give him some food and send him on his way."

"Yes ma'am, I tried that, but he doan want food. He want to see the head of the house, so I expect that is you nowadays." Mandy had read the document on the plate. "This man has got a real odd way of talking. He might be from a foreign country."

"Does he look Spanish by any chance?"

"No ma'am."

Isabella plucked the document from the plate, folded it, looked around for someplace to put it and finally tucked it into her bosom.

She followed Mandy to the back door.

At first sight of the suffering on the ruined but handsome face of the man in the torn, filthy clothes who stood on the back step outside her house, Isabella's heart went flowing to him. When he opened his mouth and spoke to her, she had the sudden, irrational thought that the angels might have sent him to replace Bushkin. She was drawn deeply into his presence by the sound of his voice, the lovely, educated English accent that made her think of a different world. But Isabella had spent the last five years among confidence men and swindlers of all sorts. She knew to be wary.

"Ah, Señora, I was not prepared to be met by such a beauty. I am enchanted," Varney said. "If you would be so kind, I need a word with the head of the house."

"I am the head of the house. What is it you want?"

"You're so young and beautiful, I wouldn't have guessed. Please forgive my appearance. I was waylaid by thugs, beaten, and robbed."

"What is your name?"

"I am Edmund Varney, the novelist."

"Really?"

"You know my work?"

"Well, actually no, but I admire the literary life, the life of the mind and heart and the soul. What on earth is an English novelist doing here in east Texas?"

"I am seeking a meal and a drink of cool water," Varney said.

Varney knew that somewhere behind him the young rebel captain and the fortune-telling girl were entering the corral and the barn to saddle three horses. The captain would whistle when they were ready. Varney was scouting the house to see what opposition they could expect, which so far was none except for the black yard-man with the musket. This exotic Spanish woman was looking at him with a pitying curiosity. He noticed the piece of paper that extruded from her entrancing bosom. Varney was thinking this was a woman he would like to become better acquainted with, a fine piece of luck.

Isabella looked at the purple knots on Varney's head, at the tangled mass of gray hair around his ears, at his earring, at his large gray eyes that showed pain and weariness, at the wretched state of his clothing, at the crusted mud and blood on his face and hands.

"First we must get you a bath," she said. "Upstairs is an entire closet of excellent suits that I believe should be just your size."

Eleven

WHEN HE LEFT THE COURTROOM in the foundry after denouncing the English writer as a false friend and a horse thief, Tom Custer mounted the chestnut Arabian mare Athena and rode back to his tent in the Federal camp on Shoal Creek.

Athena felt light to his fingers on the reins and comforting to his seat in the saddle. She was graceful and sure of foot. The feel of her power between his legs soothed Custer's temper. Athena seemed always to know where she was going. She knew where Custer wanted her to go before he knew himself.

That second Medal of Honor charge, at Sayler's Creek in Virginia, Athena had leaped the first rebel barricade in a storm of explosions, smoke, and gunshots that was like being inside a Roman candle. She found herself and her rider facing a second rebel barricade that bristled with rifles, bayonets and cannons. Instantly Athena plunged toward the second barricade, and Custer was floating into a scene of insanity. He saw the red-bearded rebel flag-bearer screaming curses. A bullet tore through Custer's cheek. It felt like a punch from a fist. He reeled in the saddle but somehow Athena made an adjustment that kept Custer from falling. Custer fired his pistol into the flag-bearer's breast from a distance of two feet and grabbed the Virginia colors out of the dying man's hands. To capture the enemy's flag meant capturing his manhood and taking away his identity. There were seconds of wildly blurring, exploding images, and then

Athena was flying back over the second barricade, then the first barricade, and Tom was racing toward the forward position of the Sixth Michigan Cavalry, where he could see his brother, the commanding general whose golden hair draped onto his shoulders beneath a hat with three black ostrich feathers stuck into the left side of the band. Tom remembered shouting with his mouth pouring blood, "Armstrong, the damned rebels have killed me, but I've got their flag again."

Now Athena was carrying Tom Custer among the Seventh Cavalry tents in Austin to his own quarters on the bank of the creek, where he could hear the water flowing and could smell the bass and perch and catfish that the soldiers and the local boys hauled onto the shore with their cane poles.

Many troopers from the Sixth Michigan volunteers had followed the example of their commander, Gen. George Armstrong Custer, and transferred into the Seventh Cavalry regulars, signing on for extended tours that would take them as occupiers into the far corner of rebel country. Every soldier in the Seventh Cavalry was a volunteer who saw the war ending and didn't want to go back home, or had no home outside of the army. Some were immigrants who were learning English.

Custer dismounted in front of his tent. He scratched Athena's ears and then kissed the white patch above her nose. She nuzzled his face. He stepped into the shade of the tent, took two sugar cubes out of a glass jar, and let Athena lick the sugar out of his palm. He loved this horse and felt he was in her debt. She thrust her muzzle into his hand. Her nostrils flared as she tasted the sugar. Her eyes showed pleasure. Custer combed his fingers through her mane and scratched her coppery coat.

"I'm going to have a little nap," he whispered to Athena.

He told his orderly, a hometown boy from New Rumley, to give Athena a good rubdown and turn her out in the corral. It was barely noon, but Tom Custer was taking the heat of the day off. He was sick with a hangover from drinking whiskey all evening and most of the night, for three nights in a row, with that two-faced Englishman.

Custer stripped off his uniform blouse and hung it over a wooden chair that had a cowhide seat. Even here in the shade of the tent, the day was turning hot. Custer found it hard to understand how people could want to live in such a climate as he had observed in his first week in Texas with the advance party. He sat on his cot and pulled off his boots. He was wearing white socks, blue uniform pants that had been tailored to fit, and a white sleeveless undershirt that exposed the tattoo on his right shoulder—the United States flag and the initials T. W. C.

With his brother Armstrong and sister-in-law Libby not here to modulate him, Tom had been drinking heavily. He blamed his thirst on Texas and on the bullet that had gone through his cheek. That the bullet went in his mouth and came out the side of his face without breaking his teeth or ruining his looks made life all the weirder and gave him more reason to reach for the bottle. Those six days in Virginia in April had cast a haze of unreality over everything and made it uncomfortable for him to live with himself. The first Medal of Honor charge, at the Namozine church, had jarred his life into a different sense of things. It wasn't that the charge at the church was his introduction to the elephant. As an aide on his brother's staff, Tom had been in the heat of the fighting at the Wilderness and through the Shenandoah Valley. But suddenly that day at the Namozine church, Tom broke away from his brother on the Arabian mare Athena and rallied the faltering troopers and led them in a mad charge into the cannon smoke. Later he thought: did I lead the charge, or did Athena lead it? But in the few minutes when it was happening, he had no thought of anything at all. They counted up what he had done at the church—killed six rebels with pistol and saber, and captured eight shocked and exhausted barefoot men, who wore ragged pieces of gray uniform, and he brought the battle flag of their Virginia regiment to his brother as a trophy. Could all this really have happened and left him intact? Before Tom could fit this behavior into his understanding of life, his brother led the Sixth Michigan to a wooded stream called Sayler's Creek, and it all happened again, except this time he got shot in the face. Tom Custer was twenty years old, but he had begun to feel he had been around forever.

He had begun to feel the same way about his horse, Athena. She had been around forever also. He had ridden Athena for only a week before the first charge at the church. The horse had been a gift from his brother, the General, who had taken her from the owner of a Virginia plantation who died fighting on the lawn in front of his own home. Tom wasn't sure how his brother knew the horse had been named Athena, but it hadn't mattered until last night when the Englishman told him in the saloon that Athena was the goddess of war and wisdom in ancient Greece. Now Tom was having unsettling but somehow reassuring feelings that this horse knew more than he did about things that mattered.

Custer's eyes fell on the Englishman's book that lay on his trunk beside his cot. He picked up *By the Sword* and opened it to the flyleaf, where he read, 'To my new friend, Tom. With admiration, Edmund Varney,' scrawled in ink by the author. What a disappointment the Englishman had turned out to be. Custer had enjoyed the company of the garrulous old man who was full of interesting stories on topics that Tom cared about, like horses, war, and women. Custer had read the first twenty pages of the novel and flipped through the rest, reading a page here and there. Varney had warned him this was one of those fictional stories, but what Custer read sounded like the truth. The first half of the book appeared to take place in India, and the last half seemed to be concerned with the retreat and destruction of a large British force in Afghanistan. The story was narrated by an Englishman who sounded like Varney. Where does the fiction come in? Custer wondered. On page twenty was a description of the execution of a prince in the Punjab. In a public square before a cheering crowd, the executioner cut off in turn each of the prince's hands and feet, castrated him, cut open his belly and tore out his bowels, pierced his eyeballs with needles, and still he lived. Finally they chopped off his head, and he gave up. Would Varney make that up as a fictional story? Custer wondered. No, that must be true. What kind of mind would invent a story like that? The truth is uglier than fiction dares to be.

Custer tossed the book back onto the trunk. He swung his legs up onto the cot and lay on his back, shielding his eyes with a forearm. He wished for a breeze, but this was the stillness of midafternoon. Custer was thinking back to last night and beginning to remember something crazy that Varney had said toward the last. What was it? The scene began coming back to him. Varney had leaned close and looked Custer in the eyes and said Athena had once been his, Varney's, war horse years ago in India and Afghanistan. That story was a fiction of Varney's mind, Custer reasoned, because he had examined Athena's teeth and inspected her form as soon as she came into his possession, and he made her to be seven years old, exactly prime for a horse of Arabian lineage. But Varney had repeated his ridiculous claim. Now Custer remembered it wasn't that Varney asked to ride Athena. It was more like Varney had said he was going to repossess Athena. He was going to ride her. He was going to take her away. But he hadn't said anything about going to Mexico, had he? Custer had figured the old Englishman had gotten insanely drunk, to be talking like that. Custer didn't take him seriously. No man alive would dare to get onto Tom Custer's horse without consent.

Yet Varney clearly had done so. Tom was trying to remember Varney leaving the saloon, but he couldn't see it, and the rest of the night was a blank. Tom didn't know if he had passed out, or if whiskey had simply washed away his memory. Tom had been having mornings of waking up feeling remorse and regret about things he couldn't remember from the night before. Maybe I had gone to pee and came back and didn't realize he had left, Custer thought. It wasn't until Tom woke up on his own cot this morning and couldn't remember how he got there that Captain Leatherwood appeared at the tent flap with Athena on the reins and told him she had been stolen but was now recovered. Until then Tom didn't know she was gone, which shamed him. Tom had known Captain Leatherwood for about three months, since the captain was released from a hospital and assigned to the Sixth Michigan. Captain Leatherwood had volunteered for the Seventh Cavalry and was sent to Austin with the advance party to command the prison and organize the military police, who so far appeared to be his three nephews. Leatherwood was the senior Seventh Cavalry officer so far to arrive in Austin, but Tom Custer was the officer who had command of the company of troopers. Custer was chagrined to have his own horse returned to him by a fellow officer with seventeen years' service in the regulars. Tom resolved that he would not have more than two drinks tonight. Tomorrow he would be up at dawn and take a patrol out to investigate reports of guerrillas south of town.

He told himself he would quit drinking and playing cards in the saloons when his brother Armstrong arrived in Austin with Armstrong's wife Libby. She traveled with Armstrong when at all possible, even to the scenes of some of the great battles of the war. Off duty, Tom and Armstrong and Libby were like children together.

Armstrong, at twenty-four, was the eldest. They wrestled and played tag, roughhoused and sang songs and played jokes on each other. But on duty Armstrong insisted on being addressed as, "General Custer, sir." It was not easy being the general's brother. Armstrong was harder on Tom than on the other junior officers and demanded more of him.

Tom Custer slapped a fly that was crawling on his cheek. He had almost drifted into sleep before he heard the buzz and felt the tickling of the fly's feet on his skin. He thought about Varney again. So maybe Varney hadn't been a false friend so much as crazy drunk enough to try such a stupid thing as to claim he owned Athena and to ride away from Dutch John's on her. No matter how you tried to justify it, what Varney did was horse theft. Being drunk was no excuse for stealing a horse, not even a horse you drunkenly believed you used to own. There was no acceptable excuse for betraying a friend, either. But Tom had liked Varney and was flattered that a famous writer would want to write his true life-story for a British magazine. Varney had said there might be a book later.

Tom hadn't yet learned what the judge had decided to do with Varney, but he was too sick to care at the moment. If hanging was the verdict for the writer, Tom would intervene and stop it. He would overrule the judge by the authority of the Seventh Cavalry. He would take a squad of troopers and save Varney from the gallows. Tom didn't expect Captain Leatherwood would object to sparing Varney's life. That rebel officer was the man Captain Leatherwood wanted. Back in Virginia, Tom had heard Captain Leatherwood had been nearly disemboweled in a fight in the Smoky Mountains, and this morning he had heard from his orderly that the rebel officer in the courtroom was the warrior who wielded the saber. Tom had made a quick study of the tall, pale, shaggy-haired man in the butternut coat sitting on the pew separated from Edmund Varney by an interesting looking colored girl in a turban and bright blue blouse. He caught the rebel looking back at him. Their eyes met for a long second. Tom felt he had seen that rebel's face. He had seen hundreds, thousands of faces like his, maybe even this exact same face. Tom had killed this face. If called upon to kill it again, he would do so.

Custer fell asleep. When he was sleeping off a whiskey binge he didn't dream. He just blacked out.

Some while later he was shaken awake by a hand on his bare, tattooed shoulder. Custer opened his eyes and looked up into the face of Captain Leatherwood, who had taken off his campaign hat to duck into the tent. This was the second time today the captain had waked him. Leatherwood was sweating and breathing hard, as if he had been running.

"What the hell is it this time?" Custer said.

"The horse thief and the rebel bastard and the colored girl have murdered Private Dubcek and escaped into the woods down near Bastrop," said Captain Leatherwood. "I'm putting together a squad to go after them."

Custer planted his feet on the floor and stood up.

"I'm leading it," he said.

Twelve

THERE WERE NO HORSES WORTH RIDING in the barn or in the corral at Bushkin's Landing.

"Two old mules fit for pulling a plow or a wagon very slowly, and one fat old nag that is permanently out to pasture," Flora said.

"From the stuff lying around it looks like these empty stalls used to be for the saddle horses," said Robin. "I'm guessing the owners of this place left here in a hurry on their good horses."

"There's somebody here. The old romancer is in the house talking to somebody. I saw a woman come to the door and invite him in," Flora said.

"Go find him if you want," Robin said. "I'm leaving. Good luck to you both."

"How you intend to go about leaving, hey?"

"By using my feet to start with."

"You see that sign down there?" said Flora. "Doesn't that say Bushkin's Landing? Doesn't that sound like boats to you?"

"I was thinking boat when we first started toward the river," he said. Her question annoyed him. "But I don't see a boat anywhere, do you?"

"Maybe the romancer has found one," she said.

Flora started walking toward the big white house. After a moment, Robin followed her. She looked around for the black man with the musket she had seen standing with Varney at the door. Apparently the black man had gone inside with the romancer. As they passed the small building where the cooking was done they smelled baking pastry. An old hound dog, asleep by the porch, opened an eye at the approach of Flora and Robin and decided they were not worth the effort of a bark in the warm sun of early afternoon. Flora started to bang on the door, but Robin lifted a hand to stop her.

"Listen," he whispered.

"What is it?"

"I'm not sure."

Rising up on his toes, Robin peered through the high, small window. Flora watched his face. Slowly he shook his head. He settled back onto his heels. Robin interlaced the fingers of his two hands to form a stirrup and gestured for her to take a look. She planted a bare right foot into the stirrup and lifted herself, bracing with a hand against his shoulder. She looked into the window.

Inside the house in a large back room with a linoleum covered floor, Varney sat in a four-legged tub, splashing happily while Mandy poured in another bucket of water. Sara the cook scrubbed Varney's back with a long handled brush. Varney's head was a meringue of soap. Joseph leaned against the wall, both hands on the musket to be ready if the situation should suddenly change for the worse. Isabella Bushkin kept her back turned modestly. She was admiring a handsome gray coat with matching trousers that she had hung on a hanger on a hook. Hanging beside the suit of clothing was a white cotton shirt, long-sleeved, snowy clean. None saw the faces of first Robin and then Flora appear in the window.

"I think this will look wonderful on you," Isabella said. "Bushkin had a superb tailor in New York. He was a prissy old gentleman who had trained on Savile Row and never let you forget it. This is a fine piece of wool from Scotland, lightweight to go with the Texas climate, though God knows for eight or nine months of the year it is difficult to find a decent cloth airy enough for the sweltering climate of this damned place. The shirt was made in Boston, cotton from India. Here we are living in fabulous cotton country, but we wear cotton from India. Why? Because it is finer quality?"

"Southern cotton is blockaded," Varney said. "You don't have the mills to turn out the finished thing."

"Even before the war, in New York we chose Indian cotton."

"Indian cotton is the finest," Varney said.

"Do you know India?"

"I spent twelve years, no, fourteen years in India," said Varney.

"I would love to have the experience of India someday," she said.

"No reason why you shouldn't realize that desire," Varney said. He rubbed a lather of soap into his face, dipped a straight razor into the bath water and began to shave, straining to see himself in a hand mirror that fogged up. "The climate in Calcutta is the same as here."

"When I was a child I used to hear stories of India from my grandfather Marcus."

"Was he a soldier?"

"He was a banker. He did business with the East India Company. They are in charge of all Indian commerce, I believe. The British army works for them. Grandfather said it was a very genteel life in India for the Englishman."

"Very genteel, except for when the natives decide to cut off your head," Varney said. "The Crown more or less runs the show there now, since the mutiny. I can tell you places to go where you will see astonishing things that will make you believe in the invisible world, and other places where you will eat superb food in opulent safety. Perhaps Señor Bushkin will take you on a tour of India."

"Not Señor Bushkin. Senator Bushkin."

"Senator? What kind of senator?"

"Bushkin is in the Texas congress. Two years ago he was a delegate to the Confederacy, but that proved too much of a challenge for his political skills," Isabella said.

She brushed her fingers against the lapels of the hanging jacket as if Bushkin were still wearing it and she was inspecting him before a political rally or an evening at the tables. She imagined what might be the look on Bushkin's face if he had changed his mind and returned and was suddenly to enter the room now. The picture made Isabella smile. She turned her face a bit, putting her nose in profile to the English writer sloshing in the tub.

"Where is Senator Bushkin today?" Varney asked.

Mandy poured another bucket of water onto his head and began rinsing his hair.

"He has gone to Mexico."

"Going to Mexico is quite the fashion in Texas these days," Varney said. "In fact, I am on my way to Mexico myself. I'm gathering material for my new novel."

"A new novel? How exciting."

"Yes, the research has been rather exciting so far. Fair warning, Señora…"

"Isabella, please."

"Isabella, I am getting out of the tub now."

Varney stood up and looked down at the bath water, which had turned brown. Mandy handed him a towel and turned her head as he stepped out onto the floor. Sara began rubbing away the rings on the tub. Joseph the yard-man leaned against the wall and wished he was outside smoking his pipe.

"If you don't like this gray suit, there are a dozen other suits upstairs. You can have your choice. Take them all if you wish," said Isabella.

Varney dried himself with the towel and then wrapped it around his waist. Isabella turned and saw that he had a chestful of gray hair, now matted and wet, and the long gray hair on his bruised head was dripping and tangled.

"Sara, get him a hair brush," Isabella said.

"They is somebody else here. I hear feets," Mandy said.

"Joseph, go and see," said Isabella.

Joseph brought his musket up to the ready position. He reached out and poked open the door that had been closed between the bathing room and the serving room that held everything for preparing food but nothing for cooking it.

Joseph was startled to look into the face of Jerod Robin. Before Joseph could react, Robin snatched the musket away from him. Flora was looking around from behind Robin's left shoulder, smiling at the sight of Varney with the towel tied around his waist, and the impressive looking Spanish woman in the riding skirt, and the three Negroes who seemed to be unalarmed.

"Who are you? What is this?" Isabella said.

"You forget about us, General Varney?" said Robin.

"Señora, these are my friends," Varney said. "May I present Captain Jerod Robin and Mademoiselle Flora Bowprie?"

"Well, then, very well," said Isabella.

"And this is Isabella Bushkin, wife of Senator Bushkin," Varney said.

"Ma'am," said Robin, touching his hat brim.

"It is my pleasure," Flora said in French.

"I am delighted to hear French spoken again," Isabella replied in French. Then in English she said, "Please, follow me into the parlor. We'll let Mr. Varney get dressed. General Varney you called him? Sara, put the kettle on. Lay out the cakes. No, first put out bread and cheese and wine for our guests. And some sausages. And cakes."

There was a couch in the parlor and several comfortable chairs on a hardwood floor that was covered by two Turkish throw rugs beneath an oil painting of the snow-peaked mountains that form the border between Spain and France. Looking at the mountains, so near to Barcelona, reminded Isabella every day of home and what a different life it might have been if she had never met Bushkin.

Isabella decided to open the bottle of wine herself. She realized she was being set up in some way. Varney had told her he had been robbed and beaten, and she had assumed he was alone and truly in need. Now there arrived a tall young blonde man wearing the remains of a Confederate uniform, and a curious colored girl wearing a turban and a bright blue shirt. Isabella needed a moment to think.

Robin said, "Allow me, please, ma'am."

He took the bottle and the corkscrew from Isabella. Robin knew he should not linger here, but a plate of bread and cheese and sausage and a glass of red wine would detain him only a few more minutes.

"My father knows your husband, the Senator, I believe," said Robin.

He opened the bottle and poured a glass of wine for Isabella.

"Your father would be?" Isabella asked.

"Dr. Junius Robin."

"Well, of course I know Dr. Robin, the planter. He is a familiar figure around the Capitol. How is his health these days?"

Robin understood the question was a way of remarking that the doctor was frequently seen drunk and was an abuser of laudanum. As one of the originals who had charged and defeated the Mexican Army at San Jacinto, Dr. Junius was forgiven much. There was a persistent rumor that he was ill with some mysterious and lethal ailment. Others said his wife had driven him mad with her pretensions of running a grand estate long after Sweetbrush had fallen on bad times.

"I haven't been home in nearly two years," Robin said.

"Oh. Then I have seen your father since you have. Senator Bushkin and I chatted with Dr. Robin in Austin a few months ago."

"Was my mother with him?"

"Why, yes. Varina is such a tall, elegant, beautiful woman. I love her voice, her English accent. Your friend Edmund Varney has similar inflections."

"They were both raised in the north of London," Robin said. "At approximately the same time, come to think of it."

Flora lifted a piece of cheese from Sara's tray and placed it between two hunks of bread.

"I could use a glass of wine, hey," she said.

Isabella watched Robin pour a glass of wine for Flora. This was quite strange if the girl was a slave. Flora pulled out a chair and sat down at the table in the place where Bushkin would have sat.

"We want to buy three of your horses," Flora said.

"Buy?" Isabella smiled.

"We will pay with U.S. dollars," said Flora.

She dug into her mustard colored skirt where the derringer was hidden. Her hand came out clutching a roll of paper money with a piece of pink elastic around it. Robin couldn't tell how much money she had, but he guessed it was several hundred dollars.

"Why don't we sit and eat and wait for your friend, Mr. Varney?" Isabella said. "I know you must be tired from your ordeal, whatever it is you are going through. How did you lose your horses?"

"They were stolen," Robin said. "Tell me this, do you even have three horses?"

"I have two horses. They're in the barn," said Isabella.

"There are no horses in the barn," Robin said.

"But of course there are."

"No ma'am."

Isabella suddenly realized Bushkin had taken both thoroughbred Kentucky saddle horses when he left for Mexico. She felt a shiver of fear at the thought he might have taken all their cash money, too. She put her wineglass on the table and went to the painting of the mountains. Despite knowing the strangers were watching, she slid the painting aside and turned the dial on the wall safe. She opened the safe door. Inside it was empty.

Slowly Isabella closed the safe door. Bushkin had a head start to Galveston, where their savings and household accounts were at the Strand Bank. But he wouldn't know how to get access to the eleven-thousand dollars she kept in her emergency private account in the Crescent City Bank of New Orleans. That was her go-home money. Bushkin didn't know the account existed. But that money was far away from where she stood at this moment.

"You're quite sure about the horses?" Isabella asked.

"Yes ma'am," said Robin.

"Well, then, there's no hurry, is there? Let's have a bit of lunch," Isabella said. "Why do you call him general?"

"It's his attitude more than anything," Robin said.

Varney entered, wearing the gray suit that had belonged to Bushkin, his feet in a pair of Bushkin's fine English boots, the collar of the white cotton shirt high on his neck. His wet hair was brushed back above his ears. His wide brow creased with lines of pleasure as he smiled and filled a glass with red wine.

"To your everlasting beauty, dear lady," Varney said, lifting his glass in a toast to Isabella. He looked into her eyes and drank the wine. Refilling the glass, Varney noticed the painting. "Could it be? The Catalan Pyrenees?"

"In the middle is Mount Perdu," said Isabella.

"And you are a Catalan?"

"My home is Barcelona," she said.

"I was in Barcelona during this past Christmas season," said Varney.

"Oh, Mr. Varney, how the thought of Barcelona makes my heart race."

Flora had spread her legs slightly to stretch her skirt and catch the crumbs that fell from her bread and cheese.

"This is very nice, but we must be moving along, hey?" she said.

They heard a sharp bang and the spray of shattering glass from the room where Sara was slicing another sausage and Mandy was loading another tray for the guests.

Joseph appeared in the doorway.

"Miz Bushkin, they's men with guns out in the yard," he said.

"Soldiers?" Varney wondered if Custer could be here already on the back of the swift Athena.

"No, they's nightrider-looking," Joseph said.

Another shot smashed a second window in the serving room. Sara and Mandy dropped to the floor amid shards of glass but were unhurt. Isabella and her lunch guests crept into the serving room and looked into the yard behind the house.

Three white men on horseback were out by the barn. They were dressed for hunting.

"Come out of your house, Bushkin," yelled one of the men. "It's time for you to pay for your sins."

"Oh my God," Isabella said. "It's Fritz Klutemeier, Bushkin's worst political enemy. He's a Unionist. Bushkin cleaned him out at the poker table in Bastrop two weeks ago."

The old hound dog got up and started ambling away from the noise. One of the men shot the dog with a rifle. The dog yelped and flipped onto his side and tried to crawl. The man shot him again.

"We'll burn the damn house down with you in it," Fritz Klutemeier yelled. "There's no way you can escape me, Bushkin."

Thirteen

ISABELLA OPENED THE BACK DOOR and stepped onto the small porch. Fritz Klutemeier and his two companions sat on their horses seventy yards from her, near the barn. Isabella didn't recognize the other two men as voters from this district. They were cold-looking men with beards and stern faces. Klutemeier was on a white horse with a black mane and a switching black tail. The German freed his long legs from the stirrups and stretched them. He cranked another bullet into his smoking carbine. Isabella could see it must have been Klutemeier who had fired the two shots into her house.

"The senator is not at home," she called out. "He has gone to Houston on business."

"You're a lying, long-nosed Spanish traitor," yelled Klutemeier in a German accent. He had emigrated from Munich.

"How dare you speak to me that way," Isabella said.

"I know he's inside the house. I saw him moving around inside," said Klutemeier. "Tell him to be a man and walk out here and take what he's got coming."

"You're asking for big trouble, Mr. Klutemeier," Isabella said.

"Yah! Trouble is right. Big trouble for a cheating, swindling traitor to America. I'll give you five minutes to send Bushkin out here, or else we'll come in and get him. Right, boys?"

The other two men nodded solemnly. Both men carried rifles

resting across their saddle pommels.

"One last time I'm telling you Senator Bushkin is not here," said Isabella.

Klutemeier lifted his carbine and fired a shot that tore a hole in the wall a few feet to Isabella's left.

"Now go in there and drag him out from under the bed or wherever he is hiding," Klutemeier said. "You got four minutes left, yah?"

Isabella whirled around and went inside and let the door slam behind her.

Sara and Mandy had fled from the back room for safety deeper inside the house. Joseph crouched beside a broken window with his musket. Varney held the Remington double-barreled 12-gauge shotgun that had belonged to the late Pvt. Huffer Dubcek.

"They have seen you and think you are Bushkin," Isabella said to Varney.

"I'll go out and deal with them," Varney said.

"No," she said. "That man is crazy. He will shoot you on sight."

"Do you have any guns?" asked Robin.

"In the closet under the stairs there's a gun cabinet. Mandy, give this man the key to the gun cabinet."

Robin opened the closet door and found the tall mahogany cabinet. He unlocked it and softly drew in his breath. Nestled into a bed of blue velvet he saw a twin set of dragoon single-action .44-caliber revolvers, made by Colt, and a Spencer repeating rifle of the model that had been issued to Federal troops in the last year of the war. At the foot of the cabinet Robin saw a box of .58-caliber rimfire cartridges for the Spencer. He grabbed a handful of cartridges and began loading them into the magazine in the butt of the rifle.

"Load these pistols," he said to Flora.

She broke open the two heavy pistols and took out the cylinders and fed bullets into them. Robin noticed that she didn't hesitate. She knows what she is doing with pistols, he thought.

"You know what I see out there?" Flora asked.

"What?" said Robin.

"I see three horses we could get."

"Yeah, I noticed that, too."

They heard Klutemeier shouting, "You got about one more minute to come out here, Bushkin, or your place goes up in smoke with you and your long-nose greaser in it."

Isabella flushed.

Varney said, "I'll kill that fool."

"No, wait. I've heard Bushkin debate him. He's a bag of wind. He'll exhaust himself and go away," said Isabella.

Peeking through the broken window, they saw the other two men holster their rifles and unstrap from their saddles two four-foot sticks of wood that had dark blobs on the ends.

"Torches," Flora said.

"You think I'm just having a joke with you, Bushkin?" shouted Klutemeier. "Time is up. Light 'em, boys."

The two men struck fire to the tar on their torches and sat back in their saddles as the flames and black smoke rose from the burning pitch. One of the men gigged his horse toward the house in a slow walk.

"If he gets close enough to throw the torch, I will blast him," Varney said, hefting the Remington shotgun.

But the man turned his horse and rode in a semicircle back toward the others near the barn, still out of effective shotgun range.

Then he casually tossed the burning torch into the hayloft of the barn.

The roof of the barn exploded into flame. Joseph the yard-man let out a wild screaming cry and dashed through the back door into the yard, running toward the mounted men. Joseph raised his musket as he ran and fired it, but the pumping motion of his arms caused the ball to bounce in the grass at the feet of the horses.

Klutemeier shot Joseph with the carbine. The bullet ripped the shirt between Joseph's shoulders and came out his back in a spray of blood. Joseph staggered three more steps forward and dropped to his knees in the yard. He remained kneeling there, his body tilted back, held upright by the heels of his shoes as he groaned and blood puddled at his feet.

"Forfeiting one damn nigger don't pay your debt or get you off of my bad side," Klutemeier shouted. "I'll have your neck in a noose, Bushkin. We'll see how your Confederacy looks from a tree limb."

Robin cocked the Spencer repeating rifle, steadied it against the windowsill and quickly but carefully aimed at the middle of Klutemeier's body. Robin squeezed the trigger. The shot spun the German sideways out of the saddle.

Klutemeier rolled over on the ground and propped himself up on his elbows and stared bug-eyed at the spreading red stain soaking his shirt front.

"Bushkin has killed me," he said in wonderment.

The man who had thrown the torch that started the barn blazing jumped down off his horse, yanked his rifle out of the saddle holster and squatted at Klutemeier's side. He tore open Klutemeier's shirt and saw the red hole pumping blood.

"He's killed Fritz," the man said.

"Let's get out of here," the other man said.

"The son of a bitch gambler has killed our cousin. Burn his house. Fry them all."

There was another bang and a puff of gray white smoke from the window. The man kneeling beside Klutemeier rocked back as a bullet from the Spencer cracked his skull and sent bits of his head flying. He collapsed onto his back, his mouth open, caught in mid-threat.

The third man flung his torch to the ground and hauled back on his reins. His horse reared. The man hung onto the saddle with both hands. The horse bucked once and then took off at a gallop up the road that led alongside the river in the direction of Bastrop. Seeing them running, the other two horses began to run, also, following the same road back to Bastrop. The white horse with the black mane was gaining on the leader as they passed from sight.

Klutemeier and his bearded companion expired in the warm yellow sunlight. Flies were already buzzing around the body of Joseph that lay halfway to the house, and the old hound dog that lay a few yards further.

Robin levered another cartridge into the chamber of the Spencer.

The walls of the back room vibrated from the noise and dishes had barely ceased rattling. The room smelled of sulfur. Varney looked at Robin and remembered Santana Leatherwood's testimony in court that the Confederate captain was a murdering savage. Not that this was actually murder, Varney thought. The shootings of Klutemeier and his companion were no doubt appropriate. There was poor Joseph lying dead in the yard. Joseph had only been trying to protect the barn—possibly he had something in the barn he was trying to save, perhaps he had come to think of Bushkin's Landing as his own territory. Maybe Joseph was fed up with being shot at, his windows shattered, his peaceful afternoon destroyed. Whatever had outraged him, he had died for it.

"Good shooting," Varney said. Robin had fired the Spencer twice from about seventy-five yards and had hit his targets, one in the breast and one in the head. Varney knew from experience how difficult that was to do. Most men caught up in violence never came close to their targets. Some never fire their weapons, not even when facing onrushing death. The rebel captain clearly had no qualms about using his weapon and was very accurate with it.

The barn was crackling with bursts of orange and black.

"They'll see this smoke from miles around," Flora said.

Watching the barn erupt in flames, Isabella pressed her palms against either side of her face and gasped. She was surprised at her own feelings. Rather than shock and grief and anger such as she had been stricken with at the sight of the ugly note Bushkin had left on the plate, Isabella was feeling giddy with euphoria. A weight was lifting from her shoulders. She realized she was now free of Bushkin and free of Bushkin's Landing—and almost finished with Texas. In weeks she could be back home in Barcelona with her family.

"Yes, we can hardly stay here any longer," said Isabella.

"Pardon? We?" Varney said.

"The Unionists around here will be coming for me, especially now with Klutemeier shot to pieces out there behind my house," said Isabella. "I want to go with you and your friends, Mr. Varney. I must leave this place at once."

"You want to go to Mexico?" Varney said.

"Not to Mexico," she said. "I need to go to Houston. May I go with you as far as possible? It's too dangerous on the road for a woman traveling alone. I can't handle the boat by myself. I wouldn't know how to begin, and there's no time to hire a crew."

Flora noticed Mandy and Sara outside bending over the body of Joseph.

"I didn't see a boat. Where is it?" said Robin.

"The shed beside the river is a covered dock. It's in there," Isabella said. "I'm running upstairs to pack a bag. I won't be a minute."

The roof of the barn collapsed in a shower of fire. Sparks drifted toward the house.

They heard Isabella's boot heels pounding up the stairs.

"We have to take her with us," Varney said. "It's only fair."

Flora and Varney were stuffing bread, cheeses, sausages and bottles of wine into a canvas sack. Flora had laid the two heavy dragoon pistols on the table with three boxes of cartridges. Robin made certain seven cartridges were loaded into the spring operated magazine in the butt of the Spencer. He put three boxes of .58-caliber brass cartridges in the side pockets of his butternut coat. They were the first big-bore cartridges ever made, and hard to come by. Robin touched the letter from Sweetbrush that was sewn into the lining. He saw Flora watching him.

"Yeah, I guess we owe her that," Robin said.

"Let's not shoot her," said Varney. "I know shooting people has solved our problems so far, but I rather adore this woman."

"Hey," said Flora, "I say she comes with us if she wants to."

Fourteen

THE BOAT TURNED OUT TO BE a thirty-foot raft with a white pine cabin on it. Painted on the cabin in green letters a foot high were the words BUSHKIN FOR SENATE.

Isabella got aboard with two suitcases, which she stowed in the cabin. Varney and Robin each grabbed a pole and pushed the flat-boat away from the dock and into the current. Varney laid down his pole and went to the stern oar that served as a rudder. Robin felt his pole jam into the hard bottom of the river. Then the pole no longer touched anything solid. Flora had gone to the bow to tie off the anchor rope and watch for floating logs. She looked back at Varney, in command at the rudder. Beyond Varney she could see the shingle roof of the big white house at Bushkin's Landing begin to steam with spumes of black smoke and speckles of orange and yellow.

Flora wrapped the rope into a coil and picked up the Spencer rifle.

"Don't take that rifle. Give it back to me," Robin said.

"I was going to keep an eye along the bank," she said.

"You can do that without this rifle," said Robin.

"Yes sir."

Robin frowned and turned his back to her and looked at the smoke and flames of the Bushkin residence as the dock and the green lawn faded behind them in the wake of the flatboat. Isabella put on a broad-brimmed straw hat with a black band that she had brought out of the cabin. She looked at her burning house and sighed. "One door closes, but another opens," she said.

"I must say, you're taking this rather splendidly," said Varney.

"Yes, well, we must find our comforts where we are now and not where we used to be or where we wish we were," she said.

"How true that is."

Standing with his fist closed around the rudder, wearing the good gray Savile Row suit with the black boots and the white India-cotton shirt with the billowing collar, the silver and jade ring glinting in his left ear, one of the dragoon pistols stuck in his belt, his hunger and his thirst satisfied for now, Varney was feeling young and vigorous in a way he hadn't felt since last night in Dutch John's saloon at the moment he decided to reclaim his horse Athena. Those like Robin who said this couldn't be the same horse, who said Athena couldn't be twenty-two years old, those people hadn't seen the marvels of life that Varney had seen—the inexplicable but true. Those who doubted this was his Athena had never ridden her and did not know her. Isabella smiled at him. He thought her nose was quite remarkable. He liked it. Such a nose on a Spaniard was aristocratic and handsome. He gazed at her bosom and returned her smile.

"How wise of you," he said.

Looking at Varney made Isabella think of an English word she admired but had never had reason to use: swashbuckler.

"Life affords no higher pleasure than that of surmounting difficulties," Isabella said.

"Then you have fallen in with the right crowd, dear lady."

Flora sat down on the toolbox in front of the cabin near the railing facing the west bank of the Colorado. She laid a dragoon pistol on the box beside her right thigh. She glanced at the tall, pale captain, who held the Spencer in his arms and moved his eyes back and forth scanning the woods along the west bank. His lips were set in a small smile. She had noticed the same tight smile on his face as he was shooting the two Germans. This was a scary man. She expected he would leave them at the next opportunity. That would be the best thing for everybody, she thought. There was a chance the army would chase the rebel captain and not press the hunt for Flora and the romancer. The rebel captain might be blamed for shooting the soldier by the time the story was told in Austin. They had already accused him of murder earlier today in the courtroom.

She searched within herself for what she felt about shooting the soldier. Flora had never shot anyone before today, but she had pulled pistols on her mother's customers and suitors if they pushed Flora too far with sexual overtures. In the maze of French Quarter streets at night Flora went armed with a small pistol and a razor, as did her mother, Mama Marie Bowprie. Her father Henri Bowprie carried a two-barrel derringer in a leather holster under his vest and taught his daughter to shoot pistols at an early age. The sign outside their shop on the Rue Iberville that said APPRENEZ VOTRE FUTUR ICI drew more peculiar customers, it seemed, than visited other fortune-tellers in the Quarter, and some became violent after hearing their futures revealed. Henri had wanted to change the sign, make it American and more friendly, simply say PSYCHIC READINGS, but Mama Marie was, after all, the one with the major psychic gift. She knew best. When Mama Marie began dying of cancer, she needed Henri to come back to her and help her recover her health before it was too late.

Mama Marie believed her bitter period of grief and anger over Henri abandoning them had caused her cancer. She had thought horribly hateful thoughts about him and had fouled her system into producing cancer. If she had imagined herself into sickness, she believed she must be able to reverse the process and imagine herself into being cured and healthy again. Mama Marie believed it wasn't only her brain that had memory; her body was a mind of its own, and all the parts of her body had their own memories, their own minds that could be changed in her favor. But this cure that she sought would require the presence of Henri. She must see his face and look into his eyes and read his heart before she could lift all the curses she had laid upon him. By lifting the curses she would rid herself of this illness she had imagined her way into.

Six years he had been gone. In the early months there had been a letter from Houston, then San Antonio. Henri was starting a business of digging water wells. Next he was going to open a freight line. A year later a letter came from Santa Fe, where Henri was entering the mercantile trade. He believed his wife and daughter would be welcome out west among the Spaniards and Indians, whereas Mama Marie and Flora would have been forbidden among the whites in Houston. Henri would send for them to come to Santa Fe soon. But the next letter came from Houston again. Henri was going to open a hotel in Houston. After a few months a letter arrived from Austin. Henri had decided the capital city of Texas was a better choice for his hotel. Henri wrote that the Confederacy was winning the war and Lincoln would be asking for peace. Austin would be a boom town. Now years had gone by without a letter, no word at all from Henri. Mama Marie's patience wore out. Hateful thoughts and curses filled her blood with anger that caused her body to break down into cancer. Dr. Gilbert, a tiny man from a pharmacy two blocks away, could not specifically locate the cancer, but he agreed with Mama Marie that she was ill. He prescribed opium. Mama Marie refused it. Drugs were not the cure that she needed. The cure would require action on her part. She believed she had begun getting sick the day she hired Amelie, the voodoo woman, to put a curse on Henri that would cause him piercing headaches and eventually blindness and painful death unless the curse was lifted by Mama Marie in person, face to face. Later Mama Marie realized there had been too dreadful an outpouring of anger in her curse, and the evil in it had rebounded. She felt the evil had landed in her abdomen. The cancer inside her grew from the seed of anger she had planted in herself. She must meet Henri face to face and forgive him or she would be killed by the evil she had called up.

Flora asked her mother to do a Far-See on Henri. When she went into her mood, Mama Marie could do a Far-See and tell you what was on the parlor table in a boarding house in Richmond, Virginia; or a Far-See could tell what was hidden behind the altar of a church in St. Petersburg, Russia; or a Far-See would reveal where the body of a murdered miner was buried in the gold fields of California. Mama Marie's eyes would roll up into her head when she went into her mood. There were pearls in the whites of Mama Marie's eyes that Flora feared she should not be seeing; she felt they were some secret connection to a realm outside this world.

"Mama, why don't you do a Far-See on daddy, hey?" Flora had asked. "Find out where he is and I will go and bring him home."

"You're too young to make such a journey," said Mama Marie.

"Sixteen is the same age as you were when you married daddy."

"Child, you don't need to remind me that I am old and fading away."

"Mama, you are not old. You are young and beautiful. We need for you to get well. Do a Far-See on daddy, and I will take the wagon and go and fetch him back here."

They were in Mama Marie's bedroom on the second floor of the old house with the crooked wrought iron balcony above the future-telling sign on Rue Iberville. Mama Marie was in bed in the middle of the afternoon, and Flora was fanning her with a palm fan in the sticky heat.

"Can't do a Far-See on a moving target," Mama Marie had said.

"Then let's take different cities and do a Far-See on them one at a time and hope daddy shows up in one of them."

"The Far-See is a gift not to be overused."

"But you do Far-Sees for rich women."

"No, I tell their fortunes and for a fee I make prophesy. I locate missing objects. But the knowledge of how to do those things comes from my own mind. The Far-See comes from somewhere that is outside of me and vastly bigger than I can understand. I am afraid of it. Each time I go into a Far-See I might not come back."

"Mama, don't be trying to fool me. I have seen you do Far-Sees for rich women looking for their pearls. You can certainly do Far-Sees for yourself to find daddy."

"Very well, then. I will do a Far-See on Negril. Your father had a fancy for a woman there before he met me. It could be he has gone back to her."

"Mama, he's not in Jamaica."

"Step back, child, but keep that fan going, move that air." Mama Marie's eyes rolled up beneath her lids and the pearls appeared in the whites. Her head rose up off the pillow and after a moment she began to speak in a soft faraway voice. "Coming down from the mountain on the steep trail, it's so green and wet, it has been raining and it is hot. The coffee is growing, and the sugarcane and the tall ganja bushes. Down below, the waves crawl onto the beaches and the little birds run in the water. There she is in the pink shack with the tin roof. She is selling carvings of wood shaped like pigs. She is fat now. Who is that man she is with? He is wearing a fine straw hat. Is he a European? I can't make out his face. Who is he? Now he is turning. His face is becoming clear. Is it Henri? No, no, it is not Henri. This is an ugly man. She wanted Henri but she has wound up with a brute instead. He is bad to her. He beats her. She is planning to murder him."

"Mama? Mama? Are you playing with me?"

"The fan, child. Fan the air." Mama Marie's dark face and shoulders and arms glistened with sweat. She went deeper into her mood. "I am seeing Houston. I see planks laid in the muddy streets for people to walk across. It is very hot here. Mosquitoes swarm in clouds. Tall people are walking in the rain. I am looking at a hotel on a street corner. The hotel is three stories high. The windows are open. I see people through the windows. They are making love. I am searching their bedrooms. I do not see Henri." Mama Marie droned on in her trance voice. She described the look of the buildings, the colors on the signs, the clothes people wore, the horses standing in the mud. The longer she talked, the more she sweated, the weaker she became. Mama Marie had taught Flora that we all are born with the psychic power to some extent, and she had helped Flora to develop her own powers into the art of future-telling. But the power to Far-See was a gift given to a very special few, and it came with a price. The further she went into Far-Seeing, the more it drained her spirit away from this world and into another.

Henri was not spotted on this day in Houston, though he might be in some other part of town, but the search exhausted Mama Marie. She flopped back onto the bed gasping for water. Flora put a glass of water to Mama Marie's cracked lips as her mother slipped into a deep sleep. Flora felt her mother's warm forehead and wiped her face with a wet cloth. Flora wondered whether to run get the doctor who lived above the pharmacy, or if she should fetch the parish priest, Father Julian. Mama Marie was born and raised a Catholic in Jamaica and went to mass and confession regularly in her youth, but she had backslid after Henri brought her to New Orleans and now she went to church only occasionally. She had told Father Julian's fortune one morning in the confessional booth. Whatever she had told him, Flora could see that Mama Marie had made a good friend of the priest. Mama Marie had taken lovers all along, but after

Henri? Might it be that if Flora should find her father she would find the answer to the questions of why did neither of you return to me? Why have you left me alone in the world?

Water gurgled along the side of the boat as the current picked up. A turtle slid off a log and plopped into the water. Flora saw fishes gliding and darting two feet below the surface. Mama Marie had told her never to take tomorrow for granted; you might not be here tomorrow. Even the greatest of the fortune-tellers cannot be sure of his own future. Mama Marie's sudden passing enforced that belief. The soldier Flora had shot, he never dreamed when he woke up this morning in his tent that a girl he had never met would kill him before lunch, nor did Flora when she had walked into the courtroom seeking justice.

She trailed her scarf in the water and then washed her face with it. This river didn't smell like the river at home, the Mississippi. This water smelled like what you would pour out of a pitcher at a restaurant. The Mississippi smelled of a thousand mile journey.

Flora looked up and saw the Spanish woman standing above her.

"Mind if I sit beside you?" Isabella asked.

Flora moved over to make room.

"Thank you." Isabella sat. She smoothed her riding skirt and inspected a stain. "Well, too bad about this skirt. This is the first time I have worn it, and now it appears to have some kind of blot on it. This must be Joseph's blood. Poor Joseph."

"You didn't go look at Joseph's body. Those two colored women did. How would you get his blood on you?"

"I didn't own him, you should know that. I don't own slaves."

Flora said nothing.

"I wouldn't want you to think I'm a slave owner or approve of slavery," Isabella said.

"All right."

"How do you happen to speak French?" Isabella asked in French.

"I was born to it," Flora answered in French.

"Ah, it feels good to speak French again. It's been so long. I am out of practice." Isabella switched back to the English she spoke with a Spanish accent. "This boat wasn't meant for traveling. Really it was more of a floating sign board for my husband."

"He took off, hey?"

"Like a cur."

Flora laughed.

"I'm sorry for laughing," Flora said. "I expected you to defend him."

"I had Bushkin on the right track until this damn war intruded. I might have made him the governor."

They passed under a giant cypress that rose from the edge of the water with branches that hung over and scraped the roof of the cabin. Robin pushed his pole against the tree to fend it off and yelled for Varney to steer into the channel.

Isabella slipped back into French and lowered her voice. "If you're in trouble with these men, I mean if you're their prisoner against your will for some reason, I can help you get away."

"How could you help me?" Flora asked in French.

"I'm going to Spain. I'll take you with me as my personal attendant."

"You want me to be your body servant?"

"Think of it as my personal assistant, not as any sort of maid, though there may be some maid sort of duties come up."

"Why would you do that? You barely know me."

"You're a lovely girl and quite bright. We would do well together."

"I'm not their prisoner," Flora said.

"What are you then?"

"I tell futures for money."

"What sort of futures?"

"I tell people what will happen to them in the future."

Isabella smiled.

"You mean like a gypsy?"

"No," said Flora. "I have the gift."

"Sorry," Isabella said, still in French. "You're even cleverer than I had thought. It must be rather uncomfortable to have one's future told for money. Why would I pay if you tell me bad news?"

"You pay up front."

Captain Robin came around the cabin and walked past them toward the bow.

"What can we expect ahead? Are there rapids?" he asked Isabella.

"This river is navigable to the Gulf, but not always," she said.

"I asked about rapids."

"Well, yes, a few," Isabella said.

Flora was the first to feel it because of her bare feet. "Hey!" she said, lifting her right foot and looking down at an eighth of an inch of river water that was rising through the deck.

Fifteen

TROOPERS OF COMPANY C FORMED UP in three ranks on the grassy field in front of the headquarters tent near the edge of Shoal Creek. There were thirty-three of them sweating in their blue wool uniform blouses in the heat of the afternoon. The company master sergeant, Ivan Hooper, a farmer from Kalamazoo, Michigan, counted heads and then turned and saluted Lt. Tom Custer.

"All present or accounted for, sir. Privates Gambrel and Campbell are on sick call. Johnson, Rooney, Gruber and Israel are assigned to prison duty"—Sergeant Hooper glanced at Santana Leatherwood, who stood off to the side under an oak tree with his three nephews—"and Ransom, Whitaker, Minter, and Jenkins are on guard detail. Fleming, Nelson, and Holloway are assigned to the cook this week. I can have the kitchen police here in formation in two minutes if you need them, sir. After eating today's beans, I believe I might transfer cookie into the muck squad with a soup spoon."

The troopers laughed.

"Where is Private Cooper?" Custer asked.

"Private Cooper, get your butt out here," yelled Hooper.

Rudy Cooper, the teamster, came out of the headquarters tent where he had been describing the shooting of Pvt. Huffer Dubcek to the company clerk, who was trying to write it all down in proper order for the army records.

"Private Cooper, tell these men what happened this morning," Custer said.

"I was just now telling . . ."

"I mean out here, Cooper. Tell your comrades."

"Well, Huffer come and got me around ten o'clock and said . . ."

"Never mind all that part. Skip ahead to the shooting," said Custer.

"Huffer and me drove three prisoners to the Bastrop County line like the judge told us. Huffer got down from the wagon to help the prisoners with their gear. That high yella nigger girl was flirting and fooling with poor young Huffer. She egged him into dropping his pants—hell, Huffer ain't had a girl in at least a year I know of—and first thing I knew she yanked out a big old hogleg pistol and shot poor Huffer dead in a cold-blooded murder. There was a damn Johnny Reb that I believe is her lover, tall blonde, icy looking fellow with long hair. The reb tried his best to murder me. But I shot it out with him and managed to escape in the wagon. I believe the reb and the girl are partners in a gang. In fact, I heard them say as much."

The troopers had begun talking among themselves in anger and puzzlement at the sudden death of Huffer. Sergeant Hooper commanded them to shut up and listen.

"What about the Englishman?" asked Custer.

"The old man?"

"The third prisoner, the one with the English accent," Custer said. "What did he do?"

"I believe he is the leader of the gang," said Cooper.

"No, I'm sure he is not in their gang. I am asking if he shot at you."

"Yes sir. He fired at least three shots at me."

"With what?"

"Huffer's shotgun."

Custer paced up and down before the front rank.

"Everybody hear what Cooper said? They murdered Private Dubcek and they tried to murder Cooper," Custer said.

"That British son of a bitch stole your horse, too," said Sergeant Hooper.

Custer frowned. He didn't appreciate being reminded in front of the troopers.

"We're going after the murderers," said Custer. "I want a show of hands for five volunteers."

About twenty-five troopers raised their hands. Hooper made a mental note of the ones who didn't.

"Very well, then," Custer said. "I will choose the five."

Custer walked along each of the three ranks of troopers, pausing five times to say "You." He hadn't learned all their names yet. The Seventh Cavalry was in its organizational phase and not up to strength. Many of these men had come into the outfit only days before they were sent to Texas in the advance party. But Tom Custer believed he could judge a man's character by the look in his eye and his general demeanor. The English novelist had passed the test with high marks—unflinching gaze, confident bearing—but then had ridden off on Custer's horse, so Custer might have misread him; on the other hand maybe there was more to the old man than had yet been understood. Custer was itching to capture Edmund Varney and reopen their discussion about the horse Athena, only this time sober. As for the rebel captain and the colored girl—there should be a way to administer justice to them on the spot rather than bring them back and trust them to that Texas judge again.

Custer chose Pvt. Nathan Zucker, a burly, hairy Jew recently immigrated from Germany; Pvt. Melrose Smith, a tall redhead from Penn's Grove, New Jersey; Pvt. Horace McDonald, a lanky Scot from Scotts Hill, Tennessee; hefty, sweaty Pvt. Joseph Campesi, immigrant from Italy, and Cpl. Jim Greengrass, a darkly handsome Cherokee scout and tracker from the mountains of North Carolina.

"You five get your kit together and mount up. We're leaving here in ten minutes," Custer said. "Sergeant Hooper, you are now in command of the garrison until Captain Leatherwood and I return. Dismiss the troop."

Santana Leatherwood watched the five selected troopers trot off toward their tents to make ready for the pursuit. The young orderly from New Rumley was leading Custer's horse, Athena, toward the headquarters tent.

"Observe that horse, boys," Santana said to his three nephews, who wore their red neckerchiefs as the badges of their military prowess. As the nephews saw it, they would be going into action for the first time with the United States Army in a few minutes, and they were a little nervous and wanted to look properly threatening as proud warriors of the Home Guard. Already they had heard troopers making jokes about them; nothing had been rank enough to cause Luther or Adam to lose their heads and start bashing or shooting. But the smirks and chuckles did sting the Leatherwood pride.

"That is a horse a man could give his life for, all right," said Santana. "Looking at that horse, I almost don't blame that old fool for trying to steal her."

Athena glanced at the Leatherwoods as she walked lightly and gracefully behind the skinny orderly.

"She knows we're talking about her," Billy said.

"Watch her prance. Ain't she fancy?" said Adam.

"I'm gonna get me a horse like that someday," Luther said.

"Never will happen," said Adam.

"Will if I want it to bad enough," Luther said.

Athena looked back over her shoulder at the Leatherwoods.

"She's making eyes at me," said Luther. "Just like a woman."

"How would you know? No woman ever made eyes at you," Adam said.

"I'm gonna whip your ass, brother," said Luther.

"Never will happen," Adam said.

Santana loosened the cord on his campaign hat and hooked it beneath his chin. Few things looked more stupid than a cavalryman losing his hat.

"You boys mount up," he said to his nephews. "Jerod Robin is out there waiting for us. This time I am going to finish him for good."

Mounted on the high-stepping Athena, Lt. Tom Custer led the pursuit detail out of the Shoal Creek camp at a trot. Corporal Greengrass, the scout, rode beside him. Santana and his nephews rode in a bunch at the rear. After the horses got warmed up, Custer would increase the pace to a lope. They had many miles to go on the Bastrop road through the pine forest and needed to conserve the strength of their horses.

As they rode, Santana was remembering the last time he had set out with a detachment of troopers looking for Jerod Robin. That was six months ago on Christmas Eve in the Tennessee mountains. The snow fell steadily and sometimes came in gusts that blew cold wet ice into his face from rocky crevices. Santana was a lieutenant then, leading a detail of twenty-five troopers from the Third Cavalry, all of them armed with new Spencer repeating rifles. They were on the track of a band of Confederate guerrillas, some thirty to forty of them, who had become known to Federals by the nickname Robin's Raiders. Santana had asked for the assignment when he learned the Robin they were after was Jerod from Sweetbrush. Before daylight on Christmas Eve morning, a breathless figure wrapped in blankets and clinging to a mule had entered the clearing where Santana was camped with his men. The man's nose was smashed and his frozen face was blue and swollen. He had bitten his tongue almost in half and could not speak.

Santana and his troopers had laid the man out of the whistling wind in the shelter of a lean-to against a boulder and tried to bring him around with hot soup and coffee, neither of which the man could manage with his lacerated tongue.

"I wonder who beat the stuffing out of this poor fellow?" said the corporal who had once worked in a pharmacy and was pressed into duty as the medicine man.

"Can't you get any words out of him?" Santana said.

"Look at his tongue, lieutenant. If it wasn't frozen, half of it would fall out of his mouth. Think how that is going to hurt when he defrosts."

Santana knelt beside the man and looked into eyes that were cloudy under iced lashes.

"Mister, can you write?" Santana asked.

The man held up his right hand. His fingers were twisted into a purple claw. Santana took off his gloves and felt in his coat pockets for a pencil.

"Build up that fire," Santana said. "Get some heat on his hand."

It was nearly an hour before the man recovered enough to grasp the pencil, but by then he also began to form words. It sounded as if he was talking with his fist in his mouth. Santana brushed snow off a map and the man drew an X on the town of Snow Hill. On the map he printed ROBINS RADERS.

Between yelps of pain as his body temperature warmed, the man told his story. He was a carpenter from Snow Hill, four miles away up a rough track into the mountains. About thirty Confederates had taken Snow Hill hostage and were threatening to burn the town and hang its leaders unless they were bought off with gold. The rebel commander was a tall man who seemed to be crazy. His name was Robin. He was very angry with the whole town. The carpenter had stood up to him, and Robin hit him in the face with the butt of a rifle. Robin hit him twice and then kicked him, the carpenter said, and left him lying in the alley between the hardware store and the Four Doves restaurant.

"You say Robin is crazy?" asked the pharmacist.

The carpenter nodded and pointed at his nose and at his tongue as if this proved it.

"He's crazy with fear of facing retribution when I get hold of him," Santana said.

"Do you know him?"

"From way back," Santana said.

The bad blood had begun after the 1836 revolution when two heroes of Texas—Pastor Horry Leatherwood and Dr. Junius Robin—found that the land grants that were their reward from the Republic overlapped. Each man had received three sections of land, 1,920 acres, with a deed signed by Sam Houston, first president of the Republic. Dr. Junius Robin, who had immigrated to Texas from Knoxville, Tennessee, and settled in San Antonio one year before the revolution, used his land grant to start his plantation, marry his English bride, and build the house known as Sweetbrush. Horry Leatherwood had come to Texas from Georgia two years before the revolution with his four-year-old brother Santana and eleven kinsmen of the Leatherwood clan. Horry used his land grant to make a home for the Zanzibar Church and start the town of Gethsemane.

The two men were friends and comrades until a clerk in the Land Office, doing research for real estate speculators, discovered that the same one hundred acres along Big Neck Bayou was included in each of their deeds. The land had been part of a Spanish Royal Grant, the past ownership was murky, and the present plats had been misdrawn. Pastor Horry suggested they split it fifty acres each; instead, Dr. Junius filed suit in the district court for the entire one hundred acres, contending he needed the entire bayou frontage for his cotton business.

The suit stayed in court for ten years. Texas had become a state in the Union, Santana Leatherwood had become a teenager and joined the Federal army to invade Mexico, and Jerod Robin was the six-year-old heir to Sweetbrush before the suit was settled in favor of Dr. Robin. By this time the two heroes had long since become enemies. Pastor Horry swore that Dr. Robin, a frequent traveler to Austin and a patron of politicians, had bought the judge. Pastor Horry and all of the Leatherwoods were insulted by the verdict.

Pastor Horry's lawyers filed appeal after appeal but lost them all the way to the Supreme Court. Santana had always wondered why his older brother, who was a passionate preacher and quick to anger and violence, held back from confronting Dr. Junius Robin with a physical assault. Dr. Robin was a saloon brawler and could have been drawn into a mortal beating or a legal shooting. But Pastor Horry had never called him out. It wasn't because Pastor Horry was afraid. Santana suspected the reason there had not been an outbreak of violence between the Leatherwoods and the Robin family was the presence of Varina Hotchkiss, the tall, beautiful mother of Jerod. Santana had wondered if Pastor Horry might have been infatuated. Otherwise, why would the Leatherwoods have been restrained from beating the arrogance out of the young Jerod Robin?

Now in the snow in the mountains of Tennessee there was nothing to prevent Santana from revenging the honor of the Leatherwoods, and there was a patriotic reason for him to do so. Robin's Raiders needed to be stamped out. He hadn't seen Jerod when Santana had been home on leave five years ago, but he knew Jerod had grown tall like his mother. He knew Jerod would not be taken without a desperate struggle. Robin's Raiders had been hitting Federal supply lines, tearing up railroad tracks, cutting wires. Only the strongest of men could survive a raider's life of hard riding, no sleep, erratic food, cold, rain, ice, snow, leading their horses knee-deep in mud, in relentless danger. Santana was surprised that Jerod had turned out to be such a man, but there was no denying that he had.

Clouds were hiding the moon and snow was falling as Santana led his detail up the rocky mountain-road through tall pines that were white with crust. They came to a pass that looked down on the valley where the town of Snow Hill lay in bits and pieces of moonlight. Santana and his scout dismounted and crept closer. They could hear shouts and curses from the town. Lights shone from windows. You would expect, Santana thought, to be hearing voices singing carols and hymns on Christmas Eve, not rebel thugs yelling insults and blasphemies. Santana and his scout, on their bellies in the snow, reached a ledge from which they could see the square that was crowded with men with guns. The men were carrying a large object out of a building. Santana studied the group and picked out a tall figure wearing an overcoat and a slouch hat that must be Jerod Robin. The tall man was directing activities in the square. He ordered the large object to be placed in front of him near a bonfire. There was more shouting, and Santana saw the men in the square turn toward a stand of trees at the western edge. Santana shifted his attention to see what they were looking at.

Three men were standing on sawhorses. Around their necks were ropes that were slung over tree limbs.

"You see that?" whispered the scout.

"I see. How many rebs you make it?"

"Maybe thirty."

"Range?"

"From here, three hundred yards. I see another ledge down there at about one hundred sixty out."

"We'll put ten snipers on that closer ledge and pump those rebs in the street full of Spencer rounds," Santana whispered. "The rest of us will charge them after the third volley."

"How about those three poor bastards with the ropes around their necks?"

"I believe they're praying for us to hurry up."

As he spoke Santana saw the tall figure down in the square at Snow Hill lift an arm in a signal and the three sawhorses were yanked one by one from under the three men. The three bodies began to jerk and dance.

Riding along, remembering, Santana heard his nephew Billy's voice.

"Uncle Santana."

Santana ignored him. Billy had been told to call him captain if there were troopers within hearing. Santana pulled his thoughts from Snow Hill back to the road to Bastrop. He realized he was feeling a pain in his left side, the location of his only remaining kidney. The pain was from thinking about Jerod Robin more than from his body pounding in the saddle. They were loping along the Bastrop road, entering the tall pines. Red dust from the five troopers riding in front, and from Lt. Tom Custer on the magnificent Arabian mare Athena, drifted back onto Santana and his three nephews. He felt sweat rolling down from inside his hatband.

"Captain Leatherwood," Billy said, riding up beside his uncle.

"What is it?"

"Why are we going this direction?" Billy asked.

"What do you mean?"

"Jerod Robin will be running home to Sweetbrush, won't he? Why don't we just go straight there?"

"Use your brain, Billy."

"That's what I'm trying to do, I think."

"The army wants to get that colored girl, too, and that old horse thief."

"Jerod Robin wouldn't stick with them two. He'd be running home to his mother."

"You're with the Seventh Cavalry now, Billy. You've got to learn to follow orders whether they make sense to you or not."

"But I'm right, though, ain't I?"

"Don't worry about it, Billy. Just follow orders. We'll catch up to Robin soon."

The road was leading them into the darkness of the pine forest. Custer slowed the detail to a trot. He sent Corporal Greengrass ahead to scout the road. The tall pines reminded Santana of Tennessee. He felt sure Billy was right that Jerod Robin would be running for Sweetbrush. But Billy had never really understood about following orders.

Sixteen

"IF WE CAN MAKE IT ANOTHER MILE, there's a place called Burroughs' Cove, where we can put ashore and maybe hire another boat," Isabella said, with river water sloshing around the soles of her boots.

"I don't know if we can stay floating that long," said Flora.

"What kind of place is it?" Robin asked.

Standing in the bow, Robin shoved a drifting log aside with his pole. They felt the thunk as the log hit the raft and slid off into the swiftly flowing water.

"It's a general store with a dock," Isabella said. "I know the proprietors, man and wife, Fred and Ellen Burroughs. They voted for Bushkin."

"They would have boats for hire?" Robin was skeptical.

"No, not actually. But one of their customers might be persuaded."

"What can we expect to find there?" Robin asked.

"Maybe a fishing boat or two, maybe something bigger, just people otherwise."

"Is there any law operating around here? Would there be a sheriff on duty at the store?" Robin asked.

"Our sheriff was shot to death last week."

"Would they be likely to have horses at Burroughs' Cove?" Robin asked.

"They might," Isabella said.

Robin was deciding to give up the idea of escaping by the river. He held the Spencer rifle under his right arm and looked down at the water that was now forming a sheen over the deck. With this rifle and a decent horse he could make it to Sweetbrush in time to do what needed to be done before the Federals would inevitably come looking for him there. If he moved swiftly enough, he could go to Sweetbrush and Gethsemane and resolve problems that perhaps a Spencer rifle would be needed to resolve. Then he could be gone to Mexico or Central America for as many years as it took for this week's actions to be lost in the passing of time. If the colored girl, Flora, hadn't shot and killed that trooper—well, but she did, it had happened. The shot had changed the situations with Laura and the baby and with his mother and father as surely as with everything else; there was no wishing it away. Robin felt the stock of the Spencer against his ribs. Spencer rifles had ravished his men at Snow Hill. He knew what he could do with this rifle.

"What do you think, romancer?" called Flora.

"It's a glorious day," Varney shouted.

"I mean do you think we will sink, hey?"

"I expect so, yes," Varney laughed. Aroused as his romancer impulses were by the thrill of steering a sinking boat, pursued by enemies, he couldn't keep his mind from straying to associated scenes from his past. His romancer's mind was open to the whim of the unbidden. Varney was attuned to the invisible.

This river they were slowly sinking into, this Colorado, had its charm, its lovely green pools, clear in the shallows, riffles in the currents, trees thick along the banks, circles of insects landing in the water. He had heard the Colorado could be a mile wide during flood, but where they were today it was less than a hundred yards from shore to shore. He saw blue crabs in the shallows, and herons and an egret dined on them. An alligator dozed in the sun on a sandbar. But what Varney's mind summoned was the memory of another river—a truly topsy river—the mighty Indus, so wide that natives called it the ocean, flowing down from the Himalayas to the Arabian Sea, its waters full of giant catfish and crocodiles, its banks alive with wild boars and tigers and buffalo and herds of wild camels. Of the five rivers of the Punjab, the Indus was the colossus that formed the western boundary of India. Alexander the Great and his army had bled there two thousand years ago. To the east of the river in India was Lahore, but to the west, across the Indus, lay Afghanistan and the mysterious and forebidding city of Kabul, all but unknown to westerners.

After falling in love and marrying a sixteen-year-old Sikh girl, to the deep displeasure of his military comrades, Varney had resigned from his regiment and entered the employ of Ranjit Singh, the Maharajah of the Punjab, the Lion of Lahore, Lord of the Five Rivers. Ranjit Singh was a tiny one-eyed man with a gray beard that covered a face pitted by smallpox. On a band around his skinny little wrist he wore the fabled Kohinoor diamond. The wife of a British diplomat said he looked like an old mouse with gray whiskers and one white eye. He already had five officers from France in his service. They wore beards and crimson turbans and striking costumes. During an all-night banquet at Ranjit Singh's palace in Lahore, they drank homebrew of grape, orange, and raisin wine mixed with the powder of crushed pearls, and the Maharajah offered Varney command of his cavalry, which could mean, in the twisting fortunes of the east, that Varney might someday have to fight against Her Majesty's army, in which he had recently been an officer.

Varney accepted. He signed a formal contract for four years. His first assignment was to go to Kabul in the guise of a wealthy western traveler. He was to settle in and spy for Ranjit Singh, who always kept his one eye on the treasures of Kabul. Varney had heard the saying that when Allah made the world he had a huge pile of rocks left over, so he used them to make Afghanistan. But Varney found the Kabul valley to be a vast fertile carpet of green. The walled city smelled of apple and peach orchards and rose gardens, its air fragrant with the perfume of flowers, its streets lined with willows, poplars, cypresses and lime trees. The smell of roasting kebabs floated through the teeming streets of the bazaar where Varney wandered eating cups of icy grape sherbet.

Varney had crossed the Indus standing at the rudder of a flatboat much like the Bushkin vessel in size, but with six oarsmen. He made his way with an escort of Shiite Mohammedan mercenaries and a baggage train of camels across the wilderness into the ancient walled city, with its wealth of gold and jewels, and its famous herds of the finest horses in the world. The legendary Turcoman horses could be bought in Kabul. Varney admired the silk-brocade cloaks of Kabul nobles, with curved swords in their sashes and rubies in their cashmere turbans. Varney explored Kabul's fabulous hanging gardens and feasted on its fruits and melons. He was sprinkled with rosewater and powdered musk. Varney returned to Lahore and devised a plan for the Sikhs to invade Kabul. He brought his young Sikh bride Aliya into Ranjit Singh's palace in Lahore, where she was treated with the deference and respect due a daughter of a neighboring, currently peaceful, prince. At a ceremony in the palace Aliyah pierced Varney's left ear and placed the jade and silver ring in the lobe as a symbol of her eternal love.

Two years later, after Ranjit Singh had established a hold in Kabul, the British broke their promise to the Maharajah and entered Afghanistan with an army of sixteen thousand that included household. Through an agreement with the East India Company, Ranjit Singh's forces withdrew but Varney's wife Aliya lingered in their villa in Kabul because her dreamer's heart was enchanted by her gardens and her poet friends and the views of the snowy peaks of the Hindu Kush.

The British played polo and cricket on holy days, ate bacon and pork chops, exhibited their women's naked faces, did not understand local languages, staged theatricals that mixed the sexes in public, greased their bullets with pig grease, and had no idea or care that they were offending the populace by their presence. Mounted on his chestnut Arabian mare Athena, Varney slipped into Kabul during the beginning of the uprising and escorted Aliya and her servants and bodyguards out of the city and through the snows of the Khyber Pass and onto the road to Lahore before Varney turned back and rode into the mountains with his Sikhs to scout the British defeat and retreat. A few hours after Varney rode away, his wife's party, several of them Afghans, encountered a company of angry British hussars.

* * * * *

"Hey, romancer, can you swim?" Flora said.

"Like a porpoise, my dear," said Varney.

He had enjoyed playing the spy for Ranjit Singh. As a child he had discovered that he had been born to be a spy. He was never an outsider, never spurned by any group he wished to be a part of, but was always an observer taking notes in his head on what he saw around him, trying to make sense of the human situation. In a way he felt he was standing between the people who were talking to him and the people he was talking to—Edmund's personality was on display, but at his core he was the observer wondering what could be the reasons for it all. This had led him into reading philosophy at Oxford, into the military and, quite naturally, into romancing on the pages of a book and a periodical.

By the Sword came first. The murder of his wife drove him to pick up a pen. The book began pouring out of him in gushes, with the invisible guiding his hand. In a fever of romancing, Varney dug into the small fortune he brought home from India—a reward from Ranjit Singh, who had ransomed Varney from the Ghilzais. He bought the Holly Bush pub in Hampstead on a hill above the heath and the red-brick house where Varney had been born.

On the second floor of the pub, Varney opened an office and started publishing the *Holly Bush Journal*. His desk sat beside windows that offered a view of the misty roofs of London far below in the distance. He kept the manuscript of *By the Sword* in a drawer in his desk and worked on it in frenzied bursts. Varney hired an editor for his magazine. He hired a secretary. Ranjit Singh had employed scores of people, many of them women, called newswriters, who gathered information and sold it to him. Newswriters roamed throughout the Punjab to find stories for the Maharajah's enlightenment. Varney told his editor to use the newswriter concept in building up the *Journal*'s content. He persuaded news agents to handle his *Journal*, and hired boys to peddle it on the streets. He encouraged and printed submissions from newswriters and from other romancers and paid them small fees which they were generally glad to get. Varney wrote essays on politics, on art, on food, on behavior. He wrote a nostalgic piece wondering at the whereabouts of the actress Varina Hotchkiss and said he had been in love with her when he was a student. He published regularly a gardening column written in iambic pentameter by a poet from Cambridge. The *Journal* was well received; it even turned a profit, incredible for such a publication. Varney's father—the Major—was proud of him. His mother, Felicity, lectured the cooks in the kitchen of his pub, and the Holly Bush shepherd's pie became a neighborhood attraction. If Varney had paused in his romancing during this period to wonder if he, himself, was happy, he would have said, yes, he was topsys.

Then *By the Sword* was published.

Most novels do not attract much, if any, public attention. But by the time copies of the first, special edition of *By the Sword* came from the printer in their handsome red leather covers, Varney had become well known from the success of his magazine and his own writings in it.

Almost at once Varney was accosted on the Hampstead high street by a veteran of his old regiment who had not served with Varney but nevertheless denounced him for having written a book full of lies, and accused him of being a traitor to his country. Varney happened to be walking at the time with Crichton, the editor of his magazine. The editor stepped between them and urged Varney not to fight. "Ye must get ready for this, Edmund," the editor said. "If ye'd fight every loudmouth who hates yer book, ye'll be busy doing nothing else."

"My book is the truth," Varney said.

"In yer eyes, not in thers."

The Major quit speaking to him and banned him from the three-story red brick home beside the heath. His mother, Felicity, was hurt by what she read in the book, and sent Varney a note to tell him how very disappointed she was to discover her son had been married to a brown Sikh woman who was a hater of the Queen. Varney wrote a letter to his mother claiming that the narrator of his book was a romancer, not the real Edmund. In time his mother softened and would meet him for tea at a restaurant on New End Road, but the Major never did forgive him and died a year ago of a sudden rush of blood to the brain. In the Major's will, Varney was left thirty pieces of silver.

Patriots broke into the Holly Bush pub twice in predawn hooliganism, smashed up the furniture, climbed the stairs and wrecked the office of the *Journal* and turned over Varney's desk, kicking his papers around. Lord Rothermere denounced him in parliament, shouting that Varney's tale of the slaughter of a British army and the murder of an Indian princess by British hussars was a treasonous fiction. Boys peddling the *Journal* were beaten up. News agents were threatened, some of their windows broken. His printer hired armed men to guard the presses. Newspapers published editorials demanding that Varney be run out of England. Groups of patriots harassed patrons at the Holly Bush pub. Varney began carrying a stout brass-knobbed cane that he would rush downstairs and use to thrash troublemakers.

But the louder the outcry, the more copies of *By the Sword* were printed and sold. The *Journal* continued to flourish in its own modest way. Crichton's desk was piled with stacks of submissions from romancers and newswriters who were excited to find what they hoped would be a fearless outlet for their writings. The famous critic Henry Bertram published a piece in *The Englishman* called "In Defense of Edmund Varney," praising the author's literary style as "vivid, vigorous, and perceptive" and the book as "wildly imaginative." Varney began to be invited to literary salons. He dined at Thomas Carlyle's flat in Cheyne Row. He met Wilkie Collins, Charlotte Brontë, and Thomas De Quincey. All were fascinated by his tales of the East. Varney had lunch with the great Charles Dickens at the Metropolitan Club, where some members pointedly turned their backs when Varney entered, but a few actually smiled and nodded. Dickens admitted to being a regular reader of the *Holly Bush Journal* and chuckled in good humor when Varney invited him to submit a story to the magazine. Dickens offered a toast and said he would try to think of something.

At a dinner party in Chelsea, Varney met Alfred Lord Tennyson, who advised Varney to pay no heed to those who criticized his work for errors of fact; in his eulogy for the poet Arthur Henry Hallam, Tennyson had misplaced his friend's tomb. "My dear Edmund, it is always preferable to pretend you misplace things on purpose for artistic effect." But, Varney had said, the events in his book had in fact occurred.

"In one form or another, I am sure," Tennyson replied. He had written a famous poem about the slaughter of the 13th Hussars Light Brigade in a foolish charge at Balaclava in the Crimea. "Let me show you how to do it."

Tennyson recited the final stanza of the poem in the manner of a teacher giving Varney a lesson in writing.

"When can their glory fade?
Oh the wild charge they made!
All the world wondered.
Honor the Light Brigade,
Noble six hundred!"

The poet acknowledged the murmurs of approval and flutters of applause from the crowd that had gathered to listen.

"My dead lancers are seen as heroes, unlike yours. I'll tell you what has half the nation at your throat, Edmund—there's no nobility to your dead soldiers."

* * * * *

On the boat on the river Varney heard Robin's voice shouting at him.

"Hey, Varney, watch what you're doing."

"Over there, romancer. Look over there," cried Flora.

Varney's mind snapped back to the present.

He saw Flora and Isabella each with a tin can, rapidly scooping water from the deck and flinging it over the side. He realized the river had crept up around his ankles, which were encased in Bushkin's fine boots. The tall rebel captain stood in the bow with his rifle, jabbing his pole into the water trying to find bottom, and waving toward the west bank, where a gap in the foliage marked the junction of a creek that flowed into the river.

Varney glimpsed some kind of dock with a sign on it a few yards up the creek. There was a boat with a sail tied at the dock, and he saw figures come out of a low shed and walk onto the dock and begin pointing toward the flatboat where Varney's hand was on the tiller.

Varney pushed hard on the rudder, turning the boat to the right in the heavy current, trying to make it to shore before they swept past Burroughs' Cove, or else sank. No time for romancing just now; the real thing had intruded yet again as with a sharp, loud crack, the rudder broke in half.

Seventeen

WHEN IT BECAME OBVIOUS TO HER that the Bushkin boat was going under and that the English novelist at the helm had overshot the cove, Isabella tossed her tin can aside and scrambled toward the cabin.

She heard the crack of the rudder as it snapped. She was thrown into the sloshing flood on the deck, but she clawed her way to her feet and yanked open the cabin door. First on her mind was to save the brown Italian leather suitcase with silver buckles that contained her personal papers—her passport, the secret bank book that Bushkin hadn't known about, five hundred dollars in twenty-dollar "double eagle" gold coins, the deed to Bushkin's Landing, a small beribboned bundle of letters from an admirer Bushkin hadn't known about, a photograph of Isabella with her father, mother, and three brothers taken at the estate of Grandfather Marcus, a room-service menu from the Broadway Palace Hotel that was a memory of happy days, a schedule of steamship departures from New Orleans, and a single pressed rose that Bushkin had given her the night they first made love years ago in Barcelona.

The other suitcase, a canvas affair with leather straps and buckles, was full of clothes and footwear. It would hurt to lose the Paris gowns and the Ballard shoes, but those could be replaced. She grabbed the brown leather suitcase and struggled toward the door as the cabin listed sharply and water rushed up to her knees. Varney appeared in the doorway and reached for her.

"Señora," he said, "you must hurry."

"I can't swim," she said.

"Cling to me," he said. "Drop that suitcase."

"The case goes with me."

She pushed past Varney and sloshed onto the deck. She saw Robin stuffing cartridges for the Spencer into the pockets of his coat. The fortune-telling girl held one of the dragoon pistols in her left hand, and with her right she hoisted herself onto the top of the toolbox. Varney had managed to turn the flatboat at an angle toward the shore, sliding twenty or thirty yards past the entrance to the creek at Burroughs' Cove.

"Go away! Go back!" cried a voice from the dock in the cove.

Isabella saw that the screech was coming from Ellen Burroughs, who ran onto the dock beside her husband Fred. Ellen was a hefty woman who was proud of the tank of fishing worms in rich soil that she kept inside the general store at Burroughs Cove, and loved plunging both hands into the soil and coming up with squirming worms between her fingers to fill the bucket she would carry out to the dock, where she and Fred sat and fished all day if the weather was right and few if any customers showed up at the store.

"Get back, Isabella! Get back!" Fred shouted.

Before Isabella could answer, she was knocked off her feet as the sinking flatboat slammed into a submerged sandbar forty feet from the bank.

Unprepared for the sudden blow, all four passengers fell. Robin's boots flew out from under him, and he struck his head against the railing, but he held tight to the Spencer rifle. Flora toppled off the toolbox and landed with a splash on her back in the river beside the boat. Varney slid forward, clutching the shattered rudder, and slammed into the wall of the cabin. Blood gushed down the front of Bushkin's fine white Indian-cotton shirt.

Flora splashed in the river for a moment and then stood up. She felt the sand oozing between her toes as the river flowed knee-deep around her.

"We can walk ashore," she shouted.

"No! No!" yelled Ellen and Fred from the dock. "Don't come here."

Flora glanced at them, wondering if they might be suffering from cholera or the pox, and then looked back at the flatboat, which was settling gently onto the sandbar. She saw Isabella holding a brown suitcase and trying to rip up the front of Varney's shirt so she could hold it against his broken nose and stanch the blood. Varney lifted his head and turned his face to the sky and pressed two fingers high up on the bridge of his nose; this was not the first or even the second time this beak had been broken. Isabella noticed blood on the earring in his left ear. The river crept up their legs.

"Go away!" yelled Ellen.

Onto the dock behind Ellen and Fred walked two men. Flora saw there were two or three other men further back at the door and windows of the general store, but these first two grabbed her attention because she recognized them at once. These were the men who had stolen her wagon, her mules and all her worldly goods.

"Aw come on in, everybody is welcome here," said the big man in a voice that rumbled up from the earth. He came up behind the owners of the store and made Ellen look small. Beneath his wide-brimmed black hat, his face was an unmatched set of dark eyes, blunt nose, and big teeth amid a thick brown beard. A military jacket from some alien army stretched around two-thirds of his enormous torso. Beneath the jacket he wore a white undershirt from which tufts of hair stuck out. He was bow-legged, in the way of big men who move with deceptive agility. To his right—the crown of his head level with the big man's nose—slouched a pale creature, blinking, thin face and neck sheltered from the sun by a dish towel that he wore fastened to his head with a band that went around just above his ears so that, except for his extreme whiteness, he would have looked like an Arab wearing a kaffiyah. He wore a vest made of some type of leather, with his upper body bare beneath it. In his right hand he held a three-pound Bowie knife, its blade hovering a few inches from Fred's neck.

"Isabella, stay on your boat and get out of here. This is Bloody Bill Terhune. He'll take everthing you got," yelled Ellen.

The pale Arab flicked his knife blade and drew blood from a shallow two-inch scratch near Fred's jugular. Fred was a skinny old man with leathery skin, and he didn't bleed easily.

"Ow! Hey, that was uncalled for!" Fred howled.

Flora aimed the dragoon pistol with both hands, cocked the hammer, and pointed the front sight into the middle of the big man's chest.

"I want my mules and my wagon back," said Flora.

"Who the hell would you be?" Bloody Bill asked, squinting down toward the girl who had risen from the river.

"I know how to use this pistol, mister," said Flora.

"It's the fortune-teller from yesterday morning," the Arab said.

"Tell you what, Little Ned. You edge off that way and I'll edge off this way. She can't shoot both of us before one of us gets her."

Bloody Bill laughed.

Flora thought of firing a warning shot over his head to show she was to be taken seriously in this matter, but it occurred to her that the sound of exploding powder would most likely cause them all to start shooting at the same time, including the men she could see in the store; her future in that event would be easy to foretell, it would be so short.

"I'm warning you, mister. Return my mules and my wagon and the rest of my goods, or..." She paused. She didn't want to talk herself into a place with no way out.

"Well, gypsy girl, that is going to be very hard to do," said Bloody Bill.

"What have you done with them?" Flora said, her hands beginning to wobble at the effort of keeping the heavy pistol steady.

"What did we do with her mules and her wagon, Little Ned?"

The Arab said, "We sold them to a Jew who was taking his family to California."

"You must get them back. Where is he?" Flora said.

"Where would the Jew be by now?" said Bloody Bill.

Little Ned lifted a forefinger to his chin and scowled in thought.

"He's been scalped by now, along with his wife and kiddies. Your wagon is burnt. Your mules are redskin dinner. I imagine that's where he is. The Jew is a piece of hair on a flagpole."

Little Ned smiled pleasantly.

"You're crazy," Flora said.

"Little Ned ain't crazy. He just acts crazy," said Bloody Bill.

"There's a difference?" Varney said.

Varney was wading on the sandbar with the other dragoon pistol in his right hand while his left held a rag of his shirt to his nose. Beside him came Isabella, holding the brown suitcase with both hands, keeping it up out of the water.

"You know why I am being friendly and welcoming to you people while you threaten me with pistols?" asked Bloody Bill.

"I know why," Varney said. "You have noticed that our sharp-shooter friend on the boat has you covered with his repeating rifle."

"He does?" said Bloody Bill.

Bloody Bill lifted a hand to shade his eyes, though the sun was at his back.

"You're right," Bloody Bill said. "I see him now."

Robin lay flat on the roof of the cabin with his Spencer sighted in on the big man and the Arab. He reckoned it a shot of fifty-five yards. It would be easy. First the big man, next the Arab, and finish with whoever came running out of the general store looking to fight. The Bushkin boat had lodged firmly into the sandbar. There was no motion from the river current that pushed against the stern. The boat made a steady platform for Robin's elbows and his hands on the rifle with his cheek feeling the cool wood of the stock. He could knock them all down in five seconds with the Spencer. He remembered how fast his men had fallen at Snow Hill when Santana Leatherwood's snipers opened fire with Spencers on Christmas Eve.

Varney sloshed toward the dock, passing Flora, who lowered the pistol from the weight of it, not from a lessening of her desire to get her mules and her wagon back. Isabella stopped next to the girl.

"Are you a man of your word?" Varney said.

He paused and looked up at Bloody Bill.

"Do I look like I am?" said Bloody Bill.

Bloody Bill's laughter rumbled. He held his sides with his elbows. He nudged Little Ned, whose pink eyes narrowed as they shifted back and forth from Robin to Varney.

"Among true warriors, even the lowest observe the code of honor of the fighting man," Varney said.

"Where on earth are you from?" asked Bloody Bill.

"I did service in India," Varney said.

"I knew you couldn't be from around here, talking like that about honor among warriors," said Bloody Bill. "You won't last long in Texas, fella."

Varney raised his pistol and aimed at the widest part of Bloody Bill. Varney's eyes were watering from his swollen nose, but this was an ample target at a range of about fifty feet. Varney hadn't shot at a human being in, what, ten or fifteen years? In India and Afghanistan, shooting at human beings had been a military necessity; they had either been the enemy, or were thought to be. Morality was not a consideration, except when he tried to make sense of it by writing in his notebook reflections that became eventually his first romance.

And now, standing on a sandbar in the Colorado River, Varney remembered the excitement, the odd twinge of pleasure he had felt when he saw his enemies fall. But he preferred to negotiate.

"Bloody Bill, is that what you're called?" Varney said.

"Some call me that."

"Bill has hanged more Yankee-lovers than I ever dreamed we had around here," said Ellen.

"He hangs the suspected ones, too," Fred said. "He takes their livestock and burns their houses."

On the roof of the boat cabin, Robin inhaled a deep breath and slowly let it out. He moved his sight from the big man to the Arab and back again, getting the feel for the sequence.

"Fred and Ellen here are good people. But they've got a rich imagination," said Bloody Bill.

"Give me your word of honor that our party will have safe passage through this place and you won't follow us when we leave," Varney said.

"All right," said Bloody Bill. "You have my word of honor."

"Don't you believe him, Mizeris Bushkin," Fred said.

"Bushkin? Would that be like in Senator Bushkin?" said Bloody Bill.

"I've heard about you, your reputation," Isabella said.

"I voted twice for your husband in the last election, and so did

Little Ned. You and us are on the same side against the niggers. It's an honor to welcome you to Burroughs' Cove. I promise no harm will come to you or your companions, not from my boys, anyhow."

The big man looked down at Flora in the water.

"Do I hear a guarantee that this gypsy girl won't shoot me?"

"You owe me for two mules and a wagon," she said.

"How do you fit in with these people?" asked Bloody Bill.

"She is with me," Isabella said. "She is my personal assistant."

"What do you think, Little Ned?" asked Bloody Bill.

Little Ned studied the people wading from the boat and then his eyes took in the rifleman on the roof of the cabin.

"They intend to do us a great misery, is what I think," Little Ned said.

Isabella boosted the suitcase up and rested it on her shoulder. The effort popped a button on her blouse.

"I will not stand here in this water any longer," she said.

Varney dabbed at his nose with the rag of a shirt. His blood had stopped flowing, but his face was smeared with it, and his eyes were beginning to swell and turn purple. He was thinking that if he was going to have to shoot this Bloody Bill fellow, he had best get at it while he could see clearly.

"See here, Bloody Bill, I am growing short of patience with you," said Varney.

"I gave you my word already. What more can I do?" Bloody Bill asked.

Varney glanced at Flora, who stood with her feet braced in the sandbar and both hands on the grip of the big pistol.

"How do you see our future working out here in this situation?" asked Varney.

"I see our side winning," Flora said.

"This is ridiculous," said Isabella. She walked toward the dock with her brown suitcase on her shoulder, her bosom straining the fabric of her blouse, her proud nose leading her toward a resolution of this standoff.

"Wait, Isabella," Varney said.

"Miz Bushkin, if that roughneck on the boat shoots me and Little

Ned, there goes four votes for your husband up in smoke," said Bloody Bill.

"That would be the Senator's problem, not mine," Isabella said.

Ellen and Fred both knelt on the dock and reached down toward Isabella to take the suitcase that she held up to them. Little Ned stared at the suitcase and rubbed a thumb along the blade of his Bowie knife.

"The ladder is around this way, as I recall," Isabella said.

Isabella climbed the ladder, water squishing out of the tops of her boots.

Varney had a flash of instinct that he should signal Captain Robin to drop Bloody Bill and the Arab before Isabella got onto the dock, but he dismissed it. There were four people shot to death in his wake already today, and not even a battle. It was only the middle of the afternoon. Not even in Afghanistan had there been a day topsys to this unless there was a battle.

He watched Fred and Ellen helping Isabella onto the dock. He looked at Flora.

"Well, the dice are thrown," he said.

"Les jeux sont fait," said Flora.

Varney waved for Robin to come in and join them.

Eighteen

BLOODY BILL HAD AN IDEA.

"Miz Bushkin and her personal assistant want to go to Galveston. Yawl two roughnecks want horses. I figure me and Little Ned and our personal assistants will escort the lady and the little yellow gypsy girl to Galveston and keep them safe from evil doers all the way. But we don't have no horses except what we are riding, so yawl roughnecks can wait right here in this store for a couple of hours while my personal assistants go off and take some horses away from the Yankee-loving citizens around here who are mistaken in their belief that the south has lost this war."

"They be celebrating a little too soon," said Little Ned. "You ain't won nothing if you can't make it stick."

"Well, what does everybody think of my plan?" Bloody Bill asked.

They were gathered inside the store. A light rain was pattering down on the dock and pocking the water of the creek. At the dock rocked Fred and Ellen's shallow draw fishing boat with its mast the size of a broomstick and its sail like a wet bed sheet. Bloody Bill had sent one member of his gang, a tall Czech immigrant named Rufus, protesting, out into the rain to watch the road coming down from Bastrop because, as Bloody Bill said, you never knew where to expect trouble to come from in times like these, but you could be sure it was coming from somewhere.

Three other gang members sprawled on the floor, smoking corncob pipes and taking a rest. They were a scabrous lot, Isabella thought, as she looked from Bloody Bill to Little Ned to the three unwashed, unshaven men on the floor. She wasn't going anywhere with them of her own volition, but she figured Bloody Bill must have known that she wasn't so stupid. Isabella finished washing blood off Varney's face. She laid three strips of adhesive tape across his nose and tenderly patted his cheek. She had taken off her boots and poured out the water. The Italian leather suitcase with silver buckles on the straps sat beside the expensive boots. Flora was at the counter picking out a piece of chewing gum from a glass jar that Fred and Ellen offered her. Water from Flora's hemp skirt dripped onto the hardwood floor and dotted her bare feet.

Robin stood in the corner with the Spencer rifle in the crook of his arm.

"I've got a better plan," he said.

After a moment of silence, Bloody Bill asked, "What's on your mind?"

Robin had been thinking about using the Spencer as his bargaining chip and taking a horse. But that would mean leaving his companions to the mercy of Bloody Bill and Little Ned and their gang. Varney was in no condition to protect them. Isabella might not be in danger of anything worse than being robbed. But Robin saw the three men on the floor leering at Flora. She turned from the glass jar and put a piece of gum into her mouth. Robin saw the look in her green eyes and again, as had happened earlier today in the wagon, something stirred within him. This mystery of attraction—how to explain it?

"First thing is, you pay this girl for her mules and her wagon," Robin said.

"What would be the second thing?" said Bloody Bill.

"The second thing is, you and your boys will tie each other up tight, hand and foot."

"I suppose the third thing is you'll steal our horses," Bloody Bill said.

"We'll pay you for them," said Flora.

"I was about to suggest that," Robin said.

"You'll probably be paying me the same amount of money as

what I pay the girl for her mules and wagon. That's my guess."

"So we could skip that step, and you can just go ahead and start tying each other up," said Robin.

Robin cocked the hammer on the Spencer.

"We're five against your one," Bloody Bill said.

"Two," said Flora.

She picked up the dragoon pistol off the counter.

"Make that three," Varney said, raising his pistol.

"What about you, Miz Bushkin? Have you turned criminal?" asked Bloody Bill.

"There must be a better plan than has been suggested so far," Isabella said.

"I got an idea," said Fred. "Why don't all of you take this mess someplace else?"

"It's getting to where nobody trusts anybody any more," Bloody Bill said.

"I blame it on the war," said Little Ned.

"Used to be, if your fellow Texan gives you his word of honor on a matter, why, you took his word and that was better than having to shoot it out." Bloody Bill moved his massive body lightly over to the only table in the place and pulled out a chair. "Why don't yawl roughnecks sit down with me here and drink a bucket of beer and get to know each other?" The chair creaked as he sat down. "Little Ned, you and your personal assistants go on outside and look to the horses, why not?"

"Don't move, any of you," Robin said.

Little Ned and the gang members eyed him warily and did not move.

"How much did you make off my mules and my wagon, hey?" Flora asked. She left the counter and came over to the table. "How much did that poor man pay you for my things?"

"Don't wave that big pistol at me, girl," said Bloody Bill, getting annoyed.

"This has gone far enough," Little Ned said.

"Get up and go see to the horses like I told you," said Bloody Bill.

"Don't do it," Robin said.

The three men sprawled on the floor looked at the repeating rifle and kept their places. Little Ned put his palm on the knob of the grip of his Bowie knife but left it there.

"Look here, now, any way this comes out it's likely to ruin our property and our business," said Fred. "I don't see why you couldn't settle this down the road someplace."

"See out there, it's quit raining," Ellen said. "Look. No more rain."

Isabella sat down at the table with Bloody Bill. Her blouse was wet and she could feel the soaked document from Bushkin against her breast.

"Gentlemen, let's not be playing macho and calling each other's bluffs until something ugly happens. My personal assistant and I are traveling together with these two men as far as the coast. I would appreciate your help, Bloody Bill, in finding for us four horses. I assume that by Yankee-lovers you mean people who didn't vote for Senator Bushkin. I will pay you handsomely, we will be gone from your life, and no one in this room needs to be harmed."

"And you will pay me for my property, hey, big man?" Flora said.

"Fat chance," said Little Ned.

"How much rope you have back there?" Robin asked.

Behind the counter, Fred and Ellen looked at each other.

"We don't have any rope," said Ellen.

"My friends Ellen and Fred ain't going to give you the rope to tie me up with," Bloody Bill said. "I'm their neighbor. Why, they couldn't exist here in this place without my friendship. Long after you folks are gone, Ellen and Fred and I and Little Ned and my personal assistants will still be living in this county. You've got no right to come sloshing through our lives, causing problems where we wasn't having none and stealing our horses and traipsing off for Galveston."

"Nobody is stealing any horses. We are buying them," Isabella said.

"At gun point? I'm surprised at you, Miz Bushkin," said Bloody Bill.

"My father and I will come back here later and settle up with you about our mules and our wagon," Flora said.

"Who's your father?" Bloody Bill looked at Varney. "This old geezer with the earring?"

It irritated Varney to be called old.

"I'll fetch the ropes and do the tying up myself. I'm rather good with knots," Varney said.

Bloody Bill clawed his fingers through his beard.

"Boys, it looks like we're in for a ruckus," he said.

The three men on the floor slowly arose, unfolding, brushing off their clothing. All three had pistols in the waistbands of their trousers. Little Ned gripped the handle of his Bowie knife and let loose a string of nervous spit into the tank of earthworms.

"Oh Lord, please don't let them do this," Ellen pleaded, looking at the ceiling. "Not indoors."

Robin's eyes flicked across the others and stopped on the face of Bloody Bill. One wrong appearing twitch of the cheek, Robin thought, and this room would explode. His finger touched the trigger lightly. He had noted at the house that Bushkin, or whomever had prized this rifle before Robin had put his hands on it, had adjusted the trigger spring so that the slightest squeeze would fire the hammer into the pin.

"What is it that you want from us, Bloody Bill?" asked Isabella.

"I'll settle for the contents of that suitcase you are toting around."

"No," Isabella said.

"Give me the suitcase and yawl can have safe passage through my territory. You'll have to go on foot, though. There ain't no regular transportation any more."

"Never," Isabella said.

"Move back away from him, Mrs. Bushkin," said Robin.

"This is crazy," Isabella said.

"You sure said that right," said Fred, ducking behind the counter where Ellen had gone to her knees and was praying.

"Suppose all of you men shoot each other. Then what?" Isabella said. "What good will horses do you when you are dead?"

"It's a matter of principle," said Bloody Bill.

"I suggest you try using your brain instead of some stupid notion of what manhood means," Isabella said. "I saw Captain Robin in action with that rifle earlier today. It's very clear to me, Bloody Bill, that you will be the first corpse in this room. Take that into consideration."

"I can't afford to back down, Miz Bushkin. My reputation will be ruined," said Bloody Bill.

"You have the reputation of being a ruthless brute," Isabella said.

"That's what I'm talking about," said Bloody Bill.

They heard a pop from outside, then seconds later another pop.

Everybody turned toward the door as Rufus shoved it open from outside. He was wet and breathing hard.

"There's Yankees out here," he yelled. "Yankee soldiers. I shot one of them. He's laying in the road just dead as hell."

Nineteen

CPL. JIM GREENGRASS LAY FACE DOWN. A bullet through his throat had opened his jugular and his blood was pouring into the narrow dirt road.

He had emerged from the forest on the road that ran through the cleared ground that Ellen had converted into a vegetable garden, and another section where the cows stood watching from near the barn. The clearing extended all the way to the building that served as dock and general store, with an attached bedroom and parlor where Fred and Ellen Burroughs lived, the whole building put together with thick cypress logs cut from along the creek that entered the river there. Corporal Greengrass had ridden out into the open, scouting, with the rest of the detail one hundred yards to his rear. He saw the tall figure of Rufus leaning against a post of the fence that wrapped around the fields of beans and tomatoes, but even though the Cherokee had survived three years of war and had won his stripes by continually proving that a man of his blood could be a warrior for the Union second to none, or almost none, his current leader, Lt. Tom Custer, being an exception, Corporal Greengrass was not immediately alert to the idea that this lazy-looking, ramshackle creature doing nothing in the middle of nowhere might be the instrument of his death.

Lt. Tom Custer sat on the Arabian mare Athena at the head of the detail and saw Greengrass fall from the saddle, and his horse rear and shy away from the thrashing body. The second shot snapped the air near Custer's ear and struck Pvt. Nathan Zucker, five yards behind, in the forehead. Zucker reeled, clutched at the air, somehow kept his seat on his horse, though his cap flew off. The hot piece of lead put a dent in Zucker's forehead but bounced off and fell onto his tunic where it scorched a hole. When he looked at the tiny thread of smoke rising from his tunic, Zucker's eyes narrowed and he fainted from shock. Custer saw the tall figure that had fired the rifle turn and run into the cypress log building. Custer felt Athena tensing beneath him, her chest swelling. She thought to charge, but she held back.

At that moment came a volley of shots from the building, and the soldiers heard a deep voice shouting, "You'll die here, you Yankee bastards, you'll die here!"

Other voices took up the cry from the building and more shots were fired, bullets buzzing around the soldiers, clipping twigs and chunks of bark off the trees.

"Dismount! Get off the road," Custer said.

To Custer it appeared his troops had ridden into an ambush. How many guerrillas there might be, he could not know.

In the shelter of the forest, Custer crept forward to the edge of the tree line and looked at the building through his spyglass. As he adjusted the focus, he felt a person kneel beside him.

"Form skirmishers, Lieutenant?" asked Santana.

"Send somebody to drag Greengrass back here with us," said Custer.

"I did already. He's dead."

"How is Zucker?"

"Hardheaded Jew, he'll be all right. Got a knot is all."

"Send the horses to the rear. Put McDonald with them."

"I sent Campesi to the rear with the horses. McDonald is a better shot."

"What else have you done, Captain?" Custer frowned.

"Brought Smith, McDonald, and the three Leatherwoods up to the edge of the woods to get in position to fire on the building."

Through the eyepiece the building became clearer. The banging of shots and the smoke from the windows continued sporadically.

Custer saw people moving around inside the building.

"You're a Texas man," Custer said. "What can we expect from these people?"

"Just what we're getting," said Santana.

"I mean, are there many of them here do you reckon? Are they out there now outflanking us?"

"The river is our left flank. They can't come that way. I put Billy Leatherwood on our right flank. He's a smart kid, always alert. They won't come around Billy without us knowing they're there."

"How many would you say?"

"I don't know if we stumbled into a nest of serious guerrillas or if these are a few sore losers."

"Shooting Greengrass makes it serious," Custer said.

Custer got the spyglass focused finally and grunted. He passed the spyglass to Santana.

"Take a look. The first window left of the door. Who do you see in there with the guerrillas?"

Santana turned the spyglass toward the building as another volley of shots racketed from the windows and voices cried insults and taunts at the Yankee soldiers.

"I think it's the old horse thief," said Santana.

"That's what I think. Looks like we've caught them."

Bullets pinged into the trees, and a flock of crows flew over the vegetable garden crying distress.

Santana kept the glass on the windows of the building. He could make out several unfamiliar forms inside the store—a huge man with a beard who was yelling insults, a couple of women, an Arab, two or three men who looked like locals. Santana got another glimpse of the British horse thief, who appeared to be arguing with a tall man. Santana adjusted focus, and yes, the tall man was Jerod Robin.

Seventh Cavalry troopers had been issued Colt .44 single-action pistols as side arms. Each man carried a breech-loading Springfield carbine in a saddle holster. They were not rapid-fire weapons like the Spencer, but at the moment no soldier was shooting anyhow. All the noise and the bullets were coming from the cypress building.

"MacDonald, Smith, you boys get ready to put some lead through those windows," Custer called.

"I see women inside," said Santana.

Custer took the spyglass. As he peered through the lens, boards were being erected across one window, and what appeared to be a table was shoved across the other. They were barricading for the fight. Custer was a little surprised at their ferocity, at the curses they were shouting, at the bushwhacking of Corporal Greengrass, who had survived the Shenandoah Valley campaign and the worst of the Wilderness only to die on a lonely dirt road in Texas.

"I can't see any women," Custer said.

"Fine. Me neither," said Santana.

Santana picked up the Springfield carbine he had propped against the trunk of an oak tree. He wished he still had the Spencer he had carried at Snow Hill. Someone had made off with it while he was in the hospital recovering from kidney surgery. This Springfield was a single-shooter, but it would take only one well-placed bullet to rid the earth of Jerod Robin. Santana almost was reluctant to kill Robin from this distance. It would be better done face-to-face, eye-to-eye, as they had been at Snow Hill when Robin took advantage of a moment of weakness and thrust a saber into Santana's side.

"Uncle Santana."

Santana scowled and turned to see Luther crawling toward him, followed by his brother Adam.

"Get back to your positions," Santana said.

"But we only got these shotguns, me and Adam and Billy. Those rebs are out of range."

"Where's Billy?"

"He's out there on the right where you put him behind a big old pecan tree."

"Suppose they come charging out of that building and run into your range and you're not ready?" said Santana.

"That's what Billy said," Luther said. "But me and Adam want to get the rifles off those two men that got shot, and then we can go hunting from way out here instead of waiting for them to charge."

"One rifle is still laying up there in the road where Greengrass was, and the other rifle belongs to Zucker, who ain't dead and will be rejoining us shortly. I want you boys to go back where you're supposed to be. You are just the same as in the army today. You have got to do what your officers tell you to do."

"I told you he'd say that," said Adam.

"You didn't either."

"Damn it, you boys get back where you belong, or I'm going to send you home to your daddy. You know how much he'll like that? Leatherwoods failing their duty?"

Luther and Adam turned without another word and scrambled through the underbrush toward their positions.

Santana looked at Tom Custer and shook his head.

"Family."

"Yeah," said Custer, "I know."

Santana sighted his Springfield on the first window to the left of the door. He had seen at least one woman in there, maybe two, and it figured the Negro girl was probably still with Robin and the British horse thief. But of course the girl was not to be spared—she had murdered a soldier—and the women, well, that's how it is at war.

Twenty

VARNEY HAD DONE THIS BEFORE.

He shucked his feet out of Bushkin's boots and stripped off the fine gray suit that was now as ruined as the clothes he had traded for it. The Indian-cotton shirt had become a bloody rag. But Bushkin's silk underpants, still wet from when the boat sank, felt sensuous and clinging, rather erotic, and so the silk underpants were all Varney was wearing as he waded into the Colorado River and began to swim upstream.

He had done this before in the Punjab in the river Sutlej, known as the river with a hundred arms. The Sutlej is where Alexander's army had stopped, the soldiers refusing to come further into India, refusing to fight any longer so far from home in a vast land full of enemies. Varney snorted as the Colorado water snuffed up the nostrils of his broken nose. His toes gripped bottom and he shoved off, gliding into a breast stroke. He was a powerful swimmer.

The rebel captain hadn't understood what Varney was doing and had made a move to stop him. As Varney studied the anger in Robin's face, he thought of Varina Hotchkiss doing Lady MacBeth. He had noticed a similarity in the expressions of Varina and her son, and the sudden rage that now flashed in his eyes had flashed in hers on the stage. Until today Varina Hotchkiss had not been on Varney's mind for decades, except for one evening a couple of years ago when he drank a few mugs of ale at a table on the sidewalk in front of the Holly Bush pub, began looking at a theatre poster for Covent Garden, and wound up the night sitting at his desk upstairs writing a piece for the *Holly Bush Journal* recalling the passion he had felt for Varina Hotchkiss and bemoaning that she had left the London stage during a triumphant run as the rich, young, romantic Lydia Languish in Richard Brinsley Sheridan's sixty-odd-year-old comedy *The Rivals*, and had mysteriously disappeared from Varney's life. By the time he finished writing the piece, Varney had fallen in love with Varina Hotchkiss all over again as he had done as a student. But he woke up in the morning with his head on the desk, a dozen empty ale mugs on the floor, and more pressing things to deal with than his memory of Varina Hotchkiss. His mind was, after all, the only place where he had control of his life.

The river water was cool and refreshing. It even seemed bracing to his nose as he plowed ahead, making strong strokes against the current. A green frog popped up beside his left ear, drawn by his jade and silver earring. Varney thought of his wife Aliyah. He could hear her delicate, childish laughter, so pure with delight. She had loved swimming in a tributary of the Sutlej near her father's palace. On a warm morning in spring, Varney and six Sikh warriors, his personal bodyguard, escorted Aliyah and her attendants three miles upstream to her favorite blue pool in a bend of the river. Upon arriving they were attacked by Mohammedan bandits who intended to kidnap Aliyah and hold her for ransom. Varney's party was pinned down by fire from long muskets. Aliyah and her attendants huddled behind the pack animals as lead balls thunked into the rigging and the flesh of the camels. The bandits were calling for them to surrender. Two Sikhs lay dead, one was wounded, the other three were fighting back with their muskets, but the bandits were hidden in the date palms. On his stomach Varney had wriggled away from the others and slithered toward the river. He heard Aliyah calling for him to come back as he entered the water, but there was no time to explain what he had to do.

* * * * *

The rebel captain, son of Varina, had accused him minutes ago of running away from the fight that was beginning. Bloody Bill had erupted with gleeful hate when the Czech opened the door and shouted the news of a dead soldier. Bloody Bill had rushed to the windows. Bellowing curses, he pulled a pistol from beneath his military tunic and began shooting across the vegetable garden up the road toward the forest, though his bullets fell well short.

Little Ned and the other gang members fetched their weapons from the corner behind the counter and started shooting. "Go home! Get out of Texas!" they shouted. "You'll die here, you bastards!"

Varney had to give Bloody Bill credit for being a man of his word, after all; he had said he hated Yankees, and now he was insanely proving it.

Varney had started for the back door that led to the dock, but Robin had stopped him. Varney saw Isabella and Flora looking at him.

"Retreating already, general?" Robin said.

"I'll come with you," said Isabella.

"Sorry," Varney said.

He dashed out the back door and onto the dock and climbed down the ladder and waded out to the stranded boat where he stripped off Bushkin's clothes and entered the river and began to swim.

This was more like it, he thought, this was a young man's life as he had known it, breast-stroking in a foreign river, hearing gunshots in ragged volleys, a black watersnake curiously observing him from a shaded pocket along the shore.

Varney considered Texas to be a strange, wild, primitive, intellectually backward area that he had never intended to visit, had never had much curiosity about. It was the dark corner of the Confederacy. He had read of the battle at the Alamo, which he would have called a classic folly except that the courageous stupidity of it had inspired the Texans to rally and throw out the Mexican government and establish their own republic, which ten years after the fall of the Alamo became the twenty-eighth state in the United States of America and promptly invaded Mexico.

Varney's intention when he had sailed from England was to visit

New York, where he had booked three lectures on the role of the British Empire in India. His speeches were peppered with blood-spattered anecdotes that he hoped would persuade a New York publisher to bring out an edition of *By the Sword*. His romance was in its twentieth printing in London, still selling around two thousand copies a year. He'd had offers from publishers in Boston and Philadelphia, but their proffered payments were such that he turned them down hoping for a grander stage in Manhattan, where Dickens had recently been so feted. Mobs of fans followed Dickens through the streets of Manhattan, hoping he would spare a few words for them. Dickens filled the theater for his readings.

Varney's lectures in New York were largely ignored by Americans but drew crowds of angry English and furious Indians. At the end of two weeks, living in a suite at the Washington Square Hotel, Varney was no closer to finding a New York publisher. He began preparing for a trip into the unknown in pursuit of the inspiration to start writing *Playing with the Mortals*, his new romance. He had decided he would be heading into Pennsylvania for a look at the battlefield of Gettysburg. Eventually he would go to Mexico, where he would hole up in a hacienda someplace, probably in the mountains, and write the book. He would find a house that had a terrace with a view across a valley, preferably with water shining in the distance, a place where he could be his creative self, listening to the muses, in comfort, for six months or a year, letting Crichton run the *Journal* until this new book was done, or maybe even longer.

Then at breakfast in the Washington Square Hotel dining room, he saw the notice in *The Times*:

Lt. T. Custer, brother of the General, received the Medal of Honor this week for action in Virginia. It was his second Medal of Honor won within six days. Lt. Custer modestly told this reporter that he owed it all to his horse, a chestnut Arabian mare he calls Athena. Custer told me, 'She is a special horse that knows how to do everything.' It is our opinion that Custer is a bashful hero, unlike his colorful brother.

Varney thought, "Athena? What if this is my Athena?"

At the very least, Custer would make an interesting piece for the *Journal*.

Virginia was to the south, Varney reasoned, the same direction as Mexico.

Varney finally found Custer in Texas. More important, he found Athena. The horse knew him right off. She was truly his Athena. He hadn't really believed it would be, but the moment he saw her he knew her. On her left hip he saw the small V branded there by some previous owner. He never had known what the V stood for, but there was no doubt in his mind that this V proved the identity of his horse. How long ago was the day he was ambushed in the Hindu Kush and lost Athena? No matter. This was his horse. Some Virginia gentleman searching the earth for rare and valuable horses must have bought her from a dealer in Afghanistan. Athena had crossed the ocean, but so had Varney. She was younger than her years, but so was he.

Five hundred yards upstream Varney swam into the shore where a small creek flowed into the river. He crawled out of the water and stood up. He was breathing hard but he felt topsys.

Custer had told him in a saloon that when he was preparing to skirmish he would send his horses to the rear. That's how Varney did it in the Queen's military in India, too, though he changed tactics when he became a mercenary.

Varney found a piece of driftwood that was three feet long and big around as his fist. It was a stout club. He couldn't have made the swim carrying a pistol. When he did it before—swam upstream in an arm of the Sutlej into a blue pool to the rear of where he knew the Mohammedan bandits were firing from—he had toted his pistol in one hand and held it up out of the water while he swam with the other arm. But he was younger then. He felt topsys now, but also he was no fool.

He heard shooting from the soldiers. Custer had opened fire. Varney counted the shots as he pushed through the brush. Only three or four rifles were firing from the Custer side, while the shooting from the cypress building came in frequent bursts. Varney hadn't heard the sound of the Spencer. Varina's son was conserving his ammunition. Varney thought of Isabella inside the building with the outlaws. He liked her spirit and good heart. Poor dear, her big mistake today was inviting him into her home and cleaning him up and feeding him. Then there was young Flora. He felt she was a messenger of some sort, and she was certainly spirited and clever.

They were worth saving, and he would find Athena back here someplace.

He figured the horses would be in a group just off the road a hundred yards or more behind Custer's skirmish line.

He heard and smelled the horses before he saw them. He parted the brush and peeked into a small hollow. There were eight horses. They made a circle around a soldier who held their reins and kept looking toward the shooting noises. The soldier, Campesi, had his back to Varney, but standing in the middle of the horses he could not be reached by Varney's club. Athena lifted her head and looked around. Their eyes met. She recognized him.

The horses began jostling each other. Campesi spoke to them in Italian and asked them to be calm. Instead the horses closed in on him. Something was wrong. Campesi ordered them in Italian to stand back and give him room and not try to kick him to death. Campesi backed out of the circle, using his Springfield as a poker, and as he got clear of the horses Varney swung the club with both hands and whacked him behind the ear.

Athena nuzzled Varney. Her eyes glowed with pleasure at seeing him. Varney walked among the other horses. He selected three to stand beside Athena. He undid the saddle girths of the other four. Swiftly he removed the bits from their mouths and stripped away their reins. Varney planted a bare foot in the stirrup and hand on the pommel and swung himself onto the back of his horse. He was sitting in Custer's saddle wearing Bushkin's silk drawers. Varney smiled. Real life was more idiosyncratic than anything he could have made up.

Varney climbed down again and picked up Campesi's Springfield rifle. Campesi's eyes were slits, but the pulse in his neck was visibly thumping. Varney unhooked the soldier's ammunition belt and slung the pouch over his shoulder. He remounted, patted Athena on the neck, and cocked the Springfield. "Now begins the tricky part, old girl," Varney said. Athena snorted and tossed her head.

Varney squeezed the trigger. Fire and smoke blasted out of the rifle with a bang magnified by the trees enclosing the hollow.

Saddles fell off the four horses that had no restraints, and they milled about for a few seconds before they began to run out of the hollow and back up the road away from the shooting. Varney held the reins of the other three horses. The trees were thick around him. The only way back to the cypress building was down the narrow red dirt road. For at least the first hundred yards, Varney would be heading into and through the soldiers. He didn't know how many soldiers there were, but he did know for certain that one of them was Tom Custer.

The noise of Varney's rifle shot and the crashing of galloping horses caused Custer and Santana to turn and look back. Could it be the guerrillas were closing in from the rear? What was Campesi shooting at? Custer and Santana had been banging away at the cypress building. The Texans inside were shooting steadily and had wounded McDonald, the meat of his right bicep torn out. Melrose Smith had laid down his rifle and was twisting a tourniquet made of a belt up near McDonald's armpit. They had heard several blasts from the shotguns of Adam and Luther Leatherwood.

Santana reached into his bullet pouch. "Damn," he said.

"What is it?" said Custer.

"I'm out of lead."

"I mean what is that shot behind us, do you think?"

"I'll go find out."

"Send one of your nephews."

Truth was, Santana had decided he couldn't trust Adam and Luther with anything important, and Billy was too far away.

"I'd better do it myself," Santana said.

Carefully keeping a tree trunk between him and the building, Santana stood up. He felt a pain in his kidney. He was always aware why he had only one kidney.

Then suddenly here they came. Santana was stunned by what he was seeing. That magnificent Arabian horse of Custer's was flying down the road toward him with some savage Indian on her back and three more U.S. cavalry horses running with her. They were on top of him in an instant. There was nothing Santana could do but jump out of the way.

As they thundered past, Santana saw it was the old horse thief riding the chestnut mare. Now Santana could conceive of Robin escaping from the cypress building. He started running in pursuit of the horses.

Lying on his stomach at the edge of the forest, Custer fired a shot at the building and saw wood chips pop off the windowsill. He heard a storm of hoofbeats behind and to his left, on the road, and McDonald was yelling in pain.

Custer rolled over and sat up. What's this? Swerving off the road and galloping madly not ten feet in front of him, pounding along the tree line and veering toward the vegetable garden, came his horse Athena. He saw Varney in his saddle. Custer slid another cartridge into the chamber and cocked the Springfield.

But he couldn't shoot Varney from here. It was too tricky an angle. He might hit Athena. He thought of the Leatherwood boys hidden in the tree line with their shotguns.

"Don't shoot the horse!" Custer yelled as he ran. "Don't shoot the horse! That's an order!"

Luther and Adam watched Varney thunder past. They had heard Custer's order, but they had already shot up their loads anyhow.

Custer ran out from the shelter of the trees and lifted his rifle. He figured there was one chance. He would take aim at a spot in front of Varney, shooting high so as not to hit Athena, and let the Englishman run into the bullet.

He was squinting along the sights down the rifle barrel, getting a picture of it, when reason told him the shot was too dangerous. There was as good a chance he would hit Athena in the head as Varney from this distance. To kill this horse would be a tragedy. Somehow soon Custer would get Athena back. This crazy old Englishman could not go much further. Custer would catch up to him.

While Custer stood in the open, lifting his rifle and aiming carefully at Varney, deciding not to shoot, inside the general store Robin stepped to the window, pushed Little Ned out of the way, hoisted the Spencer to his shoulder, put his eye on the Yankee hero, and shot him in the left hip.

Custer's first sensation was that he had been kicked. His flesh froze before it spurted pain. He stumbled forward and fell. Blood flowed from a hole in his pants. He was expecting them to finish him from the cypress building, but the guerrillas stopped shooting. Custer crawled toward the trees.

Varney and Athena and the three horses raced to the edge of the vegetable garden and began to approach the general store from the upstream side of the creek, not riding through the bean field.

At his post behind an enormous pecan tree, guarding the right flank, Billy Leatherwood heard the commotion, and he heard Custer crying not to shoot the horse. Billy realized the horses were galloping toward him. Lord Almighty, he thought, it's the Ivanhoe man.

He had been ordered not to shoot the special horse, but Billy rushed out of the woods and stumbled almost into their path and hefted his 12-gauge to blast a hole in the old Englishman who was charging toward him; this was like Ivanhoe, Billy was thinking, with the Englishman bearing down on him like a joust.

Varney saw Billy and saw the shotgun come up. Varney ducked away. Athena changed her course in one bound and struck little Billy with her chest and galloped over him, followed by the other three horses. Varney looked back and saw Billy's trampled body in a swirl of dust on the strip between the forest and the vegetable garden.

The door of the general store opened as Varney rode up.

Bloody Bill rushed out.

"By God, I'm proud to know you. You've got a friend for life named Bloody Bill. Let me shake your hand."

"I couldn't have done better myself," said Little Ned.

Varney got down off Athena and shook their hands. The others came out of the general store. Robin looked across the cleared ground to the edge of the woods where three hundred yards away three figures were crouching over the body of Billy Leatherwood. One of the three—that would be Santana—left the body of Billy and went to Custer, who had dragged himself into the trees. Robin couldn't tell how badly he had hurt Custer, but the fight had gone out of the soldiers.

Bloody Bill's gang was making for their horses in the barn.

"You shouldn't have to travel in your underpants," Bloody Bill said to Varney. He took off the military tunic that was about one-third too small for him. Varney put it on. "What army is this?" Varney asked. "Belgian," said Bloody Bill. "Don't mind the fleas."

Bloody Bill stopped a husky, sad-faced man who looked like a farmer but was the gang's expert arsonist. "Give this geezer your pants," Bloody Bill said. The man paused to think up an argument, but his comrades cried for him to hurry; they needed to be moving on. Varney put on the trousers and cinched the belt tighter. He was barefoot, but he saw Flora come out of the general store, toting that dragoon pistol and still without shoes, and Varney decided he would give a try to the barefoot style. He had gone barefoot a lot in India, despite the scorpions. When he was younger, he didn't fear scorpions. He didn't fear them now, either.

Robin watched the two figures—Adam and Luther—around their fallen kinsman. They appeared to be grieving. They were making no move to leave Billy's body. Santana had disappeared into the forest. The soldiers no longer appeared to be an immediate threat. Still, it was time to go. Robin inspected the horses.

"I suppose you'll be taking this one," Robin said, jerking a thumb toward Athena.

"She belongs to me, old son," Varney said.

"I'm taking this one," said Isabella, walking up to a racy looking Kentucky horse. She clasped her arms around the brown leather suitcase. "Mr. Varney, please help me mount."

"Dear lady, you should leave us here. You have committed no crimes. You're a person of prominence. Why get deeper into a bad situation?" Varney said.

"I should stay here?" said Isabella. "In the middle of the woods? With no money? With no house? With enemies coming for me? I believe not, Edmund. I am going to Galveston the fastest way possible, and that is to go as far as I can with you people."

Varney strapped the brown suitcase with silver buckles behind Isabella's saddle next to the bedroll that had belonged to Private McDonald.

"Please, please go away," Fred yelled from the door of the general store.

"We didn't have anything to do with this," Ellen screamed in the direction of the soldiers.

Flora brushed past Robin and went to the other two horses. She looked at them uncertainly.

"I don't ride so good, hey," she said. "What do you think?"

Robin guided her onto a black mare as her best chance of hanging on for her journey, wherever she was going. He adjusted the cavalryman's stirrups for her. Robin was still watching the two Leatherwoods standing at the edge of the woods.

"Billy is dead," Robin said to Flora.

"I expect so," she said.

"You told him."

"If he didn't change—"

Robin helped her into the saddle.

"He's got nothing to fear, actually," Varney said. "I've been there."

"God will punish him," Flora said.

"God punished him by making him Billy. Now he can set about doing better next time," said Varney.

In the distance, on the other side of the vegetable garden, the two older Leatherwood brothers picked up the body of their little brother. They carried Billy toward the road, where Santana had stepped out of the trees again and was looking toward the group in front of the general store. Robin saw another soldier appear, then another. There could be only one reason why they aren't attacking us, Robin thought. They hadn't brought enough ammunition for a full assault on a building made out of cypress logs, filled with people who were shooting back. The soldiers had expected their hunting to be swift and easy. And the Englishman had this time for sure stolen their horses, all of them.

But Robin understood the Federal army. They would keep coming until eventually they would get what they wanted. He could see that Bloody Bill and Little Ned and their gang were already fording the creek upstream from the general store and splashing off toward the south. Robin decided to follow them. If there was a road back there, outlaws would know about it.

It occurred to Robin that this was a good time for him to abandon the two females and the Englishman. They had horses now, they had weapons, and he knew Flora had money because he had seen it. After they crossed this creek and got onto whatever road or path that led away from here, he would cut loose from them and hurry on to Sweetbrush. He had grown sympathetic with all three of today's companions. He was bonded in blood with the girl and the writer through the death of the guard. He had the feeling that much of what Varney said was fabricated, or at least embellished, and the Englishman's obsession with this horse was insane, but the old man had showed courage. Varney had saved them at the general store. Robin would always owe him for that. Isabella Bushkin belonged to the Texas political class that he had spent four years defending. The fortune-telling girl, well, she had fascinated him from the moment he saw her in court. But he could make better time alone. He hoped to reach Sweetbrush and Gethsemane before the news of Billy's death arrived there.

Robin led them to the ford. He dropped back as the others entered the water, letting Varney go in front on the big chestnut mare, Isabella behind him on the Kentucky horse with her suitcase strapped to her saddle. The creek was thirty yards wide. The water bubbled fetlock-deep and swift. Robin touched Flora's elbow, helping her keep balanced as her horse shied at the clicking of hooves on slick stones under the water. His gentle touch surprised Flora. She could still feel his fingers on her knee when he had helped her into the saddle.

"I can do this," she said.

"Just the same—"

Before he could finish the sentence, his horse slipped on a rock and tumbled into the stream. The foreleg snapped like a slamming door.

Twenty-one

ROBIN DIDN'T LIKE SHOOTING THE HORSE, but a crippled animal in this forest would be torn apart within hours. He removed the army saddle and bridle and laid them beneath a tree, feeling that somehow he was making the animal more comfortable and it was the right thing to do. The others had dismounted and were watching. When Robin worked the lever on the Spencer, they looked away so as not to see the shot.

Varney wondered what the rebel captain would do next. There was a chance, Varney thought, that Varina's son would cock that Spencer again and take away a horse from one of the others. No doubt Athena would be his pick. Varney had seen how Robin looked at Athena through the courtroom door this morning, and again a few minutes ago in front of the general store.

Flora led her black mare to Robin.

"I'm not much rider anyhow," she said. "I'll hang on behind you, hey?"

Robin considered it.

"Let's try it then," he said.

The road had been an Indian trail that followed the course of the river fifty yards inland, out of the regular spring floodplain. The road was barely wide enough for two horses side by side. The main land route from Bastrop to Houston ran ten miles to the west through the plain at the edge of the pines, but they would be more likely to encounter the law in some form or other on that road.

It was about a hundred miles to Sweetbrush. Robin tried not to worry about what might happen at Sweetbrush. Getting there and doing what he should do would require every bit of his thought and effort, and imagining. What might happen after Sweetbrush was uncertain, except he had in mind to flee to Mexico. The bullet from Flora's derringer this morning had changed everything for everybody, including for people who didn't know Flora. But they soon would be meeting her unless Robin broke away from this party by tomorrow night.

Robin chuckled, imagining how his family would react if he rode up the magnolia-tree-lined boulevard that led to the two-story white main house at Sweetbrush with a sixteen-year-old colored girl clinging to his back. He imagined his wife fainting. What would his mother do? He could see Varina coming out onto the long upstairs porch, seeing him and putting on her stage airs as if delivering the second-act curtain line of a three-act play. He could hear her London voice saying, "Junius, come out here and look what our son has brought home from the war."

"What's funny?" Flora said into his ear.

"Nothing."

"That's the first time I heard you laugh."

"Some days are funnier than others."

"Tell me what you were laughing at. Was it me?"

"It's nothing."

They could hear the river constantly, and often were beside it or could see it through the trees. A large white egret stalked across the road in front of them. Water gushed over boulders at a rapid. They saw a raft of logs floating downstream, tended by two men in a small boat. In the pink light before dusk they encountered a merchant riding a mule with another mule in tow. The second mule wore a harness with a pack on each side of his body, canvas bags that the merchant told them were filled with canned goods that he intended to sell in Bastrop. The merchant saw the U.S.A. brands on the horses—except for Athena, whose golden chestnut hide remained unmarked other than the mysterious small V on her left hip. The merchant swallowed hard, thinking perhaps his luck had run out, but they let him pass. He left four cans of peaches as a toll. They rode on in the increasing dark until Robin called a halt. These horses had come all the way from Austin and were tired. "Well, thank heaven," said Isabella.

They made camp on a bluff above the river.

When they opened the bedrolls of Custer and the three troopers who had lost their horses, they found dried meat, coffee, sugar, a coffeepot, a frying pan, tin plates and cups, cornmeal, lard, bacon, potatoes, hard biscuits, and pieces of chocolate. In Custer's bedroll Varney found a comb, a mirror, and a clean blue shirt. He had been hoping for a diary or letters. Varney put on Custer's shirt. The sleeves were an inch too short and his chest and shoulders stretched the button holes past the buttons, but Varney decided to wear it. Robin staked out the horses. Flora helped him rub them down. Varney made it a point to rub down Athena, himself. The writer and Isabella built a fire and made coffee. They fried bacon and thin-sliced potatoes and opened the tins of peaches from the merchant.

Isabella was reminding herself that she believed in facing whatever life offers and making the best of things as they are. She undid the silver buckles on the straps, opened her Italian leather suitcase and took out a bottle of St. Essy Cognac, 120 years old, with the king's seal on the cork. She had been saving this bottle for opening someday when her ship sailed for Barcelona. But Bushkin's ugly document left on her lunch plate could be regarded as the same as ordering a ticket on a ship. Isabella twisted the wax seal but couldn't move it.

"Let me do that," Flora said.

The girl knelt beside Isabella, who sat next to her suitcase. From inside her hemp skirt, Flora produced a folding knife with a long blade. She took the bottle from Isabella and cut away the wax.

"See, now, this is the sort of thing you will be doing when you come to work for me," said Isabella.

Flora stopped cutting and looked at Isabella.

"Oh, I shouldn't have said that, should I?" Isabella said.

"Mrs. Bushkin—"

"Isabella, please."

"You're a nice person, but I don't foresee you in my future."

Isabella poured a generous slosh of Cognac into three of the four tin cups.

"Suit yourself," she said. "You're too young to be drinking Cognac, anyway."

"However, I am the seasoned age for a fine Cognac," said Varney, lifting his cup.

Robin picked up his cup and swished the liquid.

"I haven't had any Cognac in years," he said.

Isabella gestured toward Flora with the neck of the bottle.

"Oh, come on," Isabella said. She poured Cognac into the fourth cup and handed it to Flora. "Let's start this picnic with a toast."

"Happy days," said Varney.

He drained his cup. After a moment the others began to drink. Flora coughed.

"I was expecting something rather fancier from a literary man," Isabella said.

She poured another round.

"That wasn't a toast. That was my mantra," said Varney. He sniffed the liquor in his cup and smiled. "I do know a Texas style toast. I heard it at Dutch John's." He recited:

"Here's to the vinegaroon that jumped on the centipede's back. He looked at him with a glow and a glee and he said, 'You poisonous son of a bitch, if I don't get you, you'll get me.'"

They drank again.

"Hey, that's strong stuff," Flora said.

Isabella pushed the cork back into the bottle.

"It's a tonic for the spirit," said Isabella. "It puts a pleasing luminosity on things."

When they had finished eating, Robin tucked the Spencer under his arm, collected the four tin plates and took them down the bank to the sandy slope at the water's edge. He scrubbed the plates with sand and then rinsed them in the Colorado. Robin knew from bitter experience that stale food on plates can quickly cause stomachs to turn upside down. He thought they would use these plates at least once more before they reached Sweetbrush.

He could hear the others talking and laughing at the campfire.

The Cognac had been an excellent idea, Robin agreed. While they ate, Varney had told stories of London, of growing up in Hampstead, and attending boarding school at Westminster. Listening to him, warmed by the brandy, Robin had thought of his mother, Varina, growing up in St. John's Wood at the same time that Varney was talking about. He was hearing Varney's accent and imagining Varina as the full moon popped into view and the stars appeared. There was a gurgling gulp in the water, sixty feet out, and a splash in the dark. It was a monster fish or maybe an alligator. The river was making noises that sounded like applause. Robin stacked the four tin plates on a big rock to dry and then sat down beside them and opened his butternut coat. He propped the Spencer against the rock.

With a thumbnail he ripped the lining and took out the letter from Sweetbrush.

He could read Laura's handwriting clearly in the moonlight.

Dearest Jerod,

We need you desperately. Only you can set things right at Sweetbrush. I haven't heard from you in so long now that I wondered if you had survived. I feared you had fallen in battle. But I got word from Esther Rubicoff from Houston that her husband Jack heard that you are under care at a hospital in Knoxville where I am writing you this plea for help that also comes with my love.

Our child is ill with chronic lung congestion, and I have also been in the sickbed a time or two of late, but those problems pale beside other problems that threaten this house. The worst of the problems is your father. He has gotten into a terrible temper and is often drunk. He says he intends to murder Pastor Horry Leatherwood, and this time I think he means it. He sits at his desk in his study and broods and toys with his pistol. Woe unto me if I try to lighten his mood with a cheery remark. He never looks at his granddaughter in her crib. When I bring little Anabel, wrapped in a blanket, poor sickly thing, into his company he turns away as if afraid of catching her illness—and him a medical doctor as well as being her own blood. To be truthful, Jerod, I am afraid of your father. I think he hates me, and your daughter.

Your mother needs you.

She is doing her best to keep Sweetbrush running, but you know she is not a business person. About half of the workers are still here. I don't know where the others went, they just wandered off. Varina is not as young as she used to be, though I must say, she is as beautiful as ever. She is maintaining high spirits in the face of terrible adversity, but things are falling apart.

Sweetbrush has lost two cotton crops in a row, one to the Yankee blockade and the second was robbed by bandits who plundered a wagon train of cotton bales that was trying to reach Matamoros. Cotton prices are so high, we can be saved if this newly planted crop makes it to the speculators, but there are many perils.

Last night I heard your father yelling in a drunken rage that he was going to ride into Gethsemane and drag Pastor Horry out of his church and beat him to death in front of the whole town. The doctor and Varina had a screaming fight. He finally passed out. I fear he might do harm to her during one of these episodes. The very idea of him going into town these days is crazy. The Leatherwoods have come out of the woods in force with their Unionist beliefs. Violence is in the air. We must watch ourselves constantly. Varina did go boating on the bayou one day this week, with only her maid Mattie and the houseboy Charles to protect her, but of course Varina has always been the charmed one.

When there is business to do at the bank in Gethsemane, Varina does it. Your father is not to be trusted to go into town. Varina misses you so much, Jerod. I have seen her writing you letters that you may not have received. She expects to be hearing from you or seeing you any day now. She has been saying that for months.

My own mother—I'm talking about Thelma Boatwright, not the woman who is married now to my father—is staging charity affairs for war relief for returning soldiers who need help in becoming once again the men they were before they went to the military. She does shows at the Arts Theater in downtown Houston, usually a concert or a play, followed by a dinner at the Capital Hotel. She is begging Varina to do a reading from

'MacBeth.' I think it would be good for your mother to get out of this house for a while—baby and I would go with her—but she is afraid the roof would fall in if she leaves.

It is bitter cold here today. The sky is gray. You wouldn't think a seed would want to grow in this weather, but soon it will be time for planting. Varina is trying to find more Mexicans to work here in place of the Negroes, who have quit and walked off. Your father says the Negroes and the Mexicans will stick by him because he has given them a school to go to and he treats them as human beings with dignity, but he is being sorely disappointed. Each day when he finds another Negro has gone, it is like a pain in your father's heart. He actually thinks they love him for being nice to them.

Yesterday I brushed the leaves off your favorite bench in the arbor where you like to sit and read. I thought of you and my breath quickened.

Darling Jerod, I pray this letter finds you soon. I don't know how long I can last here.

With all my love, from your faithful wife

Laura

Robin sensed that someone was coming down the slope behind him. He reached for the rifle.

"Hey, I knew you were hiding something," Flora said.

She slid down the bank, her mustard-colored skirt riding up her thighs, her long bare legs reaching down, and her toes touching the water. She had removed her turban and shaken out her hair. Her eyes found the pieces of paper in his hand.

"I was trying to picture that it was a secret war document you were hiding, or maybe a treasure map," she said.

He surprised himself and held the letter out to share it with her as if it were a natural thing to do.

He watched her reading in the moonlight with the river lapping at her feet. Her eyes were green, he knew, but they looked gray in the pale light. He looked at the curve of her hips and at her slender fingers that held the pages from Sweetbrush.

She finished the letter and lifted her eyes.

"So what's the future for me?" he said.

"I'm not telling your future," she said.

"I don't think I want to hear it, anyhow."

He took the letter back, folded it and tucked it into the slit in the lining of his butternut coat.

"What it says in this letter about your daddy wanting to kill the preacher, is this why that soldier and his nephews hate you so much?"

"You really want to know?"

"Tell me."

Robin found that he felt the urge to talk to her. The Cognac had something to do with the feeling, he knew, but this future-telling girl was a simpatica who seemed to be inviting him to unburden himself. He had not yet talked about it with anyone, not even with the nurses at the hospital in Knoxville, where he was kept in restraints when he was brought in.

"Santana hates me because of what happened at Snow Hill last Christmas Eve."

"What did happen?"

"You heard the story Santana told the judge in court this morning."

She nodded and sat on the rock with her hands clasped around her knees, listening to him with her full attention, her eyes on his face.

"Did you believe him?"

"Yes."

"You think I'm a monster?"

"I don't know," she said.

"Varney told me this morning that Tennessee was a backwater affair. But Varney doesn't know anything about Tennessee. There are no backwater affairs in Tennessee. That is a very bitterly divided state. I know Tennessee. My father was born in Knoxville. I have kin in Tennessee. Our bunch went from Texas to Tennessee early in the war, and for much of the time we stayed there and fought there."

He paused.

"Do you have any idea what I'm talking about?" he asked.

"The war."

"In New Orleans, then, you heard about the war?"

"Of course. The Federal soldiers took over in New Orleans three years ago."

"You think I went to Tennessee to fight to defend slavery?"

"You said it was a different reason in court, but I don't know."

Robin was silent for a moment. They could hear Varney's voice from the camp above, and Isabella's laughter.

"We were behind Federal lines during the battle for Nashville last fall, raiding their supply wagons. When we couldn't break through to Nashville, our bunch went east again. We had a debt to settle in the mountains at the town of Snow Hill. Listen, I felt like I knew those people at Snow Hill. I have relatives in the county. When our bunch came through Snow Hill earlier on our way to Nashville, the people were very friendly, fed us, let us have extra corn for our horses, told us they hated the Yankees. I trusted them. Meanwhile they had sent a messenger to the Federals telling them when and where we were coming. They set up an ambush on the road to Nashville. Three of our bunch were killed in the ambush."

Her face was hidden in shadow for a moment.

"So our bunch paid a call on Snow Hill. They were shocked to see us again. The news from Nashville had made them believe we were destroyed. I was sort of out of my head by then. You said you saw it in my palm. Well, I don't know about that. I don't know how you knew it. How did you know it, anyhow?"

"It's in your eyes."

Robin stood up and moved a step closer to her.

"You're a beautiful girl," he said.

"Don't come too close," she said.

"I remember." He smiled. "The derringer."

"Go on with your story."

"How did you know to tell Billy he would be dead by nightfall?"

"I just knew. I don't know how. Please go on with your story."

"Maybe I shouldn't."

"You need to tell me."

Robin picked up a handful of pebbles and began to throw them into the river. He gazed at the moonlight playing in the flowing water.

"Go on and tell me," she said.

"I hadn't realized it was Christmas Eve until we heard them singing carols and hymns as we approached the town. It was hearing the singing, I think, that made my mind snap. These murderous bastards who had betrayed us were gathered on the street in front of the bank lifting their voices to heaven and celebrating the birth of the baby Jesus. It was easy to round them up all at once with only a few trying to fight. Nobody looks for their devils to come out of the snow on Christmas Eve. The people at Snow Hill didn't, and I didn't, either."

They heard Varney and Isabella laughing.

"Our bunch held the town for hours. We took what we wanted in the way of supplies, medicine, food for our horses. I looked them over, all the people of Snow Hill, these murderers standing in the snow singing Christmas carols in front of a painted display of the manger and the Mother and the holy child Jesus. I couldn't imagine a worse blasphemy. Each hour it was getting closer to Christmas. I thought about the three of our bunch these Snow Hill people had caused to be dead this Christmas, three brave men I had grown to love. I lost my head. I pulled three Snow Hill men out of the crowd. I chose the banker, the mayor, and the judge, the leading hypocrites. I put ropes around their necks and stood them on sawhorses under a big tree limb. I didn't even ask the banker to open the vault. Our bunch just hauled it out on wheels so we could have the pleasure of blowing it open. I told the women to take their children home. I cleared the men away so that it was just our bunch out there in the open street in front of the bank. It was dark and cold, the snow was falling, and the moon was patchy and not as bright as it is tonight."

He looked at the girl to be sure she wasn't turning away.

"So I had the banker, the mayor, and the judge with ropes around their necks. They began to beg for their lives. For the sake of God, they said, it's Christmas Eve. I looked at them and saw three devils. They were three ugly, disgusting devils. Their eyes were huge. Their mouths gaped. Evil stink came from them. I gave the signal. Our bunch kicked out the sawhorses. We hanged the devils."

Robin patted his pockets, the old habit of looking for tobacco, though he'd had no tobacco in weeks. He remembered the plug Varney had taken off the dead soldier—was that only this morning? But Varney had left everything back at Burroughs' Cove.

"We hanged them," he said.

"You hanged them," she said.

"I hanged them."

"You need a priest," she said.

"A priest?"

"If you have bad guilt, it's good to tell the priest."

"Where would I find a priest?"

"Don't you have a church?" she said.

"There's only one church in the town where I'm going, and my family does not attend it."

"What do you expect me to do?"

"Just listen to me."

She nodded.

"So I gave the signal, and three men were hanged in cold blood, guilty of being the leaders of a town of Judases. That's the way I saw it. Those three paid for the deaths of three of our bunch. It may not be perfect justice, as Judge Dingus would say, but it made sense to me. I mean, what the hell—are you going to tell a priest you murdered a soldier this morning?"

"It wasn't murder," she said.

"It's all murder," he said.

"I'm going to confess to a priest when we get to Mexico," she said.

"We?"

"The romancer and I."

"Oh yeah. Varney."

"You haven't told me why the Yankee captain hates you for Christmas Eve."

Robin glanced at the Spencer rifle.

"Our bunch was milling around in the street at Snow Hill, twenty-eight of us, showing very poor discipline, very unusual for us. We had blown open the vault and found nothing much. The three devils were hanging from the tree. The manger scene in front of the bank was knocked down by the explosion. Our bunch was going in and out of houses, loading up on sweets. Pies, cakes, cookies, cobblers, candy. Most of the town people had gathered in the little church and were singing hymns and Christmas carols again. They were afraid I was going to decide to kill all of them. The mothers hugged their children. The men tried to stand up straight and look brave. Our bunch was looting their houses but taking only their sweets and a few hams. I think the singing got to us and made us careless. Our bunch was stuffing sweets into our saddlebags and laughing and singing and saying merry Christmas and joshing with each other and then—"

Robin bent down and dipped his hands into the river and washed them.

"—where there had been twenty-eight of us, there suddenly were only seventeen. I didn't hear the shots until I saw us falling. Then I heard a volley and another volley and six more of us fell. Our horses were shot full of holes, and screaming and falling. We ran for cover against the buildings. I was seeing devils everywhere. They were real devils, wearing Federal uniforms, coming through the snow, firing Spencer rifles, shooting us down."

Robin flicked his hands in the air, drying them.

"Men were fighting all up and down the street, rolling in the snow, screaming, cursing. I killed a Federal up close with my pistol, a big man, taller than me. He was trying to slice me with his saber. He tumbled, and I got shot in the thigh. The blow knocked me down. I fell on my face in the snow.

"When I looked up, a Federal was standing over me with his pistol aimed down at my heart. He could have finished me easily. He reached up and took off his hat. He wanted to be sure I could see his face. He grinned at me. He said, 'It's me—Santana Leatherwood.'

"I said, 'Don't shoot.'

"He said, 'Are you surrendering?'

"I said, 'Yes.'

"He said, 'Let me hear you say it.'

"I said, 'I surrender.'

"He kept his pistol aimed at me, and he had a big smile on his face, but he turned his head to call out to someone, and when he did I grabbed up the saber the dead Federal had dropped. I lunged and drove the saber through the opening of his overcoat. It went in to the hilt. He got a peculiar look—how could this have happened to me?

"Five of our bunch escaped Snow Hill. We rode back toward Knoxville, where I have kin. The other four warned me I was raving. They didn't know if I had gone crazy, or if I was delirious from my wound being infected. I had painted my face blue, like I was some blood-mad Celt of old. The others jumped me one morning. They said I'd had enough. For sure they'd had enough of me. They tied and gagged me and delivered me to the hospital in Knoxville. Thank God they did. I was out of my head. I don't remember much of what I did for a while after Snow Hill. But my mind started clearing up. Then a couple of weeks ago came the letter that you read just now."

Robin extended a hand to help her up.

"Go back up to the campfire?" he asked.

"I think I'll sit here for a while longer, hey," she said.

He withdrew his hand. He tapped the four tin plates together.

"Why didn't the Yankee captain tell the judge what you did to him?" she asked.

"He's embarrassed about it. I made a fool out of him."

"You lied to him," she said.

"Yes."

"Are you ashamed?"

"I'm alive," Robin said.

"He'll come to your home looking for you."

"I know."

"You don't need me to tell your future," she said. "You're telling it to me now."

Robin lifted one foot and planted it higher on the bank, returning to the campfire. He turned and looked back at Flora as she waded into the river up to her knees. She felt the cool water soaking up her anxieties and cleansing them away.

"Is your derringer loaded?" he said.

"Hey, of course it is."

"Would you shoot me if I came down there and kissed you?"

"What do you think?"

"I think you might." He laughed and hauled himself up on the bank with the four tin plates and the Spencer rifle. Flora was standing in the river, holding her skirt above her knees, in the moonlight. Looking at her made him smile. Or maybe it was the Cognac. He hadn't figured her for a Catholic. "A priest, huh? Maybe you can find me one."

She watched his hips as he walked up toward the campfire where the romancer and Isabella were laying out their bedrolls.

Twenty-two

AN HOUR BEFORE DAWN Isabella and Flora packed the bedrolls while Varney and Robin watered and saddled the horses. Custer had been carrying a nosebag and oats for Athena, and a small bag of sugar. The romancer fed his horse Athena the rest of the oats and scratched her ears and crooned to her.

Robin glanced at Varney's bruised and swollen face.

"Your nose doesn't look too bad," Robin said.

"Anyhow, I can see around it today," said Varney.

"That was a courageous act of yours yesterday, swimming upriver and stealing their horses. I'm starting to believe you really might have been a general in India."

Varney laughed. "It's mostly all documented, my son."

"How can you stand going barefoot?"

"The tender bits are the insides of my thighs." Varney gingerly patted his thighs through the thin cotton trousers. "I wasn't toughened up for all this riding. But being back on Athena makes pain a pleasure."

"You say that horse is twenty-two years old?" said Robin.

"No, I didn't say that exactly."

"She looks a good, healthy, prime seven years old to me," said Robin.

"I may have said she is ageless."

Varney tightened the cinch and patted Athena on the hip.

"What is that brand? What does V stand for?" Robin asked.

"There is a story about Athena that she'd had many riders before me, and will have many after me. Nobody knows who put the V on her."

"You honestly believe this is your horse?"

"This is my horse without a doubt."

"Maybe this is your old horse's granddaughter."

Varney shook his head and went to fetch his bedroll. Robin looked at Athena's teeth. He lifted her lip and searched for grooves on her incisors. A horse aged ten years or more would have grooves reaching from gums to the tips of the teeth. By age twenty the grooves would be gone again. Athena's incisors were smooth, with no grooves or dental cups. Her gums were pink and tight on the teeth. It's just not possible, Robin thought. His fingers touched Custer's saddle. He thought of the boyish-looking man with the clean, starched blouse pulling on his gloves in the courtroom yesterday morning, and of the man he saw through the sights of his Spencer rifle later in the afternoon. He had hit Custer in the hip on purpose. He didn't want to kill him. He wondered if he had.

"How long before the army comes looking for you at your family estate?" Varney returned with two bedrolls and Isabella's suitcase.

"I don't know. They're not organized yet to handle the chaos. It might take a week."

"That long? But you shot Custer."

"Maybe less then, I don't know. I'm sure Santana Leatherwood will come soon. You should bypass Sweetbrush and head for Mexico on your horse. You're taking the girl with you to Mexico?"

"The girl? Flora?"

"Yeah, that girl."

"I would never bypass Sweetbrush, Captain," Varney said. "At last I get a chance to meet Varina Hotchkiss. I've waited half my life for this."

They rode through the morning, keeping to the river road. The air turned sultry, and humidity rose from the river in waves. Mosquitoes buzzed them. The southern sky began bleeding purple into the clouds. Lightning lit the horizon. They heard a distant rumble. Robin felt a gust of cool air on his face. He was sweating but a chill ran through his skin. He could feel what was coming. A thunderstorm was blowing in from the Gulf of Mexico.

"I see the ominous clouds," Isabella said. "My God, the rains in this place are fierce. You can go for months with no rain at all, and then suddenly you get a whole year's worth. It's like your monsoons in India, eh, Edmund?"

"This is the monsoon season over there," said Varney.

Isabella made a quiet gesture toward Robin and Flora, who were riding in front. Flora was sitting on two bedrolls behind the saddle with her hands on Robin's hips. Isabella raised an eyebrow and looked at Varney.

"Quite a peculiar couple," she whispered.

Varney recalled the expression on Robin's face when Robin had spoken of Flora going to Mexico with the writer: a flash of disapproval, as if it could possibly matter. Varney looked at Flora, swaying in the saddle, her skirt pulled up around her thighs, her buttocks clutched among the bedrolls, her black hair loose and frizzy. He thought of Aliyah. His mind sailed to a summer night in Lahore. He saw Aliyah stepping out of the bath. He saw her lying on the silk cushions. He realized Isabella was looking at him and expecting him to respond to whatever she had said. His mind flew back from Lahore, and his mouth made a grimace that caused Isabella to wonder if he was in pain.

"Can you keep going, Edmund?" she asked.

"Always to excess, dear lady," he said.

On the road they encountered two men pulling a wagon that had been designed for horses or mules. One man clutched each of the two long staves from which leather harness dangled. The wagon was heaped with a load that was covered by canvas. The two men wore Mexican sombreros and business suits that were splashed with mud. They were both in their forties, European, overweight, had three-day beards, and looked exhausted.

"How do you do? My name is Antoine and this is my partner Humphrey," said the taller of the two, stepping out from the traces and offering his hand.

Robin glanced down at the hand. "Your wagon is blocking our way," Robin said.

Antoine dared not let his gaze linger on any of the riders, though it was hard to look away.

"I'm sorry. Our horse died about thirty miles back down the road. Humphrey and I are on our way to Austin to open a restaurant and curio shop."

"Where have you come from?" asked Robin.

"Houston."

"Is it raining there?"

"Buckets."

Humphrey leaned back against the wagon, sweating and wiping his face with a towel.

"Torrents," Humphrey said.

"Buckets is sufficiently descriptive," said Antoine.

"Now you are editing me?" Humphrey said.

"Have it your own way then. It is raining torrents."

"Do you gentlemen know a hotel man in Houston named Henri Bowprie?" Flora asked.

"What hotel is he with?" said Antoine.

"His own. He would be owning the hotel."

"A Frenchman? Big fellow? Talks a lot with a smooth line of gab?" Antoine said.

"That sounds like him." Flora was excited.

"I believe he used to come into our restaurant two years ago. For months he came in nearly every evening, always talking about opening a hotel." Antoine was suddenly afraid he might have said too much. "Why? Is he a friend of yours?"

"Henri Bowprie is my father."

"Oh. Well, in that case, I actually don't know him at all," said Antoine.

"I suggest you tell her what you know about her father," Robin said.

"We knew a big Frenchman named Henri about three years ago when we owned Chez Rouge in Houston," said Humphrey. "He was a regular customer for a while, entertained guests, drank good wine, was drumming up money to build a new hotel on Main Street. Mind you, the war had started. There was no financing for new hotels.

Eventually Henri quit coming around. I heard he owed money to a smuggler from Galveston. Pardon me. I'm about to faint with fatigue."

Humphrey drank from a canteen.

"What happened to him? Where did he go?" asked Flora.

Antoine looked sadly at their horseless wagon.

"Who knows? We never saw him again. There's been so much coming and going and disappearing." Antoine flinched at the sound of thunder far off. "The rain is going to catch us. I thought it might go around, but, no, it's coming our way."

"If you will pardon us, we had best be moving on down the road," Humphrey said.

"What are you smuggling?" asked Varney. "Not shoes, by any chance?"

"This is restaurant equipment. Pots and pans, knives and forks, bowls and plates, whisks and—"

"Why would you be using this back road, hey?" Flora asked. "I came up on the main road a few days ago. It's much faster."

"We were hoping to avoid being stopped by robbers," said Antoine.

"Once again we are tricked by fate," Humphrey said.

"Oh, for heaven's sake, let these poor men get on their way," said Isabella, shouldering to the front on her Kentucky mare, the brown leather suitcase with silver buckles strapped atop a bedroll behind her saddle.

"I was wondering what size boots these fellows wear," Varney said.

"You might want trousers and a jacket, too," said Robin.

Flora lightly dug in her heels and the horse carried her and Robin past the two restaurant entrepreneurs, who ducked back against their wagon.

"If you see Henri Bowprie in Austin, tell him his daughter is looking for him," Flora said.

Isabella tugged at Varney's sleeve.

"Come on, Edmund. We'll soon be at Sweetbrush. I'm sure Dr. Robin will spare you some clothing. No need to punish these men any further," said Isabella.

Varney felt Athena gather herself and start moving forward, as if she had decided she agreed with Isabella. He looked back over his shoulder. Humphrey had returned into the traces of their wagon, and Antoine was pushing from the rear, struggling toward Austin.

It was another hour before the rain began.

First came one big cold drop that hit with a splat. When Robin was living in the field his raiders carried their blankets and kit rolled in waterproof tarpaulins that served as shelter from rain and wind and made a dry place to sleep on wet ground. But Custer's troopers had left their camp in Austin without a thought that the weather might change. When the rain reached them, the travelers on army horses would have no relief.

Minutes after the big drops began, the air turned cold. The sky faded to dark purple. The surface of the river became calm. The current seemed to be trying to reverse itself. A great blue heron stood on the bank looking at the approaching weather. Tiny circles began spreading on the water as the rain fell harder. A big bass leaped and fell back with a whack. The riders felt the breeze rising. With Varney in the lead on Athena, the riders and horses bowed their necks and headed into the storm.

They heard the wind howling as it struck them with sheets of rain that blew sideways. They felt suffocated. The sky turned black as night. Thunder boomed and flashes of lightning crashed around them. Hailstones the size of marbles pelted them. They unrolled the blankets from their bedrolls and used them to fend off the hail. The blankets became sodden and heavy. The road turned into a swamp that was dotted by balls of ice. The procession trudged forward. The riders could barely see the ears of their horses.

Robin felt the girl's arms clutching his waist to keep her from sliding out of the saddle in the pounding rain. They had fought in rain like this at Chickamauga in '63, but Robin thought the Feds wouldn't be out in this kind of weather merely for a chase.

There was nowhere to turn for shelter. Lightning crashed in the tops of the pines. The storm was growing stronger and seemed to be settling in for a long stay. A storm could linger over one area for days. Varney and Athena had endured monsoons in India, but never a storm more powerful than this.

Athena halted. Something was in the road ahead of them. Varney peered out from the blanket that was plastered around his head by the rain.

He could make out the shape of a donkey standing in a puddle in the road. Canvas saddlebags hung on the donkey's sides. Varney saw a heap of clothes lying in the mud beside the donkey. There was a sharp blam, and lightning lit up the scene. The heap of clothes began moving. An arm reached out. A ghostly face with big eyes stared from the hood of a raincoat.

"Help me." A woman's voice shouted through the hammering of the rain. "I'm liable to drown here."

Varney slid down off Athena and sloshed to her.

"My hip," the woman said. "I fell."

Varney supposed her to be about the same age as his mother, early seventies.

"Anything broken?" Varney said.

"I don't know."

"Let's see if we can get you on your feet," Varney said.

"I was nearly home, too, damn it," she said.

He grasped her under the armpits and lifted. She managed to stand by leaning against Varney. The other riders edged closer, ducking their heads against the smashing of the rain.

"You're a miserable looking bunch," the woman shouted.

"Truly spoken," yelled Varney.

He helped her toward the donkey, but she pulled away.

"I don't ride this beast," she shouted. "I walk and he totes. That's our bargain."

"You'll be all right now," said Varney.

"I'm not sure I can walk on this hip. Help me home," she said.

"Let's be moving," shouted Robin. The rain had battered his hat brim down all the way around his head.

"She needs our help," Varney shouted.

It crossed Varney's mind that the last time he stopped to help a stranger on the road was Christmas Eve in Spain when bandits had leaped out from behind the rocks and stolen his money and beaten him almost to death.

"We can't help her," said Robin.

"We can't leave her here," Varney yelled.

"Bless your heart," said the woman. "It's only a hundred yards behind you."

"What is?" Varney asked.

"My home."

Isabella moved to the front on her Kentucky horse, squeezing past Robin and Flora.

"What does she say?" said Isabella.

"Her home is a hundred yards back down the road."

"Impossible. There's no home along here," Isabella said.

Varney wrapped his arms around the woman's waist and lifted her into the saddle on Athena. He grabbed the donkey's rope.

"I'll take her home," shouted Varney. "Go on ahead. I'll catch up to you."

Varney boosted himself onto Athena behind the woman.

"I said go on ahead. I'll catch up to you," he yelled.

With his arms around the woman's middle, Varney turned Athena around and headed back the direction they had come. The others watched him go past. Athena plodded through the pounding rain. Varney turned and saw the others were following him. The woman squeezed his hands to get his attention.

She shouted into his ear, "The big cypress tree with the forked trunk. Turn in there."

He could see the tree but no sign of a path or trail in the darkness of the storm.

"Here," she shouted. "Turn in here."

"Where?"

"At the cypress tree, damn it. Turn in now."

Athena took the lead and walked off the road into the brush beside the tree. The brush parted. Varney could see a trail of muddy puddles leading through the forest. "Another fifty yards," shouted the woman. He had dropped the rope but the donkey followed closely. The other riders entered the path behind them. Branches scraped their faces. Water poured down through the tree limbs.

"Stop here," the woman shouted. She dug into the clothing beneath her raincoat and produced a large key. "Take this. Open the door. Go on."

"What door?" asked Varney.

"It's right in front of you," she said.

He looked where she pointed and he saw it. He would have taken it to be a section of a tree that had been scorched by lightning. It stood against what in the rain Varney had thought was a thicket, but now saw was a mound, a rising of earth that became a hill. Varney slithered down from Athena and splashed to the tree. He couldn't recognize it as a door, but he saw the keyhole at waist height concealed by a wooden shingle that had drooped a couple of inches from the beating of the rain and wind and hail, enough that the keyhole was exposed.

Varney inserted the key and turned the lock. He pushed on the shingle. The door opened inward. The door was taller than his head. He stepped down into the dim space. Inside, the fury of the storm was muffled. The air had a dank odor from the rain but was fresh and cool. Varney could see inside about twenty feet before it became too dark. He could tell it was a large room, probably more than one room. He looked at the walls and saw a drapery of glittering crystals. He realized he was standing inside a limestone cavern.

He felt Athena's nose nudging his back. She wanted in out of the rain.

Twenty-three

SHE SAID HER NAME WAS ADA PLIMPTON.

"To be honest, I wouldn't have invited you folks in out of the rain if I had known one of you is Isabella Bushkin," she said.

She was hobbling around the interior of the cavern lighting oil lamps. Athena and the two other horses and Ada's donkey were being stabled by Varney, Robin and Flora in an adjoining wing of the cavern with a trough of corn to eat and with straw to lie down on. An underground stream flowed through the cavern near the horses. In the middle of the large room, on a Persian carpet, there was a cherry wood dining table that had known a stately home. A round tin tub three feet deep and six feet across stood against a white limestone wall that was decorated by Indian pictographs of hunters and bears. Another wall was a mosaic of shellfish fossils. In an alcove the size of a box car were half a dozen single beds with mattresses on iron frames. A tall wardrobe closet with a mirrored door sat on four curled feet beside the entrance to the sleeping alcove.

Isabella was sitting on her suitcase, soaked and exhausted, looking around the cavern at the furnishings—a potbellied stove, a settee, several chairs from different periods and tastes, two couches, an armoire painted rose-pink, a bookcase full of books, a kitchen cabinet with shelves of pots and pans.

"Do I know you?" Isabella asked.

"I saw you at a political rally in Galveston several years ago. Then about a year ago I saw you at another political rally in Bastrop. I went to Bastrop to hear for myself that you and your husband haven't learned a damn thing from this war you people brought on."

Ada Plimpton twisted the handle of a faucet that protruded from a pipe that ran down the limestone wall from the ceiling. Water began gushing into the tub.

"I have a tank up above that collects and holds water from a spring in the side of the hill. A very fine engineer built it for me when he was staying here in the early days before the vigilantes grabbed him and sent him off to die. He vented the stove for me, too. He got shot in Pennsylvania, of all the damn places for a Texas man to go to find death."

Ada limped away from the tub and left the water running. One drop fell from the darkness above and clung to her forehead. The roar of the storm was faint inside the cavern. Ada limped toward the pink armoire. She was a small woman, gray and thin. She hung her raincoat on a hook. She was wearing a blue velvet dress. "Damn, I am wet. It feels like the whole world must be all wet."

"How's that hip?" asked Varney, coming in from the horses.

"Let's take a look," she said.

Ada began unbuttoning the dress.

"I wear this dress when I go to the store eight miles from here to buy supplies. The fellow who owns the store says I look good in this color. I remind him of someone he used to love."

Ada undid the last button and stepped out of the dress and tossed it aside.

"See there?" she said, pointing to the blue and purple welt on her naked left hip. She looked at Varney. "See that bruise? My butt looks as bad as your face."

Ada laughed. Naked, she padded back to the tub and turned off the flow of water from the faucet. The tub was full.

"Who's been beating on you, anyhow, Mister—what did you say your name was? Forney?"

"Edmund Varney."

Robin and Flora entered from the area of the cavern where they had been tending to the horses. They saw the nude Ada standing beside the tub.

191

"You look like four drowned rats," Ada said. "You can catch pneumonia if you want to, but I am going to soak in this spring water which is warm and full of minerals and has healed cripples. After a soak, I'll build a fire and dry my clothes and anybody else's clothes that wants me to."

"Let's build the fire now," said Robin.

"Be sure to open the flue when you do," Ada said.

She climbed into the tub and sank into the water with a contented sigh. She ducked her head under and came up combing her hair back with her fingers.

"What are you talking about? I didn't have anything to do with starting this war. I hate this war," Isabella said.

"So you say now your side has lost," said Ada.

Ada raised an elbow to the rim of the tub and peered over it at Varney.

"That wardrobe and a couple of trunks are full of clothes from men who won't need them any more. You should find a decent fit."

"It's very kind of you," Varney said.

He peeled the Belgian army tunic off of his body. Robin was packing the stove with wood and kindling. Isabella stood up abruptly. She found herself growing angry. All the drastic things that had happened to her since Bushkin left that document on her lunch plate yesterday, she had borne with the humor and dignity she had learned from being a beautiful woman with a long nose. But life had finally sent this crone to nag her into losing her temper. Isabella undid the silver buckles and opened her suitcase. She scraped aside the oilskin-wrapped packets of papers. Her hands found the half bottle of Cognac. She paused. She rolled the bottle aside and dug further into the suitcase and came up with a folded piece of white silk.

Isabella flapped the silk and held up a peignoir that she had bought in Houston last Christmas season. An entire shipload of goods from Paris had arrived by way of Mexico. She had been saving the lingerie for a special occasion that she decided had arrived.

"Hey, that's lovely," said Flora. Her mother had favored such lingerie. Mama Marie would lie around the apartment in her scanties on hot afternoons when the future-telling parlor was closed for siesta.

"It's something dry to slip into," Isabella said.

Isabella draped the lingerie atop the suitcase. She unbuttoned her blouse and took it off. A crinkled piece of something fell from her bosom onto the cavern floor. She picked it up. It was the document from Bushkin, now a sodden unreadable wad. Robin was tinkering with the stove and pretending not to look at her. Varney and Flora were staring at Isabella's breasts.

"Put this in the fire for me, please, Captain," she said. She tossed the wad of paper to Robin.

Isabella sat down on the suitcase and struggled to pull off her wet boots.

"Allow me," said Varney.

Isabella leaned back and lifted her legs. Varney took hold of her right ankle.

"Rule of the house," Ada said. "No sex indoors. It's an absolute rule. I can't allow it broken. We never would have lasted if I let sex go on in here."

"Who are you? What is this place?" said Isabella. Boots off, she stood up and stepped out of her skirt. She peeled off her underpants and lobbed them onto the pile beside the suitcase. She touched a hand into the water of the tub. She nodded. "This is a very nice temperature."

"Mother nature heats it for me," Ada said.

Isabella got into the tub and sat down.

"You have no right to blame this war on me," Isabella said.

"A year ago in Bastrop your husband made a speech claiming the Confederacy was just about to win the war, if only Texas could round up more troops to throw into battle," said Ada.

A year ago, Robin thought, was the time of the fights at the Wilderness, Spotsylvania and Cold Harbor. Bodies had stacked up high at those places. Wave after wave of men had rushed full face into double charges of nails and scrap iron that exploded into them from cannons at point-blank range. There were rumors that the will of the North had been broken by so much bloodshed, and a truce was in the works.

Robin lit a flame in the tinder. Where had Santana gone, he wondered? Custer was either dead or badly wounded. Most likely,

Santana had taken Custer back to Austin, which would mean more time for Robin at Sweetbrush. But Santana may have gone home to his brother with Billy's body. Robin put the wad Isabella had tossed him into the fire and closed the stove lid. He glanced at the two women in the tub.

"That was the senator speaking, not me," Isabella said.

"You stood beside him and smiled and carried on like it was the truth he was saying," said Ada.

"So answer my question. What kind of place is this?" Isabella asked.

"You could call it a boarding house for brush men," said Ada. "That's why I wouldn't have invited you in here if I had recognized you in the storm. I'm trusting you not to betray me to the vigilantes."

"The war is over," Isabella said.

"Don't fool yourself," said Ada. "Vigilantes are never gone for good."

"Is there room in the tub for one more?" Flora asked.

"For you there is, child," said Ada.

Flora took off her blue blouse and dropped it beside Isabella's wet clothes. She pulled down her hemp skirt. Robin and Varney stared. Her body was smoothly muscled. Flora climbed into the tub and sank below the water. Her head emerged, black hair dripping. She smiled. "Hey, this is heaven."

Ada sat up and frowned at Varney, who had begun undoing the belt at the waist of his trousers.

"Keep your pants on, Varney," Ada said.

"I'm just going to have a soak," he said.

"Later," said Ada. "You and the soldier can have a soak when the women are done with it. I don't allow mixed bathing in here. Putting men and women together in warm water naked is the wrong thing to do in a place like this."

Ada leaned her neck against the rim of the tub.

"There's no need for you to stand there and gape at us, Varney," she said. "You must have seen nude women before. Why don't you go read a book or something? No, why don't you look through those trunks and the wardrobe and find yourself some clean garments. You go ahead and start drying clothes, soldier. You have no reason to keep looking over here. There are blankets on the beds in the bunk room. You men get out of your wet clothes and wrap yourself in blankets. I don't allow naked men parading through here."

Varney grinned and went to find the trunks. This old woman could command a regiment.

Ada turned to Isabella.

"After your husband's speech in Bastrop the vigilantes got inspired to search the forest again and caught two of my boarders and hanged them, so what I am saying to you is from my heart," Ada said.

"I don't understand," said Flora. "What is a brushman?"

"A brushman is a draft dodger," Isabella said.

"In some eyes, child, a brushman is a patriot," said Ada.

"What do you mean by draft?" Flora asked.

"A collection of fools calling themselves my government passed a law that requires all Texas men between the ages of eighteen and thirty-six to go to war and die to defend a few Texas men's rights to make slaves out of human beings," said Ada. "How about you, soldier? Did they draft you into the military?"

Robin was halfway to the bunk room. He had taken off his butternut coat and was looking for a stout hanger for it. He stopped and looked back at Ada.

"I volunteered," he said. "I would have been ashamed not to."

"Your neighbors would have shamed you?" Ada said.

"My family owns slaves," said Robin.

"So you fought for the cause?" Ada said.

"I fought for my family," said Robin.

The three women watched Robin walk into the bunk room, where they could see Varney, bare-chested, opening the lid of a steamer trunk.

"I have to admire a man who knows what he believes in fighting for and goes and fights for it," Ada said. "I hate a man who loves war and promotes war but won't go to war himself. Like these politicians who tell the public that one Texan can whip ten Yankees but are scared to go to the front themselves to find out."

"Senator Bushkin never said any such thing," said Isabella.

"I heard two of his speeches in person and read about some others. Senator Bushkin thinks he's bomb-proof," Ada said.

"Not any more he doesn't. He has run off to Mexico," said Isabella.

"I'm not surprised. I'm sorry for you, I think. You should have known he would leave you." Ada's attitude softened. Flora scooped both hands into the water and poured it onto her face, tasting the salty minerals. "Are you a slave, child? Do you belong to one of these people?"

"I am born free."

"What do you mean I should have known he would leave me?" Isabella said.

"Men don't last," said Ada.

"Surely some of them do," Isabella said.

"Some of the bad ones hang around too long, but all the good men go away or die," said Ada.

"Sounds like men have run out on you, too, hey?" Flora said.

"Child, I've had my heart broken deeply," said Ada.

"My mother used to call me 'child.' You talk like her." Flora cocked her head and looked closely at Ada, wondering if this body could be the receptacle into which Mama Marie's spirit had flown. "But you don't sound like her or look anything like her."

"This old bag of bones ain't really me," Ada cackled. "I don't look in the mirror any more because the mirror doesn't recognize me. I'm a middle aged beauty. I don't know who that old woman is who wears my blue dress."

"How do you happen to be running a boarding house for draft dodgers, or patriots, or whatever you want to call them?" asked Isabella.

"Anton Kobler," Ada said.

"Pardon me?" said Isabella. She lay back in the tub, feeling warm and drowsy. The mineral water was improving her humor. "Is that a person, or an east Texas dessert?"

"Anton was both," Ada said.

"He was your lover," said Flora.

"You must be a mind reader, child," Ada said.

Flora laughed.

"I guess it shows on my face when I think about Anton," said Ada. She glanced at Isabella. "You look skeptical. Do you think I'm too far along in age to have a lover?"

"Heavens no, not me," said Isabella.

"I'll tell you something you may not yet have realized," Ada said. "When you turn loose the vigilantes, you can't know where and when they're going to stop. It might be your own head in the basket before long. Just look at Bushkin now—fleeing for his life. He was a fat cat. Now he is a running dog."

"What are you picking on Bushkin for? He was marching in the parade, but he wasn't at the front of it. Bushkin hated vigilantes. He was opposed to slavery in his own way. He was, all in all, a pretty good man, or I thought so until yesterday," said Isabella. "As a senator, he was representing the view of his constituents. In that speech that you refer to, he was telling the voters what they wanted to hear."

"You should have made him tell them the truth," Ada said. "Slavery is evil. War is bad. In a long fight thirty Yankees are going to whip ten Texans. Worst of all, idiotic vigilantes get encouraged by stupid speeches from men like your husband."

"Did the vigilantes hang Anton Kobler?" asked Flora.

"I don't know if you have ever been in love," Ada said. "I don't mean love somebody. I mean totally in love."

Isabella smiled and nodded. She remembered the incredible breathless feeling when she was introduced to Bushkin at a ball in Barcelona. "Indeed," she said.

"No, but I believe in it," said Flora.

"I came to Texas from Baltimore with my husband in the first year of the republic—that would have been twenty-eight years ago, child," Ada said. "My husband, Randolph, and I came to Texas for the same reason most everybody did—land. It was too crowded in Baltimore. Lord knows what a horror Baltimore must be by now today, with so many people. Randolph's trade was doctoring animals. Randolph was peculiar in the head, but his heart was pure and sweet. He could lay his hands on a sick animal and the creature would look at him and recognize that Randolph really wanted to help. That feeling had a powerful effect on the cure, I am sure."

Ada stood up and waded to the faucet and released more water into the tub. They could faintly hear the thunder and the blasting of the rain outside. One of the cavalry horses nickered.

"We rented an adobe house on Military Plaza in San Antonio, and Randolph hung out his shingle." Ada shut off the faucet and sat down in the tub again. Isabella closed her eyes and listened. She wondered where Bushkin might be at this minute. "You would be surprised how many sick animals were in San Antonio when we got there. Randolph made his reputation in town right away when he cured cattle of the screwworm. The screwworm ordinarily kills a beast, but Randolph dug the worms and eggs out with a pen knife and plastered the wounds with hot tar, and it worked."

Isabella opened her eyes.

"You're Dr. Plimpton's wife?" Isabella said.

"You know Randolph?"

"I've heard of him. What on earth are you doing helping draft dodgers?"

"Patriots," said Ada.

"Dr. Plimpton is a Unionist?"

"Randolph doesn't know there's a war. He's got the dementia. But if he did know, he would be a Union man, I am sure."

"But he's still practicing. I heard him mentioned only recently."

"He's a good animal doctor. That's the purpose of his life. I left him ten years ago. He doesn't remember I'm gone, bless him. He knew it when I first left him, though, and it hurt him, that sweet man. He wouldn't divorce me. I asked him. I know his sensitive feelings hurt when people found out about me and Anton Kobler, but he wouldn't divorce me. I tried to explain it to him without hurting him worse, but you can't really do that. I was in the grip of love's power. I wanted Anton Kobler."

"Who is he? Anybody I would have heard of?" asked Isabella.

"I told you his name. Anton Kobler."

"I mean, what does he do? San Antonio is a large city. What sort of business is Kobler in?"

"He's the son in Kobler & Son. They make buggies. It was fifteen years ago when Anton came to our office to hire my husband. The Kobler family raises coach horses. They raise goats. They raise homing pigeons. That was Anton's area of fascination, the homing pigeons. Two of his prize fantails had taken sick. He brought them to our office in a bamboo cage. The birds were lying on the floor of the cage. I thought they were kaput. I told Anton that my husband wasn't Jesus who could raise the dead. Then Anton turned his big brown moist eyes on me, and I was never again the same person. The power of love overwhelmed me. I was shocked. I thought I had been in love before, but when I met Anton I realized I had never been in love until the moment he looked at me."

"He was younger than you, hey?" Flora said.

"Another good guess, child," Ada said. "He was nineteen years old. I was fifty-seven. Randolph cured Anton's birds. They were constipated. Who would ever guess a pigeon could be constipated? Randolph figured it out immediately. He smelled their breath. He stuck his finger up their butts. Well, you don't need to hear all the details. By the time those birds got regular again, I was totally in love with Anton and he with me. Many people believe we have lived other lives before this one, and will live other lives after this one. I think this must be so. I think we remember pieces from other lives that we couldn't know otherwise. Our bodies may cross paths with someone we have loved in another life, and our souls recognize each other. I have racked my brain and prayed to heaven for an explanation of how Anton and I, as unlikely a couple as you can picture, would have fallen in love with each other, and I believe this is the answer. Anton and I are soul mates—the rest of this world be damned."

"But Anton is dead," said Flora.

"No, child, he's not dead."

"I think he is," Flora said.

"Go on," said Isabella. "You meet this beautiful young man and fall in love and then what?"

"We hid it for five years. We would meet now and then when my husband was out on a call. San Antonio is not as big as you may think it is when it comes to hiding a love affair in the Anglo community. There were suspicions, but we got by with it because nobody could believe their eyes. Eventually we were exposed by Anton's mother, who walked in on us one afternoon in the stable with the coach horses. That was embarrassing, let me tell you. The community was outraged. Poor Randolph was just beginning to get the dementia, but he had enough sense to know I had been unfaithful to him. Anton and I left San Antonio in a Kobler buggy. We settled on a farm outside the town of Smithville. It was a piece of land that had been deeded to Randolph to settle a debt. Randolph gave it to me when I left him. It was only forty acres, but it had a decent house on it, and Anton and I weren't much interested in farming, anyway.

"People would give us curious looks when we went into Smithville to buy supplies, and I heard that the Baptist preacher was searching to find what it says in the Bible about a young man and an older woman—the answer is the Bible says it is all right, as long as she's not his mother or his sister." Ada cackled. "Anton and I were happy. We raised beautiful homing pigeons. Those are amazing birds. We would ship them down to the border and they'd be released, and Anton and I would watch the sky at our place and here the birds would come, flying right back to our home. It gave me a warm, happy feeling in my heart to see those birds returning to us from so far away.

"One morning the recruiter came to our house and demanded that Anton join the army and go fight against the United States government. Anton refused. Some of our neighbors already despised and feared us for being odd. Now they began to show it. They hung a sign on our gate that said TRAITORS. They shot two of our dogs. They poisoned our milk cow. When we went to the store in Smithville for groceries and feed, you would have thought we had red spots all over us. Anton was far from the only man in our county who refused to enlist. But we were newcomers, strangers, and odd. You ever feel hated? It knocks the wind out of you. You must know what I mean, Mrs. Bushkin, being the wife of a politician."

"I know the feeling," Isabella said.

"Then the draft law was passed. Anton was at the top of the list in our county. In those early days of the war there was a provision that if you owned twenty slaves you were exempt from the draft, or you could hire somebody for $500 to go to war in your place. Anton didn't own any slaves, of course—the Koblers, being Germans, didn't take to the idea of slavery. Anton's father gave him money to hire substitutes several times over. By this time, though, Anton and I were a scandal. Nobody in our county would touch Anton's money. So Anton went to the brush.

"Oh my, how the flag-waving frauds chased after Anton. They searched the forest from our farm to the river. They spied on me. They intercepted our mail. When they couldn't find Anton, they threatened me. They called me a witch and a whore and a crazy person. Courage in a woman is often mistaken for insanity. They said they'd burn us out. I was at the end of my string. I didn't know what to do. Other men from the county were disappearing into the brush, too. It was like coon hunting for the vigilantes. They'd tree a brushman with hounds. They'd shoot him or hang him. If he'd been a popular fellow, or was lucky, they might load him into a wagon in chains and send him off to the front. Later in the war when the need for soldiers got truly desperate, it became the patriotic thing to do to hurry a captured brushman into battle instead of wasting his bones by swinging them from a tree."

"But by then you had found this hideout," said Flora.

"You're a perceptive child."

"She's a fortune-teller," Isabella said.

"Oh yes?" Ada smiled. "I could use some advice from you, child."

"Anton is dead. Go back to Randolph," said Flora.

"Why do you insist he is dead?" Ada asked.

"In the wall near the horses I saw a nook that has a framed photograph of a handsome young man with a mustache. The photograph sits on an altar cloth that has a silver cross on it. That is a shrine to Anton. You know he is dead."

Ada nodded. She breathed deeply and splashed water in her own face.

"Go back to Randolph?" Ada asked.

"He loves you and he needs you," said Flora.

"And he doesn't know you've been gone," Isabella said.

"The neighbors know," said Ada.

"It's not the neighbors who will be paying your bills in your old age, or, rather, as you continue to mature," Isabella said.

"Randolph is demented," said Ada. "I'd be taking advantage of his sweet nature."

"He'd be benefiting from yours," said Flora.

"How would you see this turning out, child?" Ada asked. "I mean if I were to go back to Randolph?"

"You will make it good," said Flora.

Ada looked at Flora and then at Isabella.

"I'm glad to have your company," she said. "I don't know why you people were riding in this kind of weather, but we're lucky we ran into each other. I'm getting out of the tub now and putting on dry clothes. I'll bring blankets for you two to wrap up in. I don't allow lacy lingerie in here, Mrs. Bushkin."

Ada stood up and climbed onto the floor of the cavern and shook herself dry in the light from the oil lamps.

"That lingerie rule is because I haven't had any lingerie in years," she said. "I wonder if Randolph kept all my things?"

Twenty-four

AFTER LEAVING ADA PLIMPTON'S cavern the following morning, they crossed the swollen Colorado on a ferry operated by tow chains, turned east, forded three creeks, and camped for a night on the banks of the Brazos. By midafternoon of the next day, they were a mile from Sweetbrush.

Varney on Athena and Isabella on the cavalry horse, with her battered suitcase, were riding side by side on a muddy track that ran between cotton fields where water glistened in wide pools from the storm that had pounded the area for three days before finally passing through. The afternoon was warm and humid, but Varney wore a gray wool suit that he had selected from a trunk at Ada Plimpton's cavern. On his feet were black leather boots that had been fashioned for a vanished brush man by a cobbler in San Antonio. Isabella thought Varney made a striking figure on the coppery Arabian mare, with his gray hair combed back into a senatorial ducktail, bruises under each eye almost like theatrical makeup, and a purple welt on the bridge of his nose.

Isabella was feeling pretty good about things. The warm mineral soak in the cavern had reminded her to look on the bright side. Each morning brought her one day closer to going home to Spain. She was counting on Dr. Robin to help her arrange the transfer of her funds from the bank in New Orleans to a bank in Houston so she could put her hands on the U.S. cash dollars and Federal securities all the sooner—no trading in Confederate money or worthless bonds. Dr. Robin had given generously to finance the careers of several politicians that she knew of, all of them secessionists. Bushkin had never asked the Sweetbrush planter for a contribution or a favor. When asking needed to be done, Isabella did it.

"You have actually met Varina Hotchkiss, then?" asked Varney.

"I have been in her company in Austin when the legislature was in session. The last time I saw her was a few months ago in Houston at the theatre," Isabella said.

"She was acting?"

"No, she was in the audience with a lady friend. I merely said hello to her in the lobby after the show. Bushkin was in a rush to get to the hotel bar."

"What did you see?"

"It was an amateur production of King Lear with a cast entirely of women, done for the war effort. The first act lasted two hours. There were dead women actors all over the stage." She laughed. "It was all I could do to keep Bushkin in his seat. He will happily sit at a poker table for twenty-four straight hours, but five hours of theatre is an ordeal for him."

"Dr. Robin didn't attend the theatre with her?"

"Not this night. She was with a woman who organizes charities."

Riding a few yards to their rear came Jerod Robin. Flora was mounted behind him on the black mare, just as he had imagined his arrival might be. But it didn't seem funny to him now. What he was seeing caused a knot in his stomach. In the fields on either side of the track the cotton should have been a foot high. There should have been men in the rows with hoes fighting the weeds. Today the rows were mud, but he could see weeds poking up from puddles among the beaten-down plants. There were no workers in sight anywhere, only the watery fields under a polished sky.

"I've been thinking," Robin said in a voice soft enough that only Flora could hear him.

Flora leaned forward, her chin against his shoulder, and waited.

"When we come in sight of the house, don't be putting your arms around my waist like you are now," he said.

She released him and sat back.

"I could just jump down and trot alongside you," she said.

"At Sweetbrush, I'll get you a good horse and whatever else you need, and you and Varney can be off for Mexico. You need to go across the border and into the mountains as fast as possible."

"How about you?" she said.

"I have things to do here."

"This is a very dangerous place for you," she said.

"This is my home."

"You're ashamed for your people to see me riding with you this way?" she said.

"I'm just talking about the hugging, that's all."

"You want me to get down off the horse right now?"

"Stay where you are," he said.

Ahead and to the right Robin saw a dull glint off the tin roofs of buildings that housed the cotton gin and the cotton press and the plows and hoes and other equipment. Beyond these buildings stood the barns and pens for the farm animals. As the riders came closer, Robin could see cattle in the fields, and at last he saw people, three black workers, standing at the door of one of the barns. The three looked around curiously at Robin and his companions, but they did not wave or hail him. He didn't recognize them.

The track the riders had been following through the cotton fields turned into a muddy road that ran beside the quarters. Twenty cabins of white pine with red brick chimneys lined the north side of the road. At a few of the cabins women and children watched from porches or windows as the riders passed. Chickens squawked in the road. Behind the row of cabins were acres of vegetable gardens and fruit trees, an area of beehives and then the sugarcane fields began.

An old black man with a white beard slammed the door of an outhouse and hobbled toward the road, pointing at the riders with his cane.

"Don't yawl be causing trouble here now," he hollered.

"Pappy, it's me," said Robin.

"Who is me?" the old man said, squinting up at the man on horseback with the girl mounted behind him.

"It's Jerod Robin, Pappy." Robin slid out of the saddle and took a step toward the old man, who retreated and lifted his cane to ward off any attack. "Don't be afraid. It's just Jerod."

"Jerod is in the crazy house."

"No, I'm here, Pappy. It's really me. Where is everybody?"

"I can't see very good. Take off your hat," said the old man.

Robin took off his hat.

"Well, drop my drawers," the old man said.

"How have you been, Pappy?"

"Ninety-three just the other day."

"You been taking good care of the doctor?" Pappy had been Dr. Junius Robin's personal servant, and he doubled as the butler when duty called for parties or special guests. Pappy had been in the house when Jerod was born. Jerod knew Pappy couldn't be ninety-three, but he might be eighty-three. "I don't know what he'd do without you."

"How'd you get out of the crazy house?"

"It was a hospital. I'm all right now. Listen, Pappy, we're going on to the big house. Where is everybody? Who's the foreman these days?"

Pappy studied the captain's face.

"Are you sure you're little Jerod? You do favor him, but Doctor Junius said his son is locked up in the crazy house in Tennessee."

Robin mounted his horse. Pappy looked up at Flora, sitting in her perch amid the bedrolls.

"You coming the wrong way, girl. Most is going the other direction," Pappy said.

"Take care of yourself, Pappy," Jerod said.

Robin rode to catch up with Varney and Isabella, who had stopped in the road and were looking ahead to the carriage house and stable, where they could see half a dozen horses in the corral. A woman with a broom was standing in the front door of the carriage house looking back at them. A black man with a pitchfork appeared in the big door of the stable and called to someone. In a moment another man stepped into the doorway and looked at the newcomers.

"Around this way," Robin said. "Let's go in by the front."

Robin led them along a road that turned off to the south and passed under a bower of gardenia bushes that still dripped from the storm. The gardens beyond the bower were lush and green, Victorian in layout but almost tropical in growth. Yellow forsythia bloomed among honeysuckle and beds of roses. The air carried the fishy, oily smells from nearby Big Neck Bayou.

The road curved back to the right, bordered by hedges six feet high of blue hydrangeas, and merged into a boulevard with a narrow green median down the center, with fourteen magnolia trees planted on either side. White lilies lay in pools in the ditches.

At the end of the road, where it made a circle around a marble fountain, stood the big white house, two stories high with a pitched roof, wraparound porches upstairs and down, green shutters with French doors and fluted Corinthian columns all across the front.

This was Sweetbrush.

Robin had pictured this sight in his mind so often over the last nearly two years that, now that it was real, it seemed unreal. The house rose up out of surrounding greenery—the gardens, the moss hanging from the trees, the bougainvillea, the trumpet vines—with a commanding presence. From the gold roadrunner on the weathervane at the peak of the roof to the ornate carvings on the support columns of the porches down to the engraved brass knobs on the double doors in front, the house announced itself as out of the ordinary and now perhaps out of its own time.

The big house at Sweetbrush had stood for twenty-six years. It was built the year before Jerod Robin was born. Varina Hotchkiss had drawn the plans on the kitchen table of the cottage that was the owners' residence at Sweetbrush when Varina arrived in Texas from London newly married to Dr. Junius. The doctor had started planting cotton two years earlier on land that he had been awarded by the Republic of Texas, and on more land that he bought with inherited money from Tennessee. Dr. Junius had brought Pappy with him from Knoxville to San Antonio when he came to Texas to overthrow the Mexicans. Pappy had been at San Jacinto and had tended Dr. Junius's horses and goods while the Texans charged on foot across the field at Peggy McCormack's farm and routed the Mexicans and their leader, Santa Anna. When he received his bounty of land from the Republic, Dr. Junius summoned five more slaves from the old Robin family place outside Knoxville. Then the doctor traveled to the markets in New Orleans and returned to Texas with ten more slaves—six men and four women, all of breeding age and good quality, worth the nine-thousand dollars he had paid for the lot.

Working in the fields with his shirt off and a hoe in his hands with this crew, Dr. Junius put in the first crop at Sweetbrush. He planted seeds, chopped weeds, picked the cotton at harvest, worked at the gin and on the press, helped make the bales, shipped cotton from Galveston to mills in England, and when he saw financial success coming to his plantation, Dr. Junius gave himself a celebratory business trip to visit the British mills. He sailed from Galveston to London, where an event he could not have dreamed of led to the building of the big house at Sweetbrush, this monument to Victorian architecture as imagined by someone who had played Titania in Midsummer Night's Dream.

Robin felt a surge of amazement at the thought that he would in minutes be seeing his daughter for the first time. It was a confusing sensation. When he and Laura were married four years ago they both took it as a matter of course that they would have children. Jerod had not really wanted a baby, but he hadn't not wanted one. The patterns and cycles of life dictated that he should have children, and Sweetbrush should have an heir. He felt he was too young at twenty-one, and Laura, at age eighteen, was too young to be forced into the responsibility for children. But it was expected of them. When he left for the war the first time, they had thought Laura might be pregnant. She wasn't. Jerod came home on leave nearly two years ago, and by this time both he and Laura believed they did want children. Jerod had seen so much wreckage and waste and blood that he hoped future generations would rise to cleanse the country from ruin and devastation. Jerod was at Sweetbrush on medical leave for two months, recuperating from a broken ankle and a bayonet wound in the right bicep and a fever that came from infection. Laura thought the act of sex was totally undignified—making like monkeys, she called it—but she accepted it as a requirement for motherhood. By the time he returned to war, they had reason to believe she was pregnant. A letter that reached him in Virginia confirmed that their daughter had been born in their bedroom at Sweetbrush. That would have been a year ago. Now at last he was about to see her.

"Jerod! Darling Jerod!"

The double doors flew open and Varina Hotchkiss rushed out and ran down the steps and hurried toward her son with her arms outflung.

Jerod swung down off the horse and met his mother beside the marble fountain in the turning circle. They crashed together and wrapped each other in their long arms and hugged. Varina pulled back and stared into her son's eyes and took his face in her hands and kissed him on each cheek, on each eye, and then on the lips.

Varney and Isabella dismounted while the mother and son were embracing, but Flora remained sitting amid the bedrolls on the black mare.

"My son, my son, I have prayed every day that you would come back to me," Varina said.

"Mother," he said. "You look wonderful."

"Are you well? It took us the longest time to discover you were in a hospital. I tried to write, but you know—" Varina shrugged and smiled at her dyslexia— "I have that problem with the words."

Jerod had seen his mother reading and learning plays by painfully copying out the entire text, word for word, three times and memorizing it so that she would not have to consult the pages again but would have the play in her mind to savor.

"I should have written you," he said. "I'm sorry."

Jerod looked past her toward the door. His eyes scanned the windows.

"Who are your companions?" said Varina. Her eyes widened. "Mrs. Bushkin! Isabella! My God, what has happened to you?"

"This damned war," Isabella said. "You can't imagine how happy I am to see you again, Varina."

Varney stepped forward and bowed.

"This is Edmund Varney, the novelist," said Jerod.

Varina's mouth opened and she touched her lips in surprise.

"Oh yes? *By the Sword*, the *Holly Bush Journal*, of course," Varina said, extending a hand to Varney. "A fellow Londoner."

He kissed the back of her hand and smiled, his eyes alight with pleasure.

"This is the greatest moment of my life," he said. "At last I meet the brilliant, glorious Varina Hotchkiss."

"I read the flattering article you wrote about me in the *Holly Bush Journal*. My sister sent it to me," said Varina. "It's nice to be so pleasantly remembered."

Varina looked up at Flora, who sat on the horse. A shiver of distress passed across Flora's features. She closed her eyes.

"And who is this?" Varina asked.

Flora opened her eyes. She was receiving a bad impression. Something was more wrong here than the damaged cotton crop Jerod had pointed out to her in the fields.

"My name is Flora Bowprie."

"She's passing through," Jerod said. "I met all of them on the road."

"Come in the house, Flora. You must be hungry. Everyone come into the house. Welcome to Sweetbrush."

"Where is Laura?" asked Jerod.

Varina took his arm and led him toward the door.

"The horses?" Varney said. "Horses come first, you know."

Varina leaned back her head, her yellow hair draping down her back, cupped a hand to her mouth and yelled in a voice that would have carried to the top row in any theatre in the world.

"Brainey, you little scamp! Where the hell are you?"

A Negro boy of about twelve came running around the corner tucking in his shirttail.

"Ma'am!" he said.

"Stable these horses," Varina said.

"Yes ma'am."

"I'll go with him and see to my own horse," said Varney. "No offense, Brainey, but I like to do it myself."

"I'll go with you," Flora said.

"Well, not me," said Isabella. She untied her Italian leather suitcase with the silver buckles and held it in her arms. "I'm all for planting my sore behind on a pillow and having a glass or two of wine."

"Please, hurry and join us, Mr. Varney," Varina called to the procession that was walking toward the stable. "You, too, Flora, dear." Varina looked at Jerod. "Edmund Varney, indeed. What is he doing here?"

"He's going to Mexico to write a book," said Isabella.

They walked up the steps. Through the open door Jerod expected to see Laura coming down the stairs with their child.

"Where is she?" Jerod said. "Where is Laura?"

"Let's get comfortable first," said Varina. She clapped her hands, and a middle-aged Negro woman wearing a white calico dress with a blue apron came into the foyer. "Mattie, please take Mrs. Bushkin's suitcase."

"I'll follow along behind her," Isabella said. "I need to wash."

Jerod went into the parlor with his mother. Above the fireplace hung a portrait of Varina and Dr. Junius done by Gerard du Plessy from London. The carpet on the hardwood floor was thick and soft under Jerod's boots. He tracked mud on it. The furniture was Victorian rosewood and mahogany, overstuffed, with green velvet drapes pulled back from lacy curtains to reveal tall windows that looked into the gardens.

"Your father has gone hunting with the foreman," said Varina. "I'll send someone to fetch him."

"Mother," Jerod said. "What's the matter with Laura?"

"She's fine. She's in Houston with her mother. Would you like a drink?"

"The baby is with her, then?"

"Darling." Varina took her son's hands and squeezed them. "Your daughter is dead."

Twenty-five

"SHE WAS NEVER A STRONG CHILD," Varina said.

Jerod's legs felt weak. He sat on a red plush rosewood sofa between cushions with his hands on his knees, holding his hat and looking up at his mother. He realized he felt no authentic emotion at hearing about the death of the child he never knew, only a kind of dumb wonderment that now he would never even have a memory of her.

"It was pneumonia. She died ten days ago. We buried her in the garden at the chapel," Varina said.

Varina opened an enamel box and took out a Turkish cigarette. The first match she used crumbled in the humidity. She put down the cigarette and took her son's hand. She sighed and shook her head.

"Who performed the service?" Jerod asked.

"Laura's mother came and brought her preacher from Houston, an Episcopalian gentleman, Father Garvey. It was a lovely ceremony. Your father was quite nice to everyone all day. Junius did love that child, you know, in his own way. He was deeply moved at the loss. The next morning Laura returned to Houston with her mother. Darling, I rather doubt Laura will be coming back here to Sweetbrush."

"What do you mean?"

"Laura doesn't like it here," said Varina. "She is afraid of the Leatherwoods. She is afraid of your father. She hates being out in the country. She prefers to live in Houston with her mother and the friends she grew up with. She wants a social life."

Jerod nodded. He knew Laura in her heart had never felt at home at Sweetbrush. It was Varina and her friend Thelma Boatwright, Laura's mother, who had matched Jerod and Laura in the first place. Varina and Thelma had become close friends through a mutual interest in theatre. They encouraged their son and daughter to meet while Laura was a student at Mrs. Baker's Preparatory Academy being drilled in French and piano lessons.

"Laura says your baby wouldn't have died if we had been close to some of the good doctors in Houston. She might be right. We will never know. But Laura is not coming back to Sweetbrush unless you go into Houston and kidnap her, which would be a dashing but unwise thing to do," said Varina.

"Is she divorcing me?"

"I don't know. You could romance her. In time you might change her mind."

Mattie the housemaid came in and smiled at Jerod.

"I'm glad to see you again," she said.

"Thank you, Mattie. I'm glad to see you, too."

"Mrs. Bushkin is in the blue bedroom," Mattie said to Varina. "We are fixing her a tub. You should know she is looking through the closets."

"Encourage her to wear anything she fancies," said Varina.

Varina went to the marble-topped rosewood sideboard on which were glasses and bottles of whiskey, sherry, and red wine. She poured a glass of whiskey and gave it to Jerod, who was still sitting on the couch.

"So I suppose you have a decision to make," Varina said.

He sipped the whiskey.

"Mother," he said. "I'm in trouble. I have to leave the country for a while. I have to go soon. Before I go, what can I do to help you here?"

"What sort of trouble?" asked Varina.

"I'm accused of crimes. The law is after me. Santana Leatherwood and the Yankee army are after me." He finished the drink. "I'll be gone for a while. I can see things are not good around here. I'm worried about you. What can I do?"

"Go see Pastor Horry and call off this feud," she said.

Varina sat down beside him on the sofa and looked into his eyes.

"I mean it," she said. "Tell Horry he can have the land he wants, and more land on top of that. Apologize for these years of anger. Tell him you are speaking for our family."

"I can't do that."

"Jerod, darling, we have lost the war. Sweetbrush cannot survive unless we make friends with the Leatherwoods."

"Mother, I can't."

"We need peace here."

"The doctor will have to make his peace with Pastor Horry. This started as their feud. As long my father lives, this is his place, not mine."

Jerod stood up. A button was dangling from his butternut coat. He tore the button off and dropped it on the table.

"I'm going upstairs to get some clean clothes on for a change," he said. He looked down at his mother and noticed wrinkles in her forehead. "I can't apologize to the Leatherwoods. I'm sorry. I'm too deep into it. If you ask me to go shoot Pastor Horry, I would do that. But I can't apologize to the Leatherwoods."

Varney appeared in the parlor doorway as Jerod was walking toward the staircase. The romancer had washed his face and slicked back his hair and was smiling with anticipation.

"Where's the girl?" Jerod asked.

"Flora?"

"Yes, that girl," Jerod said.

"She's in the stable. She won't come in this house."

"Why not?"

"Something to do with slavery," Varney said.

Varney watched the young captain go up the stairs, then turned back to the parlor and saw Varina Hotchkiss sitting on the sofa, her long legs gracefully crossed beneath the full skirt, and her yellow hair flowing down either side of her handsome face. This moment would rate as topsys.

"I say, fate is cruel that you were raised in St. John's Wood and I grew up virtually next door in Hampstead, and we have never met until now," Varney said.

She stood up and smiled.

"Would you like a whiskey?" she asked. "Or sherry?"

"Most kind of you. Whiskey, please." He watched her move to the sideboard. She still had the glow of a star. "I'm interested to learn that one of my readers sent you my column, which means that at least one person in London knew where you had gone."

"Many people knew, Mr. Varney."

"If you would call me Edmund, I would melt at your feet," he said.

"In this climate, Edmund, a Hampsteadian easily melts."

He accepted a glass of whiskey and noted that their eyes were on the same level. He wasn't sure who was taller.

"I should tell you," she said, "We call this squirrel whiskey. It's made so deep in the woods that squirrels fall into the open tubs of mash."

"I do taste squirrel now you mention it," he said, licking his lips. "I came to see you play Lydia Languish in *The Rivals* the night you abandoned the stage."

"I know. You wrote about it."

"I was in love with you."

"So you have written."

"You are very powerfully attracting me at this moment."

"Please, Edmund." She laughed. "There's no need to flatter me. I am already happy to have a literary man from London in my parlor."

"I must ask—why did you leave the theatre suddenly that night and never return?"

Varina glanced out the window into the garden. She thought it might have started raining again, but it was only a humid breeze that was stirring the roses.

"You speculated on that in your column," Varina said. "Reading it I was surprised that you failed to see what should have been the most obvious motive. I fell in love. I met a wealthy young doctor from Texas and fell in love. There's no mystery about it except for the mystery of love itself."

"But why the sudden exit?"

"His ship was about to sail when I made up my mind."

"You gave up the theatre for love?"

"I did."

"You came to this god-awful place for love?"

"Edmund, please, you look comically aghast. Please, sit down. Let me refresh your glass."

"I have long suspected that actors are insane," Varney said. He lowered his aching body onto the sofa. He took the second whiskey from Varina and looked up at the face that had enchanted him on nights when he had sat in the dark watching her. "Going about in costumes saying other people's words and pretending to be someone else, is that sane behavior?"

Varina picked a cigarette from the box. Varney leaped up and struck the match. He held it to her cigarette.

"I don't mean that I disapprove," he said. "I am fascinated."

"You're a bit cuckoo yourself," she said.

"Exactly."

"I know about your novel that put you in the stew."

"Have you read it?" he asked.

"My husband burned it."

Varney lit a Turkish cigarette for himself and looked at Varina through the smoke.

"Whatever for?" he asked.

"His British friends who own the mills told him your book is treasonous."

She smiled gloriously.

"But he didn't get angry and burn your book until he saw the column you wrote about me in the *Holly Bush Journal*. Junius is very jealous. He imagines that you and I may have had a love affair before he met me."

"If he is jealous of every man who fell in love with you in London, he has far more enemies there than friends," Varney said. "Did he bother to read my book for himself?"

"He read some of it, I am sure."

Isabella came in. She was wearing a green silk dress with a low-cut bodice and a full skirt that brushed the floor. Mattie had let the dress out at the waist. Isabella had pulled her dark hair back into a bun and was looking regal.

"I can almost smell the ocean from here," she said.

* * * * *

Flora sat on a hay bale in the barn.

She thought about her father, Henri. She had prayed that she would find him, but maybe it would not happen in this lifetime. In a stall nearby, Athena knocked a hoof against the boards and snorted. The two army horses had been turned loose in the corral, but the old romancer had rubbed Athena and crooned to her and put her in the stall before he went to the house.

Flora reached under her skirt. She pulled out her roll of paper money that was bound by a silver clip. She counted $2,723 in Federal notes. The lease payment on the APPRENEZ VOTRE FUTUR ICI building would take her a long way and keep her in fair comfort. She tucked the money away again. Flora leaned against the wall and tried to rest. She felt uneasy here. She saw a shadow and looked up and saw Jerod Robin standing in the double doorway. He wore a brown sack suit, a blue cotton shirt with a collar, a new pair of boots and a fresh shave. He had brushed his blonde hair back above his ears, and his sleepy blue eyes seemed refreshed.

"Come inside and eat," he said. "We'll pack you a bag, get you some clothes and shoes and a good horse."

Athena snorted in her stall.

"Not that horse, but a good, strong, gentle pacer that is easy to ride and eats up the miles," said Jerod.

"That's kind of you," she said.

"You get under my skin. You know that?"

She nodded.

"Mattie is serving dinner early. Come into the house and sit with us and eat," he said. "You'll enjoy my mother."

"Your mother is beautiful, but I'm not coming inside."

"What's wrong with you? Are you sick?"

"I feel fine."

Jerod grunted. "Look at you. You need clean clothes. You need shoes. You need food."

"Where is your wife?" she asked.

"Why?"

"You showed me her letter to you. She was in pain. How is your little girl?"

"The baby is dead. My wife is gone. That chapter is over. Some homecoming. You finally find the stream and step in it, but the water has moved on." Jerod had a thought. "Did you see this coming?"

"No, but I felt it when we rode up to the house."

"How do you feel something like that?" he said.

"You know how," she said. "It just comes over you all the sudden. You get the strong feelings, I know. I can tell that you do."

"The truth is, I don't know what I feel," he said.

He looked at her bare feet propped up on the bale. He looked into her green eyes.

"Please get up off that bale and come inside," he said.

"What's the old romancer doing?"

"Entertaining the ladies, I am sure."

"Please tell him I am out here waiting on him to go to Mexico," she said.

"Tell him yourself while you eat."

"I don't feel right being cooked for and served by people you own."

"Flora?" he said.

She smiled. He had never called her by name before.

"I was looking around and thinking how most of this was built by people you own, and it makes me uncomfortable," she said.

"My father and mother built this."

"Slaves built it."

"Well." He paused. "Now that I think deeper into it, I can't see any good reason why I should give a damn what becomes of you. I don't care what you do," he said. "You've already caused me a world of trouble. So you can sit out here the rest of the day and all damn night if that's what pleases you."

She watched him walking back toward the house. There was a rustling noise behind her and the boy Varina Hotchkiss had called Brainey appeared from between stalls.

"Master, he mad," Brainey said.

"He's not your master."

"Yes, he be. The doctor, he the real master, though. He the master over all."

"Is he the master over his wife?"

Brainey's eyes widened and his mouth made a circle of amusement.

"He pee in his pants," Brainey said. "She doan like it."

A bell clanged from the rear of the house.

"Dinner time," Brainey said.

Growing up in the French Quarter, Flora had eaten dinner with Mama Marie and often with Henri at the hour of eight o'clock. They would often sit at the table until past ten. Here the shadows were growing long but the sun was still yellow above the horizon beyond the jungle along the bayou.

"The doctor pees in his pants?" she said.

"And he cries, too. I saw he. I saw he cry like a baby."

"What was he crying about?"

"I doan know. I'm hungry now. I'm going to dinner," Brainey said.

"Do you eat at the table with the master?" she asked.

Brainey stared at her. His mouth circled up again and he wheezed laughter. Then he ran down the aisle and out of the stable and toward the house, his cotton pants flapping, his feet splaying out. Flora listened to the old romancer's horse chewing straw in the stall. She raised her feet up onto the hay bale and leaned against the wall and settled in to wait.

Twenty-six

THEY GATHERED AROUND THE DINING TABLE. The drapes were pulled back, and the windows were open on a bright afternoon. Mattie and a young maid unfamiliar to Jerod laid out a meal of roast chicken, mashed potatoes, cream gravy, black-eyed peas, sliced tomatoes, and buttermilk biscuits. Isabella rubbed the brown cherry arms of her chair and noted that the Empire furniture could use a good polishing. The glass in the doors of the china cabinet was smudged with a handprint, she had remarked to herself while admiring the gold leaf plates stacked on the three shelves. She supposed help was hard to keep now at a place like Sweetbrush.

As they ate, Isabella described for Varina the events of the last three days from her point of view—Bushkin fleeing for Mexico, Klutemeier and two Unionists attacking and burning Bushkin's Landing, the trip down the river on the boat and the encounter with Bloody Bill, the fight with the Yankee army at Burroughs' Cove, the storm and the shelter in Ada Plimpton's cavern. Isabella presented Jerod's shooting of the two Germans in the most heroic way she could, as saving her life. She didn't mention the death of Billy Leatherwood or realize Jerod had shot Tom Custer, but she described Jerod's performance against the Yankee soldiers as courageous. When she told of Edmund Varney swimming up the river and stealing the army horses, Varina laughed and touched Varney's hand lightly as he raised a wineglass to his lips.

"There was a scene like that in *By the Sword*," she said.

"Then you did read my book?" said Varney.

"Of course I did," she said.

Jerod looked at his mother, knowing the effort it took her to read or write. She had explained to him that she thought in pictures, not so much in words. She would see words written back to front, out of order, with letters of the alphabet that she mistook for other letters. When she was faced with writing a personal letter, she puzzled it out. The last letter Jerod received from her, last autumn, she said her condition was getting worse at writing, though she had improved a bit at reading. "They say many geniuses are dyslexic," she wrote to him in a flowing pen that gave no hint of the labor behind it. "So I will pretend that I am a genius and this is the price God extracts from me."

"I would love to see Edmund's novel," Isabella said. "May I read it?"

"I'm afraid it's been, um, loaned out," said Varina. "I'm sorry."

"Do you think my book is treasonous?" Varney asked.

"I read it as a love story. I wept when she was murdered by the soldiers. For me what you did is art, and art is not treason," she said.

"Art certainly stirs the brutes up against it, though," said Isabella.

The young black servant girl brought in the coffeepot to refill their cups with real coffee, from Mexico. Jerod idly wondered at the girl's status on earth. Legally she would soon be declared free, and then what? When he left for the war four years ago, there were eight household servants to staff the twelve-room Sweetbrush mansion, including three in the kitchen. Today, near as he could tell, there were four, plus the boy Brainey.

Jerod wondered what Flora was doing.

"Surely, you must have realized by now that Texas is a mistake," Varney said, smiling at Varina. "You belong at home in London, in the theatre."

"My husband believes Texas will survive all this and become a world power as an independent nation eventually. I wouldn't want to rush away at the first intermission and miss the rest of the play," she said.

"I take it your husband is a doctor of economic philosophy?" said Varney.

"Junius is a physician," she said.

"Does he still practice?" asked Isabella.

"He has never practiced medicine except during the revolution. Junius came straight to Texas after he received his medical diploma and right away got into the revolt against Mexico. I believe he did practice a bit after the revolution until he got his land grant," Varina said. "But once he started planting, this became his life."

"What is his university?" asked Varney.

"Transylvania University," Varina said.

"Pardon?" said Varney. "He was schooled in Europe?"

"Transylvania University is in Lexington, Kentucky," Varina said. "When Junius was there, at Morrison College, Transylvania University was the rival of Yale and Harvard. U.S. Senator Henry Clay taught the law there, and his cousin Cassius Clay studied there; he is the emancipationist who seems to have won out in the long run. Cassius inspired and encouraged Junius to open a school here and educate slaves. Stephen Austin came from Transylvania University to organize his settlement in Texas. Confederate President Jefferson Davis and General Albert Sidney Johnston were schoolmates of Junius at Transylvania University. I love saying that name. Transylvania, Transylvania University."

"I had no idea," Varney said.

"You'll appreciate the irony. Transylvania University was established on thirty-eight thousand acres taken away from the British Empire during the American Revolution. I went to Lexington with Junius to a reunion. It's the loveliest campus, three thousand wooded acres with green fields and pastures and thoroughbred horses and white board fences, and flowers everywhere."

"The great Varina Hotchkiss has become a Texas patriot. I would never have believed it possible," said Varney.

"I do remember London, Edmund. Coal smoke, soot, mud, frozen slush, a walk-up flat in Soho, shivering cold in the dressing room while I'm doing makeup by the blind-making light of an oil lamp—we didn't have gas lights in the dressing rooms for fear of fire or asphyxiation. I remember dirty wigs and the smell of ammonia. I would put on the mask of Lady Macbeth and fit myself into her costume and step into the foot lights and become Lady Macbeth for five hours. I would emotionally work myself up to suicide every night. When the applause was done I would get drunk at a café and chatter with everyone and eventually go back through the stinking fog to my flat in Old Compton Street, nearly always alone."

"Nonsense," Varney said. "You were a star. Men lusted for you. They pursued you."

"I was twenty years old," she said, "but I wasn't stupid. I explored the stage-door Romeos for a while, before I gave them up and stuck with my art to keep me warm. My mum and dad owned a newsagent in St. John's Wood—it's in the family yet—my married sister is the mysterious source who sent me your column in the *Holly Bush Journal* as she had sent me your novel earlier."

"If only I had known you were available," said Varney.

"I was just the opposite of available, Edmund."

"How did you meet him?" Isabella asked.

"Have you seen *The Rivals*?"

"I saw it in New York."

"The doctor fell in love with Lydia Languish," Varina said.

"Lydia is a hopelessly idealistic romantic, but young and beautiful and very rich," said Isabella.

"Well, I was far from rich," Varina laughed.

She looked across the table at her son.

"Darling, you haven't said a word," she said.

"I've been eating with both hands," said Jerod.

Mattie came in with a steaming bowl of hot peach cobbler, a pitcher of cream and a serving spoon.

"The doctor just now rode up out back," Mattie said.

Jerod pushed back his chair and stood up. He felt a rush of breath around his heart. Varina crumpled her napkin and dropped it on her plate. She nodded at Jerod, who stepped over behind her and pulled out her chair as she rose. She smiled down at Isabella and Varney.

"Please excuse us," she said.

Varina and her son walked through the house to the covered porch in the rear. They could see Dr. Junius handing the reins of his horse to the boy Brainey. The doctor was saying something to Lucas, the foreman, a slender black man, who was still mounted. The doctor was tall and heavy-shouldered. In the heat of the afternoon he wore boots, trousers, and a white undershirt spattered with mud.

"By God, I won't have it!" they heard Dr. Junius shout. "You go and tell them I won't hear of it!"

"Just trying to stay on your good side, boss," said Lucas.

"Pull your father aside and visit with him. You need to understand," Varina said.

Dr. Junius took off his straw hat and wiped his face. There was a smear of mud on his cheek. His hair was longer and grayer than Jerod had remembered. Trotting up behind the doctor on a mule came the boy who had delivered him the message to come home, but had forgotten why the doctor was wanted. The boy was carrying the doctor's shotgun and held a dead goose by the neck.

"Go on back to the quarters now, Lucas, and tell them what I said." Dr. Junius's voice carried across the yard for the benefit of anyone who might be hiding and listening. "If they want to come to me with something reasonable, I'll listen. But this damn fool idea is out of the God-damned question."

The doctor turned and started toward the house, his boots squishing in the grass. He looked up and saw them standing on the porch. He squinted at them, unsure.

"Hello? Could that be you? Jerod?"

Jerod met him at the bottom step. Jerod was prepared to embrace him, but instead the doctor extended a hand with a grin and a look into Jerod's eyes.

"It's good to see you, son," the doctor said.

"Good to see you, too."

"I wrote you two letters. I guess you didn't get them."

"They never caught up with me."

"Well, I didn't hear from you, either," the doctor said.

Jerod nodded.

"I heard from a friend in Knoxville that you had cracked up," the doctor said.

"I got shot, but I'm fine now," Jerod said.

"I want to hear all about it, son." He grasped Jerod by the elbow and looked up at Varina on the porch. "The coloreds want to have a meeting and decide how much land we're supposed to give each one of them. Some son of a bitch has been telling them the Yankee army is on its way here to turn everything over to the colored people."

"Do you have enough workers to handle the crop?" Jerod asked.

"The storm pretty much took the cotton. We've got enough workers to handle what's left," said the doctor. He looked at Varina. "The son of a bitch who stirs these people up is that preacher. Lucas tells me he has started letting coloreds into his church and they hear that venom he preaches and they come back here and plot how they can own Sweetbrush."

"Horry preaches the New Testament," Varina said.

"Show me where it says in the New Testament that we have to divide up our property and give it to the coloreds. You can't find that anywhere in the Book. Horry preaches from a Bible he wrote himself. He's no friend of the coloreds."

"He has invited coloreds to attend his church, but they haven't done it yet. They're afraid to go into town."

"How do you know? Are you standing up for him?" said Dr. Junius.

"Mattie told me. We have guests, Junius. Senator Bushkin's wife is here, and a man from London. You'll want to clean up a bit. Jerod can visit with you while you wash," Varina said.

Jerod followed his father up the back stairs. At the landing on the second floor, Jerod turned to the right and took a step toward the master bedroom before he realized his father had turned to the left and was walking toward the guest wing. Jerod waited a moment to see if his father had made an absent-minded mistake. But his father continued to the largest of the guest bedrooms, turned the knob and went inside.

The doctor sailed his hat into an armchair.

"I'm sorry about your baby girl," said Dr. Junius. He sat down on the spread of the canopy bed that had two dozen roses carved into its cherry wood headboard. The doctor had tracked mud across the hardwood floor and onto the rug beside the bed, where he began removing his boots. "Her whole life, she was never quite right. We did our best, of course. I'm truly sorry about the baby."

"I appreciate it," Jerod said.

The doctor raised his beefy arms and skinned out of his undershirt. Old white and purple scars crawled across his chest under the mat of gray hair. Dr. Junius had received some of the wounds fighting the Mexicans and the rest in brawls.

"I'm not going to try to fool you. I'm not sorry Laura has gone home to her mother," said the doctor. "Laura didn't fit here. Your mother picked her out for you because Laura is pretty and dumb and no competition, but it turns out the girl is weak. You're better off without her."

The doctor took off his trousers and walked in his underpants into the adjoining room. It was a bathing room with a cast iron tub, a long marble counter with a sink, a mirror and a water pitcher. Behind an Oriental screen Jerod could see a mahogany armchair with the seat hollowed out and a porcelain chamber pot beneath it.

"How bad are things here?" Jerod asked.

"What do you mean?" The doctor looked up from washing his face in the sink. "Bad? No, we're doing fine. If it wasn't for sons of bitches like Horry Leatherwood, my life would be just fine. One day soon I'm going to remove him from the equation."

Dr. Junius looked at himself in the mirror.

"I'm looking old," the doctor said.

"You look fine."

Dr. Junius opened a cabinet door. Off a shelf he took a bottle of laudanum and a pint of brandy. He poured laudanum into a silver spoon and sucked it down. He sipped brandy as a chaser.

"Does away with the aches and pains," the doctor said. "I've been having headaches. I got out the old medical books and diagnosed myself. I am suffering from a terminal termination of life sooner or later." He laughed. "It's a shock when the finger points at me."

"What are you talking about?"

"Mortality. It intrudes on my thoughts these days." He picked up a bone-handled comb and ran it through his hair. "Did you hear that Sam Houston died?" asked the doctor.

"That was more than a year ago, Dad," Jerod said.

"Was it? Seems like last week to me. Old Sam got us into this mess. He lived long enough to see what a mistake it was to steer us into the United States. But we aren't beaten. We're going to bring back the Republic, son. We're going to survive this madness and come out on top as a world power. We'll make a lasting peace with the Mexicans. We'll make alliances with England and France and Germany. Houston will be the biggest city in the world. Galveston will be the biggest port in the world."

"Is this the right time for that?" asked Jerod.

"It's always the right time. We just have to stay the course and not let the Unionists deter us again. Lamar is the man we should have listened to—Texas from here to the Pacific."

The doctor sloshed the remaining water from the pitcher onto his chest.

"Pappy!" he yelled. "Pappy, I need a towel!"

"Pappy is at the quarters," Jerod said.

Jerod pulled a large white cotton towel off a wood dowel rack and gave it to his father. The doctor wiped his face and chest with the towel. He looked at the laudanum bottle, shrugged and poured an inch of the milky liquid into a glass. He drank it, then reached for the brandy and drank two swigs from the bottle. He looked at Jerod, waiting for a rebuke, but saw no disapproval. Jerod's expression was one of curiosity.

"What's this about you being in the hospital in Knoxville?" asked the doctor.

"I got shot in the thigh and I was out of my head for a while with fever."

"You cracked up, didn't you?" the doctor said. He tossed the towel onto the counter and walked into the bedroom. He pulled open a bureau drawer and took out clean underpants. Jerod noticed the underpants had not been ironed. The doctor stepped out of his underpants and stood naked, looking at his son. "Hell, cracking up is not anything to be ashamed of. Men get tired, they get hurt, they crack up. You put your finger over one leak and another one pops up. It's human. You've got those medals you won at Shiloh and Chancellorsville to wag in their face if anybody thinks you're a coward."

"Have you heard that I stuck Santana Leatherwood with a saber?"

"This whole county has heard about that. I wish you had killed him," the doctor said as he put on the clean underpants and went to the closet, where Jerod could see his father's clothes on hangers.

"Did you hear the circumstances?"

"You ran into each other at Snow Hill in Tennessee, and he shot you but you got the best of him."

"Is there more?"

"That's all I heard on the grapevine. I want you to tell me about it when we get time."

Jerod realized Santana must not have told even his brother that Jerod had surrendered before the stabbing. He must not have told anyone.

"I'm proud to have you home," said Dr. Junius. "We've got a huge job ahead of us. We've got to get the railroads up and running. We've got to elect new politicians all across the board. We've got to get the army and navy organized and the bankers in place. We'll need to issue currency. My God, the prices are going mad. I've been approached to run for president of the Republic. I don't think I'll do that, but I'm willing to serve in the office until we can hold our elections."

"Who offered you the office?"

"Patriots. Right-thinking men and women. I'll fill you in when we have time to sit down for a visit on strategy."

"I'm leaving the country in two days," Jerod said. "Santana Leatherwood and the army are coming to arrest me."

"For what?"

"I ran into him in Austin and some laws were broken."

"No Leatherwood is going to come on this property and arrest you," said the doctor.

"It'll be the Yankee Army."

"What can I do to help you?" the doctor said.

"Mother wants to make peace with Pastor Horry," Jerod said.

His father glared at him. "That's not why I am sleeping in here."

"I never supposed it was."

"She says I gag and snort during the night and keep her awake."

The doctor stuffed in the tail of his linen shirt and buttoned his trousers.

"The hell with Horry Leatherwood," he said. "I'm just the man to send him there."

Dr. Junius put on a frock coat with satin lapels and inspected himself in the mirror on the closet door. The coat draped nicely on his torso and his muscular buttocks. He nodded with approval at his reflection.

"All the same, I have to leave the country," Jerod said. "I can't stay and fight Santana here. The Yankee Army would wreck this place. You might want to think about making peace with Pastor Horry instead of murdering him."

"Why would you call it murder?"

"You go looking for a man to kill him, and do it, it's murder," Jerod said.

"I'll make him a fair fight. That's the best I can do," said the doctor.

He felt the inside pocket of his jacket and found a slender Mexican cheroot. He stuck it into his lips and frowned at his son. "I wonder where Pappy has gone off to? Pappy was at my call for thirty-five years, and now I can't find him when I want him. There's precious little loyalty left in the world. Who is downstairs? Mrs. Bushkin and some fellow from London? Let's go down and entertain them in Sweetbrush style."

A chill struck Jerod's breast as he watched Dr. Junius go through the bedroom door with smoke puffing from the cheroot in his mouth. Jerod caught his breath and felt his heart pounding. It was a sensation he recognized from the war, not fear but awareness that death was near. Suddenly he had a vision of the doctor's body lying cold on the earth. Jerod touched his fingers to his forehead and shut his eyes and tried to erase the image. He followed his father down the stairs.

Twenty-seven

"A GANG OF FIFTY MEN WITH GUNS broke into the state treasury building in Austin two weeks ago and made off with most of the state's gold and silver," Isabella was saying over coffee after their meal. "They shot a few citizens on the street. There may be law in Texas, but where is the order? Looking back, I believe the news of that event may be what frightened Bushkin into planning his escape even before he heard the Yankee army is going to hang him."

She poured a spoonful of brandy into her coffee and stirred it.

"What are you going to do now?" asked Varina.

"I'm going home to Barcelona."

"I wish you would stay in Texas. Assume the senator's office. We need you," Varina said.

"With the Unionists threatening to murder me in Bastrop?"

"Move the senator's office to Houston for a while. You speak as the senator. You don't need to go back to Bastrop. Wait and see how things play out," said Varina. "We have many friends in Houston who will protect you. I think you will soon find there are more Texans in Bastrop than there are Unionists."

"Don't listen to her, Isabella," Varney said. "Texas will never be better than semibarbaric."

Varina laughed.

"I mean no disrespect to the Spanish," Varina said, "but wasn't it near Barcelona where you were robbed and beaten, Edmund? My sister mailed me the essay you wrote about it in the *Holly Bush Journal*. You said Spain was populated by cruel, sullen, conniving brutes. Surely you have a better opinion of us Texans than that."

Mattie entered with a silver tray to clear the dishes off the table.

"The roast chicken is fit for a rajah, Mattie," said Varney.

"Thank you."

She looked at his earring as she picked up his empty plate and the empty cobbler bowl from in front of him. She had noticed his earring when he first arrived. The shine of silver and jade in his car had inspired her to put on a clean calico dress.

"Pastor Horry is preaching tonight," Mattie said to Varina. "You ask me to tell you when he do."

"This is a special service?"

"No ma'am, it's a regular Wednesday night preaching except the word is out if we show up he won't turn us away," Mattie said.

"Are you going?" Varina asked.

"It ain't likely that people like me can go into that town at night with any degree of safety," said Mattie.

"I'll take you," Varney said.

"Edmund, you don't know what you're saying," said Isabella.

"This woman needs an escort to church and back," Varney said. "I'm happy to take her. What do you think, Mattie?"

"I don't know," Mattie said, looking at Varina.

"You don't understand what you are getting into, Edmund," said Isabella.

"Exactly the way I like it," Varney said. "I'll discover it as I go along."

"The preaching starts at seven," said Mattie.

"What is it, four or five miles to town?" Varney said. "We'll plan to leave here at five o'clock sharp. I'd like to dawdle a bit en route and gawk at the sights. I have never seen Texas before and doubt I shall ever return."

"Miz Varina?" said Mattie.

"It's nearly five o'clock already," Varina said. "The doctor will want his supper."

"His chicken is in the oven staying warm. The new girl can serve it."

"Aren't you afraid?" asked Varina.

"Yes ma'am. I sure am," Mattie said.

They heard boots coming down the staircase. Varina touched her lips with her napkin.

"Mattie, go and fetch the doctor's supper," she said. "We'll give Mr. Varney a few minutes to come to his senses."

Mattie hurried out of the dining room. They heard her voice and the voices of the doctor and Jerod in the hall.

"Edmund, are you drunk?" Varina said.

"I should like to see this preacher I have been hearing about," said Varney.

Dr. Junius Robin strode into the room, his shoulders back, his chest out, the cheroot clinched in his teeth in a wide grin.

"Mrs. Bushkin," he said, removing the cheroot and bowing at Isabella's chair. "You do us an honor with your visit."

"The honor is mine," smiled Isabella.

"And how is the senator's health?"

"He has gone to Mexico to preserve it."

The doctor frowned and pursed his lips. Another one gone. But he hadn't counted on Bushkin to do anything important in the new order. The doctor looked at the man sitting to the right of Varina. The doctor's gaze took in the swollen nose, the bruised face and the earring. The man studied the doctor's face at the same moment, and their eyes locked. The man stood up at the table.

"This is Edmund Varney, from London," Varina said. "Mr. Varney, my husband, Dr. Junius Robin."

Varney was prepared for any reaction from the doctor except what happened.

"Welcome, Mr. Varney. Welcome to Sweetbrush," the doctor said. He walked around behind his wife's chair and shook Varney's hand. "By God, it makes my blood rush with excitement to know we have ties with London again. Please assure your colleagues that we are open for business and ready to deal."

"Why, thank you," said Varney.

"You're drinking coffee. Wouldn't you rather have tea? Varina, why didn't you serve this man tea? Mattie! Mattie!"

"Thank you. I prefer coffee today," Varney said.

Jerod lingered in the doorway watching them.

"We do have tea, you know. Fifty dollars a pound by the time it runs the blockade, but it's Varina's favorite. I believe the sun is over the yard arm. Could I interest anyone in joining me for a drink?"

Mattie came in with the doctor's dinner plate on the silver tray. She laid out his food as he went to the marble-topped sideboard on which sat the bottles and glasses.

"I'll have a whiskey," said Varney.

"Good man," the doctor said.

On her way out of the dining room, Mattie looked at Varney and shrugged. She hadn't made up her mind.

Dr. Junius poured whiskey into two glasses and handed one to Varney.

"Here's to Queen Victoria and King Cotton," said the doctor.

He touched his glass against Varney's. Both men drained their whiskeys. The doctor poured two more.

"Junius, your food is getting cold," Varina said.

"Not hungry, dear. Not hungry at all." He placed an open palm against Varney's back and gently guided him toward the French doors that opened into the garden. "I know the name, Edmund Varney. Quite familiar. Portrush Mills, is it? Or Pemberton-Curry? Well, no matter. In Texas there is plenty for all. Come and look at our gardens, Mr. Varney. My wife designs them."

They stepped onto the grass in the shadows of tall hedges. The rush of humid air brought sweat to Varney's face. He could smell flowers and a hint of dung, a pungent aroma that reminded him of Kabul. They heard a whippoorwill calling from the thickets along Big Neck Bayou.

"Lovely," Varney said.

"I do a bit of boxing, myself," said the doctor.

"You look very fit."

"From the looks of you, you need to learn to duck." Dr. Junius chuckled. He called to the house. "Jerod, bring that bottle out here and join us."

They walked on the grass toward the far end of the garden where Varney could see a white picket gate and beyond it two Negro men in conversation. The two men saw the doctor coming with Varney and quickly separated and walked away.

"These bruises are the result of a boating accident," said Varney.

"I could teach you to box. The next time you have a boating accident, it won't hurt half so much. Don't be offended, please. I am joking. Ah, here is Jerod at last with refreshments. May I pour, Mr. Varney?"

"One last tiny one, please."

The doctor filled their glasses and gave the bottle back to Jerod.

"I trust you have found your bedroom satisfactory and hope you will have a pleasant visit with us," Dr. Junius said. "I am eager to hear the news from London. I met my wife there. We were married at a chapel in Southampton."

"Your wife is a very beautiful woman," said Varney.

"The old girl has held up well, hasn't she?"

The doctor offered the bottle again, but Varney declined. The doctor poured himself an inch of whiskey and held it up to his nose. He inhaled sharply, clearing his sinuses. He stirred a finger in the glass and put a drop of whiskey at each nostril.

Varney swatted a mosquito that bit his cheek. The slap sent a shock of pain through his skull. He groaned.

"I am a member of the Gentlemen's Boxing Society in Houston. I would be proud to take you there as my guest," Dr. Junius said.

"I'm not much in the mood to do any boxing just now," said Varney.

"I mean, we could go watch the fights. Challenge night is a good show. Members issue challenges to one another a month ahead of time and the suspense builds up to fight night. The wagers are quite large. Friday nights the coloreds fight for pay. I could take you into Houston this Friday."

The doctor snorted, whiffing whiskey up his nose.

"Feel this air?" the doctor said. "I swear the air gets thick as wool."

Jerod thought he saw his father lose his balance for an instant.

Jerod reached out to steady him, but the doctor pulled back and straightened his shoulders.

"What's the matter with you?" Dr. Junius asked his son.

"Sorry," said Jerod.

The doctor walked across the grass and stepped onto a path paved with crushed oyster shells. He waved for Varney and Jerod to follow. They crunched past beds of roses and trellises of bougainvillea that glistened with wetness. At the white picket gate Dr. Junius stopped and waited for them to catch up.

The doctor pointed to a white pine building with a tin roof. Through an open door they could see machinery. Jerod didn't like seeing the door open and no one around.

"That's the big gin in there," Junius said to Varney. "That honey will be ginning around the clock to meet world demand, you wait and see. We'll be much better than before the war at producing cotton. Texas cotton will be the finest cotton in the world. We'll grow enough cotton to put pants on every savage in Africa, and we'll never run out. We have God's bounty here in Texas."

Varney mashed a mosquito on the back of his hand and wiped a drop of blood off his thumb. Looking at the sky above the roof of the building, Varney judged it to be very near five o'clock.

"I wonder if I might ask a favor?" said Varney.

"Of course. For our visitor from London, anything that you wish is yours."

"I may want to borrow a horse and buggy for a few hours."

"You want to have a look around the place by yourself? I would suggest you take Jerod with you and go well armed. The atmosphere is uncertain, so far as random acts of violence are concerned."

"Who should I watch out for?" asked Varney.

"Everybody. But this is a temporary situation. Our trade routes will be open again soon. British mills will be turning out Texas cotton in a few months."

Dr. Junius squinted with pain and bit his lip. He limped toward a marble bench that sat on a path between beds of roses and tulips. The doctor dropped heavily onto the bench and sighed. Jerod stood beside him and looked down at the struggle in his father's face as the doctor regained his presence of mind.

"It's nothing. Just a twinge I get," the doctor said.

Varney sat down on the bench beside the doctor. He stretched his arms above his head and yawned.

"Makes me lazy, this humidity," said Varney.

"In this climate you can hear and feel the crops growing," the doctor said.

"What's the attitude in the town toward business? What sort of man is the mayor?" asked Varney, with a quick glance at the young Robin. Jerod started to speak, but he swallowed his words. "Is he enthusiastic and trustworthy?"

"We're going to replace the mayor," Dr. Junius said.

"What is his flaw?" asked Varney.

"He's not planter-minded. He doesn't fit. They threw him out of Georgia thirty years ago for his radical religious beliefs. He walked to Texas with a horde of white-trash kinfolks. After our revolution he built his infernal church here and the town grew up around it. There's too many Leatherwoods to get him voted out of office. We'll have to remove him in a more direct fashion."

"I'm curious what could be his religious beliefs that were too strange for Georgia?" Varney asked.

"He preaches heretical nonsense. He says Jesus was a reincarnation of some ancient god. That's just the start of it. People gather at his feet and swallow this guff. I went to his church in the early days, but we had a falling out over a piece of land and a personal matter. I believe Horry Leatherwood is an impediment to progress. I am going to remove him. Don't worry about the mayor standing in anybody's path."

"He's a preacher, is he?"

"A preacher with a gun," Jerod said.

"He's a mean old son of a bitch," said the doctor. "But he's only flesh and bone. Don't let him change your mind about doing business here. The Leatherwoods control the town, and the road to the coast, but I don't have to ship cotton through the town. I'm going to develop Big Neck Bayou into a channel for shipping cotton by barges, six hundred bales per barge, with a port right here at Sweetbrush."

Through one of the ornamental windows that had been cut into the hedge, Varney could see the carriage house and the stable. He noticed Flora Bowprie coming out of the stable. She was talking to Mattie, who had put on a bonnet and was carrying a book. Mattie glanced at the house, starting toward an oyster-shell path lined with whitewashed stones that led to the back door.

"I know, I know, the popular belief around the world is that Texas is prostrate, devastated by this war for state's rights that we had to fight, this war that was forced on us. But popular belief has the character of a dog. Show the people a piece of beef and watch them wag their tails. As soon as Texas signs a few hundred million dollars in cotton contracts, popular belief will come around to fervently believing that we will flourish as a republic, friendly with but independent of the United States. No more of these punishing alliances we let Sam Houston goad us into when we joined the Union. We fought for the right to be free and independent Texans. By God we rose up and overthrew the Mexicans. We bled for our republic. If we had never joined the Union, we wouldn't have had to fight the damned federal government to defend our freedom. My son followed the Bonnie Blue Flag into battle to defend our honor and our right to live free."

"Why didn't you go with him?" asked Varney.

"What?" the doctor said. "Go where?"

"To the war."

"I stayed here to run the plantation," the doctor said.

"You were a hero of the revolution. I can imagine you would have made a valuable general," said Varney. "Varina could have run the plantation."

"Varina?"

"She's a strong, intelligent person," Varney said.

"Yes, of course she is. What are you getting at?" asked the doctor.

Varney stood up. He felt sweat sticking his shirt to his chest.

"I'd like to take that buggy now, if you don't mind," Varney said.

Dr. Junius placed the heels of his hands on the bench and hefted himself to his feet. Jerod thought the doctor might be about to pitch forward, but his father straightened up and eyed Varney with growing suspicion.

"You take a rather familiar attitude toward my wife for someone you just met," the doctor said.

"I saw her on the stage long years ago. I feel I know her much better than I actually do. May I ask the boy called Brainey to rig up a buggy for me?"

"Are you a broker, or do you represent a mill?" asked the doctor.

"Neither, I'm afraid. I'm just passing through on a trip from New York to Mexico. I'll be out of your life tomorrow. Right now, I'd love the use of a buggy."

Dr. Junius fastened his eyes on Varney's earring, and then slowly examined the noble brow, the swollen nose, and the glittery gray eyes.

"Who the hell are you?" asked the doctor.

Jerod stepped between the two men.

"He's with me, Dad."

Varina came out of the French doors, her hair flowing onto her shoulders, and walked rapidly toward them. Isabella remained in the doorway with her coffee cup.

"I'm merely a traveler relying on your hospitality," Varney said.

"He's my guest," Jerod said. "Come on, Mr. Varney. I'll fix you up with that buggy."

"I know your name. Who are you?" the doctor persisted, staring at Varney. The doctor turned to his wife. "Who is this man?"

"Mr. Varney is an author," she said.

The realization hit the doctor's mind like an open-handed slap. He took a step back.

"How do you look at yourself in the mirror?" the doctor said to Varney.

"What right do you have to burn my book?" Varney said.

"I am assured that the Royal Hussars never murdered an Indian princess or massacred a party of innocent travelers," said the doctor. His face was turning pink. "To write that they did is treason. I'm surprised you are not in prison."

"Why should you care what I write?"

"I love England. British mills are my best customers and very good friends."

"Did you read my book?" Varney asked.

"I read every lying, stinking word of it. The British withdrawal from Kabul was orderly and successful. Your account is a wretched lie. Did you turn traitor just for the money, or do you think you are God, who can change history?"

"Junius, mind your manners," Varina said.

"You would side with him, wouldn't you?" said the doctor. "This weak-minded, artistic-looking bastard with the earring in his ear? He wrote that he's in love with you, so why wouldn't you side with this liar?"

The doctor unbuttoned his collar and breathed deeply, trying to fill his lungs. Sweat ran down his forehead.

"I'm putting you on notice, doctor," Varney said. "I may be a writer of romances, but I am from a military family, a former officer in Her Majesty's Hussars, and I am not known to stand for being insulted."

"Meaning what?" said Dr. Junius.

"One more crack from you is over the limit."

"Let's step out to the barn," the doctor said.

"No boxing, I have a bit of a headache," said Varney. "I choose pistols rather than fists."

"Then pistols it is, by God," the doctor said.

Jerod looked at his mother.

"Stop it, Junius," she said. "And you, Mr. Varney, I won't have you threatening anyone with a pistol at this house or on this property. Mattie has gone to the stable to wait for you. You had better leave now."

"Mattie?" said the doctor. "What does Mattie have to do with anything?"

"Mr. Varney is taking her to church," Varina said.

The doctor gasped and lurched toward Varney, but before Jerod could interfere the doctor staggered sideways to a white iron bench, ripping open the front of his shirt with one hand while the other clawed at his throat. His clothes were drenched with sweat. He made gagging sounds and the whites of his eyeballs rolled.

"Help me get him inside," Varina said to her son. She called out. "Isabella, come and help. Edmund, you must leave."

"Is he having a heart attack?" asked Jerod.

"I don't know. Let's get him into bed," Varina said.

Varina and Jerod each took an arm over their shoulders and struggled to lift the doctor off the bench. His head sagged onto his heaving chest. Isabella rushed up and got on Varina's side and helped to haul him up. He was groaning and gasping for breath.

Varina turned her famously blue eyes onto Varney.

"Tell Pastor Horry that Mattie has come to church with my blessing," she said.

Twenty-eight

FROM THE DOORWAY TO THE STABLE, Flora Bowprie and Mattie could see the commotion beyond the hedges, but they couldn't tell what was happening. They heard the doctor shouting, and then the anger was replaced by cries of alarm. Flora worried that something had gone wrong with Varney. She was relieved to see the old romancer come out of the white picket gate and stride toward the stable, with the boy Brainey running out in front.

"The old master, he fall out!" Brainey said, rushing through a mist of mosquitoes that hung over a water trough. He pulled the tarpaulin off a four-wheel buggy just inside the stable door and sent a shower of dust and straw into the air. "He spin around and go whooooo!"

"Is he dead?" asked Mattie.

"The old master, he doan ever die. That's what he tole me."

"Damn these nasty monsters," Varney said. He waded through the mosquitoes, slapping himself and wincing. "Hello, Flora, my dear. Mosquitoes have always found me irresistible. Mattie, are you ready to go?"

He walked past them and went to the stall where he could see Athena's perfect head with the white blaze between her eyes. She nickered a greeting. Varney offered her his hand to smell, rubbed her muzzle and scratched her cheekbone. So she could see him clearly, he stood a bit to the side away from the blind spot horses have straight ahead.

"I guess I'm ready. I mean I believe I'm ready. I believe God wants me to do this," said Mattie, holding the Bible against her stomach. Her bonnet had a purple ribbon hanging down in back.

"What happened in the yard?" Flora asked.

"Dr. Robin blew his stack," Varney said.

Brainey led a black gelding with a blonde forelock to the buggy.

"This is a Gelderlander warmblood," said Brainey. "The old master love this horse."

"You know your horses," Varney said.

"I do, I do. That chestnut Arabian of yours is the most good-looking horse I ever saw," said Brainey. "How come you not be riding her into town?"

"I lost my horse to the wild Ghilzais once before. The way I hear it, this town is full of wild Ghilzais."

"Doan know no Ghilzais," Brainey said, hitching the Gelderlander to the buggy. "But it loaded with Leatherwoods and Zanzibarians."

The buggy was a phaeton, a light, swift carriage that seated two on leather upholstery with a folding leather top.

"Miz Varina, she like this buggy best. She take it when she go into town," said Brainey.

"Does she go into town very often?" asked Varney.

"More than likely," Brainey said. "Mattie go with her."

"Lucas gone with her to the bank. He allowed to have a gun," said Mattie. She looked anxiously at the buggy. "Please, Lord, help me keep strong."

Flora went to the stall where Varney was feeding a carrot to Athena.

"When do we leave for Mexico, hey?" she asked.

"Dawn tomorrow. I promise," said Varney.

"I'll guard your horse until you get back," she said.

"I am counting on you to do that. You better get something to eat."

"Mattie brought me some chicken and potatoes. I'll stay right here with your horse."

"Don't sleep in the stall. She's liable to get restless and step on you."

"If you don't come back, can I have her?" asked Flora.

"Why, bless your heart, of course you can. But I am coming back."

Varney hugged Flora. She was surprised, but the way he did it did not feel lewd to her, and she squeezed him in return. The last man who had hugged her was her father Henri.

The carriage squeaked as Mattie climbed into her seat. Varney noticed a small brass plaque on the foot board that said Kobler & Son. Varney made a clicking sound with his tongue and rattled the reins. The carriage rolled out of the stable onto the crushed-shell path that led to the boulevard through the magnolia trees. Looking back, he saw Flora and Brainey standing in the entrance. They waved.

With a humid breeze in his face, fanned by the motion of the trotting horse, Varney steered the buggy onto the red-dirt road that led into the dense growth around Big Neck Bayou. Mattie tied the purple ribbon under her chin to hold her bonnet tight. The afternoon light was peach-colored as it fell through purple clouds beyond the passing green foliage. A flight of two hundred white ibises, the light glowing violet and green and copper on their wings, their bills hanging like dippers, coasted in to land on the water among the tall bald-cypress trees. The air smelled rich and fertile. A parade of mosquitoes dived at Varney's face and hands.

"Were you born here at Sweetbrush?" Varney asked. He knew she couldn't have been, because she was older than the Texas revolution by several years, but the question made her smile.

"I was born at Knoxville, Tennessee, to the estate of Colonel Rodney Robin and his wife, Miz Jessica, may they rest in peace. I came to Sweetbrush as a child with my mama, who died, and my daddy, who ran off," she said. "They caught him in the forest and tied him to a tree and whipped him."

"Dr. Robin whipped him?"

"No, the doctor wouldn't do that. He was real distressed when he heard what they had done. It was a bunch of white men that go around looking for coloreds to hurt."

"You were a child when this happened?" asked Varney.

"Oh, no. This was three weeks ago. My daddy never got over the whipping. We buried him the other morning. Miz Varina read the Book over him at the grave."

She showed Varney her Bible.

"I'm a natural born church woman," she said. "But we didn't have no church except at the chapel at Sweetbrush. The Zanzibar Church is the only church in town, and coloreds have never been welcome until now, if we really are welcome now, which I am going to find out."

"Why are there no other churches?"

"Pastor Horry won't allow it. Other preachers have come to town and tried to preach, but Pastor Horry runs them off."

"He can't stop them from preaching, can he?"

"He'll shoot their ass. The Leatherwoods can stop anything they want to stop."

"What does Dr. Junius have against Pastor Horry?"

"They are feuding."

"But what about?"

Mattie glanced from side to side as the buggy rolled between the trunks of cypress trees that rose out of sight. Swampy water sprayed from the wheels while they crossed flooded Big Neck Bayou on a stout oak bridge forty yards wide.

"You from a foreign country, are you not?" she said in a low tone.

"I'm from England," said Varney.

"You going back home right away?"

"I'll be in Mexico for a while first."

"But you not lingering here?"

"Not a chance. I'll be gone tomorrow."

"Then in return for you doing me this favor I will tell you the truth about what I think. I think they are feuding over Miz Varina."

Varney's eyebrows lifted. He had not considered that might be the case.

"Why do you think so?" he asked.

"I'm not saying nothing more," she said.

An alligator floated up and lay on the surface of the bayou, enormous eyes watching the carriage go past.

"Has she been seeing the preacher right along?" asked Varney.

"I never said she's been seeing him. I never said that at all. You forget I ever spoke up on this matter."

To forestall further questions, Mattie opened her Bible and began reading aloud as the buggy clattered off the bridge and bounced into the crunchy dirt of the road through the forest that was looking tropical to Varney. He saw orchids growing in the brush, and tall mounds of red ants. A pair of wood ducks fluttered down into the swamp and settled among the herons and ibises and other ducks. The birds were putting up a squawking, shrieking racket, and bullfrogs honked.

"'Though I speak with the tongues of men and of angels, and have not charity, I am become as sounding brass, or a tinkling cymbal. And though I have the gift of prophecy, and understand all mysteries, and all knowledge, and though I have all faith, so that I could remove mountains, and have not charity, I am nothing.'"

She closed her Bible and looked at Varney.

"That's God's truth," she said. "My daddy used to quote that verse from memory."

"The translator should have said love rather than charity, but well enough," he said.

"Translator?"

"The scribe who translated your edition of Corinthians into English probably debated between charity and love, and chose charity. That's fine. People understand the concept of charity far better than they understand love."

"God wrote the Bible," Mattie said. "What are you thinking?"

"If God were going to put it in writing, love is the proper word."

"God did put it in writing and He chose charity. Here it is in God's own words," she said. "The high-and-mighty that don't have charity are nothing in the eyes of God."

They bumped through a puddle. In the little streams along the ditches crawfish darted in swirls of sand. Water dripped from the canopy in shafts of peach light, but Varney did not stop to raise the leather top.

"The passage you read just now, is that Pastor Horry's message?" asked Varney.

"I don't know his message. I'm going to hear him because he has a real church."

"The chapel at Sweetbrush is as real to God as Pastor Horry's church," Varney said.

"How would you know? What kind of religion are you that wears an earring?"

Varney smiled. Sweating, he took off his gray wool suit coat and folded it in his lap as he drove the buggy. Mattie noticed the grip of the pistol sticking out of his waistband.

"I have learned so much from my visit to the afterlife that I can't call myself any particular religion. God is. That's the whole story in two words," Varney said.

"Uh-oh. Look yonder," said Mattie.

Two men walked out of the trees. They led their horses into the middle of the road and stopped, facing the oncoming carriage. They wore straw hats and short-sleeve shirts. Varney tugged the dragoon pistol out of his waist and hid it under his coat in his lap.

"Do you know them?" Varney asked as the carriage drew closer. "Is this a robbery?"

"They look like being from the town," she said.

With his fingers Varney tugged the reins. The Gelderlander smelled the men and halted. The horse's ears pricked forward at the possibility of danger. The taller man grinned at them from inside a thick red beard. He lifted a hand in a stop signal. His companion carried a 10-gauge shotgun with the barrel sawed off to twelve inches.

"Hidy," the tall man said.

"Good afternoon," said Varney.

"Where are you heading with that nigger?" the man said.

Beneath the wool jacket Varney's finger found the trigger.

"Miss Mattie and I are going to church," said Varney.

"That's a hoot," the man said, grinning. He spat and wiped his beard.

"This nigger and this buggy both belong to Dr. Robin. I suppose you've got a written note from him attesting that this nigger is free to come and go," the man with the shotgun said.

"It's our duty to stop ne'er-do-wells from fleeing work and to catch them if they try it," said the red-bearded man.

"If you got a freedom letter from Dr. Robin on this woman, then it will be a one-dollar toll fee to use this road," the other man said.

"I am attending the Zanzibar Church tonight," Mattie said loudly.

"The church don't have a nigger section in it," said the red beard.

"Tonight they will," Mattie said.

"Let me see if I have the toll fee in my pocket," Varney said. He lifted his hand from beneath his jacket and the big dragoon pistol was aiming at the man with the shotgun. "Look what I found—a road pass." He cocked the pistol.

But both men were looking past Varney and Mattie. Back down the road, cantering on a sorrel thoroughbred so similar in color that for an instant Varney feared he was riding Athena, Jerod Robin was drawing the Spencer rifle out of its scabbard and cranking the lever action.

"Ain't that the young Robin?" said the red beard.

"What do you suppose that means?" the man with the shotgun said.

"I ain't messing with him," said red beard. He glanced at Varney and Mattie. "If you're running from this crazy son of a bitch, have a short, happy life." He stuck a shoe in the stirrup and grabbed the horn and heaved himself into the saddle. "I guarantee you young Robin ain't on his way to no church."

The two men jabbed their heels into the flanks of their horses and disappeared into the trees.

Jerod rode past the carriage and quickly scouted along the road to make sure the men were gone. He sat holding the Spencer upright with his right arm as Varney drove the carriage up to him, and then fell into pace alongside as they proceeded along the road, which was growing dark now from the foliage that hid the sinking sun. They could hear birds settling into the trees.

"What are you doing here?" Varney asked.

"I owe you," said Jerod.

"How's your father?"

"He's up and around. He says he hyperventilated. I think you better not come back to the house."

"I'm coming back for my horse and for the girl," Varney said.

"Yeah. Just stay away from my father."

Upon seeing the humans, three pied-billed grebes silently submerged beneath the ripples left by a muskrat swimming among starbursts of spider lilies in the marsh on the left of the road. The odor of gas oozed from pads where green frogs floated in the swamp. For two miles along the road cypress trees stood in a foot of water in a jungle of fronds and orchids and brightly colored birds. This was not the Texas that Varney would have pictured if he had ever given Texas much thought, and certainly not the Texas he had known in the green and brown hills of Austin. This could as well have been tropical India.

"Mattie, are you sure you want to do this?" Jerod asked after a while.

"Yes, I am," she said.

"How much farther?" asked Varney.

"The road takes a curve to the right up ahead. The town comes on you all the sudden," Jerod said.

"Do you suppose the preacher knows what happened to his son Billy?" asked Varney.

"I think not. Telegraph wires are down."

"I feel it's up to me to tell him," Varney said.

"No, you won't," said Jerod.

"I'll tell him Billy died bravely and with dignity. That's the trick," Varney said.

"Little Billy Leatherwood is dead?" said Mattie.

"He's in the afterlife," Varney said. "No reason for alarm."

"You'll regret it if you tell him about Billy. It doesn't take a fortune telling girl to know that," said Jerod. "Pastor Horry is no man to toy with."

They slurped through a stretch of oily mud that spotted the carriage and smeared the horses up to their knees. A swarm of yellow butterflies swirled across in front of his eyes and then, even though he had been warned by Jerod that the town would appear suddenly, Varney was surprised to blink and see Gethsemane open up before him, hacked out of the jungle—wagons, chickens, people, horses, pigs moving in the muddy streets between houses and commercial buildings in a ripe, green, steamy clearing ten blocks from north to south and five blocks from east to west, dominated in the center by a two-story yellow-brick building with a steeply pitched red-tile roof and a blood-red sign that said ZANZIBAR CHURCH.

Twenty-nine

THEY WERE STRUCK BY THE VIVID HUES of green surrounding the town of Gethsemane—lime green, purple green, yellow green, green green, incredibly intense colors emerging from and into the jungle-like thicket as if from another dimension. Vines were creeping out into the foundations and onto the walls of the bank, the law offices, the mercantile and hardware stores, the blacksmith shop, the livery, the apothecary, the neatly shuttered homes built of pine and painted in pastel shades of yellow, ochre, pale blue, reminding Varney of a rubber plantation village he had visited in southern India.

A high, keening sound whined from the three story, tin-sided sawmill on the east side of town, convenient to the road that had been a buggy path as they were coming from Sweetbrush. But now the path expanded into a highway wide enough for two heavy wagons loaded with lumber to pass on their way to and from the lumberyards in Houston thirty miles to the south.

Men wearing wide-brimmed straw hats, short-sleeved shirts and denim trousers came out of the sawmill as the work day was ending, and the screaming of the saws began to fall silent. Racks of hardwood logs piled up beside racks of pines waiting for the next wagon caravan. The smell of sawdust hung in the air. Chickens were scratching in the mud or roosting in the trees. Sea gulls drifted in from the Gulf of Mexico, strutted and cried on the rooftops and dived for scraps in the garbage behind the café. Women wearing long dresses and bonnets strolled on the plank sidewalks. Children shouted at each other as they played games with rubber balls and hoops between the houses. Older boys were stacking sawed planks into neat rows on the loading dock. Jerod Robin recognized some of the boys. Four years ago these boys had walked the four-and-a-half miles along the road to the Sweetbrush school where Jerod taught.

Jerod, Varney, and Mattie were aware that the news of their arrival was spreading through the town. Mattie sat up straight and clutched her Bible. Jerod had tucked his Spencer rifle back into its scabbard. His eyes were sweeping the faces, making a count of Leatherwoods. Jerod hadn't been in Gethsemane since before the war. The town had grown double in population, he guessed, up to maybe a thousand people. Jerod saw eight or ten men and boys and six women he took to be Leatherwoods. There was a certain way the Leatherwoods carried themselves, an assurance that they were physically capable, had good teeth and were better looking than most. Jerod noted that each Leatherwood he picked out also stared back at him. He could see his name registering in their minds. They seemed more curious about him than hostile. Everybody in town— Unionists, Confederate sympathizers, Leatherwoods, immigrants, Zanzibarians and unbelievers—recognized Jerod as the man who had stabbed Santana Leatherwood with a saber.

As the buggy rolled slowly onward, with Jerod riding beside it, a few people began to follow, and then more joined in the train, and soon a crowd of a hundred, and growing, trailed along behind the three new arrivals.

The Zanzibar Church of the True Believer was three blocks into town, on the corner, the only brick building in Gethsemane. The sign above the door stuck out into the street like a theatre marquee that said ZANZIBAR CHURCH in blood-red letters two feet high with OF THE TRUE BELIEVER in smaller red letters underneath.

Varney tugged the reins, and the black Gelderlander halted the buggy at the front door of the church.

The crowd gathered behind the buggy and began edging forward in a semicircle, closing around the three visitors. Jerod heard his name repeated by several voices. He saw Leatherwood men approaching either side of the buggy. Jerod felt that Pastor

Horry was watching him, probably from the windows of his office on the second floor.

Looking up, Jerod saw one of the windows sliding open. Pastor Horry stuck his head out the window. His hair was cropped close to his skull, and his face had a lean, aesthetic look. His jaws twitched with muscle as he spoke down to them, but his mouth was smiling with good Leatherwood teeth.

"I'm glad to see you, Sister Mattie," Pastor Horry said. His voice resounded over the street. "I'll be right down to greet you."

Varney hopped down from the buggy and walked around the Gelderlander and took Mattie's hand. He helped her find footing on a plank through the mud. The crowd watched them. Jerod sat on his horse with the butt of the Spencer touching his right knee.

Mattie's heels clattered as she stepped onto the wooden porch in front of the church, with Varney close beside her. Varney saw a small sign in gold letters an inch high painted on a glass pane in the door of the church. This sign said Town Hall, Mayor's Office.

Pastor Horry opened the door and came out. He looked at Mattie and his dark eyes sparkled. His short, dark hair was lightly dusted with gray. He wore a white cotton shirt with no collar. His shoulders were wide, but his torso was lean, and he gave the impression of agility and sinewy strength. He was sixty years old, his skin browned and creased by the sun. On his wide leather belt hung a U.S. Army holster with a .45 caliber Walker Colt cap-and-ball revolver in it. The holster flap was open.

"Welcome, Sister, to the Rock of the Truth," the preacher said.

"Thank you," said Mattie.

Pastor Horry raised his powerful arms to the crowd.

"The preaching starts in thirty minutes," he said. "You people go about your business, and don't be concerned with this colored woman coming among us. There are three hundred seats inside this church for believers, and we will joyfully make room for any and all coloreds who feel the call. And any of you white or Mexican heathens within sound of my voice, you are welcome, too. We are all the same family when we celebrate the truth of the living Jesus."

As the people dispersed, Pastor Horry called to a boy wearing a felt cap.

"Charlie, take Miss Hotchkiss's carriage to the livery. See to her horse."

He turned his attention to Jerod.

"You can get down and come inside, Jerod," he said.

"I'll have to bring my rifle with me. I'd hate for it to get stolen," Jerod said.

"I don't blame you," said Pastor Horry. "Charlie, take Captain Robin's horse along, too. Tell Sammy to have them ready to leave here in two hours. That sound all right to you, Jerod? Do you trust me for two hours?"

"Yes sir," said Jerod.

The preacher turned to Varney and looked him up and down.

"Who would you be?" the preacher asked.

"Edmund Varney," said Varney. There was no sign of recognition on the preacher's face, only a questioning. Varney always half expected strangers might have heard of *By the Sword*. "I am instructed to tell you Mattie has come here with the blessing of Varina Hotchkiss."

"Are you a cotton buyer?" the preacher asked.

Before Varney could answer, Jerod said, "He's a British citizen, passing through. I met him on the road."

"With the earring you look like a pirate who has lost his ship," the preacher laughed. "Come inside. We'll visit for a while before the sermon."

Varney paused in the entrance, impressed by the auditorium that occupied the downstairs of the church building. He had expected to see benches, but instead there were theatre seats with red velvet-covered cushions, backs, and arms. The two aisles were wide enough to drive a wagon down, and there was three feet of space between the rows, plenty of room for the audience to stand and move about and walk to the aisles. At the front of the auditorium on a stage stood the pulpit, a polished mahogany rostrum with behind it a stained-glass window of Jesus praying in the garden at Gethsemane, and hanging on the wall an ivory cross seven feet tall and five feet wide, representing, Varney thought, the death of at least one mighty elephant.

"I think it's best for you to come upstairs and wait in my office, Sister Mattie," Pastor Horry said. "I have a fresh batch of lemonade the good ladies have whipped up for me—it even has a chunk of ice in it."

"I don't want to make trouble," Mattie said.

"Why, of course you do, Sister Mattie. You want to make good trouble, the kind of trouble the living Jesus would make," the preacher said.

Pastor Horry's office was up one flight of stairs at the end of a hallway, past other doors that led to offices whose desks and chairs sat empty but were littered with papers that indicated business. In the preacher's office they found a handsome woman stirring a pitcher of lemonade. A wiry, whiskery man wearing a vest over a pink shirt with balloon sleeves jumped up from a chair in front of the preacher's large gleaming oak desk.

"Excuse me, Mayor," the man said. "It poorly reflects on my good sense if I become a nuisance to your honorable self, but if the mood should fall upon you in the immediacy of the moment I would be pleased if you would sign my license and collect the city's due fee from my satchel—"

"Come back tomorrow," said the preacher.

"I have high hopes I might be onto the road into Houston by early in the morrow, by which I mean to say before daybreak," the man said.

The preacher spread the document on his desk and read it. He pulled a rubber stamp from a drawer and pressed it against an ink pad. He looked at the man whose pink shirt was staining purple with sweat.

"The city licensing fee for building, opening and maintaining a public bath house is, ah, fifty dollars up front and, ah, twelve dollars a month thereafter, to be paid in specie, no paper money," said Pastor Horry.

The man wiped his mouth with a handkerchief and shook his head.

"That is an awfully steep penalty," the man said. "In Houston City we have no licensing fees to pay."

"Then go back to Houston," said the preacher, pinching the document between his fingers to rip it in half. "They need bathing in Houston worse than we do."

"I accept the fee," the man said. He opened his leather satchel and reached inside. "Thank you, Mayor, for granting me your favors."

Pastor Horry stamped the document.

"Pay Mrs. Twilliger," said the preacher. "Do it in her office, not mine."

When the woman had taken the entrepreneur down the hall, Pastor Horry turned to Mattie and said, "Sister Mattie, would you pour us each a glass of lemonade? Take one for yourself."

She frowned, but she laid her Bible on the desk and did as he asked. Pastor Horry walked over and looked out a window and nodded with satisfaction at what he saw. The sky was pale with clouds. The light was dying. Lamps were flickering into life in homes. The windows of the shops and offices were going dark. A bell tinkled as a cow plodded down the street, tended by a small boy. People strolled along the plank sidewalks. The crowd had scattered, as the preacher had ordered, but in a few minutes three hundred Zanzabarians would pour in from the darkness and fill the auditorium downstairs.

The preacher gazed out the window while Mattie served the lemonade. He tasted the glass she gave him, and a small piece of ice touched his tongue. He nodded and smiled at Mattie. He looked at Varney and Jerod, who were still standing. Jerod held the Spencer rifle in the crook of his right arm.

"Everybody sit down, please. You take that arm chair in the corner, Sister Mattie," the preacher said. "Open your Bible and read up on the Gospel of Matthew. My lesson as is often the case is the Sermon on the Mount." He watched Jerod and Varney turn two maple chairs away from a card table. "Tell me, Jerod, how is your mother?"

"She sent me here to ask you to make peace between our houses," Jerod said.

"You are asking for peace? You recently tried to kill my brother."

"My mother reminds us that the war is over now," Jerod said.

His father's behavior had persuaded Jerod that his mother was correct—the old man had lost his grip. It was now Jerod's responsibility to speak for Sweetbrush. Apparently Santana had told no one the entire story of their encounter at Snow Hill. Could it be Santana hadn't heard Jerod's surrender? Blood mad chaos had stormed all around them at Snow Hill, gunshots and screaming, and Jerod had been crazed out of his head. It could be that he had only imagined surrendering for an instant before he saw the chance to strike with the saber, and had never said so out loud. But, no, three mornings ago in the prison yard Santana had uttered the insult that Jerod was without honor.

"What does your father say to this?" asked the preacher.

"I have presumed to speak in his behalf."

"Is the old bastard sick, or just too drunk to come here himself?"

"I'm speaking for my mother, too. I'm offering to settle the dispute between our families. As a show of good faith, we will deed you a section of land, a full six hundred and forty acres, and thirty acres of frontage on Big Neck Bayou. I must have an answer tonight, your word on the matter."

The preacher opened the door of a wardrobe closet and studied the three coats hanging in wooden hangers on a wooden pole.

"I'll have to think about this. My dispute with Junius is as old as you are. What's the sudden rush?"

"I'm a fugitive from the war," Jerod said. "I'm heading for the border tomorrow. I need to know this is settled."

Watching Pastor Horry select a white linen coat from the closet and slip smoothly into it over his wide shoulders, the coat needing to fit over the U.S. Army holster and the pistol at the preacher's hip, Varney decided not to confess the death of little Billy. The preacher did reach down and snap the holster flap shut, but this man who was about to lecture on the Sermon on the Mount did not entirely project love.

"May I inquire about your earring?" Pastor Horry said, looking at Varney.

"It was put in my ear to stay for life by my late wife. It is a symbol of love and devotion in her Sikh tribe," Varney said.

"What the devil is a Sikh?" asked the preacher.

"It's a religion that grew up in the Punjab in India four hundred years ago. A Hindu drowned in the river Bain and his body was lost in the deep water. They mourned his death, but he reappeared three days later. He now had a glow around his form and a divine light in his eyes. Everyone could see he had profoundly changed. Crowds gathered around to hear what he had learned in the afterlife. He told them, 'I have learned there is one God. There is no Hindu, there is no Mohammedan.'"

"What was this fellow's name?"

"Guru Nanak was his name. He gave his possessions to the poor and spent the rest of his time on earth roaming India and into Afghanistan and Tibet and as far south as the island of Ceylon. He wore the robes of a pilgrim and went to Mecca, Medina and Baghdad, singing songs about the one God. Sikh men are ferocious warriors, because they don't fear the afterlife," said Varney.

Varney mashed a mosquito on his wrist and looked at the blob of blood on his thumb.

"I say, you do grow them big here," Varney said.

Pastor Horry had begun taking a greater interest in Varney, realizing this was no ordinary, predatory land scout or cotton buyer who happened to have an earring and a British accent.

"You spoke of your late wife?"

"I have been fifteen years without her now," said Varney.

"My wife died giving birth to my youngest son about the same time ago," the preacher said. "I sympathize with your loss. Why have you never remarried?"

"No one has filled the bill," said Varney.

"Same with me," the preacher said. He fumbled in a pocket on the front of his trousers and pulled out a gold watch. He unsnapped the lid. "They'll be stomping their feet downstairs in a few minutes. My people are eager to hear the Rock of the Truth. Left to their own devices, people behave like pigs. They know they need regulating. They demand to be constantly inspired to work up the goodness it takes to get into heaven. Without a strong person to lead them in the right direction, people veer off into hell nearly every time. This Guru Nanak, he sounds like to me an incarnation of Jesus the Christ."

"Guru Nanak says we are all children of God," said Varney.

"That's what Jesus would say, all right," Pastor Horry said.

They heard rumbling from downstairs and the banging of a door. Jerod looked out the window and saw a crowd at the intersection as people hurried toward the church. He glanced at Mattie, who sat erectly with her hands clasped, watching the preacher and the Englishman.

"Jesus is his name. The Christ is a title," Pastor Horry said. "The Christ has incarnated into this world many times under different names in different ages to tell us the rules and inspire us to live up to God's intention for the human race."

He picked up a cigar from his desk, tried to strike a match that fizzled and then tossed the cigar back into a pine scented box.

"Zoroaster, Hermes, Apollo, the Buddha, Krishna—those are names of the Christ. 'What has been done will be done again. There is nothing new under the sun,' says Ecclesiastes in the old Bible of the Jews. In the Gospel of John, Jesus says lest a man be born again he shall not see the Kingdom of God. He's telling us to wake up from our material sleep and realize the Kingdom of God is in this world, if we would love each other. The Christ incarnated and preached his message to the Mohammedans, he preached to the Hindus, he preached to the Buddhists, he preached to the damned Chinese, he preached to the Mexicans, he preached to the Italians and he used up several incarnations trying to convince the Jews to love everybody."

"How did you get inspired to do this?" Varney asked.

"As a boy in Georgia I climbed a mountain and looked into a beautiful red sunset and the Lord sent me a vision that I must go west and found a town called Gethsemane and start a church and lead people into trying to live by the teaching of the living Jesus, not the crucified Jesus. I'm not a perfect human being. I don't practice what I preach. I sin and fall short over and over. The sin of anger often overcomes me. But Jesus could incarnate into town today and walk into this room and look at me and say, 'This old son of a bitch is trying to do the right thing.'"

Mrs. Twilliger opened the door and looked in from the hall.

"Where do you want me to put Sister Mattie?" she asked.

"Put Sister Mattie in the middle of the front row. Seat these two gentlemen on either side of her," said the preacher.

He poured a glass of water. He unscrewed the top of a salt shaker and used a forefinger to pry out a gob of salt that was waxy from the humidity.

"It's not the crucifixion that's so all-fired important," Pastor

Horry said. "It's the resurrection. People were crucified right and left in those days, but Jesus is the only man who died on the cross and came back in three days—the Christ incarnated again—and walked right into their faces with holy electricity glowing out of him, and he said if you want proof, just look at me. Just touch me—I am the Holy Ghost in the Flesh. If Jesus hadn't got up and come out of that tomb, he'd be remembered today as a great Hebrew prophet, but I wouldn't be preaching his Word. But he did come back from the dead, which makes all the difference."

The preacher stirred salt into his glass and tipped it into his mouth. His cheeks swelled. He gargled and spat into a basin.

"The Iron Jackets and the Catholics worship the crucified Jesus because their churches say believing he died for their sins will keep them from going to hell. But that's all they have to do—believe, have faith. Good works are not required. Zanzabarians try to follow the teaching of the living Jesus from the Sermon on the Mount. That is the hard way to get to heaven."

He looked at Varney for a reaction.

"You know how you catch a movement out of the corner of your eye, and you look, but nothing is there?" said Varney.

"Yes, I have seen such flashes," Pastor Horry said.

"Actually, something really is there. It's the quiet people from the afterlife."

Pastor Horry spat into the basin again.

"Are you talking to me about angels?" he said.

"The moment comes when it's as if you have been living in a theatre but didn't know it until a scrim suddenly rises on the stage and suddenly you see the quiet people revealed in another dimension. If you see the quiet people, and they don't go away when you blink, you are what we call dead. That's how simple death is. You don't need to move a muscle and you are instantly in a wholly different dimension that is separated from you now only by the blink of your eye."

"You sound like you have been there," said the preacher.

"I died and the quiet people showed me into the afterlife," Varney said.

"What did you see?"

"I saw worlds and more worlds above them and below them, and there are a hundred thousand skies over them. I saw universe beyond universe. There are no boundaries or limits to God. I haven't been able to find words for what I saw. I am trying, but it's as if I am a worm under the crust of the earth trying to explain the stars to the other worms. That's what I hear in theological discussions—worms debating each other about the stars. What terms could I use that you might understand? Guru Nanak returned from the afterlife saying a mortal cannot write an account of God because God does not finish."

"You experienced this with your own soul?" asked the preacher.

"I did," Varney said.

"You truly believe this happened to you?" asked the preacher.

"I used to wonder if I have a soul. Now I know for sure. This is not a matter of faith."

"You didn't see any people on the other side? You didn't see any friends or relatives?"

"The quiet people were with me. They didn't say anything. I understood. There was no need somehow. But they were very well dressed."

"Were you in heaven, or in hell?" the preacher asked.

"The afterlife is far greater than either of those concepts. Hell or heaven don't exist in the afterlife."

Pastor Horry looked into Varney's eyes. "Were you afraid?"

"I felt excited but calm and curious," Varney said. "I was joyful. I wanted to stay. One of these days you'll see for yourself."

"Inevitably," said the preacher.

Mrs. Twilliger opened the door again. They could hear an organ playing a hymn downstairs. The church vibrated with the energy of the music and of people moving and breathing and touching and gossiping.

"What if a new preacher shows up here that people think is an incarnation of the Christ?" said Varney.

Pastor Horry said, "He'd be a fake, and I'd put a bullet in him."

"It's an overflow house, very nice for a Wednesday," Mrs. Twilliger said. "I'd best escort our guests to their seats."

Jerod kept his Spencer rifle at his side, with the butt under his armpit so as to conceal the weapon as much as possible as they went down the stairs and into the crowded auditorium. It seemed wrong to carry a rifle into church, but Pastor Horry was wearing his pistol outside his pants. Varney had the Dragoon revolver in his belt, covered by his suit coat. Jerod noted other weapons among the congregation, mostly pistols—a nod, he supposed, to the example of their preacher.

The crowd was standing and singing, clapping their hands and thumping their feet on the floor, to rollicking organ music played by a skinny red-haired woman wearing a scarlet dress. Seeing the black woman enter the auditorium with a stranger and a tall straw haired man they knew to be Jerod Robin, they hushed the singing and clapping. Their feet stayed planted. The organ music paused until the crowd saw Pastor Horry march in behind the visitors.

"Play on, play on," the preacher roared.

Mrs. Twilliger had left printed pasteboard signs that said RESERVED in three plush, red theatre seats in the middle on the front row. Mattie stood between Varney and Jerod for the singing. Pastor Horry mounted the steps to the pulpit. He smiled out at the lustily singing open mouths of the audience. Pastor Horry had the knack, Varney thought, of seeming to look at and smile at each individual in the audience. He was an impressive man in his white linen coat, brown skinned and darkly handsome.

"Praise Jesus, the Rock of the Truth," Pastor Horry said, raising his hands in a benediction, as the hymn ended.

"Praise Jesus, the Rock of the Truth," the crowd repeated. They made a great rustling sound as they sat down.

Pastor Horry's eyes swept the hall, seeming to linger at each face.

"The first race of which we have any consciousness, which is the great power of ancient times, is spoken of in the story of Noah in the Bible of the Jews," he said. His voice filled the room. "Today we know this race by the term Negro. In ancient times this race was the greatest of all races. There has never been a civilization that has been any greater than the civilization of ancient times which was created by the Negro race. In all the various powers of humanity the most wonderful of all is the power that was perfected by ancient culture and civilization and religious wisdom and knowledge of the ancient Negroes. The contribution of this great race in the past is present with us now. It is in our consciousness, and it has to do with the physical nature of man. Without this material nature, you and I would not exist. We are indebted to the ancients for the great gift, the perfect gift, of the physical nature of man, the physical powers which are now present in us and which were the result of tremendous effort, long eons of time of struggling and suffering on the part of this ancient race called Negro."

Pastor Horry paused. The room was silent. The preacher looked down and smiled at Mattie.

"Welcome to the Zanzibar Church, Sister Mattie," he said.

Mattie held the Bible against her chest. Tears rolled down her cheeks.

"Praise Jesus, the Rock of the Truth," the crowd chanted and stamped their feet.

Pastor Horry let them go on for a moment, and then raised a hand for silence.

"People in the world today are interested in Jesus on the day he was born so we can have Christmas and on the day he was crucified so we can go to heaven on his bleeding back. But the three years he walked among us and spoke to us from his heart, people in the world today don't take that part of Jesus seriously," said Pastor Horry. "We turn a tin ear to what Jesus really said."

He watched the faces of the audience.

"Jesus in his time was famous throughout Syria, and great multitudes of people came to see him from Galilee, and from Decapolis and from Jerusalem and from Judea and from beyond Jordan. Seeing the multitudes gathering to hear his teaching, Jesus went up onto a mountain and composed his thoughts into his central message. When he was ready he stood before the crowd in his white robe and opened his heart and gave the people the Rock of the Truth."

Pastor Horry turned the pages of the large leather-bound Bible on the rostrum.

"Jesus told the crowd at the mountain that day that there is no room at the table in heaven for hypocrites who claim to be one way but act another," he said. "If you are a fornicator in private—and, believe me, you better do your fornicating in private in this town—

but loudly decry fornication by others, you can knock on the door to heaven until your knuckles bleed, but Jesus won't hear you. If you sneak off to a gambling den in Houston and wager your treasure in secret while here at home you righteously, publicly denounce gambling by others, you might think you are ahead of the game, but on Judgment Day you'll roll a craps. If I preach love but act with hate, I am lower than a serpent in the eyes of Jesus. Jesus can't stand a hypocrite. Where does Jesus say this? Jesus says it in his Sermon on the Mount as reported in the Gospel of Matthew."

Pastor Horry began to read from the Bible.

"Judge not, that ye be not judged," he said. He looked at Jerod.

"For with what judgment ye judge, ye shall be judged; and with what measure ye mete, it shall be measured to you again."

The preacher looked out at his congregation.

"Jesus means free ranging morality judges, not judges in our justice system," he said. "He's talking to you and me. I'm disgusted with fools who claim God is on their side. Let me tell you something about God," he glanced at Varney on the front row. "God is not on your side or my side, or our side or their side. God doesn't take sides. God is God. If you want to be on God's side, you must follow what Jesus the Christ says in the Sermon on the Mount, which is the Rock of the Truth."

Pastor Horry began reading again.

"And why beholdest thou the mote that is in thy brother's eye, but considerest not the beam that is in thine own eye?

"Thou hypocrite, first cast out the beam out of thine own eye; and then shalt thou see clearly to cast out the mote out of thy brother's eye."

Pastor Horry traced a finger along a column of text in the Bible.

"Jesus says when you pray do not sound a trumpet before thee, as the hypocrites do in the synagogues and in the streets, that they may be seen of men. The hypocrites love to pray loudly in the synagogues and in the streets so everybody can see how holy they claim to be. When thou prayest, says Jesus, go in thy closet and shut thy door and pray to thy Father which is in secret; and thy Father which seeth in secret shall reward thee openly."

Mattie had opened her Bible and was following the preacher's quotations. Her eyes moved as he skipped forward in the book.

Pastor Horry stepped away from the rostrum and stood with his shoulders back and his hands on his hips and glared at his audience.

"These are not the words of Horry Leatherwood," he said. "This is Jesus the Christ himself speaking out of his own mouth from his own heart. He is talking to you and me, personally. Is there a man in the room who cares to stand up and tell me that Jesus the Christ is full of bull shit? Jesus is wrong? Jesus didn't really mean what he said on the mountain that day? He was a Jewish confidence man stringing us along? Is that why we killed him? It wasn't just the Jews and Romans that crucified Jesus the Christ—it is all of us, over and over, day after day."

A bearded man on the back row leaped up and yelled, "Jesus is the Rock of the Truth."

The Zanzabarians arose and stamped their feet and chanted, "Jesus is the Rock of the Truth." Varney and Jerod stood also, on either side of Mattie, who began chanting with the crowd. During the excitement, Mrs. Twilliger hurried in from the side entrance and passed an envelope to the preacher. She whispered to him and rushed out again.

He silenced the crowd and gestured for them to sit.

"Jesus wants us to come into our church and sing and stamp our feet to praise the Lord in our Zanzibarian way," Pastor Horry said. "He is telling us that loving God and doing the right thing must be in our heart. Bragging to the world how holy you are won't get you into heaven, but it will land you in hell if you are lying about it. You must match your deeds to your words. Hypocrites may think they are pulling a mask over the eyes of God, but they'll wake up one awful morning with their ass on fire."

The preacher looked at the envelope Mrs. Twilliger had given him. He started to put it into his pocket but didn't.

"We bring on our own suffering," he said. "Jesus said the great law is simply to love one another. But we do not really intend to do that. We're only interested in getting things for ourselves, being a success, having money, having pleasure, trying to figure out what happens when we are no longer here. We don't realize that all the secrets of all the great mysteries of life would be revealed if we simply would love."

The preacher tore open the envelope. He quickly read the one sheet of paper. Wrinkles crossed his forehead. He sucked in a breath and held it. He glanced at Jerod and Varney.

The preacher's chest swelled. He lifted his eyes to the room and slowly exhaled.

"I have been informed that my son Billy has died suddenly," he said.

A gasp went up in the room, a sob. Varney realized that Billy had been popular in Gethsemane.

"In your prayers tonight, please remember Billy. In the Zanzibar Church we don't make a spectacle out of death, but when we go alone to pray in the silence where we find God is really listening to us, we open our hearts and weep all we need to."

The preacher turned to the skinny woman in the scarlet dress who had been sitting at the bench of the organ. "Sister Catherine, please play, 'Come We That Love the Lord.'"

Jerod saw a dozen Leatherwood men leave their seats and gather by the main entrance inside the auditorium. Sister Catherine banged away at the organ and the crowd stood and sang lustily and stomped their feet, rattling the stained glass window, shaking the ivory cross.

Varney leaned close to Mattie and said, "Stick by me, whatever happens."

Pastor Horry came down from the podium and motioned for the three of them to follow him. They went up the stairs and along the hall into the preacher's office. Half a dozen Leatherwood men appeared in the hallway. The Leatherwoods muttered angrily. Pastor Horry waved for his kinsmen to stay back and shut the office door in their faces.

The preacher read aloud the note a messenger had delivered from Santana Leatherwood:

Dear Brother Horry

Billy has been killed. He was trampled by a horse ridden by a British horse thief we are chasing. Billy died bravely doing his duty. We are bringing his body home to bury in the plot beside his mother. I am tracking Jerod Robin for two murders, maybe four. I expect he has run home to his mother. I hope to be in Gethsemane by Friday. Adam and Luther are with me, also some regular soldiers.

Respectfully, Santana

Pastor Horry looked at the page to make sure of what he was reading. He noticed a line he hadn't seen earlier. "Here is a post script. Santana says, 'The horse that killed Billy is a beautiful chestnut Arabian mare belonging to Lt. Tom Custer.'"

Pastor Horry unbuckled his belt and laid his pistol and holster on his desk. He entwined his fingers into a double fist and rolled his eyes up to the ceiling.

"I'm trying, Jesus," he said.

Jerod moved to one of the windows. The street was dark except for lamps shining in two buildings. A nighthawk flitted past the window. The air smelled salty with breeze from the Gulf. The church was vibrating from the stamping and singing in the auditorium.

"That rifle isn't going to solve your problem tonight, Jerod," the preacher said.

"I didn't murder anybody," Jerod said.

"You've turned out to be a fine looking young man. You strongly favor your mother. Any brains you've got, you got from her," the preacher said.

He opened a drawer in a file cabinet and found a Manila paper folder that he tossed onto his desk.

"In the Sermon on the Mount, Jesus says blessed are the peacemakers. I was just coming to that radical notion in tonight's sermon. I've thought this over, Jerod. Here is my offer. You can get this done and be off to Mexico ahead of Santana and the army. I want you to bring Junius Robin into town tomorrow at first light. I want Junius to shake my hand in public on the street in front of my church, and apologize."

Jerod shook his head. "He won't do it."

"You can keep the section of land, but I want forty acres on Big Neck Bayou. In return as my own show of good faith," Pastor Horry said, slapping a palm on the folder, "I will tear up and burn these papers"

"What are they?" Jerod asked.

"Your mother has borrowed eleven thousand dollars from the Gethsemane Bank to keep your plantation going. This is the record. I can tear it up."

The preacher turned to Varney.

"So you're the horse thief."

"I did not steal the horse," said Varney. "The horse belongs to me."

"I expect you to show up in town tomorrow morning on that horse with Jerod and the old man," the preacher said. "With the help of the living Jesus, I might be able to make myself forgive you for the death of Billy. But I am going to kill your horse."

Thirty

PASTOR HORRY ORDERED the livery to deliver Varina Hotchkiss's buggy and Jerod's horse to the back door, while inside the church Sister Catherine hammered her organ and led the Zanzibarians in stamping and singing.

Jerod, Mattie, and Varney moved swiftly down the dark street. They could feel the deeper blackness of the thicket pressing in around the town. When they reached the road to Sweetbrush, they urged their horses into speed. They flew along the dark tunnel through the jungle of foliage and the forests of hardwoods in swamps bursting with plant and animal and fish and reptile and insect life in the blackness among pockets of moonlight. They rattled across the bridge over Big Neck Bayou. Lights shone in the windows downstairs at the big house, and upstairs in the bedrooms being occupied by Dr. Junius Robin, Varina Hotchkiss, and Isabella Bushkin.

"It has been jolly fun getting to know you, Captain Robin," Varney said, hopping out of the buggy at the stable door.

The boy Brainey ran out of the stable to take the horses and the carriage inside. Varney saw Flora coming from the stalls as Mattie untied her bonnet and whipped it off her head.

"You're heading for Mexico?" said Jerod.

"I believe the word is pronto," Varney said. "I've got to get Athena away from here before the preacher comes looking for her."

"I guess I don't need to tell you not to go back south through Gethsemane," Jerod said. "There's a road that heads due west through San Felipe and then on to Gonzales, down to Floresville, and then it's a long, straight, hot ride to the border. Brainey will scout the San Felipe road for a few miles to make sure the Leatherwoods don't have it staked out."

Jerod pulled the Spencer rifle out of its scabbard.

"Take care of my horse," he said to the boy, "and fix these people up with whatever they need. Mattie, you give him a hand. Load up a packhorse with food for a week, a tent, water bags—"

"I'd like to say goodbye to your mother," said Varney.

"I'll tell her. Maybe she'll come out. I'll get a rifle for each of you from the gun case, and ammunition."

"Pick out a horse for me that I can handle," said Flora.

"What do you think, Brainey? The Morgan?"

"I'll catch up the Morgan," Brainey said. "He's in the pasture with those two horses that got the U.S. brands."

"If you get past the Leatherwoods on your horses, your trouble is just starting," said Jerod, looking at Varney. He glanced at Flora. "The way south through the chaparral is bandit country, even before the war."

"What are you going to do?" Flora asked.

"I don't exactly know," Jerod said.

"Listen, old son, I wish you the best," said Varney, sticking out his right hand.

"I hope you get that new book written," Jerod said.

They shook hands, and Varney hurried toward the stall where his horse had poked her head out and was looking at him.

"You watch out for yourself, hey?" said Flora.

Jerod felt her green eyes on his face. He bent forward and kissed her on the lips. She didn't back away. He put his left arm around her and drew her against him and kissed her again. "I've wanted to do that," he said.

Abruptly he turned away from her and walked to the stable door, where he encountered Isabella. She was coming from the house, in a hurry, hugging one of Varina's dressing gowns around her body. She looked back over her shoulder, up at the second floor. Jerod couldn't help but notice her nose.

"Your mother needs you up there," Isabella said.

Jerod nodded and continued on the path toward the house.

Isabella stepped into the stable. Flora came to the door and watched Jerod's back as he walked away. Varney led Athena out of her stall. He picked up a brush and gently scratched her golden shoulders. Varney discarded the McClellan military saddle in favor of a more comfortable western saddle he found in the tack room. The new saddle lay on a plaid blanket in the aisle. Isabella pursed her lips and puffed at a gnat from the storm of insects that hovered in the glow around the coal-oil lanterns that lit the interior.

"Whatever did you do to make Dr. Robin so furious?" asked Isabella.

"Told him the truth," Varney said.

Isabella watched him brushing his horse. She saw Varney composed and lit in the shadows like a painting by Velasquez.

"I won't be going on with you," she said. "Dr. Robin is handling my financial matter, and Varina is arranging my transport to Galveston."

"You're a lovely woman. I apologize for the trouble I brought to your door," said Varney.

"I wonder what might have happened if at the party where I met Bushkin, I had met you instead?" she said.

"Perhaps we will see each other again," said Varney.

"Would you come to visit me in Barcelona?"

"Dear lady," Varney said. He paused and looked at her. "How can I find you?"

Watching from the stable, Flora saw the dark figure of Jerod go up the steps onto the porch. She heard the screen door slam. She could feel the heat from Jerod's lips, and his arm around her body.

Jerod passed through the kitchen. Mattie and the young black girl were packing bread, jerked meat, and cans of pork and beans into two canvas bags. He went up the back stairs, but the guest bedroom used by the doctor was empty, the covers ripped off the bed and thrown onto the floor. Jerod and the women had carried and dragged Dr. Junius into the master bedroom after his attack in the garden. To Jerod it looked as if his father's heart was failing. But Isabella emptied a sheaf of bills and invoices out of a paper bag on Varina's Bonaparte writing desk. As a child Isabella had seen Grandfather Marcus have fits like this. When she held the open paper bag to the doctor's mouth, his eyes rolled up at her and he nodded that he understood what to do. Ten minutes of the doctor breathing into the bag and sucking the gases back down his throat and he was on his feet again and shouting at Varina and stumbling back into the guest bedroom that had become his own. Jerod had left then to catch up with Varney and Mattie and make the request his mother had asked him to make.

The French doors on the upstairs porch were open. Jerod could hear his mother's voice from down the hall at the master bedroom. He smelled a whiff of fishy air from Big Neck Bayou. Birds were setting up a serenade in the magnolia trees that lined the boulevard out front. He remembered Laura standing in their room—his room again now, a room just like this, at the other end of the hall—promising she would stay at Sweetbrush and raise their child here, no matter what, and looking sad about it. Well, he thought, the water has moved on.

Walking along the hall toward the master bedroom, Jerod heard them arguing.

"I tell you, there is nothing physically or mentally wrong with me," the doctor was saying. "I simply lost my temper and breathed out all my carbon dioxide. I am fine now."

"Why are your hands trembling?" Varina asked.

"I'm a little tired," he said. "I need a drink."

The doctor was sitting on the bed when Jerod entered. Varina was standing at one of the screened French doors that opened onto the second-floor porch. There was a nervous stillness in the air, like the detritus of combat. The doctor's shirt was unbuttoned and he was barefoot.

"Where's that English son of a bitch now?" he asked Jerod. "Is he off the property yet?"

"He's leaving," Jerod said.

"I should have boxed him on the jaw. I could have laid him out with one punch," said the doctor.

"Varney is a brave man," Jerod said.

"Did you know he is in love with your mother?" asked the doctor.

"Yes, sort of," Jerod said.

"For God's sake, Junius, I never saw Edmund Varney in my life before this afternoon," said Varina.

"I don't believe you. You're acting. I can't believe anything you say," the doctor said.

Varina shrugged. She sighed.

"Tell him where you have been, Jerod," she said.

"I went to see Pastor Horry," said Jerod.

The doctor's eyes were uncomprehending.

"You—" He looked back and forth between Jerod and his mother. "You—?"

"What did Horry say?" Varina asked.

"What did Horry say about what?" Dr. Junius jumped to his feet, staggered a bit and straightened himself. "What the hell are you talking to Horry about?"

"You'd better have a drink," Varina said.

She reached for the velvet pull cord. Jerod knew the two women downstairs were busy packing for Varney and Flora. Jerod said, "I'll get it." He went to the guest room that the doctor was occupying and fetched the bottle of whiskey off the sideboard. He hesitated, and then picked up the bottle of laudanum. He was hoping Varina would tell the doctor about his mission, but returning to the master bedroom he saw they had hardly moved. The doctor looked confused. He was trying to close his shirt, but he couldn't fit the buttons into the slits.

Varina took the bottle, poured a glassful and handed it to the doctor, who also reached for the laudanum. Dr. Junius swigged the milky liquid, swallowed, scowled, and washed it down with the whiskey.

"All right," the doctor said. "I'm all right."

"Tell him," said Varina.

"Tell me what?"

Jerod hesitated.

"Tell me what, damn it?"

"I offered Pastor Horry some land to make peace with us," Jerod said.

The doctor nodded dumbly as he digested the information.

"What did Horry say?" asked Varina.

"He's willing."

"You're plotting against me," the doctor said to his wife. "You waited for Jerod to do the dirty work."

"I'm trying to save this place from going under, Junius. Listen to reason. We will survive and prosper, like you say, but it's going to take a long time, many years. I'm with you, Junius. We will make Sweetbrush cotton the best that there is in the world, but we need to work with the town and the bank, and that means the Leatherwoods. Forget the past. Horry is willing," she said.

"No, by God. No," said the doctor.

"We need to settle this tonight," Jerod said.

"You don't know what she is asking me to do," said the doctor.

"It's only forty acres on the bayou that he wants," Jerod said. He decided not to mention the eleven-thousand-dollar loan at the bank. But he could not avoid the other demand. "You and I are going to town at daylight. Pastor Horry will meet us in front of the church. You are to shake his hand and apologize."

"Never!" the doctor shouted.

"Please, Junius," said Varina.

The doctor's face turned gray with rage.

"You whore!" he shouted. "You're plotting to steal my land!"

He drew back his right arm to slap his wife, but Jerod stepped between them.

"Don't ever do that again," Jerod said roughly.

"You're ganging up on me!" the doctor shouted. "I knew one day this would happen." He shoved Jerod with two hands to the chest. "Get away from me. I don't trust you. Now you're acting like Horry's bastard. That's who you might be, you know—you might be Horry's bastard."

"Junius, don't do this," Varina said.

"Your mother made love with Horry Leatherwood. Tell him, Varina. Admit it. Jerod might be Horry's son as well as he might be mine. Is that the truth, or not?"

"Jerod is your son," she said.

"But you can't be sure," the doctor said.

"I'm sure," she said.

"No, you can't be sure. The son of a bitch showed up here at this house the night you were born, Jerod. Looking after his own, he was," the doctor said.

"It was only one afternoon, so long ago," she said to Jerod.

"You've been seeing him again," the doctor said. "I know you have. The servants know. What a laugh it would be in the quarters for me to go shake that son of a bitch's hand, and apologize. You'd enjoy that, wouldn't you? Making fun of me? Well, it will never happen! I'll kill him before I'll shake his hand. I'll kill you before I'll apologize to him for being his cuckold!"

"You've said enough," Jerod said.

"Talking like Horry's bastard," said the doctor.

Jerod knocked him down.

The doctor fell with a crash that rattled the painted oriental crockery on the mantel. He rose up on his elbows and wheezed. Varina knelt beside him and pressed her long fingers against the flesh of his chest. She felt his beating heart. Jerod's right hand throbbed.

"Junius, let me help you into bed. You're not well," she said. "I'll send to Houston for Dr. Ward."

Jerod looked down at the red blotch on the doctor's left cheek where the blow had landed. Jerod wanted to say he was sorry, but the words wouldn't come out.

"Get away from me," the doctor said.

He grasped the frame of the bed, tendons straining in his forearms, and pulled himself to his feet.

"I'll meet Horry Leatherwood in town at first light, all right," he said. "I'll blow his greasy head off."

The doctor looked past Jerod toward the hall door and his eyes widened.

"What's this?" he said.

Flora Bowprie appeared in the doorway. She had wrapped a saffron scarf around her head in a turban. She wore trousers, leather chaps and a pair of tall boots to protect her legs from the thorns of the chaparral. The dragoon pistol was in a holster on her belt. Her green eyes found Jerod.

"They're here," she said.

"Who are you talking about?" said Varina.

"Brainey was in the pasture and he saw them coming. The Leatherwoods and the soldiers. They're here," Flora said.

Thirty-one

VARNEY AND THE BOY BRAINEY led Athena and the Morgan to the stable door. The horses were saddled, snorting and ready to go. Mattie had brought two rifles and ammunition from the house according to Jerod's instruction. The packhorse was being loaded by Mattie and the servant girl. Isabella hurried around the stable blowing out the lanterns, leaving them in darkness as rain clouds misted across the moon.

"I couldn't tell how many they was, maybe ten or twelve in all," Brainey whispered. "I saw two of those Leatherwood brothers—they give me the willies—and I think another Leatherwood, older, and some soldiers. Some is colored. Can you imagine? They stopped in the pasture and carried on and cussed a streak when they saw the two horses with the U.S. brands. They are really mad. Is your name Marty?"

"Varney."

"That's the name they said—Varney. They don't like you," Brainey whispered.

"Colored soldiers here?" asked Mattie.

"Sounded colored to me," Brainey said.

Mattie buckled the final strap on the canvas bags and patted the horse on the rump.

"Done," she said.

Isabella joined them at the entrance. She had shed the dressing gown because of the humidity. Sweat glistened on her breasts in the low-cut negligee she had borrowed from Varina and was close to spilling out of.

"Edmund, you can't wait any longer on that girl. The soldiers will be here any moment," Isabella said.

"I'm not leaving without her," said Varney.

"It's you they want for stealing their horses," Isabella said. "They don't care about her."

"She killed one of them on Monday," said Varney.

"Oh," Isabella said. She hadn't heard that part of their tale.

"Woooo," said Brainey, very impressed.

"I heard something out there, like horses," Mattie said.

"Edmund, darling, you must get going," said Isabella.

"Not yet," Varney said.

"Are you sure you know where the road is?" asked Isabella.

"Brainey is going to guide us," Varney said.

He held out a hand to the boy and helped him get a foot into the stirrup and vault himself onto Athena's back. Brainey grinned. This was some animal. Varney stood beside his horse. He wore a black felt hat he had found in the stable. He inspected the loads in his dragoon pistol. He wished he had some tobacco.

"I know I hear something," said Mattie.

They looked at the big house where lights still glowed in the windows. Moonlight splashed the gardens. The tall hedges threw shadows across the beds of flowers. They smelled honeysuckle in the damp air. Birds were calling from the trees and the shrubbery. Varney figured the birds would let him know when the soldiers were coming close.

"What can she be doing up there?" Isabella said.

"Here she be," said Brainey.

Flora dashed down the path, her chaps flapping and her boot heels crunching in the oyster shells. She ducked inside the stable.

"Is he coming?" Varney asked.

"I don't know. He grabbed that big rifle, hey," she said.

"Mount up," Varney said. "We are leaving."

"I hope to see you in Barcelona, then. Ask anyone on the Ramblas where my family lives," Isabella said.

Varney turned to Isabella and kissed her. Flora noted that it was nothing like the way the old romancer had hugged herself this afternoon. This was more the kiss that Flora, with her French Quarter upbringing, would have expected from a romancer. Isabella clasped both hands behind his head and thrust her body against him. They made suckling noises. Flora had never kissed anyone that way, but she had heard it going on in the next room. It had been nearly that way when Jerod kissed her just now, but he had broken it off too soon.

Varney stepped away from Isabella and smiled. He mounted Athena. The boy Brainey was sitting in front of the saddle, on the horse's shoulders and neck. Isabella handed Varney the rope tied to the halter of the packhorse. Flora adjusted herself in the saddle. She felt the stirrups through the toes of her boots.

"Wait," Brainey whispered.

"Behind the gate. Look there. What is that?" whispered Mattie.

Several men on horseback appeared in the moonlight near the white picket gate at the end of the garden. Varney couldn't quite make them out. He was straining to see them when Flora said, "It's the two brothers from the courtroom, and I think three soldiers."

"Watching the back door means they are already in front," Varney said. "Sit still a minute." He looked up at the lights in the second floor bedroom windows. "Let's see what happens."

In the master bedroom, the doctor wrestled away from Varina, who was trying to restrain him. He opened the drawer in the nightstand and took out a Colts revolver. Jerod doused the lamps and picked up his Spencer rifle from the doorway and went to the French doors and looked down into the circle drive in front of the house. He saw four soldiers on horseback coming down the boulevard between the magnolia trees. Three were Negroes, and their officer was white. They halted at the fountain. Jerod could see that the officer in the lead was Santana Leatherwood, with his wide-brimmed campaign hat tilted forward. He was wearing yellow leather gloves. Moonlight caught the silver captain's-bars on his epaulets, and the two rows of silver conchos and the silver spurs on his boots.

"Jerod, you must get away from here," Varina said.

He cranked a .58-caliber round into the Spencer.

"I'll cover for you," said the doctor. "Is that Santana down there with those coloreds?"

"It's him."

"I'll keep them busy. You go out the back," the doctor said.

"Stay away from the doors," Jerod said. "Mother, get down behind the bed."

Jerod could see the three black troopers had their carbines in hand. He wondered if Flora and Varney had escaped. He feared they hadn't had time. Jerod saw the troopers raise their carbines. He realized they were going to shoot.

They fired six quick shots into the downstairs windows, setting off a crashing of glass in the windows and lamps and mirrors and pottery, and a great raucous outcry from the birds in the trees.

"The sons of bitches," the doctor said.

"Hello, the house," called Santana.

Santana flicked a yellow glove and the troopers blasted six more bullets into the French doors off the upstairs porch. Two rounds tore into the master bedroom, shattering Varina's vanity table and ripping the canvas of a landscape painting Varina had bought in Paris.

"Come out of there, Jerod, or we'll burn you out," shouted Santana.

"He's not here," Varina yelled.

"That you, Miz Hotchkiss? Show yourself to me," shouted Santana.

"Don't go out there," Jerod whispered.

Jerod was behind the upright beam between two doors. He raised his Spencer and put the sights on Santana's chest.

Varina opened the screen and stepped onto the porch.

"Jerod has gone to Mexico," she said.

"Funny thing. My messenger saw him in town an hour ago," said Santana.

"He went to see your brother. The feud is over. The war is over. Let Jerod alone," she said.

"Sorry, ma'am, but even as beautiful as you are tonight, I have to wonder if you are lying to me. Lying does run in your family," said Santana.

"Go on, Jerod. Make a run for it," Dr. Robin said.

The doctor threw open the screen doors and strode onto the porch. He shoved Varina aside, hard enough that she fell down. The doctor squared his shoulders and raised his pistol and aimed at Santana, who had stayed back out of pistol range in the moonlight.

"Get off my property, Leatherwood! This is my Texas that I fought for! This is my home! Death to traitors!" the doctor shouted, and started shooting. The bullets spanged off the marble fountain and whined into the night.

"Knock him down, Simpson," Santana said.

One of the black troopers laid an eye on the sights of his carbine and shot the doctor in the upper right chest. The bullet broke his collarbone. The doctor dropped his pistol and staggered backward. He tumbled through the screen door into the bedroom on his back. Varina scrambled in behind him on her hands and knees. Jerod had his sights on Santana's heart all the while, but he did not squeeze the trigger.

"Santana, I've got you dead. You can't move fast enough to save yourself," Jerod called.

The troopers aimed their carbines at the sound of Jerod's voice.

"Hold it," Santana said to them. He raised a yellow glove and the troopers stopped. "Why are you telling me about it, Jerod?"

"I want to make a deal with you," shouted Jerod. He kept the sights on Santana's heart.

"I did that before. Look what it cost me."

The doctor was moaning on the floor. Varina tore his shirt open and frowned at the purple wound. Blood was puddling on the carpet beneath the doctor. Varina found the laudanum bottle and pried open his mouth and poured in the rest of the elixir.

"Promise me on your word of honor that you will spare the house," Jerod shouted. "You won't try to arrest my family. I'm the one who killed that trooper on the Bastrop road. The girl didn't do it. Don't keep after her."

"What about Custer's horse?"

"It's not my horse."

"Where is the old thief?"

"I don't know. We split up."

"What, an hour ago?"

"That's right," Jerod yelled. "He's gone."

Santana stood in his stirrups and looked around. Adam and Luther must be close to the rear of the house by now, with troopers to back them up.

"What would I get in return, besides you not drilling me at this moment?" yelled Santana.

"I will surrender."

"You what? I didn't hear."

"I'm coming out and giving up to you, Santana. Don't move. You won't know if I've still got you dead in my sights until you see me come out the front door."

"I won't wait long," Santana shouted. "Some of these troopers were with Sherman going to the sea. They know how to treat a place like this, and they like doing it."

Jerod stepped back from the French doors into the dark room. He looked at his father's twitching fingers. The doctor's head lay in Varina's lap, and her yellow hair touched her husband's face as she bent and said, "Junius, can you hear me?" She looked up at Jerod. "He's dying."

Jerod stripped the linen case off of a pillow and tied the white cloth to the barrel of his Spencer rifle.

"He is your father, you know," Varina said. "You do believe me, don't you?"

"Mother," Jerod said, "this is the best I can do."

He leaned down and kissed her on the lips. The doctor's eyelids fluttered. Varina squeezed Jerod's hand. "I love you, Jerod."

"I love you," Jerod said. He turned and went out of the master bedroom and walked down the hall and then down the central staircase and stepped on broken glass in the entrance hallway. A lamp was lit in the parlor. He got a glimpse of the new servant girl hiding behind the sofa watching him pass.

The tall double doors were already open on the warm night. Jerod pushed open the screen and stepped onto the porch between the columns. He held up the Spencer rifle with the white flag on it. He saw the white Leatherwood smile break across Santana's face.

"Keep that flag waving and walk to me," Santana said.

Santana and the black troopers sat on their horses forty yards from the house, beyond the fountain. Jerod kept a finger on the trigger as he waved the white flag.

"Are we in agreement?" Jerod said, thirty yards out.

"You wouldn't try to make a fool out of me again, would you?" Santana said.

"Just tell me you will spare my family and the house and the girl," said Jerod.

"And you will do what, again?"

"I surrender," Jerod said, twenty yards away.

"Say what?"

"I surrender."

"Done," Santana said.

Santana climbed down off his horse and stood watching Jerod approaching. The three black troopers shifted nervously, their carbines ready, as they saw Jerod's right hand on the trigger action of the rifle. Santana loosed his chin strap and with a thumb nudged the campaign hat up a couple of inches onto his forehead. The two men looked into each other's eyes warily.

Jerod lifted the Spencer rifle into the parade position of present arms, holding it across his chest with both hands, the white pillow case hanging from the muzzle.

He offered the weapon to Santana in a formal military manner.

"Let this be the end of it," Jerod said.

Santana accepted the Spencer rifle. He hefted it and rubbed his fingers on the walnut stock.

"Nice gesture," Santana said.

Santana moved back half a step to get leverage and then moved his right shoulder into the blow as he swung the butt of the rifle against Jerod's jaw. Jerod's hat flew off. He dropped to one knee. His jaw drooped. A spot of blood dripped out of his mouth. His eyes were dazed. Santana moved back another step to make room and launched a kick into Jerod's stomach with the toe of his black boot.

Jerod doubled over and coughed. The troopers watched their captain kick Jerod again, in the chest this time. Jerod toppled over onto his back. Santana looked down at Jerod's mouth that was twisting in pain. Santana smiled. He lifted his right knee, raised the heel of his boot to Jerod's face, and gouged a slash down Jerod's right cheek with the rowels of his big Mexican silver spurs. Blood poured onto Jerod's face. Santana lifted his left knee and put the heel of his boot to Jerod's other cheek. The spur tore open Jerod's flesh.

Santana raised up and smiled down at Jerod.

"That's for making a fool of me," Santana said. "For my kidney, I will hang you at sunup. We'll make a ceremony out of it."

Santana looked at the house. His eyes went to the second floor porch. He wondered if Adam and Luther had ever gotten into position, or if they had wandered off again.

Inside the entrance to the stable, Varney and Flora were mounted, listening to the sounds of the night, trying to guess what might be the right moment for them to make a dash for the road to Mexico. Flora was watching the back door of the house, hoping Jerod would come running out, and that he had not been shot in the fusillade. Isabella and Mattie crouched on either side of the entrance.

"You better get off here, friend. This is going to be tricky," Varney said to the boy Brainey, who sat on Athena's broad shoulders. Varney felt the war horse between his legs, the power of her.

"I go with you. I never been to Mexico," Brainey said.

"Not this trip, amigo," said Varney.

Brainey hopped down. "You go behind the gate and past the gin and take the road west where the big purple flowers are," Brainey said. He stared admiringly at Athena. "She look real fast."

Varney smelled a noxious gassy odor. He glanced around to see if coal oil had spilled from one of the lamps. The odor was growing stronger. It seemed to be seeping from the trees.

"Hey, there they go," said Flora.

In the moonlit gardens behind the house they saw Adam and Luther running away. In a moment the rear of the house shattered into a roar of explosion and flame.

A cloud of black dynamite smoke erupted. Huge red and yellow flames ate up the pine walls of Sweetbrush. Fire crackled up the steep roof and reached into the sky.

"Now," Flora said. "We better go now, hey?"

"Varina Hotchkiss is in there!" Varney said.

He leaped off of Athena and ran down the oyster-shell path toward the burning house.

"My suitcase!" shrieked Isabella. She ran behind Varney, holding her nightgown up to her knees and crashing through the oyster shells.

The servant girl met them at the door. Her dress was scorched and her hair sparkled with little fires. Looking dazed, she stepped aside for them. Varney could see the kitchen was a flaming array of splinters and smashed glass. Dirty grey smoke filled the downstairs of the house. Varney and Isabella coughed and covered their faces as they went up the back stairs. The smoke grew worse with each step upward. Floral wallpaper was peeling off in smoking strips.

At the top of the stairs Isabella turned left and ran toward the guest bedroom where on the bed lay her Italian leather suitcase with the silver buckles that enclosed her passport, bank books, and love letters. Varney made his way through the flames and smoke to the right along the hall. Coal-oil lamps were exploding into fire. Glass cracked and the pine wood screamed. The smoke was suffocating and seared his lungs.

The door to the master bedroom dangled from one hinge. The walls were burning. Smoke billowed through the room and out the French doors and across the porch and into the sky. Varney found Varina Hotchkiss sitting with her back against the bureau, stunned, choking in the smoke, her eyes red, and her yellow hair smeared with soot and ash. Dr. Junius sprawled on his face a few feet away.

Varney picked her up by the armpits. She was surprisingly light beneath the smoldering gown. Her face was touching his. Her hair spread on his shoulder. He got her turned around and she almost fell again. A board from the ceiling crashed down and burned on the carpet. Varney slipped around in front of Varina and draped her arms around his neck. Clutching her arms, he bent his knees and she rose onto his back, her long legs hanging limply down against his. Varney bowed his head and plunged forward into the flames.

He felt Varina's head knock against his and realized she was conscious as he carried her toward the door. He looked down and saw that the doctor was trying to crawl using his left hand, his right shoulder grotesquely dislocated, his shirt bloody and charred with a dozen smoking wisps of fire. The doctor clawed the floor and looked up and caught Varney's glance. They stared into each other's eyes. Varney's mind flashed to the phrase—that little spark of celestial fire called conscience—but he couldn't remember if he had written that, or if someone else had and he had stolen it for *By the Sword*.

The flames soared a hundred feet high. The jungle was lit up. The people from the quarters stood at the edge of the light and watched the big house burn. They gazed in wonder at the black soldiers in Yankee uniforms. White-bearded Pappy leaned on his cane and wondered why it had taken the world so long to come to an end. The troopers sat on their horses far back from the fire.

Jerod lay unconscious in the grass in the shadow of the marble fountain. Santana stood with his arms folded watching flames crackling up the roof of the house he had always resented and hated. He imagined the glow of the flames could be seen in Gethsemane. He smiled.

"Buggy approaching, Captain," called one of the troopers.

Pastor Horry Leatherwood sat in the front passenger seat of a six seat carriage driven by Charlie from the livery. Two buckskin carriage horses trotted in tandem along the boulevard between the magnolia trees, whose leaves were catching sparks and ashes. Pastor Horry jumped out of the wagon and ran to Santana.

"How did this happen?" Pastor Horry yelled above the blasting and rumbling of the fire.

"I don't know," Santana said.

"Where is Varina?" shouted the preacher.

"The old bitch is in the fire somewhere," Santana yelled.

"Around in back," a trooper called. "There's a woman."

Pastor Horry and Santana circled around the flames toward the stable, where they saw the boy Brainey guiding frightened horses out and turning them loose in the pasture. Isabella staggered out the back door of the house with the suitcase in her arms. She fell and a trooper ran forward to help her up. She shook loose of the soldier and marched along the oyster shells, her hair tangled, her face smudged, her nose proudly leading her slightly behind her breasts.

A moment later the screen door banged open and Varney came out with Varina. She was on her feet now. He had an arm around her waist, and she leaned against him. They stumbled down the back porch steps.

"It's him. It's the horse thief who rode down Billy," said Santana.

"I have forgiven him for that," the preacher said. "Let him go."

"What? You can't forgive him. He's a murderer and a horse thief," said Santana. "The army will have him."

"Let him go," the preacher said.

Varney guided Varina to Isabella, who had put down her suitcase and turned back when she saw them come out. The preacher wore his white linen coat. Falling ashes spotted his shoulders. Varney's eyes darted at the faces. He tried to get a discreet look at the stable entrance. He wondered where Jerod had gone, and if Flora was still waiting. He wondered if Flora was holding the reins to Athena in the darkness inside the stable.

The old romancer released Varina into the arms of Isabella. He looked at the two women—Varina with her yellow hair matted by ash, Isabella with her splendid profile and generous eyes. They were beauties. He loved them both. But he understood what his karma now required.

"I'll be right back with the doctor," he said.

Varney turned and ran along the oyster shells between the white rocks back into the house.

Timbers were crashing in flames. Resin was popping like gunshots. A curtain of fire hid the back stairs. Varney ran through the house and up the broad stairway in front. He heard the chandelier tinkling and smashing in the dining room. Fire gushed out of doorways. Paintings were ablaze. Varney had an instant of his mind trying to relate this to something he had done before, but nothing quite fit. He was breaking new ground here. This was topsys.

Floorboards were burning in the upstairs hall. Varney swam into the smoke. He felt the incredible heat searing his flesh. A gust of scalding sour breath struck his cheek. Yellow flames blocked the door into the master bedroom. The doctor had to be inside, maybe had crawled closer to the door. The fire boomed and hissed. Varney tried to breathe. He raised his left arm to cover his face and plunged into the room.

In the master bedroom there was no fire. All was in perfect order. The bed was covered with a Persian quilt. Sunlight reflected from Varina's dressing mirror. The French doors were open to a crisp yellow and green afternoon with a breeze that stirred the drapes. Birds were singing in the garden. The doctor was nowhere to be seen. But there were six people in the room, four men and two women. They were fashionably dressed in modern London style. They might have been in the lobby of Claridge's. They were looking around the master bedroom, picking up and inspecting items, poking into the closet. A man in a velvet waistcoat turned away from admiring the eighteenth-century landscape on the wall. He smiled at Varney. The old romancer felt a rush of joy. He recognized who they were. They were the quiet people.

The roof collapsed with a thundering showering fiery roar. Varina and Isabella stood watching arm in arm. The soldiers gathered around the edge of the firelight in the rear of the house and slapped at swarms of moths. Adam and Luther looked in awe at the blaze. The people from the quarter pressed forward to see. Pastor Horry and Santana were fascinated by the spectacle. In the darkness the creatures hushed.

The fire and smoke and hubbub covered Flora as she slipped out the back door of the stable riding the Morgan into the corral, holding Varney's chestnut mare by the reins, not knowing what to do. She let Athena more or less guide them. They left the corral and crossed the road through the bougainvillea and picked a path quietly in a westerly direction, keeping in the darkness beyond the flames. Flora was remembering the bad feeling she'd had approaching this house yesterday between the magnolias. Now the old romancer was in there in the flames. She had seen him run into the house the second time. She didn't know what had happened to Jerod. She kept watching the burning house and hoping she would see one of them come out—Jerod or the old romancer, either one— and then she saw Jerod sitting up and leaning against the marble fountain in the shadow.

Thirty-two

THE BELLS WERE CLANGING in the towers of the Parroquia, the pink granite Gothic cathedral with twisting spires and winged gargoyles that made Jerod think of a wizard's castle in a picture book. The eccentricities of the parish church reminded him of home, in that it had been designed the same way Varina Hotchkiss had imagined the Victorian mansion at Sweetbrush: by drawing a sketch of it.

Bells began sounding before daylight in the many churches in San Miguel de Allende, summoning workers into the fields, and they rang periodically all day and into the night. After six months of living in San Miguel, Jerod was accustomed to the bells and found them comforting. They were a sign of continuity. The bells had been ringing for three hundred years, and they would ring again tomorrow.

In a world that is broken, continuity matters. He chose not to believe what his father had accused his mother of. Jerod had decided Dr. Junius could never have trusted someone who could love someone like him.

Jerod was sitting at a sidewalk table in front of Rosa's café on the Jardín with a pistol in his lap that was covered by a copy of the *New York Times* newspaper only twelve days old. People crowded into the plaza in the cool, bright sunshine. Shops and improvised booths were piled with nuts, candy, toys, flowers, wreaths and Christmas candles. Carpenters nailed together a platform for a band concert in the center of the Jardín.

The waiter brought him coffee with cream, bread and butter, a pot of apricot jam, two fried eggs, and black beans with salsa. Jerod had the same breakfast at Rosa's every midmorning at about the same time. He had heard yesterday that a gringo stranger had checked in at the Hotel Colón on Calle de San Francisco and was asking about him. Jerod had been expecting Santana Leatherwood to show up sooner or later. There was no use trying to hide, even in a town as large as San Miguel. Now that Santana had gotten this close, he would have to be dealt with.

Jerod tore off a hunk of bread and smeared butter and jam on it. He could feel the cold weight of the pistol in his lap. He breathed the high desert air and smiled at the purity of it. He could smell flowers from the window boxes and gardens. The blue misty Guanajuato mountains rose on the horizon. Jerod sipped the hot coffee and watched the faces moving in the plaza and on the sidewalks.

Santana's timing couldn't be deliberate, Jerod knew, but it was something to think about. One year ago today they had fought at Snow Hill. So much water had moved on since that day, and yet here they were again.

Jerod's eyes continued to move around the plaza as he ate. Statues of saints and generals looked down from niches in walls that were gouged by old bullets and cannonballs. Church bells rang in the Oratorio. Two dozen schoolgirls in blue uniforms marched across the plaza. A donkey cart rolled past the municipal building followed by two policemen interested in its contents. Three men carried a lemon tree, with dirt hanging from its roots, past Jerod's table. Jerod poured salsa on his eggs and beans and picked up a fork, and then saw him.

A gringo limped into the plaza, coming out of the Calle de Mesones. He wore a brown suit and a wide-brim felt hat and carried a mahogany cane which he leaned on as he studied the perimeter of the plaza. His eyes fell upon Rosa's café and then upon Jerod sitting at the table. The gringo was nearly a block away, but it was clear where his attention had gone. He began to limp along the sidewalk, his left hand heavy on the cane, the people dodging around him. He was coming to Jerod's table.

He was Tom Custer.

Jerod finished his eggs and beans and wiped the yellow remains off the plate with the last of his bread. He drank the rest of his coffee and looked up as Custer was twenty feet away. The brass tip of Custer's cane scraped into the sidewalk. Jerod's right hand dipped beneath the table. He noticed the bullet wound on Custer's cheek had healed but left a pale blotch of a scar on his boyish face.

"You are Captain Jerod Robin?" Custer asked.

"I was expecting someone else," Jerod said.

"I have come to get my horse," said Custer.

"Would you join me for a cup of coffee?" Jerod asked.

"I would, thank you," said Custer.

He pulled out a chair opposite Jerod. Custer sighed as he lowered himself into the chair, leaning on the cane, stretching out his left leg. He arranged himself on the chair with his left leg sticking straight toward the sidewalk. Jerod signaled the waiter to bring two coffees.

"You want food?" Jerod said.

"Not hungry, thank you," said Custer.

"It was me who shot you at Burroughs' Cove," Jerod said.

"I figured as much," said Custer.

"So if you want revenge, I will accommodate you," Jerod said.

Custer took off his hat and patted his forehead with a napkin. The strain of sitting had brought sweat to his face. Custer's long hair was parted in the middle and swept behind his ears and hung down to his shoulders in back.

"You can take your hand off that pistol under the table," said Custer. "All I want is my horse."

"Your word of honor?"

"My word, yes."

The waiter poured two cups of coffee and left the pot on the table. Jerod put the pistol into his belt and used both hands on the cream and sugar. Custer took his coffee black. Custer looked at the two scars on Jerod's cheeks. They were ugly red worms about three inches long.

"Captain Leatherwood has been transferred into the Indian Territories," Custer said.

"You can see he put his mark on me," said Jerod.

"Yes, I heard that he did."

Custer winced as the bells of the Parroquia began clanging again.

"It takes a while to get used to this, I suppose," Custer said. "Do you ever get used to it?"

"I can never go home," said Jerod.

"There's nothing I can do about that part of it," Custer said.

"How did you find me?" Jerod asked.

"My outfit is in Houston now. I put on civilian clothes and went to see your mother do a reading from Shakespeare at the Civic Hall for a charity for war veterans. She is a very beautiful woman, and I am told she is a great actress. I'm afraid I fell asleep. It was the fault of the writing, not the acting."

Jerod smiled. "I'm sure it was."

Custer reached down with his left hand and lifted his leg at the knee to relieve a pain. He settled back against the wrought-iron chair.

"After the reading I went to a party at the Capital Hotel. Your former wife was there. Your mother passed through the party. The crowd applauded her. She was with some Spanish woman politician. A ship had come in with champagne from France. There was a lot of drinking and dancing. Well, no dancing for me. I might be done with dancing."

Custer refilled his coffee cup.

"Do I need to tell you that your name was on many lips in that room—stories about the war, stories about murders and fires. Violent stuff, mostly. I kept my ears open. I heard several people say they thought you had gone to San Miguel."

Custer gestured toward the plaza, where vendors were selling cotton candy and bottles of orange soda. A lone musician blew notes on a cornet, warming up.

"Smart choice of places," Custer said. "I like it here. Since you can't go home again, you could do a lot worse than this ringside table."

"Did you meet Laura?" asked Jerod.

"We were introduced. I understand that since she divorced you, she is quite the belle around town."

"What do you mean by that?" Jerod asked.

"Only that she is popular in society and has many suitors. Or she would have many suitors if they weren't afraid you will come back and bury them." Custer made the hint of a grin that barely moved his mustache. "Don't squint at me. I don't want anything of yours. I want my horse is all."

Custer shifted painfully in his chair.

"The first time I got shot it didn't hurt much," Custer said. "This time it hurt like hell."

"Yeah. It hurts," said Jerod.

"Laid up, I did a lot of thinking. I decided to make a life out of the army. I really need my horse back."

"Let's take a walk," said Jerod.

The streets of San Miguel were winding and abrupt, a cobblestone maze of sunny courtyards behind walls. Carved doors in rust-colored walls became gateways into gardens of geraniums and poinsettias. Custer limped along beside Jerod, his cane tapping on the cobblestones. They went uphill on Calle de Correa. Custer had difficulty walking on the cobblestones and the cracked sidewalks. Jerod caught Custer's elbow to keep him from stumbling when they turned onto the street called Barranca.

"I wonder where the crazy old Englishman is right now," said Custer.

"You mean besides dead?"

"He used to go on about the afterlife," Custer said. "I just wonder where he is right now."

"Did you read his book?" asked Jerod.

"I read it while I was laid up in bed with this broken hip. It's a fictional thing."

"I heard him say every word of it is true," Jerod said.

"He also says Athena is about twenty-five years old. There's no way that could be true, is there?"

"I have to wonder," said Jerod.

"Anyhow, I brought the old man's book with me. I'll trade it for the horse. I tore out the title page that he autographed to me. I'll keep that to remember him by, but you can have the rest of the book."

Four blocks from the Jardín they stopped at an oak door in a chocolate brown wall. The top of the wall was lined with jagged glass among flowers in pots. Shuttered windows looked down from the second floor, and above them in the roof garden were more flowers and hanging fronds.

Using a black-iron door-knocker, Jerod rapped three times and waited. A wagon loaded with straw mats and pulled by a burro bumped on the cobblestones and went down the hill toward the stream that flowed through a park. Women were washing laundry in the stream. Jerod rapped three times more.

The eye port opened, and then closed. Dogs began barking inside. They heard the bolt rattling on the other side of the door. The door swung inward, and Flora Bowprie was standing in the entrance between two German shepherd dogs. She wore a purple headband and a white cotton shirt over a purple skirt that touched her ankles. Her feet were bare, her toes holding the tile floor. Tom Custer was taken by her cat-eyed look that he had noted in the courtroom, but the first thing he noticed about her now was that she was pregnant.

Tom had observed the course of several pregnancies in his family in Ohio. He guessed the girl was about six months along.

"You remember Flora," said Jerod.

"Of course," Custer said. He took off his hat and made a slight bow. He saw that she had a derringer hidden in her right hand. "I come in peace."

Flora stepped around them and looked up and down Barranca. Church bells were ringing again.

"If you are looking for Captain Leatherwood, he won't be coming here any time soon, I promise," said Custer.

"Nobody is following you?" she said.

"I swear," said Custer.

Flora spoke to the dogs in Spanish and they returned to their favorite spots in the shade under the balcony that jutted into the small courtyard. She led Custer down six brick steps into the courtyard. He labored with the descent. She reached out to help him but thought better of it. He would have been insulted. Jerod slammed shut the bolt in the oak door behind them.

They crossed between the pots of blooming flowers on the brick floor of the courtyard and went through an archway into the kitchen. A kettle was hissing on the stove. Half a dozen poster-size pieces of paper were spread on the round oak table. Jerod pushed the papers aside and gestured for Custer to sit. Pulling out his leather-backed chair, Custer saw the posters were hand printed in English, French and Spanish. In English the poster said: HENRI BOWPRIE YOUR DAUGHTER IS HERE INQUIRE ROSA'S CAFÉ.

"You want a bottle of beer?" Flora asked the visitor.

"Could I have coffee, please?" Custer said. "If I start drinking beer, there's no telling how this will turn out."

"You'll have to deal with Flora about the horse," said Jerod. "Varney gave the horse to her before he ran into the fire."

"I understand you are some kind of fortune-teller," Custer said, watching Flora pour coffee into three cups decorated with flying birds.

"Professionally," she said.

"I'll pay you to tell my fortune," said Custer.

"I don't work on Christmas Eve," she said.

Through an arched doorway in the pale-blue wall, Custer could see a small Christmas tree on a table in the parlor. A tin star glinted on top of the tree, and the limbs were decorated with colored glass balls and peppermint candy.

"About the horse, then," said Custer. "Although Athena is my horse, and I have had God's own amount of trouble over her, I am willing to pay you a reasonable reward for taking care of her for me."

"Why would you come all this way for a horse?" Flora asked.

"Haven't you ever loved anything this much?" said Custer.

"Yes, I have."

"I owe a lot to this horse. I admire this horse. I love this horse. I need this horse."

Flora fastened her green eyes on him and he had the uncomfortable feeling that he was being read.

"What do you think?" she asked Jerod.

"It's all up to you," he said.

"All right." Flora stood up from the table. "Come with me." Her skirt swished and her hips moved as she glided on bare feet across the polished floor. "Come out to the stable."

The kitchen doors opened onto a tile walk that led to a half acre of ground inside adobe brick walls that were studded on top with broken glass. Flora unlatched a gate and they entered the stable yard, the German shepherd dogs following. The dogs drank from the water trough beside the dusty, yellow-brick stable. Straw was scattered across the stable entrance. Chickens dug frantically in the dirt and scolded each other. A cat sat by the fence and watched.

Flora whistled. "Athena," she called.

They walked to the stable entrance.

"Oh, excuse me," Flora smiled.

Inside they saw the beautiful chestnut Arabian mare, her coat glowing with health, her eyes wide and bright, and her profile sensuously powerful, smacking her lips with pleasure as she nursed her skinny, awkward, long-legged foal.

The foal had four white feet and a brindle stripe between her eyes and a birthmark in the shape of a V on her left hip, a copy of her mother. Custer guessed the foal to be about three weeks old.

"How could this be?" Custer said.

"Somewhere last January she got pregnant with a pureblood Arabian stud. That's the only possibility, isn't it?" Jerod said.

"Unless she just reproduces," said Custer, only halfway joking. "It was March when I first got her in Virginia. I don't know where she was before then."

"Varney said this horse always belongs to warriors," said Jerod. "If that is so, she should be yours. But the decision is Flora's."

Custer walked into the stable and rubbed Athena's nose and scratched her neck. She smelled his hands and nuzzled against his face and hair. It was clear that she remembered him fondly. The foal splayed out her legs on knobby knees and slurped loudly at her mother's breast. Bells began ringing from three more churches.

"We can't separate them," Flora said. "The foal is too young."

Custer nodded. "It's six or eight months before she should be weaned. A year or more these two should be together. I'll get hold of a big wagon with a roof on it and pack it with straw and hire some teamsters and haul the two horses back to Texas, taking very good care of this foal, if you will allow me."

"You'll need ten men with guns to escort you," Jerod said.

"I'll hire as many as it takes." Custer grew excited at the idea. "Between Athena and her daughter, I can ride a great war-horse for the rest of my army career, and long after," he said.

The Parroquia was four blocks away but when the mighty bells from its towers and spires joined the bells of the other churches, at least eight of them now ringing, the pealing became noticeably louder and deeper and the vibrations raised goose bumps on Custer's arms.

"Christmas Eve," Jerod said. "They're calling the faithful."

"We're going to mass tonight," Flora reminded him.

"I remember," Jerod said.

"You want to go with us?" Flora asked Custer.

"I better not. I'm a Presbyterian."

The foal finished her meal and wobbled forward toward the stable entrance. Athena bobbed her head and made a soft grunting sound. The foal stopped and steadied herself and looked out at the three humans, trying to get them identified.

"You take the two horses and you are totally done with us, hey?" said Flora.

"Me, personally, I am, yes. I can't in honesty speak for the army."

"Go find yourself a proper wagon," Flora said. "Come back here when you are ready to travel, and the two horses will be yours."

"Thank you," said Custer. He held his hat against his chest and bowed toward her. He looked at Jerod. Custer held out his right hand. "I'm glad we never met in the field before Burroughs' Cove. I know you could have killed me that day. I was waiting, expecting you to do it."

Jerod shook his hand. "Can you find your way back to the hotel?"

"Walk me past your dogs, and I can make it the rest of the way," said Custer.

"Bring us the old man's book when you come back," Jerod said.

In the evening Flora and Jerod went up the stairs onto the roof of their house and sat on wicker chairs in the garden and watched